INTO *the* LIGHT

THREE RIVERS BOOK ONE

New York Times and *USA Today* Bestselling Author

Jasinda Wilder

INTO *the* LIGHT

THREE RIVERS BOOK ONE

1

Bear

THE JARRING BUZZ OF THE KLAXON MAKES MY hands shake; it's a sound that's defined my days for the last ten years.

This is the last time I'll ever hear it.

Guard Jacobsen pulls the cell door open. "C'mon, Bear. Time to go."

I clench my hands into fists to hide the shaking. Rise to my feet. Let out a breath. "One minute, please."

Jacobsen nods, leaning against the frame of my cell, thumbs hooked into his belt. Jacobsen is one of the good ones. A big man with unruly blond hair and a constant five o'clock shadow, he's talkative and quick with a joke and tends to use his size and rapport with the prisoners to quell any issues rather than his billy club.

I turn to Matt, my cellmate for the last six and a half years. He stands by the bunks, visibly fighting emotion.

"Appreciate you, Matt. All you've done for me." I put out a hand.

Matt takes it, squeezing hard before pulling me into a rough embrace, whacking me on the back. "I'm glad as hell you're gettin' out, but fuck me, I'm gonna miss your big ass, brother."

I thump him back a few times, pulling away without releasing his hand. "Gonna miss you too." Matt clears his throat a couple of times, tugging at the neck of his bright orange Michigan Department of Corrections jumpsuit. "Give 'em hell, man."

I snort. "My hellraisin' days are behind me." I grip his shoulder and shake him gently. "So are yours."

He shoves at me. "Aw fuck off, Bear. You know what I meant."

"Yeah."

"Gotta go, Olafsson," Jacobsen says. "Ride's waiting."

"Comin'," I say over my shoulder. "See ya 'round, Matt."

"See ya 'round, Bear."

We both say it, knowing it's untrue.

I nod once more, turn, and exit the cell, pacing a few steps down the hallway before pausing to wait for Jacobsen to close the cell. Hurts like hell, leaving behind the first real friend I've ever had. I refuse to look back, knowing if the situation was reversed, Matt would do the same.

Jacobsen gives me a little shove. "Move along, Olafsson." It's friendly, disguised as rough.

As I pass cell after cell, prisoners reach through the

bars and I tap my knuckles against theirs, greet each man by name, and give him a nod.

Down through the dayroom and to R and R, where I'm processed for release: strip out of my jumpsuit and dress in my street clothes. They fit like shit—the last time I wore them was ten years ago, and I've put on a fuck-ton of muscle since then. The jeans constrict my thighs and my junk and rise around my ankles, the floppy brown leather belt doesn't fit even on the last hole, and the shirt fits like I'm doing my best Chris Farley "Fat Guy in a Little Coat" impression. My other belongings, which now feel like they belong to someone else, include a long-dead Nokia flip phone, eighty-six dollars and seventy-seven cents, a pack of now-stale gum, and an expired state ID card.

The sum total of my belongings as a human on this earth.

Once I'm changed, Jacobsen, against protocol, accompanies me to the gate. "Better not ever see your ass again, Olaffson, you hear me?"

I nod. "Yes sir. I hear you. You won't."

He fixes me with a hard, stern glare. "Serious as a fuckin' heart attack. You got a once-in-a-lifetime shot at turning your life around with this work-release program, Bear. *Don't* fuck it up."

"I know it. I won't. Got my word on that."

Jacobsen nods. "Good." He shakes my hand. "Have a good life."

I let out a short sigh. "Do my best."

Jacobsen turns and twirls his hand in the air over his head; a loud buzz precedes the gate sliding open. For a minute, I can't move, sure that a swarm of guards is going to rush me and haul me back to the box.

Jacobsen gives me a hard shove, forcing me to trip and stumble across the threshold. "Get the fuck outta here, Olafsson. Tired of lookin' at your ugly fuckin' mug, already."

I walk backward and give him a nod. "I'm going."

He hooks his thumbs in his gear belt, watching as I cross the road to the big silver F-250 idling on the shoulder. When I round the hood, he gives me a wave, which I return, and then he strolls back to the R and R room. Another buzz announces the closing of the gate, which I watch slide closed with my hand on the truck's door handle.

Once the gate is closed, I let out a sigh.

It's real.

I'm a free man.

I open the door and settle into the passenger seat—the cab smells like old coffee, leather, diesel fumes, and grease. The truck is older than my prison stay: ten years, eleven months, and eighteen days. The gray leather is cracked and worn, the dash is peeling, and the analog radio is tuned to a local hard rock station, the volume low enough I can just barely make out the sounds of Nirvana. The stock manual gear shifter has been replaced with a huge wrench; the stainless steel of the handle is tarnished and worn from long use.

In the driver's seat is my boss and work-release supervisor, Riley Crowe. At six-three, he's an inch shorter than me and lighter by a good fifty pounds. His hair is neatly cut, swept back and to the right, glossy black. Clean-shaven, with eyes so pale blue they're almost white, and shocking in their intensity. He's dressed in worn, faded, dirty blue jeans, battered Wolverine work boots, and a filthy white T-shirt stretched across a muscular chest.

He grins at me. "You're a free man, Bear. How's it feel?"

I shrug a shoulder. "Not sure yet. Only been two minutes."

He laughs, backhanding my chest. "Tell you one thing—you need new clothes. Those fit like shit."

I nod. "Put on a few pounds on the inside, I guess."

"A *few*?" He cackles sarcastically, shoving the shifter into first and feathering the throttle, making the big diesel engine groan.

A few miles later, Riley glances at me. "So. You know how this is gonna work?"

I shrug. "I guess."

"Might as well go over it again, now that you're officially out on parole. You've put in three years in my program, which got you a shit-load of good-time credit. That plus your overall behavior on the inside means you're out on parole ten years into your twenty-five-year sentence."

"Yes sir." None of this is news to me, obviously.

"So now that you're out, you're gonna continue to work for me as part of the conditions of your parole. You'll still have to report to your parole officer once a month, but as long as you stay good with me, you can skip the bi-weekly check-ins. Now, the official work-release program stipulates you work for me for a period of five years total, so you owe me another two. Your pay, as you're obviously aware, has gone in part to pay off your stay. The rest has been put into an escrow account for you. Now that you're out, I'll hook you up with the bank and get you a card. You have enough to put down a deposit on an apartment, which we've already set up for you—you just gotta sign some papers and pay the deposit. You'll need a ride eventually, but until you can get one, I'll pick you up and drop you off—your apartment is on the way for me." He glances at me. "Got all that?"

I nod. "Got it." I rub my palms on my jeans. "I'm grateful, Riley. Thank you."

Riley nods. "I've been where you are. I built this program to be what I wish I'd had when I got out."

"It's the best thing that's ever happened to me," I say, watching the familiar sights slide past the window.

I've made this drive every day for three years—from Holbrook State Correctional Facility to Three Rivers, a journey of a little under an hour. Until today, however, the journey has been in a Department of Corrections bus, with an armed deputy watching my every move. Until today, at the end of the workday, I boarded the bus back to the prison, process back in, and rejoin Gen Pop for chow time and then rec time before we're put back in our cells.

Today, everything is different.

No bus. No deputy. No jumpsuit. No going back to Gen Pop. No more chow line. No more rec yard. No more long late-night talks with Matt. No more lifting in the yard with Gregg, LaShawn, and Antonio.

Sensing my need for quiet time to process the coming changes, Riley turns up the radio and cuts the chatter, left wrist dangling over the wheel, his right hand resting on the wrench shifter handle.

The hour drive passes quickly, and soon the highway angles west, the open farmland and clumps of forest giving way to roadside parks on the left and RV campgrounds on the right, and then the campgrounds and state parks give way to five and ten-acre homesteads on the right, and on the left the sky opens up and gives you occasional glimpses of Lake Michigan.

Another few minutes and the highway runs right up against the shoreline, Lake Michigan rippling blue and green and gray, stretching into the horizon. On the right, the large parcels subdivide into one- and two-acre parcels, with winding neighborhoods behind them.

Three Rivers is a small town in Northern Michigan, on the west coast of the state north of Traverse City. Perched right on the shoreline, the downtown area has seen a boom of expansion in the three years I've been coming here on work release, with an influx of young families, new businesses, and entrepreneurs quickly transforming the once-sleepy lakeside small town into a bustling, exciting up-and-coming community. It's cute and quaint—what I've seen of it, at least, as the bus winds through the downtown and into the industrial area where Crowe Demolitions and Crowe Construction have their equipment yard and headquarters.

We're nearing downtown now, passing through a short stretch of beachside resorts and hotels and inns, mom-and-pop diners, fudge shops, kayak, jet ski, and paddleboard rental shops, and the marina, with sprawling neighborhoods climbing the steep hills east of the shoreline and highway. With every mile, the buildings get closer together and the steep hills settle and smooth out. And then, abruptly, the four-lane state highway narrows to one lane in each direction and becomes Main Street, still running parallel to the shoreline. On the left is the beach, with parking lots just off the road, state park-run bathrooms, and city-owned concessions buildings dotting the lots at regular intervals; beyond the parking lot and bathrooms is a wide swath of grass sprinkled liberally with benches, grills, and picnic tables, eventually giving way to sand and then the water.

On the other side of Main Street is the town itself. Parking lots run alongside the road with businesses beyond them, cross streets running perpendicular to Main Street crammed with restaurants, shops and stores, cafes, and bars. The downtown area itself isn't especially big, containing only a square mile or two, but the rest of suburban Three Rivers is actually fairly sizeable, sprawling out along the shoreline and extending several miles to the east in suburbs, industrial complexes, and shopping centers. Cutting through the town and emptying into Lake Michigan are the three rivers that give the town its name: Crooked Trout, Red Bottom, and Michigami. Some five or so miles north of where it narrowed, Main Street widens back into a four-lane highway and continues northward, eventually reaching Mackinaw City and the Mackinac Bridge.

Riley makes a right onto Compass Street; here, breweries abound, sitting on the Michigami River, interspersed with fancy restaurants. The further east we go, the more the landscape changes, shifting from bustling downtown and its attendant sprawl to quiet, tree-lined neighborhoods, elementary schools, and play parks with slides, jungle gyms, and sandboxes. This, too, shifts after a while, giving way to industrial complexes—warehouses, manufacturing facilities, dentist and doctor offices, accountants, tax professionals, law offices, and the like. And then eastward beyond that is Division Boulevard, running parallel to Main Street, a wide, busy four-lane road lined with places like Target, Best Buy, Meijer, Applebee's, Chili's, car dealerships, and strip malls.

Riley pulls into the Target parking lot and shuts off the engine. "C'mon, big guy. Let's get you some clothes that actually fit."

I follow him into the store, where he grabs a red shopping cart and beelines for the men's clothing section.

"What size are you?" he asks, eying me. "Quadruple XL?"

I shrug. "Dunno."

"Guess you'll have to try a few sizes, then." He grabs a few T-shirts and jeans in various sizes and then directs me to the changing rooms. I try things on until I find my sizes, and then Riley makes some selections for me—I let him choose, because I have no clue. Haven't worn anything but orange jumpsuits in ten years.

With a few changes of clothes in the cart, he grabs some personal effects like deodorant, a hairbrush, a five-in-one bottle of shampoo and whatever else, a toothbrush and tube of toothpaste, and a pair of work boots.

As we wait to check out, I glance at him. "I don't have money for all this."

Riley shrugs. "Yeah you do, just not with you. I got you covered. We'll sort it all out later. Don't worry about it."

After making the purchases, I change into the new clothes in the bathroom, take a long piss, and wash my hands. I examine myself in the mirror for the first time in a while: prison mirrors leave something to be desired, to say the least.

Standing six-four-and-a-half in my socks, I have bright red hair that's currently loose and shaggy around my shoulders, wavy and frizzy and tangled. My beard matches in color and overall appearance, hanging to mid-chest, bushy and wild. My eyes are somewhere between green and gray. I've always been a big guy, but with nothing to do in prison but eat, lift, talk, and sleep, I've packed on a massive amount of muscle over the last decade, and probably weigh at least two-sixty-five, if not more, most of it solid muscle, although I do have a decent layer of padding sheathing my muscles.

All in all, I look…scary. I was into tattoos before I went inside, so my arms and torso are covered in ink. A lot of it was gang-related imagery, which I either altered or covered on the inside with prison ink.

I throw away the old clothes and exit the bathroom, feeling a little more human now that my clothes fit. Riley is waiting by the exit, chatting with a beautiful woman in her thirties.

"Bear, come say hi to my friend." Riley waves me over. "Jess, this is Bear, he works for me. Bear, this is Jess. She runs the office for Felix and me."

As I approach, Jess's eyes widen and she backs up a step, involuntarily. She's tall and willowy, with long brown hair shot through with blonde highlights and soft brown eyes.

"Ummm…hi?" Her greeting comes out like a question.

"Nice to meet you, Jess," I murmur, keeping my distance and my hands in my hip pockets; I glance at Riley. "Meet you at the truck."

I amble away, self-conscious after her reaction.

I've always had sharp hearing, so I can't help overhearing her as I walk away.

"Jesus, Rye, where'd you find a monster like that?"

"He's in my program," Riley answers. "He's a good dude."

"If you say so," Jess mutters, sounding doubtful. "He's the biggest person I've ever seen."

"Should see what he can do with a ten-pound sledge."

"Looks like he could demo a house with his bare hands," Jess says.

Riley laughs. "Yeah, he probably could."

I lose the rest as I leave hearing range.

I feel her eyes on my back and unconsciously hunch my shoulders.

I should be used to it—I've been bigger than everyone my whole life. Now, though, with the amount of muscle prison put on my already huge frame? I think Jess's reaction is gonna be something I'm gonna have to just accept.

I'm a monster: an ex-con; a violent offender.

I do my best to shrug it off, leaning against Riley's truck. A red SUV pulls in beside the truck, and a tiny Asian woman emerges, helping a little kid out of a blue booster seat; she scoops him up with a scared glance at me and hustles away.

"Mommy? Was that man a giant?" the little boy asks, watching me over his mother's shoulder.

"Hush, baby," she murmurs to him. "Don't stare."

With an irritated growl, I rake my hair back. Women and children are terrified of me just from being near me. When Three River locals discover what I was convicted of—

Forget it.

Focus on the here and now.

I hear Matt's voice in my head, reminding me to breathe, and focus on what I can control.

Riley swaggers up to the truck and yanks the back door open, tossing the Target bags on the back seat, which is already littered with fast food trash, folders stuffed full of documents, a black and yellow Dewalt bag full of tools, work gloves, Mt. Dew bottles, and who knows what else.

"Don't mind Jess," Riley says, slamming the door closed and hopping behind the wheel. "She's a sheltered little white-bread girl who's never left Three Rivers."

I shrug as I latch the seatbelt across my chest. "It's fine."

"I keep waiting for her and Felix to hook up, but my brother is a pussy-ass dipshit, apparently. I know he likes her and I know he knows she likes him, but he won't pull the trigger."

"She's pretty," I say.

Riley just nods and shrugs one shoulder. "She is."

Felix is Riley's older brother, and owner of Crowe Construction, the counterpart to Riley's Crowe Demolitions. Felix builds spec homes, and he and Riley also work together flipping homes—Riley does the demo, Felix renovates, and then they sell it and split the profits.

Riley grins at me. "Yeah, she is. Not my type, though. Sweet girl, but I like 'em with a bit more spark, y'know?"

I shrug. "Sure."

I have no idea.

I haven't spoken to a woman who wasn't in uniform in ten years. And the first woman I did talk to, just now, literally backed away from me. And that's before she knew anything about me.

The rest of the day is spent getting me settled: we go to the credit union where my savings are held, and I get a temporary checkbook and pick a debit card, which will be mailed to Riley's office since I don't have an address yet.

Next, he takes me to an apartment complex back toward town, near the industrial area.

Foxwood Commons is a massive apartment complex running along Tompkins Road between Main Street and Division; the buildings are long and low, three stories, beige brick with faded green shingle roofs and matching shutters, balconies connecting the buildings at the second and third levels, with a fenced-off swimming pool serving the whole complex, and laundry facilities for each building. Riley walks me through the process of signing a six-month lease and writing a check for the first and last months' rent, and then I'm given keys to my very first home.

It's on the far north end of the complex, a third-floor unit, one bedroom and one bathroom with a tiny living room and galley kitchen, threadbare tan carpet in desperate need of replacement, Formica counters and laminate flooring, popcorn ceilings, and battered twenty-year-old appliances.

Riley stands in the living room with a sour look on his face. "Well, Bear, it ain't much, and it ain't exactly the Ritz, I know, but—"

"Beats the shit out of a ten-by-twelve prison cell," I cut in.

He laughs and claps my shoulder. "You said it." He sets my bags of purchases on the floor. "You'll need some furniture, I guess. C'mon. I know where we can get some cheap."

"Why are you doing all this?" I ask as we descend the stairs.

He waits to answer until he's behind the wheel again. "When I got out, I had Mom, Dad, and Felix. Felix let me crash on his couch and gave me work on his clean-up crew. But several guys I was on the inside with didn't have that support. They got out and didn't have dick. Nowhere to go. No one to help them. What're they supposed to do? Where are they supposed to go? That's why recidivism is so fucking high in this country. Prison is about punishment, not reformation. I watched a good half a dozen guys I did time with end up right back on the inside within weeks or months and a couple within fuckin' *days*—because they had no fuckin' *options*." He lets out an angry sigh. "I vowed that when I had the ability, I was gonna do something about it. So, after I got the company going, I put the program together. I don't have the time or wherewithal to help a lot of people, but I do what I can for the guys who go through my program. I figure if I can help you develop skills while you're on the inside, pay you enough to have something to live on when you get out, help you find somewhere to live, and then give you a job, you're not gonna go back in. Do it right once, and that's all you need." He looks at me. "It's a bridge, Bear. A bridge from prison to real life as a responsible member of society."

"Can't ever thank you enough."

"You can—stay on the path, man." He cuts a sharp, insightful glance at me. "Stay clean. Do good work. Be a good person. Don't go back to prison. And maybe pay it forward a little. *That's* how you thank me."

We spend an hour at a resale shop, picking out a bed, dresser, couch, and coffee table—we have to make two trips to get it all from the store to the apartment in the back of his pickup.

By the time we've gotten my apartment set up, it's almost five o'clock.

Riley glances at his phone. "Guys are about to knock off for the day. Whaddya say we check in and grab a bite?"

"Sounds good."

I'm overwhelmed. It's been a whirlwind of a day, and I've barely had time to think, let alone process everything that's happened. But I go along without a word because what else am I supposed to do?

I greet the guys on my crew, mostly guys with checkered pasts like myself—rough dudes with criminal records suited to the work of demolitions. Riley takes us to a dive bar not far from the worksite. The other guys all get beer, but I'm not ready to try booze yet, so I stick to ice water. The cheeseburger is the best thing I've ever eaten. The guys all watch me devour it, likely each of them remembering their first meal on the outside.

After sitting at the table with the crew, sipping ice water and watching them chat and laugh and hurl playful insults at each other for a couple of hours, the gathering breaks up and Riley drives me back to the apartment. He parks outside my building with the engine idling.

"So. First day of work as a free man tomorrow. I'll be here to get you at seven-thirty. Cool?"

"Sounds good," I answer. "Thanks for everything."

He holds out his fist, and I tap my knuckles against his. "Hey. One thing, Bear. First night alone might be rough. Just, you know, don't do anything dumb, yeah?"

"I'm good. See you in the morning." I give him a chin lift as I close the door and head up to my new place.

Close the door.

Sit on the couch in the peace and quiet for a few minutes.

Now what? It's just past eight in the evening, and I have no clue what to do with myself. No TV, no phone, no books, no friends, nothing to lift with. No cellmate to talk to.

It's dead quiet. Still. Stifling.

Yeah…I'm gonna need something to do in my off-hours so I don't go crazy. The first order of business is gonna be some books, some sort of weight-lifting equipment, and probably somewhere to go or something to do that's not gonna get me in trouble.

I end up laying in bed fully dressed, listening to traffic rush past outside, mind wandering and spinning.

Eventually, I fall asleep, knowing I'll wake up at dawn regardless.

Freedom is trickier than I'd expected.

2

Noelle

"AND THEN HE JUST LEAVES. JUST LIKE THAT! Can you believe it? He just leaves. Who *does* that?" Shelly Crawford, the client in my chair, chatters nonstop as I apply the dye to her hair.

I don't exactly tune it out, more just let it wash over me, occasionally offering up an encouraging word or two to keep her going. With Shelly, it's easy enough. Her current diatribe is about her latest online dating fiasco, one in a long series of them. She has terrible taste in men and never seems to learn.

She keeps chittering away as I let the dye set. I'm only half listening, the rest of my mind going back to my attempt at dating, a fiasco of epic proportions. He was a guy I met during a short-lived experiment with going to the gym, an attempt to shrink my backside a little. He was cute, seemed nice, and when we exchanged numbers and texted a little, he didn't even send any dick picks. The actual date, though? Horrific. He talked about himself the whole time, his financial portfolio, his workout splits, his favorite lifts, and his fantasy football picks. No question about me. He didn't even offer to pay for me and then tried to stick his tongue down my throat in the parking lot.

Nope.

That was several months ago, and I haven't even tried to date anyone since.

Such is my luck. I've been in a funk ever since my divorce from Brennan. I mean, good riddance—he was cheating on me with no fewer than three different women, but still. We were married. I thought I loved him; I thought he loved me. So yeah, Nat and Nik warned me he was skeezy. Nate and Noah told me they saw him making out with a girl at the ice rink over the winter. The flags were there; I just didn't see them. Didn't want to? Chose not to? I don't know. It doesn't make finding out the man you thought you were going to love forever was a philandering scumbag any easier.

I haven't been able to find my balance ever since— and that was over a year ago.

I rinse Shelly out and set about styling her long, voluminous, shiny, now-platinum blonde hair—no sign of the infringing gray strands. She's still yammering on about some reality show she's been watching, and I *um-hum* and *no way* in all the right places—a skill I've long since mastered after twelve years as a cosmetologist. I got my cosmetology degree a few months out of high school, got a job at a salon, and have been cutting and styling hair ever since—now I lease a chair here in Lux Locks Salon in downtown Three Rivers.

The dream, of course, is to have my own salon. I'm close, too. I almost have all the funds I'll need, and I have the formal business plan, and I've been scouting possible locations for months. The trouble is that Three Rivers real estate isn't cheap, especially downtown, which is where I want to be. I could easily get a space on Division over on the other side of town, but I'm not willing to compromise on the dream of having a salon right in the action. I just have to keep waiting for the right space to come along, and I know it will.

Someday. I hope.

My phone buzzes in my back pocket just as I'm putting the finishing touches on Shelly's hair. I wrap it up, cash her out, and then head in back to check the message before my next appointment shows up—Kelly, the salon owner, has a strict no phones out on the floor policy.

The message is a text in the thread between my sisters and me, creatively named *THE GIRLS.*

> **NIK: Mom and Dad want us all to come over for dinner tonight. 7 pm.**
>
> **NAT: I won't be done with my rounds till 730. I'll swing by then.**
>
> **ME: I'll be there. Thanks for the heads up, Nik.**
>
> **Nik gives my message the thumbs up.**
>
> **NAT: what about the boys?**
>
> **NIK: they're already going to be there. Mom told me to tell you two.**

The bell over the door dings, announcing my next client, so I shove the phone back in my pocket and head out onto the floor. My client is Abby Sheffield, an every-two-week regular who comes in for a color touch-up, blowout, and a mani-pedi; she tips like a boss, and I enjoy talking to her, so the four-hour appointment goes by fast and takes me through the rest of the day. She always books the next appointment that day, so the big time block is always reserved well ahead of time. Some of the girls don't like the long bookings, preferring to turn the chair over faster, but I do enjoy them. I like getting to know my clients and the longer blocks allow that. I pay closer attention, honestly. It's the quick cut-and-color with the every-few-months clients I tend to tune out. Maybe I shouldn't, but hey. I make the rules, right? No one ever complains that I'm not paying attention. I've always been able to multitask well, splitting my attention into different tasks.

Once Abby is done, I close up my station and head home. I don't have to be at Mom and Dad's for another hour and a half, so I change into yoga pants, a tank top, a hoodie, and sneakers and go for a walk. I put in my AirPods, crank my favorite playlist, and head out.

I rent a tiny Craftsman a few blocks from down-town—close enough that I can walk or ride a bike to work in nice weather but away from the bustle of downtown, so it's quiet. I'm in the zone, tuned into the music and the rhythm of the walk, arms swinging, feeling good.

I've tried gym memberships, yoga, Zumba, dance classes, and spin classes, and even I borrowed Nikki's Peloton while she was on vacation, and the only thing that I do consistently and enjoy is walking. I'll never be some skinny, jacked CrossFit athlete with a snatched waist, but I think I look pretty good. I walk three or four miles at a brisk pace almost every day, except in torrential downpours or the most brutal of winter days—when that happens, especially in winter, I borrow Nat's gym card and walk the track at the Y.

I catch a glimpse of myself in the glass of a storm door as I pass a house: five-seven and...curvy. I'm not fat or overweight by BMI standards, I just tend to carry some cushion around the hips and thighs, although my bust isn't exactly small, either. My ass does look pretty good in the yoga pants, if I do say so myself.

I'm a true ginger with ivory skin, liberal freckles, and kelly-green eyes to go with it, courtesy of recessive genes since no one else in my family has red hair or green eyes. Everyone else—Mom, Dad, Nat and Nik, and Nathan and Noah—are blond with either brown eyes or blue. It fits, though. Nat and Nik are identical twins and older than me by four years, and Nathan and Noah are also identical twins and younger than me by four years—I'm thirty, making Nat and Nik thirty-four and the boys twenty-six. I'm smack dab in the middle and unlike any of them. The running joke in the family is that Mom had a secret affair with the mailman. It's only a joke because it's patently untrue: Mom and Dad have had the same mail carrier for forty years, a sweet old Black lady named Helen.

As usual, I'm lost in my thoughts and only half paying attention. Thus, when something warm and heavy hits my legs, I'm shocked and knocked off-balance. I hit the sidewalk hard, scraping my palms and ripping the knees of my yoga pants.

"What the heck?" I yelp, rolling to my butt. "Where did *you* come from?"

My assailant is a dog. Medium size, it looks like a lab-pit mix, with short brown fur, floppy ears, and big brown eyes. No collar, skinny, and dirty. It looks up at me pathetically, wriggling its tail even as it hunkers down in fear.

I hold still, extending the back of my hand toward the pup. "Hiya, friend. You lost?"

I catch a glimpse of its undercarriage—a female. She wriggles and shimmies toward me, afraid and trying to show submission. She sniffs my hand, sniffs again, and then licks.

"I can't bring you home, but I can bring you to the shelter. How about that? You seem like a sweet girl. I'm sure someone will bring you home." I carefully move to my feet, realizing only as I look around that I'm only a few doors down from home. "Come on, girl. I'll help you."

She seems to understand and follows me down the sidewalk to my house. I grab my purse, ignoring the stinging on my skinned palms, and then grab a bungee cord from the garage to use as a makeshift leash. The dog waits for me at the end of my driveway and lets me wrap the bungee around her neck and secure the hook. She's clearly had a home and training because she jumps up into the backseat of my aged-but-serviceable CR-V without hesitation.

The drive to the animal rescue is less than fifteen minutes, but the eager, sweet little dog can't sit still, leaping from the front seat to the back and then to the front again, trying to crawl onto my lap even though she's *definitely* too big to be a lap dog, drooling on me and smearing drool on my window.

"You're a lot, girly, you know that?" I rub her floppy ears as we park behind Three Rivers Animal Rescue. "But I guess some people could say the same about me, huh? Brennan sure got annoyed with me a lot."

The dog gives a little bark, grinning at me.

"You know, you're right. Frick him. We don't need to even think about stupid, dumb-dumb loser-butt Brennan Engler. Do we? No, we don't." She ruffs again, flipping at me with her long pink tongue. "Okay, sweet girl. Let's go inside."

She hops onto my seat and waits for me to grab her makeshift leash before making the jump to the ground. I bring her inside, and she seems perfectly at ease, looking around and panting happily as I wait at the counter.

The rescue is a cacophony of animal sounds, mostly a chorus of barking dogs. The dog sits at my feet, looking up at me occasionally.

I look back down at her. "You know, you sure are sweet, aren't you? I'd love to keep you, but my landlord has a strict no-dogs policy. Plus, I work so much I'm rarely home, and that wouldn't be fair to you, would it?"

She whines at me as if understanding and slumps down to her belly, chin on her paws.

A door opens and a middle-aged woman comes to the counter; she's short and plump with a bouffant bottle-blond bob and chunky costume jewelry, wearing mom jeans and a baggy T-shirt, with a blue vest emblazoned with a cat and dog logo and the words "Three Rivers Animal Rescue."

"Hi!" She's loud and effusive. "I'm Gloria." She leans over, resting her prominent chest on the counter. "And who do we have here?"

"She literally knocked me over just now. I was walking near my house over on Elm near First Street. She's a stray, but she's been trained. Good on the leash, jumped right in the car. She's a sweet girl, I just can't have dogs where I live."

Gloria comes around from behind the counter and approaches the dog carefully, letting her sniff before crouching to say hi. The dog greets her with kisses and a puppy grin.

"Oh, she *is* a darling, isn't she? Too bad you can't take her, huh?"

I give the dog a ruffle of her ears. "I really wish I could, but my landlord has a very strict policy."

"Well, don't you worry. We have plenty of space, and I think I know someone who just might be a good home for this girl." Gloria clips a collar around the dog's neck and then a short lead. "I'll take her back."

"That's it? I don't need to do anything else?" I ask.

"Nope, we're good."

A digital bell chimes as the door behind me opens. I feel…I don't know. A tingle down my spine. A frisson of something electric.

Frowning, I glance over my shoulder to assess the source of the feeling.

"Oh." I blink in shock at the mammoth, terrifying human being standing just inside the doorway. "Um. Hi."

"Mmm." He juts his chin up with a terse grunt that barely counts as communication.

At five-seven, I'm not exactly pint-sized, and nor am I diminutively built. So I'm not used to feeling tiny.

But this man.

Dear goodness.

He's a colossus.

At least six inches taller than me, maybe even more like eight, he's not just tall. I mean, he *is* tall, but he's just... freaking enormous. His shoulders are titanic boulders bulging at the seams of his dirt-smeared black T-shirt, which bears the logo of Crowe Demolitions on the left breast. The shirt is so big I could wear it as a nightgown, and I'd probably swim in it. Yet on him, it's skin-tight.

His arms?

Lordy. Literally the size of my thighs. His chest is massive and hard, bulging with muscle and tapering to his waist. I've read the term "tree-trunk legs" before but never really visualized it until now. They're veritable sequoias sheathed in dirty, faded denim. His boots are probably as long from toe to heel as my arm is from fingertips to elbow.

The shock doesn't stop there.

He's a ginger. Bright red hair, and a *lot* of it. It's loose and wild and in desperate need of care. It's obvious he just let it grow and doesn't really know much, if anything, about caring for it. If I had to guess, I'd say he either washes it with bar soap or has one of those all-in-one bottles.

And his beard. Dear goodness, his beard. It's a real-deal mountain man thing, bushy and chaotic, hanging to his chest in an explosion of red.

My fingers itch to get all up in his business, washing, trimming, braiding.

Yet, behind and beneath the wildman hair and beard, he has deep, probing hazel eyes somewhere between green and gray. He gazes down at me, assessing me—he seems almost...shy? Not fearful, but...I can't place it.

"Didn't mean to startle you." His voice is the rattling rumble of an approaching freight train, low and quiet and powerful.

"I...no, you didn't. Well, you did, but it's fine." I smile up at him.

His brows knit at my smile as if he's puzzled by it. And that's when I get it—given his size and shocking appearance, he's probably used to people shying away from him. The tattoos wreathing his forearms and disappearing under his sleeves probably don't help, either.

I stick my hand out at him. "I'm Noelle Harper."

At first, he just stares at my hand like he doesn't know what to do with it. And then, very slowly, he lifts his hand toward mine. And holy freaking crap, his hand is... I've run out of synonyms for "huge." It could engulf both of mine and when his fingers curl around mine and his palm touches mine, his hands are as rough as cinderblocks. His grip is darned near delicate, though, as if he knows exactly how powerful he is and how to modulate his grip.

"Bear."

I blink up at him. "Bear? That's your name?"

"Yup."

"Like, for real? It's not a nickname?"

He just shakes his head.

"Bear, huh? Well, it certainly suits you." I try to see around his Godzilla thighs. "You're not bringing anything in. Adopting?"

"Volunteering."

"Oh. Really?"

"Yup."

I can't help but laugh a little. "You don't talk much, do you?"

Another shake of his big, shaggy head.

The door to the back opens and Gloria emerges, leash

in hand, putting a cell phone in her vest pocket and then looking up.

"Wow. Hi." She blinks at Bear, clears her throat. "How…um. How can I help you?"

I'm nosy and curious, so I stay to watch the exchange.

Bear slips past me to the counter—that tingling on my skin explodes all over again as he nears me. "I'd like to volunteer. Work with the dogs."

Gloria stares at him for so long that it's awkward. "You…what?"

"I'd like to help. Volunteer." He repeats himself patiently, no sign of awkwardness, no sign that he even notices her reactions to him.

She swallows hard. "I…we…yes. Yes. Let's see." She ducks to peer under the counter and comes up with a clipboard with a stack of tear-off volunteer forms. "Just fill this out. I, um…I do need help in the back. It's just me right now, and we're almost full up. I can't man the counter and clean up."

"No people. Just the dogs," Bear rumbles.

I almost laugh, but manage to hold it in.

Gloria watches him fill the form out; he hesitates when he gets to the section about prior convictions; I have good eyes and can read the form from where I'm standing.

He looks up at her. "I have a record. I work for Riley Crowe. He will vouch for my character."

Gloria opens her mouth, closes it, and opens it again. "I…I see. I would have to speak to Mr. Crowe. But…if you're okay staying in the back, I think we could make it work. I…I mean no offense, Mr. Bear."

The corner of his mouth twitches. "Just Bear. I'd rather stay in back anyway. Not good with people."

Gloria's mouth flaps again, and then she reads whatever he wrote on the form regarding priors her eyes widen. "Um…"

"Paroled. Good time credits and work release. Won't be trouble."

"But…but…." She's white as a sheet.

Bear sighs and takes a step backward. "Nevermind. I understand."

Gloria sets the clipboard down, looking at him. "You don't…you don't seem…"

"I just want to spend time with the dogs. I won't be trouble." He sounds…almost sad. Or resigned.

"I really do need the help. My last helper turned out to be terrified of dogs and quit after a week." Gloria looks down at the form, then at Bear again. "If Riley Crowe gives you a good reference, then that's good enough for me. I know Riley. He's had his share of trouble, but he's turned things around in recent years. And that program of his seems to be doing well."

Bear nods. "Changed my life. I owe him a lot."

"You're in the program?"

He nods again. "Three years. Got out a month ago."

Gloria seems to soften, then. "You like dogs?"

A shrug of one heavy shoulder. "Always wanted one. Cellmate used to be a trainer. Taught me some things."

"Wonderful. If you'd like to wait while I call Riley, you can start today, if you'd like." Gloria withdraws her phone, gesturing at a blue plastic chair in the corner.

"I'll wait. Thank you."

Gloria bustles into the back, phone to hear ear already. Bear doesn't move for the chair, I notice, although he does give it an appraising glance, clearly deciding not to risk it.

He looks at me, then. "Still here."

I blush. "Yeah, um…" I shrug, grinning. "I'm just nosy. It was nice to meet you, Mr. Bear."

That lip quirk again—like the start of a smile, quickly abandoned. "Just Bear."

"I almost laughed when she said that." I know I should go, but he's a fascinating person, and the tingle I feel around him is sort of addictive. "It's really your given name?"

He pulls a folded stack of cash out of his pocket, an ID on top, the whole held together with a rubber band. He shows me the ID—not a driver's license, I notice.

Bear Olaffson. It's his real name.

"Wow. Pretty cool." I smile at him again, hoping to get another of those lip twitches out of him; no such luck. "Well, Mr. Bear Olafsson, I should go. But it was nice to meet you. Maybe I'll see you around?"

"Maybe, Noelle Harper." His eyes scan my face, flick quickly over my body and back to my eyes. "Hopefully."

I blush at his attention, his gaze—at the "hopefully."

"I play Trivia at The Cellar every Friday night with some friends," I blurt. "You should come. It's fun."

"Trivia?"

"Yeah, you know, random facts?"

He peers at me, thinking. "I don't drink."

I shrug. "No problem. A couple of my friends are sober, too. It's still fun." I grin at him. "You can just sit there and watch. Maybe that'll stop the randos from hitting on us."

"I could do that."

"See you Friday, then?" The tingle of hope and excitement is intoxicating.

There's just something about the guy. Despite his size,

appearance, and whatever he wrote down on that form that rattled Gloria so badly, I don't feel even a hint of fear. The opposite.

He nods. "Friday."

I hold out my hand for another handshake, just because I want to feel his hands on mine again—it's a rush, how his massive, cinder-block hands are so gentle. He frowns, taking mine and turning it over to look at the palm.

"You're hurt."

"Oh, it's nothing. A stray bumped into me and I scraped my hands. A little Neosporin and I'll be good as new." I swallow hard as he holds onto my hand, his thumb delicately brushing the scrapes. "I'm fine, I swear."

"Wash 'em out. Don't want an infection." His eyes flick to mine.

"I will," I whisper. My phone buzzes in my back pocket, and I jolt, shocked. Fish it out. "Crap! I'm late for dinner. I gotta go, Bear. I'll see you Friday!"

"See you Friday, Noelle."

I back up out the door, waving, holding his gaze till the last second.

Suddenly, Friday can't come too soon.

3

Bear

NERVES JANGLE THROUGH ME, WHICH FREAKS ME
out; I don't get nervous. All the gnarly shit I've
been through? Nothing fazes me.

Walking into this bar?

Very much fazed.

Why am I here? What do I think is going to happen?
Noelle, a gorgeous, sweet, friendly, normal, well-adjusted
girl, is going to…what? Fall in love with my big, surly,
fucked-up self? Not fucking likely.

I rub my sweaty palms on my jeans, staring at the door
of The Cellar. An historic establishment in Three Rivers,
The Cellar occupies the main floor of the former Opera
House, a red brick building with elaborate stained glass

windows and an arched front door. A large white keystone block features the date the building was dedicated: 1832.

Within, I can hear the buzz and hum of conversation, a faint thud of music, the blare of TVs. Cars rush behind me in both directions on the other side of the full parking lot. As I stand near the doorway, debating simply walking back home, a gaggle of twenty-something women click on heels and boots toward me from the parking lot, clustered together and giggling. I feel their eyes on me, and the whispers and giggles feel like needles in my skin.

I shuffle away from the door so I don't crowd them as they enter. " 'Scuse me."

One of the girls, her hair elaborately curled and pinned, makeup caked on, lips bright red, skirt barely covering her ass, fake tits pushed up to her chin, winks at me. "I'd climb that tree," she stage-whispers to her friend as they scuttle past me through the door.

"Holly!" Her friend shrieks, and then simpers at me. "Sorry, my friend is a slut."

Any possible response is dried up, leaving my tongue fused to the roof of my mouth. I just stare at them, brow furrowed, molars grinding in furious embarrassment.

With another flurry of whispers and giggles, the girls enter the bar and vanish into the crowd.

"Fuck this," I mutter to myself.

I turn and head back in the direction of Tompkins Road, toward home. I make it approximately six steps when I hear the door open behind me, emitting the noise of the bar's interior. Feet slap pavement, and then Noelle is beside me, grabbing my arm.

"Hey, Bear, I thought I saw you out here." Her voice is at once soft and bright, friendly and musical.

"Uh, yeah." I sigh, annoyed at myself.

Brilliant response, loser.

She pivots to stand in front of me as if she could pose an obstacle to my forward progress; yet, I find myself stopping.

Looking down at her, mesmerized by her vivid green eyes, obsessed with an adorable spray of freckles dotting her creamy skin on her cheekbones and nose, my breath comes short, and my skin feels too tight around my bones.

"You weren't planning on ghosting me, were you?" She smiles up at me, the glint in her eyes turning her words into a tease.

"Uhhh…" I roll a shoulder. "Not ghosting. Just…"

"Not good with crowds?" She guesses, her gaze going soft, the smile still curving her plump pink lips.

God, she's beautiful. Her hair is copper and gold, whereas mine is rust and old blood. The aforementioned brilliant green eyes and milky skin. And her body—fuck. I force myself to hold her eyes instead of ogling her tits.

She's dressed in khaki shorts that cling to her thick, soft, muscular thighs and generous, heart-shaped ass; her shirt is a sapphire V-neck with sleeves so short it's almost a tank top but not quite. The hem doesn't quite meet the waist of her shorts, occasionally offering a glimpse of her belly. Her cleavage is generous enough to draw my gaze as if by fishhook and line, yet in no way excessive or showy.

"No," I murmur, eventually. "Not good with crowds."

She grabs my hand and pulls me back toward The Cellar. "Well, you can't chicken out now, buddy boy. I've already saved you a seat in the corner. C'mon!"

Maybe it's the way she so fearlessly grabs my giant paw and tugs at me, maybe it's the challenge in her words, but I allow her to pull me to the door. I grab the elaborate twist of wrought iron that is the door handle and open the door for her. She keeps hold of my hand, tugging me into the darkened interior; being late spring, the sun is still setting at seven, sending lances of sunlight through the stained glass windows. The Cellar is packed, and people jostle me and bump into me and bounce off me as Noelle tries to weave a path through the shoulder-to-shoulder crowd by the bar.

I edge in front of her to take the lead, using my sheer bulk and intimidating presence to forge a path; as usual, the crowd parts for me.

Noelle giggles. "Well, *that's* a handy trick." She leans against my back, soft breasts pressing into me; she points at a table in the far back corner. "That's us, there."

I angle for the table, mouth dry at the innocent contact, heart hammering.

Don't read anything into it, I tell myself. She's just being nice. It means nothing. How could it?

There are five people at the table, three women and two men. All five sets of eyes widen comically as I approach with Noelle clinging to my arm as if we're walking the red carpet together.

I remind myself that the only reason she's holding onto me like this is so she doesn't get sucked away by the crowd. Best not to let silly things like hope and attraction run away with me. Stay focused on reality. Gorgeous girls like her don't go for grumpy beasts like me.

Even when we reach the table, however, she doesn't let go. She glances up at me, her smile bright and eager and intoxicating. "Bear, these are my friends." She points to each person in turn. "Kyle, Ashlynn, Raina, Thomas, and Colin."

Kyle is in her thirties, with long, loose, wavy dark brown hair and light brown eyes, dressed in a tight, revealing little red dress. Ashlynn is around the same age, with artificially silver hair cropped short and styled in an artfully messy mop, hazel eyes, wearing a thin, clingy forest green shorts-jumpsuit thing, her earlobes rimmed with innumerable silver hoops. Raina has thick black hair in a loose braid down her back, dark eyes, and skin that hints at Middle Eastern heritage of some sort, wearing a pale purple sweater and dark wash blue jeans. Thomas and Colin are a gay couple; Thomas is slender and effeminate, with voluminous blond hair in a swept-back pompadour, dressed in a bubblegum pink velour tracksuit; Colin is dark-haired and more conservative, clean-cut, and wearing pressed khakis and a white button down. They sit close, hip to hip and shoulder to shoulder, Thomas's hand tucked around Colin's arm, much like Noelle's is around mine.

"We've been best friends since elementary school," Noelle says to me, guiding me to a spot on the bench side of the booth, at the very end so I have plenty of space for my bulk and my long legs. "We all went to cosmetology school together."

I sweep the group with my eyes, nodding once. "Nice to meet you guys."

"Lovely to meet you," Thomas says, in an arch, crisp voice, his eyes twinkling as if he has some inside joke he's not sharing. "So, No-No, darling. Where did you meet this stunning specimen of a man?"

I can't tell if he's mocking me or not.

Noelle sits in a chair close to me, her legs perpendicular to mine. "At the animal rescue. I found a stray and brought her in, and Bear here was signing up to volunteer."

"Welcome to the fam, Mr. Bear," Thomas says.

I shoot a look at Noelle, who is spluttering in laughter. "Just Bear."

"I didn't say anything, I swear," she says. "That was all him."

Thomas frowns. "Did I miss something?"

I'm saved from having to explain as a waitress comes by to take our orders. Kyle orders a spicy margarita, Ashlynn gets a Cosmo, Raina a Diet Coke, Thomas a club soda with lime, Colin a Manhattan, and Noelle a glass of white wine. I get a glass of ice water. After drinks are ordered, Raina asks for an order of chips and guac and a side of soft pretzels.

This group has clearly known each other their whole lives. They shift from topic to topic rapidly, and sometimes several conversations are happening all at once. I mainly follow Noelle's side of the conversation—she moves seamlessly from a conversation about haircutting with Ashlynn to a discussion about dog breeds with Colin to a series of increasingly corny and lewd jokes and references with Kyle. Yet somehow, I don't feel left out, even if I have nothing to add. She glances at me every so often, smiling, laughing, nudging my thigh with her knee—reminders of her presence, indications that she's not forgotten about me.

I don't know what to make of it.

I like it, though.

Drinks come, and the appetizers not long after. Since I only got a glass of ice water, I don't assume I'm invited to eat anything.

Noelle, after a few minutes, leans toward me. "Not hungry?"

I shrug. "Not my food."

She rolls her eyes, snagging a soft pretzel rod, and touches it to my lips. "Don't be silly."

I take the snack and munch on it. "Thank you," I say, after chewing and swallowing.

She pats my knee. "You're funny."

I frown, unsure what I did that was funny. "Okay."

For some reason, this makes her laugh even more.

After that, she seems to think it's her job to feed me. She scoops guac onto a chip and shoves it into my mouth every so often, much to the amusement of her friends. I don't get the sense of being mocked, though. More like they just don't know what to make of me, or more likely, what Noelle was thinking when she brought me along.

After a good thirty minutes of chatting and snacking, I've had three glasses of ice water, necessitating a trip to the restroom. I take care of business, wash my hands, and push through the crowd back to the table.

A pair of young men have crowded into the space where I was sitting, ignoring Thomas and Colin as if they didn't exist, clearly harassing the women. Raina looks uncomfortable, Ashlynn looks ready to throw silverware at them, Kyle is trying to slink under the table, and Noelle is scanning the crowd, looking for me.

I let my feet fall heavily on the creaky hardwood floors behind the two little douchebags. I cross my arms over my chest and wait.

One of them, dressed in expensive jeans and a pale blue polo with the collar popped, reeking of expensive cologne and entitlement, shoots a glance over his shoulder without seeing me. "Go away, dude. I'm talking to these lovely ladies."

I let out an irritated sigh that's part growl.

This gets his attention. He straightens, turns, and looks up at me. Pales.

I lean down and put my face closer to his. "Fuck—*off*."

The twinkie little douchebag grabs his buddy and drags him backward away from the table and into the crowd without a word.

Noelle sighs in relief, and so does everyone else. "Thanks, Bear. Idiots like that are so darned annoying."

"He probably sends unsolicited dick pics," Ashlynn says.

"Oh for sure," Kyle adds. "And he probably thinks it's gonna make every woman swoon at his feet."

"The popped collar?" Thomas says, snarky and acidic. "As *if*. That's *so* early aughts. And it was never cool in the first place."

Colin just nods at me. "Thank you."

I just shrug. "Yup."

Thomas giggles. "You're really committed to the strong silent type bit, aren't you?"

I've never heard a man giggle before. It's funny—I almost smile. I just nod instead. "I guess."

"So, Bear. What brings you to Three Rivers?" Ashlynn asks, elbows propped on the table, chin on her fists.

"Work."

"What do you do?" she asks.

"I work for Crowe Demolitions." I hope she'll leave it at that.

Thomas fans his face. "Ohmygod. Riley Crowe. Colin, I love you to bits, you know that, but if Riley fucking Crowe ever turned gay, I'd leave you for him in a heartbeat. That man is sex on toast."

Colin just rolls his eyes. "Riley Crowe is a shameless manwhore."

"Well, duh," Thomas shoots back. "He's a himbo, but he's hot as balls."

Raina snickers. "Balls aren't hot, Thomas. They're wrinkly, hairy, saggy, and weird."

"That's just because you haven't found the right balls," Thomas answers. "When the right balls come along, I promise, honey, you'll want to lick them all day long."

Raina just fakes a retch. "I'm gonna be sick."

Kyle snorts. "You're such a prude, Raina."

"I'm not a prude! It's just—who licks balls? No one! You just end up with pubes in your mouth." She makes a disgusted face, shaking her head. "No thanks. Been there, done that, bought the T-shirt, and burned it."

"That's because you don't actually *lick* them," Thomas says. "It's more like a nice, soft suckling motion. Right, honey?" He nuzzles into Colin.

Colin blushes. "Who wants another round?"

Thomas just giggles again. "You're so predictable. You can take the boy out of church, but you can't take the church out of the boy, even if he is gayer than Elton John."

Noelle moves from her chair to perch on the edge of the bench beside me, leaning into me. "My friends are perverts, Bear. I hope you're not easily offended."

I shift over to give her more room, but she only follows me, shoving herself against my side. "They're funny."

"Thanks for handling those two jerks."

"My pleasure."

"Is that how everyone reacts to you?" She looks up at me as she asks the question, all of her attention focused on me.

That too-tight feeling comes back, and my mouth goes dry again. "Usually. I scare people."

"You don't scare me," she says.

I don't know what to say. "Probably should." It's the wrong thing to say, but it's the truth.

"Why? Because of your size? Or because of whatever it was you wrote down on the form?"

"Both."

"Well, I'm not afraid of you."

"You don't know anything about me."

She smiles. "Nope. Not yet. How about you tell me something?"

"Like what?"

She touches my left forearm, where I had a tattoo blacked out. "Like what was under here."

Hesitating for a moment, I sigh. "A bad tattoo."

"Bad in terms of content or quality?"

"Both."

"What was it?" Curiosity, interest—no judgment.

"Gang affiliation." It's as much as I can manage, right now.

She examines me, searching my face with those bright green eyes. "And you're not in the gang anymore, so you covered it up?"

"Right."

"What kind of a gang was it?"

"The bad kind." That's only partially true.

They kept me alive. Gave me a home. A family. They also used me, got me into trouble, and put me in prison. I don't say any of that, though. I don't have the words for any of it. And if a sweet, innocent girl like her knew even half the truth, she *would* be afraid.

A burly, blond, bearded man wearing a flat cap taps a microphone. "Welcome to Trivia Night at The Cellar, everyone!" A chorus of hoots, hollers, and applause greet this. "You all know the rules by now, but I'll review for those who might be new. One person answers for the team. The first team to ten points wins the round, and the first team to win three rounds gets a two-hundred-and-fifty dollar gift card redeemable here at The Cellar. Remember, no googling! Now, is everyone ready? Our first category is pop culture."

Over the next three hours, Noelle and her friends win two rounds, battling another table for the third round. Oddly enough, I end up contributing answers twice and find myself enjoying the evening. Mainly because Noelle stays close to me the whole time, some part of her touching me at all times—a hand, a knee, a thigh against mine.

It's intoxicating—*she's* intoxicating. Hypnotic. Always laughing, joking with her friends, always with a smile. And even though I rarely speak, she never pushes me and never seems to think it's awkward.

Even her friends seem comfortable with me. Colin is almost as quiet as I am, and Thomas obviously adores him.

The other team ends up winning since none of us knew the name of a famous fountain in Rome. Our team groans when the other team comes up with the correct answer and the win, but no one seems especially upset.

Colin is the first to stand up. "I have to work early, guys. Can we go, Tommy?"

Thomas rolls his eyes. "Fine, be all responsible and shit." He stands up with his boyfriend and blows kisses to the group—including me. "Love you all. See you next week!"

Thomas playfully shoves Colin through the crowd, goosing his ass a few times along the way, which Colin plays along with, acting primly outraged.

"C'mon, girls, we might as well go, too," Ashlynn says. "If I have another Cosmo, I'll need a ride home, and god knows the ride-share options in this town are few and far between."

"No shit," Raina says, examining the long receipt and digging cash out of her purse. "The last time I got drunk on Trivia night, I waited for my Uber for over an hour. I could have walked home faster than that."

I follow the girls out of the bar, accompanying them across the parking lot.

Kyle glances at me over her shoulder as we reach the far side of the lot and a cluster of cars all parked together. "Nice to have a bodyguard no one will fuck with. I've never liked this parking lot at night."

Noelle grins up at me. "I'm glad you came, Bear."

I nod. "I had fun. Thank you for inviting me."

I wait as she chats with her friends for a few minutes, and the other three get in their cars and drive off, leaving Noelle and me alone in the lot under a wide pool of amber light from a street lamp.

"Did you really have fun?" she asks.

I nod. "Yes. Never been to a trivia night."

She grins, shrugging. "It's just a fun excuse to get together and hang out every week."

"Almost won tonight," I say.

"Almost." She looks up at me. "So. When will I see you again?"

I swallow hard. "Dunno. Next Friday?"

"When do you volunteer at the rescue?"

"Most nights after work. I help Gloria clean up and feed everyone before she closes up for the night. Wash the dogs. Walk 'em around play with 'em."

"Maybe I'll stop by and help one night this week." She looks hopeful.

It's hard not to read anything into the way she's acting toward me. Hard not to let the little seed of hope germinate.

"I'd like that."

She smiles at me, and my heart pounds. "See you soon?"

"Sure will. Drive safe."

She squeezes my hand. "Where's your car?" She looks around the now empty lot.

I shrug. "Walked. I live close."

"Want a ride?"

I shrug again. "It's okay. Not even a ten-minute walk. I'm good."

She looks almost disappointed, which is ridiculous. But it makes me rethink. "If you're sure."

"No need to go out of your way."

She pats my arm. "It's not, I promise."

I lick my lips, hesitate another moment, and then shrug. "Okay, then."

Her car is tiny and smells like fruit and lavender. My heart pounds the whole ride to my apartment complex, and my hands are clammy and sweaty.

I can't help staring at her lips and her small, clever hands. Her chest. Her bare thighs.

God, stop staring.

I know she caught me looking at least once, and only grins at me, a sly little smirk, but says nothing.

"See you at the shelter, Bear," she says as I unfold from her car.

"Yeah, see you."

She snickers. "You're so funny. Bye!"

She drives off, leaving me wondering what I did that was so funny.

No clue.

All I know is I like her. A lot.

And that seed of hope is germinating, despite my best efforts to kill it.

4

Noelle

I CLUTCH MY PHONE IN BOTH HANDS, TRYING LIKE crazy to keep a tight rein on hope. This space is absolutely perfect—right on Main Street between Compass and Brookline, sandwiched between a coffee shop and a photography studio. It's a blank slate, with nothing but open space, large black-and-white checkered tile flooring, and plain white walls. All I'd need are the stations and some decorations, a little counter or desk for the cash register and appointment book, and some shelving for merchandise. It has two bathrooms, a small office, and a back door to a little alley nook for breaks, with a nearby private dumpster for trash, complete with a locking fence.

I keep my voice even as the showing agent waits for my response. "It's very nice. What's the asking rent?"

Vicki, the agent, lists a number that makes my eyes water, and my eyebrow twitch.

"Is there any wiggle room on that?"

Vicki winces. "Maybe a little, but not much. You know spaces on Main Street go fast, Noelle. If you want it, I'd put in an offer soon. Like, within forty-eight hours, max. I've already shown it six times and it's only been listed a week."

"Okay, well, let me crunch some numbers and get back to you. Thanks, Vicki." I smile at her and make my exit, fighting tears of disappointment.

No way in heckle-schmeckle I can swing that rent, even if I don't pay myself. It's triple the amount I'm paying for my house, and that's just rent—add utilities for both, plus the overhead of the business itself? Forget it.

Maybe if I let go of my house and get an apartment, I could finagle the numbers enough to make it work. *Maybe.* But all the apartments are farther from downtown than I want to be. Plus, I love my house. It's cute, and it has just enough space for me and my little collection of things. It's cozy and quiet and a few blocks away from Main Street.

If only I could have a dog, it would be even more perfect. But so far, I haven't been able to get Richard to budge on that topic. My plan all along has been to make Richard an offer to buy it from him, but my investigation into comps in the area put it out of reach for a few more years, at least at my current rate of income. If I were to shell out the bucks for a place like the one I just saw, things would get even tighter.

Ugh.

"Someday," I tell myself. "Someday."

I stop in at Pints & Paninis, a cute little cafe that sells artisan sandwiches during the day and transforms into a bar in the evenings. Lucas takes my order, giving me the same hopeful smile he's given me every day for years, even after I've told him in no uncertain terms that we aren't ever going out together. I mean, he's cute, gainfully employed, and charming as all get out, but he's nineteen. A cougar I am not.

As I wait for my sandwich, I watch foot traffic on the sidewalk and cars on Main Street. A huge silver pickup stops at the traffic light at Brookline, right in front of Pints & Paninis. In it, Riley Crowe is at the wheel, lounging backward in the seat with his wrist hanging over the wheel, mirrored aviators hiding his eyes, his shiny black hair slicked back. Beside him in the passenger seat is Bear. My heart skips a beat just looking at him.

I've thought about him constantly since last Friday. I haven't had time to go see him at the shelter despite my best efforts. Every day this week, something has come up: a client needs a last-minute blowout before a big event; Mom needs help in the garden at home; Dad needs a trim; Nat needs me to feed and play with her blue and gold macaw, Patch, because she agreed to work a double shift; Nik needs me to style her hair for an interview for the prime time news anchor slot; the boys are trying out for parts in a play at the Three Rivers Theater and need me to run lines with them.

I love my family, but gosh, they all come to me when they need something, and I can't ever seem to say no. I've never been able to say to no them. I don't mind, most of the time. But it sure does get exhausting.

I'm going to go see him today, I decide, as Riley and

Bear pull away at the green light. Especially because our usual Friday night Trivia gathering has been canceled—Thomas and Colin have a wedding, Raina has a family thing, and Kyle and Ashlynn are both working late.

I take my sandwich across Main Street and eat it on a bench overlooking the water, letting my thoughts wander, as they do so often lately, back to Bear.

He was so shy and hesitant. Every time I touched him, no matter how innocently—and it was all innocent—he would look at me in shock, as if unable to figure out why I would do such a thing. Other than that brush of his thumb over the scrapes on my palm, he hasn't made physical contact of any kind with me. He won't pull away, but neither will he touch me first.

The man has secrets, that much is obvious. Deep ones. Dark ones. There's pain in his eyes. The tattoos on his arms hide scars. Yet for all that, he's gentle, quiet, and still. I feel no fear of him, even though he seems to expect it. I mean, I get it. If all you were to go on was his appearance, sure, he's intimidating as all heck. But there's more to him—a lot more. He hides it, but that just makes getting it out of him that much more of an intriguing challenge.

Finished with my lunch, I head back to the salon in time for my one o'clock with Maggie Hendricks, and her soft patter about her grandkids keeps my mind occupied—and after that, I'm so busy I have no time to think about Bear.

⊙

I'm still in my work clothes, but my last appointment ran super long—Ella came in for a blowout and ended up with a cut and color *and* a blowout, which is good for my bank account, but meant I couldn't clock out and lock up until after seven, and the shelter closes at seven-thirty.

It's quarter after by the time I park behind the shelter and go inside. I'm greeted by the welcome cacophony of barking dogs and the scent of fur and whatever else. The bell announces my presence, and Gloria hustles out.

"Why, it's Noelle Harper. Another stray?" She peers over the counter expectantly.

"Actually," I pause, clear my throat, and hope my embarrassed flush isn't too obvious. "I wanted to go back and talk to Bear for a few minutes. I thought I'd help him do whatever it is he's doing."

Gloria's eyes twinkle knowingly. "Ahh, I see. That man has been a godsend. Dogs and cats both love him, and he doesn't mind doing the dirty work. I admit I had my reservations, what with a murder conviction on his record, but after talking to Riley and watching him with the animals, it's obvious he's sweet as sugar, just a little misunderstood, maybe. Goodness knows I don't know the circumstances of his conviction, but I figure there has to be a mistake of some kind because I just can't see a man as kind and gentle and patient as he is killing anyone." Her eyes widen, and she claps a hand over her mouth. "There I go again—me and my big mouth. Forget I said anything?"

Murder conviction? Holy crappy-doodles.

But as Gloria said, there must have been a mistake.

She waves me to the back. "He's giving Roger a bath right now—the poor idiot pooped in his cage again. Just follow the howling."

As I pass her, Gloria catches my arm. "Do tread softly with that one, dear. He's one of those still-waters-run-deep types. And try to forget what I said—it wasn't my place to say anything, it's just my mouth runs away from my brain sometimes."

I pat her hand. "It's okay, Gloria. Thank you."

I push through the batwing doors—the volume increases tenfold, and I follow the sound of a howling husky to the back of the shelter; along the way, I pass dogs, cats, bunnies, parrots, and even three adorable white rats together in a cage. Another set of doors takes me to a subway-tiled room with a waist-height stainless steel wash basin running along one wall, with restaurant-style springy spray hoses at regular intervals, with hooks on the wall for clipping leashes.

Bear is at one of the stations, his broad back to me, gigantic arms flexing as he holds a writhing, shaking, yowling husky in place with one hand, scrubbing it with the other.

The husky is downright yelling, making a noise that sounds for all the world like "No! No! No!"

And Bear answers. "Yes, yes, yes. Don't talk back to me."

"Row-row-row-*ROW*!"

"I know you don't like baths. Next time, don't shit in your cage. Wait for me to walk you."

"Wow-row-*ROW*-row."

"Yes, it is your fault. You know better. I told you I'd walk you."

"Row-*row*-row-row."

"I was not too slow. I was busy, you ungrateful turd."

"*Rrrrow*."

"Rude."

I can't help the snort that escapes me at this exchange, and Bear glances at me over his shoulder.

"Oh, hey. You came."

"Hi, you. Yeah, sorry it took so long. Been a busy week." I edge closer. "Can I help?"

"You're gonna get wet."

I shrug out of my sling purse, hang it from a hook, and find a blue shelter apron on another and tie it around my waist. "A little water never hurt anyone."

"Tell that to Roger."

I move up beside Bear, snickering at the pissed-off expression on the big husky's face. "Hi there, Roger," I say, taking the dog's wet, soapy scruff from Bear so he can use both hands to finish lathering.

"Row-row."

"That sounded like hello, to me," I say.

Bear nods. "Yep. He's a talker."

"Yeah, I heard the two of you having quite the disagreement."

"Roger was being a turd."

"Row-*ROW*-row-row-row." *I wasn't being a turd.*

"Yes, you were."

"Row-row-row-*row*." *No, I was not.*

"Do you argue with dogs a lot, Bear?" I ask, giggling as Roger tries to shake off, only to huff in annoyance when Bear snags his scruff and prevents him from doing so.

"Nope. Just with this loveable dickhead."

"Row-row-row-row-row-row?" *Who are you calling a dickhead?*

"You, you dickhead." Bear glances at me. "Gotta rinse him. Hang on tight."

I clutch Roger's neck scruff with both hands, turning his face to mine. "Hold still for me, buddy, okay? The more you cooperate, the faster it'll be over."

"Row-rooooo." *Says you.*

I splutter and laugh as Bear hoses Roger with the sprayer; the dog goes apeshit, struggling against my hold as he tries to escape and shake off. "Hold still, butthead!"

"*ROW*! Row-roo-row!" *NO! Let me go!*

Bear moves behind me, momentarily framing me with his huge body, transferring the sprayer to his other hand so he can rinse Roger's other side and under-body.

My hold slips and Roger manages a few sharp shakes, spraying us with soapy water before I can grab hold again. "Sorry, sorry. His fur is slippery."

"Almost…done." Bear nudges Roger's chin up and gives his chest and belly one last spray. "Okay. On three, let him go and back up. Ready? One…two…*three*."

In unison, Bear and I back away from Roger, who gives us a scathing glare of death and doom before shaking vigorously. He leaps down and bolts around the room, then, with a wild case of the zoomies, pausing now and then to shake again—perhaps not so incidentally doing so right near us.

Bear grabs a thick white towel from a stack on a shelf and snags Roger as he zips past, hauling him around. "Time to dry off, Rog."

"ROW!" *NO!* "Row-roooo!" *I'm zooming!*

My heart melts a little, watching how gentle Bear's huge hands are as he towels the obstinate creature dry. After toweling him off, Bear and I take turns running a brush through Roger's thick fur, until he's glossy and handsome.

"How did a handsome fella like this end up here?" I ask Bear. "Do you know?"

Bear shrugs. "Huskies sound like a good idea until you have one."

"Why's that?"

He gestures at Roger, who, now that he's been released from his grooming, has resumed his maniacal zoomies. "They're too damn smart for their own good. They talk back. Endless energy. He's like this literally all the time. No off switch."

"Why Bear, that was, like, six whole sentences at once!" I tease.

He blinks at me owlishly. "What do you mean?"

I laugh. "I'm teasing you."

"Oh."

I peer up at him. "You do know that I'm just playing around, right? I'm not actually making fun of you."

He nods slowly. "I know."

"*Bear*?" Gloria's voice echoes from the front, sounding scared. "*HELP!*"

"Grab Roger." Bear hands me a leash and bolts for the front, moving faster and more gracefully than a man of his size has any right to move.

I leash Roger and walk him to the cages, finding the empty one with his name handwritten on a tag. I put him in and unclip the leash, latch the cage, and hustle for the front.

Gloria is huddled behind the counter, shaking, as no fewer than four burly, brown-uniformed county Animal Control officers struggle to contain the single most horrifying creature I've ever laid eyes on.

It's gargantuan, a barking, drooling, slavering, snarling beast the size of a lion with short, mottled-brown fur, pointed ears, and a long, whip-like tail. The mammoth animal is a killing machine with huge, crushing jaws and curved, slicing talons on his dinner-plate paws. Even with a leash muzzling his jaws closed and a spiked collar digging viciously into the thick fur at its neck, the monstrous dog is seconds from breaking loose and murdering us all.

Bear faces the beast from a couple of feet away, hands at his sides, cooly and calmly regarding the two-hundred-pound murder machine.

"His owner died," one of the officers explains between grunts of effort. "Won't respond to commands. If you guys don't take him, we're putting him down. He's fucking dangerous as hell."

Bear grunts in response, crouching. "Wait a second." He rises and inches closer. "Hold him."

"Fuckin' trying, man. This big fucker is impossible to hold." The officer is a big, thick-necked man himself, as are the other three, and even with four of the telescoping noose things around his neck, the dog is dragging all four men across the tile floor.

Bear gets ahold of the huge, terrifying dog's collar, glancing at the nametag. "Panzer."

"Yeah? So?" the officer snaps.

Bear lets the shiny gold nametag go and backs up. "Sitz." It sounds like *sits;* I assume it means sit.

Immediately, the dog ceases struggling and plops his butt onto the floor.

"Platz." *Pl-AH-ts.*

The dog, Panzer, lays on his belly. It means to lay down, I guess.

"Bleib." *Bl-eye-b.* Bear glances at the officers. "Give him some slack."

"Are you fuckin' nuts?" Bear just stares, and the officer shakes his head. "Fine. Your funeral."

They slowly ease off the pressure, until it's apparent Panzer isn't going anywhere.

"Take them off."

One by one, the animal control officers remove the hook-loop-pole-things, moving slowly and gingerly; as soon as the tools are free, their hands go to the tasers on their belts.

Bear holds Panzer's gaze. He pats his thigh. "Komm. Fuss." *K-oh-m; fooss.*

Instantly, the dog bolts forward, curls in a tight circle, and stands at Bear's side, his big ribcage against Bear's thigh.

"Braver Hund, Panzer. Braver Hund." *Br-ah-ver hoond.*

"The fuck?" one of the officers mutters. "German?"

Bear nods. "Highly trained guard dogs like this are taught in German. He won't respond to English commands because he doesn't know them."

"Fuck me. He's like a different dog entirely," the first officer says.

Bear unhooks the wicked-looking barbed collar and tosses it away. "He was hurt and scared. His owner died. He's upset."

"He destroyed the house his owner was living in. An older guy who lived alone. Neighbors eventually called the cops due to the smell. Cops called us. Could barely get this guy here."

Gloria emerges from the corner. "I don't know about that one, Bear."

Bear crouches in front of Panzer, ruffling his ear as he slips the muzzle off. "He's mine. I'll take him."

"But Bear—" Gloria shimmies around the counter and huddles behind Bear's bulk, peering nervously around him at the massive dog, who is now standing in the same place, panting and grinning happily up at Bear. "Are you *sure*? I don't know if your apartments allow dogs."

"My problem, not yours." Bear juts his chin up at the animal control officers. "Thanks, fellas. We're good."

"You're sure?" the lead officer asks, obviously skeptical.

"I'm sure. He'll stand there just like that until I say otherwise, whether it's five minutes or an hour." Bear ruffles Panzer's ears. "Sitz, Panzer."

Panzer plops his butt down and resumes panting. Bear goes around the counter and through the doors, but Panzer only watches him go with a concerned look on his face. After a moment, Panzer gives a sad little whine in his throat.

Bear reappears, and Panzer goes back to happy panting. "See?"

"Craziest shit I've ever seen, man," one officer says as they troop out the door.

Gloria rubs her face with both hands. "That was rather frightening."

"How did you know?" I ask.

"His name tag," Bear answers. "Panzer is a German word. Means tank."

"You speak German?" I ask, unable to hide my shock.

"Not really. My cellmate was German. Trained dogs professionally for the police and military as well as private owners. He taught me a few words—commands, mostly."

I have a billion questions, and I'm not sure which one to ask first, or how to ask any of them.

Gloria sighs. "Well, kids, that was about all the

excitement this old lady can handle for one day. You can go, Bear, I'll close up. Thanks for all your help today, dear."

Bear grunts and nods. "See you tomorrow."

"Are you really taking that dog home?" Gloria asks.

"Yeah. I'll figure something out."

"I'll get the adoption paperwork together for you tomorrow. You can take a bowl, leash, and some food if you'd like."

Bear doesn't smile at her, but his expression softens. He's fond of Gloria. "Thank you."

"Bear," I murmur. "You can't take him to your apartment. They don't allow dogs."

Bear just shrugs. "No one in the unit below me, or across. Be fine for one night."

"And then?"

"Dunno. Maybe he can sleep at the yard."

I frown up at him. "The yard?"

"Headquarters." He taps the logo of his work shirt— Crowe demolitions. "Equipment yard."

"Why not take him there tonight?"

"Have to ask Riley first."

"So call him and ask?"

A sigh. "No phone. Don't know his number."

I blink at him. "You don't have a cell phone?"

"Nope. No need."

Back to one and two-word answers, now, apparently.

"Well, it'll be tight quarters, but I'll drive you two home."

Bear shrugs. "Not far. I can walk."

"Bear." I take his hand. "C'mon."

He gazes down at me, at our joined hands—his fingers tighten ever so slightly around mine. "Alright."

It is indeed tight quarters in my little CR-V, what with a giant man and equally giant dog. Panzer huffs constantly, fogging the back windows until I lower one, at which point he hangs his huge head out and lolls his tongue, jowls flapping in the wind.

"He sure is funny, now that he's not acting like a murder machine," I say. "What kind of dog is he? Never seen one like him."

"Cane Corso." *CAH-ney COR-so.*

"What made you adopt him? I ask.

A shrug. "I understand him."

I glance at him, and wait—my father, a psychology professor, long ago taught me the value of a leading silence.

Bear looks at me, and then out the window. "Big, scary, unwanted, and misunderstood. People see his size and how intimidating he is and nothing else."

"Bear," I murmur. "I see you."

He shakes his head, swallowing hard. "Noelle…"

"What?"

A sigh. "I'm not…" he trails off.

"Not what, Bear?" I press.

We pull into his complex and I park in front of his building.

Bear chews on the inside of his cheek, making his mustache twitch. "A lot of things."

"Like what?" I know I'm pushing, but I can't help it.

I want to know more about him. I want to know everything. I see it all bubbling away inside him, unexpressed as if he just doesn't know how to let it out.

"I've done bad things, Noelle."

I twist in the seat to face him. "Are you going to hurt me?"

He frowns. "Never."

I shrug and smile. "Okay, then. I believe you. I feel it. I know it's true. I told you, already; I'm not scared of you."

"If you knew what I'd done…"

I swallow hard. "Gloria, she…she didn't mean to, but she sort of let it slip that you had a murder conviction. That's what she was so scared of that day we met."

Bear growls a sigh. "Manslaughter and armed robbery."

"I don't really know the difference."

A shrug. "Degrees of severity and levels of intent."

"Will you tell me about it?"

He frowns at me. "You really wanna know?"

"Yeah, I do."

At that moment, Panzer whines in his throat and gives a soft little whuff.

"He's gotta go, I think. Need to walk him."

"Okay. We can walk and talk."

We get out, and Bear gathers the leash, food and water bowls, and the small bag of kibble and deposits it all on the bottom step leading up to his unit.

Leash in hand, Bear pats his thigh. "Fuss."

Instantly, Panzer, who was waiting in the backseat with the door open, bounds out of the car, leaving it rocking on its springs, and halts at Bear's right leg.

"Gosh, he's *really* well-trained, isn't he?"

Bear nods. "Very."

We amble unhurriedly along the narrow strip of grass between the parking lot and the road circling the complex; after a few hundred feet, Panzer lifts his leg to piddle on a maple sapling. A few feet farther down, he squats to drop a dookie the size of a chihuahua. Bear digs a plastic bag from his pocket and scoops it up, twists the bag a few times, turns it inside out to put another layer of plastic around the yuck, and ties it off.

We continue on in easy silence—I can tell, somehow, that Bear is thinking about what to say, so I give him the space to think.

Ahead, a fat raccoon waddles away from the fenced-off dumpster; Panzer's whole body tightens, quivering, ears flicked upright and swiveled forward, tail stiff, but he doesn't leave Bear's heel, a soft whine his only protest.

"Braver Hund, Panzer," Bear mutters, once the raccoon is out of sight.

The dog looks up at him and whuffs quietly.

"He's amazing," I say. "I thought for sure that raccoon was dinner."

"He's a guard dog. Trained to obey his human no matter what."

We make it halfway around the complex before Bear speaks again.

"You really wanna know?"

I can't help myself—I slip my hand into his and press into his side. "I do. But only if you want to tell me. I'll still be your friend if you don't."

He peers down at me. "My...friend?"

I smile. "Yup. Friend. Ever have one of those?" I tease, poking his side; it's like poking a brick wall.

"Sort of." A thoughtful pause. "Well, yes. Matt, my cellmate. But that's a little different than normal friendship."

"I have so many questions, Bear. *So* many."

He lets one corner of his mouth curve up a little, in the closest thing to a smile I've ever seen on him. "So many, huh?"

"Like, at least sixty-seven."

A snort. "That's a lot."

"I mean, yeah. You're sort of enigmatic."

"Enigmatic?"

I'm tempted to tell him what it means, but I don't want to assume he doesn't know. Just because he's a huge guy who's been to prison doesn't mean he's stupid or uneducated.

"Very." I'm still holding onto his hand, and it's just so easy to walk with him, hand in hand, like we've done it forever.

Every so often, he twitches his hand, tightening and loosening, and looks down at our joined hands.

When he does it again, I glance up at him. "Why do you do that? Just curious."

"Do what?"

"Squeeze my hand. Look at our hands."

"Oh." He shrugs. "Make sure I'm not holding too tight. Don't wanna hurt your little hand."

I feign indignance. "My hand is not small."

He snorts and holds his palm up; I fit mine up against his, the bottoms of our palms lined up. He can curl his fingers over mine almost double. "Tiny." He glances at me as we join hands and continue walking. "I also just…." He trails off. "Never mind. It's stupid."

"What? Tell me, please."

He hesitates a moment or two and then sighs. "You, holding my hand. Gotta remind myself it's real."

My heart burns at this. "Bear…why wouldn't it be real?"

He shakes his head. "Hard to explain."

"Try me?"

A long pause. "Easier to tell you why I went to prison."

"You don't have to tell me anything," I say. "But I'd like to know everything."

"Grew up...rough," he says, after a moment of thought. "Dad died before I was born. Mom couldn't handle taking care of me, I guess, so she turned me over to the state."

"Oh my gosh, Bear. I'm so sorry. That's awful."

A shrug. "I guess. Foster home to foster home, none of them good, till I was twelve. That last family was fucked up. Mom tried to do things to me, Dad kicked the shit out of me, and their kids made fun of me and did all sorts of mean shit. So I took off."

The burn in my heart increases, and my eyes sting. "Bear, my goodness. That's...how can people be like that?"

A soft snort. "Most people are, in my experience." Another pause. "Was a street kid after that. How I ended up in the gang." He touches the tattoo I asked about. "Three-One-Three Bishops."

He looks down at me; I'm on his left, Panzer on his right. The light is fading, but with these two beside me, I couldn't possibly be any safer. All the same, I huddle closer to him, soaking up his warmth as the late spring evening turns cool.

"When I was twenty-one, I was out late with...I guess I thought he was my friend at the time. Alex. He was driving. Decided he wanted to knock over a liquor store."

"Knock over, meaning..."

"Rob. Steal cash and some booze. Supposed to be a quick in and out. I wasn't armed—never carried a gun. Didn't need to." He lapses into silence, thinking. Remembering. "Clerk got gutsy. Talked shit to Alex. Alex pulled his gun, and I tried to wrestle it away from him. I wasn't about shooting innocent people. The gun went off, and the clerk got shot."

"It wasn't even your gun, and you were trying to stop it," I protest.

He nods, shrugging. "No security camera inside. Alex was wearing gloves because it was January. I wasn't. My prints were on the gun; his weren't. We both got tagged, but he ratted on me and said it was my gun. Didn't matter what I said because they had my prints on the murder weapon. So I got the manslaughter charge, and Alex only did a nickel. I got twenty-five years."

I gape at him. "*Twenty-five years?*"

He nods. "Did just shy of eleven."

"Eleven years in prison for something you didn't do?"

A shrug. "I was there. A guy got shot. Someone had to pay."

"Aren't you angry?"

"At who?" A shake of his head. "Alex? I was, for a bit. No point, though."

"No point in being angry at getting framed and spending eleven years in prison for a crime you didn't commit?" I stop and look up at him. "I'd be so angry."

"I did a lot of bad shit before that, Noelle. Hurt a lot of people very badly." He looks down at me, gray-green eyes deep and serious. "Only if they started it, but still. Committed other crimes. Way I see it, I did the time I deserved, just not for the crime I was convicted of."

"You were an orphan. Living on the streets, homeless at twelve? I have to imagine the things you did you only did because you had to, to survive."

A shrug and a nod. "I guess. Doesn't make it right,

though." He peers into the darkness that's fallen around us, then back at me. "Prison changed me. Learned how to stop being so angry. No more fighting. No more hurting people."

I stare at him, frowning. "You seem so gentle, now, Bear. It's hard to imagine you angry and violent."

He clears his throat, looking away from me. "It's ugly. Dark. Bad. Not who I am anymore."

I cling to his hand, squeezing hard. "No, it's not."

"If you were in a gang and other people carried guns but you didn't...how did you survive?"

He shrugs, making a fist the size of an industrial wrecking ball. "When I hit people, Noelle, they break." The fist relaxes, no longer a deadly weapon, just a hand.

Panzer growls, attention on something in the darkness. He gives one big, deep, threatening bark, and there's the sound of scuffling feet on concrete and a curse as someone runs off.

"Braver Hund, Panzer."

"Not safe around here, Noelle. Not a great area."

I lean into him. "I'm with you."

He heaves a deep breath. "Question I can't answer is why."

I look up at him. The self-doubt in his voice and the implication that I shouldn't be with him breaks my heart for him. "Why not?"

He doesn't answer for a long time. We've long since come full circle back to his building, now standing near my car again. "Lotta guys out there for you, Noelle. Guys who didn't do a dime in the pen for manslaughter."

I shrug. "I suppose. I like *you*, though." I smile up at him, in the darkness.

"Weird."

I laugh at that. "It's not weird. Geez."

"Is to me."

I sigh and rub his thick, firm forearm with my other hand. "Well, fine. But it's not weird to me."

"I don't understand you, Noelle Harper."

I lift up and kiss the side of his cheek, just above the line of his beard. "Well, Bear Olafsson, we have time for you to learn. I'm not all that complicated, though, I promise."

He doesn't move for a long time, as if shocked and paralyzed by my kiss.

I'm not sure what possessed me, either, and I know this whole thing is probably crazy. My family won't get it at all. But I find myself not caring.

I've lived most of my life doing things for other people, my family in particular.

This? Getting to know Bear? It's for me.

5

Bear

RILEY GIVES TWO SHORT BLASTS ON HIS HORN, alerting me that he's there. I drain the last of my coffee, pouring more into the scratched, dented, and battered gray-green Stanley thermos I'd found at the thrift store yesterday, along with the restaurant-grade Bunn coffeemaker. Screwing the top on, I carry it to the door.

I glance back at Panzer, who is lying on the couch, watching me with his big, deep, soulful brown eyes. "Panzer, Fuss."

He stretches his forepaws on the carpet, trots forward a couple of steps, lets his hind legs down, pauses to stretch forward with one hind leg and then the other kicked out and shuddering, and then he trots to my right heel, following me out and down the steps. It's a gray day, heavy, soggy, leaden skies promising rain later.

As I approach his truck, Riley lowers his window, frowning at me. "Bear, buddy, what in the actual motherfuck is *that*?"

"Sitz," I command, and Panzer plops his big ass on the ground as I open the rear door and reorganize the back bench to make room. I pat the bench. "Komm rein." *K-oh-m r-EYE-n*—come in.

Panzer springs up onto the bench with a lithe athleticism belied by his monstrous size.

He's so big, he sits his butt and hind legs on the seat with his forelegs on the footwell, resting his chin on the console between the front seats. Riley twists in his seat, eyeing the dog warily.

I round the hood and get in. "That's Panzer."

"Like the German tanks from World War Two?"

I nod. "Means tank in German."

"I have questions." He puts the truck into reverse but doesn't back out.

"Okay."

"I repeat—what the actual motherfuck *is* that thing?"

"A dog. Cane Corso. Owner died and he got turned in by animal control. They were gonna kill him."

"And you adopted him?" Riley asks, dark brows lifting.

"Yes. He's a good dog. Doesn't deserve to die."

"Guess not, but, Bear, you can't have dogs in the apartment." He looks at Panzer, whose eyes are flicking between Riley and me. "He looks like he could take down a goddamned moose."

"Prob'ly."

"Okay, um." He pinches the bridge of his nose. "And you're planning on…what? Him coming to work with us?"

"Yes."

"Bear…"

"I tell him to lay down and stay, he'll stay put till I say otherwise. Won't bark. Won't chase nothin'."

"He won't attack anyone?" Riley asks, sounding skeptical.

"Long as they don't pose a threat to me."

"Bear, I'm not sure a whole fuckin' army could pose a threat to you," he says, chuckling.

"From your perspective. He's got a different one." I ruffle Panzer's ears. "He's a good dog. He won't be a problem."

Riley sighs, regarding the animal. "Will he bite me if I pet him?"

"Does it seem like it?" I ask. "Let him sniff the back of your hand."

Riley puts his hand near Panzer's snout, letting the dog sniff. After a couple of good whiffs, Panzer gives Riley's hand a little lick and then nudges his hand with his snout.

"Wants you to scratch his ears," I say.

Riley gives Panzer's ears a good scratching, earning a funny little groan from my new friend. "Alright. We can give it a go. But if the manager catches wind that you've got a dog up there, you'll have to figure something else out."

"Worst case, he sleeps at the yard," I say. "Rather he stays with me, though. He…he helps me."

Riley nods, clapping me on the shoulder. "I get that. Transitioning to freedom after that long on the inside isn't easy. It'd be good for you to have a companion." Another ruffle of Panzer's ears, and then he backs out of the spot and heads for Tompkins Road. "Long as he behaves, I'm cool with it."

The job site is less than ten minutes away—we swing through McDonald's on the way for breakfast; I order a couple extra sausage patties for Panzer, who wolfs them down happily, his wet black nose twitching hopefully as we eat ours.

We're working in a cul-de-sac off Manitou near Division; the homes on the street are all mid-century ranches in varying states of disrepair. Of the sixteen homes on the street, Felix and Riley own eight, the rest either abandoned and falling apart or empty and for sale—only two are occupied, and according to Riley, they're close to selling. We're in the process of demo'ing the properties owned by the brothers. We've finished two over the last week, and are starting a new one today.

The rest of the crew are already there—Larry, Eddie, Miguel, and Juan arriving together in one truck, Richie, Darius, Duane, and Anthony in another. Both trucks bear the company logo, hauling enclosed trailers full of equipment—sleds, wrecking bars, Sawzalls, angle grinders, jackhammers, wheelbarrows, tile scrapers, and a bunch of other shit.

The guys set about gathering gear, putting on high-vis vests, hardhats, and safety glasses while Riley unlocks the front door.

He stands on the stoop as we head for the door and claps his hands. "Quick change of plans today, fellas."

Before he can get anything else out, Darius raises his hand. "Question, boss." He points at Panzer, who is currently lounging on the grassy verge between the sidewalk and the road. "Why we got a big scary-ass dog?"

Riley nods at me. "Bear?"

"That's Panzer. Won't bother you. Just don't try to pet him unless I'm with you."

Darius looks at me. "Long as he stays way the hell away from me, I'm cool."

"Anyone have issues with Panzer?" Riley asks. No one else says anything. "Right. So. Last couple weeks I've been noticing that Bear tends to work ahead of everyone else."

Juan grins at me. "That's 'cuz he works like five people."

Riley chuckles. "Exactly my thinking, Juan. So, what I propose is that Bear takes a house by himself and the rest of us work together as usual. Bear, that cool with you?"

I consider the idea briefly and then nod. "Sure. Probably get more done that way."

Riley claps his hands. "Great. Guys, we're here. Bear, you tackle the one across the street. I've marked the walls that are coming out. You're going down to studs and sub-floor. Power and plumbing are both off, but watch your clearances around outlets and shit. You know the drill."

"Sure do." I grab a wheelbarrow, wrecking bar, sledge-hammer, tile scraper, and a red plastic coal shovel, toss the tools into the wheelbarrow, and then head across the street. "Panzer, komm." When we reach the property where I'll be working, I pause in the center of the patchy, overgrown front yard. "Platz. Bleib."

Panzer circles a few times clockwise, a few times coun-terclockwise, once more clockwise, and then lays down, tongue lolling and gaze alert and curious as he watches me head inside and assess the job at hand.

It's a doozy. Piss- and who-knows-what-stained car-pet, graffiti-tagged walls, water-stained ceilings, old mat-tresses, discarded needles, empty booze bottles, piles of shredded newspaper, fiberglass insulation, and bits of cloth—rat and mouse nests. I wander the house, locating the walls marked for removal, identifying the load-bearing structures, testing the floors for sagging, and poking at water stains on the ceiling with my wrecking bar.

The first step is to get rid of the trash. I put on my work gloves, fit an N95 over my face, and get to work hauling shit out to the 30-yard roll-off in the driveway. Panzer watches me come and go, chin on his paws as he dozes. Riley pops in to check on me around eleven, after three hours of work. "Damn, dude, you're really cranking in here."

I've cleared the trash and removed the marked walls, and I'm now working on pulling down the drywall to expose the studs and insulation.

"Honestly, boss, this is better for me," I say. "No one in my way slowing me down."

He claps me on the shoulder. "Lunch in an hour. Good work, bud."

As I work, I let my mind wander. It's why I like demolition so much: my body does the work, and my mind has the freedom to process things.

Mostly, it's Noelle occupying my thoughts. It's tempting to think she's interested in me. She sought me out at the shelter and invited me to hang out with her friends, and whenever we're together, she's always touching me.

I just don't know what to make of it.

I don't know how to trust it. I mean, shit, she's so far out of my league it ain't even funny. She's hot as fuck, for one thing. That thick, wavy red hair, those freckles. Her lips. Her body, Jesus. Takes everything I've got to not stare at her like a goddamned pervert. Big, round, plump tits that strain against her shirt. That glorious, tight, heart-shaped ass that sways with every step, hypnotizing me.

Her eyes. God, her eyes. The way she looks at me like she sees something worthwhile in me.

Something I have trouble seeing in myself.

My wrecking bar bites into drywall near a seam, and I lever it sideways and then yank hard, ripping a huge section away to topple to the floor. I smack the hooked end of the bar into the wall, burying it in place, and haul the section out to the dumpster, heaving it in. I'm sweaty and filthy, but I feel good, my muscles loose and warm. Now that I can work at my own pace, I get a lot more done. I was held back by the sheer amount of people coming and going; Riley likes to use his whole crew at once on a single property, working faster that way rather than splitting us up into separate crews. Each property gets done faster that way. The problem for me is I can work twice as fast as the next guy. Now that I have a whole house to myself, I can set my own pace and not worry about anyone getting my way.

I take a quick break, sipping coffee from my thermos as I lounge in the grass beside Panzer, who rests his chin on my thigh.

My mind goes back to Noelle. To the possibilities. Wondering what she wants from me. Friendship? More? What would more look like?

She has married parents and siblings. A good job. Friends. A whole life. A good, stable, clean, well-adjusted life.

Where does a giant, hairy, tattooed ex-con with blood on his hands and a closetful of skeletons fit into that life?

I don't.

Best case scenario, I'm just an interesting new

thing—a project. An anomaly in her vanilla, well-ordered life.

Best not to let my imagination run away from me. Hope is a dangerous thing. One thing you learn on the inside is acceptance. Each day is exactly the last one. No one is going to suddenly show up at your cell door and let you go. I worked my ass off to get here—avoided fights, made friends with everyone I could, and stayed away from the troublemakers. Volunteered wherever I could. Kept quiet. Obeyed the guards. Took my lumps from the guards with a quick club without complaint—god knows I can take a hell of a beating. When rumors of the opportunity for a work-release program made its way around the population, I was first in line to get evaluated for it. I was passed over the first few times—my security level was too high. But after another year and a half of doing good time, I finally got selected for the program, mainly because of Jacobsen's recommendation.

I worked like a mule during the supervised work-release period—an armed deputy accompanied me and Eddie, the other inmate from the program. The deputy monitored us, accompanied us everywhere we went, and watched everything we did. Strip searched us when we got back to the prison, making sure we hadn't smuggled in any contraband. Eddie got released on parole six months ahead of me, and now it's my turn.

The point is, it's not luck and it's not random that I'm out. I worked for it. Learned how to keep my temper in check. Learned how to defuse a violent situation rather than resorting to breaking faces the way I used to.

Now that I'm out, though, hope is a different thing. On the inside, hope is a liability.

You hope for an early release, but if you don't get it, you'll go bananas. Hope for a good cellmate but get stuck with a chatty asshole. Hope no one fucks up free time in the yard with a bullshit fight, necessitating another fucking lockdown. You hope, and hope gets crushed. So you stop hoping and just do your time. Find your rhythm. Pick the shit that gets you from one day to the next—for me, it was the meditative intensity of lifting, and talking to Matt.

On the outside, hope is a tender little seed in my gut. Tempting to water it. Watch it grow. But old habits die hard.

I have a roof over my head. I can walk out the door whenever I want. I can eat what I want when I want. No guards to give me a liver shot with a billy club just because he's having a shit day. No buzzer announcing nightly lockdown. No chow lines. No communal showers with cold water, and having to watch my back in case some jackass decides he wants to shiv me to make a point.

That's enough. It has to be. What else is there?

Panzer is sleeping behind the desk in front while Gloria and I clean cages and top off water bowls in preparation for closing. It's been a long, hard, rewarding day. I got the house almost done and then spent the evening at the shelter working on training Roger to behave. A couple came in and spent some time with him but decided he would be too much work to train. It was heartbreaking—Roger was excited when they played with him and got depressed when they left without him. So I figure I can teach him some basic commands, and maybe the next couple will take him home.

I keep an ear out for the door chime, that pesky feeling of hope percolating my gut—I want Noelle to show up again.

Seven-thirty arrives, and I've taught Roger to sit and stay and to lay down and stay. Tomorrow we'll work on *come* and *heel*.

We make sure all the cages are latched securely, all the doors are locked, and the lights are off, and then Panzer and I walk Gloria to her car.

No Noelle. Disappointment is a sour weight in my belly, which is stupid. She has better things to do than hang out at an animal shelter with me.

We walk home, Panzer and I. Once home, I pour him a big bowl of kibble and nuke a can of chili for myself. Leave my front door open for the warm late spring air, and listen to birds sing their evening songs.

Headlights rake across the parking lot, slant toward the building, and then stop and shut off. A door opens and closes. Feet stomp on the metal steps. Panzer is lying halfway out the door, big body across the threshold, nose sniffing the air. A low growl rattles his chest and the walls, and then his head lifts and his long tail starts flipping and tapping.

Noelle appears at the top of the landing. "Hey, Panzer. How ya doing, buddy?" she says in a high-pitched sing-song. She crouches in front of him, letting him sniff her as his tail picks up speed, now whipping side to side like a scythe. "You're a handsome boy, yes you are."

He licks her face, playfully nudging her hand aside

when she tries to stop him from licking her right in the mouth.

"Okay, okay," she laughs.

"Say halt," I tell her.

"Panzer, halt," Noelle says, her voice firm but still shaking with laughter. Panzer stops licking immediately, pulling his head back to look at her; she ruffles his ears. "Good boy."

His tail thumps, and he watches her as she rises to her feet in the doorway. "Can I come in?"

"Yeah, 'course."

She's wearing a pale green dress that ends just above her knees, the neckline scooping low to show a dick-hardening expanse of generous, creamy cleavage. The sleeves are short, capping at mid-bicep. Her long, strong legs are smooth and soft-looking, and her hair is twisted in a braid hanging over her right shoulder, the tip dangling just above the swell of her breast. A worn, tan leather purse hangs from her shoulder.

Her eyes are sad and red-rimmed.

I shoot to my feet and move toward her, reaching for her hand. "What's wrong?"

"Nothing, I just…" she shakes her head and sighs. "I'm just a little disappointed, is all."

"Come. Sit. Tell me about it." I pull her by the hand to my couch—a ratty, threadbare thing older than me with old, sagging springs. "Couch is a piece of shit, sorry."

Noelle sets her purse on the coffee table, a low thing of splintery oak and foggy, ring-stained glass. "It's stupid."

I lower my bulk onto the couch well to one side, giving her plenty of space to sit as close to or far from me as she wants. She plops down right beside me and kicks off her flat black leather shoes to reveal bare toes, the nails painted a muted mint green almost the same shade as her dress. Her dress settles across her thighs, pooling at her core in a tempting triangle. She leans her head back and closes her eyes.

"Sorry to show up like this," she mutters. "I just got some bad news and don't want to be alone."

"Welcome anytime," I tell her. "Was hoping I'd see you."

She sighs again, heavily, rubbing her face with both hands. "I'm sure compared to what you've been through, my silly little problems are pathetic."

I pat her knee. "Panzer—komm."

He unfolds to his feet, shakes himself, and then ambles over to Noelle, resting his heavy head on her lap. Automatically, her fingers dig into his ears and rub, scratch, and knead; his eyes roll backward in his skull and he rumbles a happy sound in his chest, tail slinking side to side in sinuous waveforms.

"He really is a sweetheart," she says.

"Yep." I stretch my arm along the back of the couch behind her head, not exactly around her shoulders, but almost. "Tell me about it."

"I expected it, but it still sucks," she says. "I saw a space a few days ago. It was way out of my budget, but it was…it was just *perfect*. I ran the numbers like fifty times, but no matter which way I looked at it, it was out of my range. And then today Kelly called and told me it's gone. I shouldn't be upset about it, you know? I mean, I knew I couldn't afford it, but I *wanted* it. I wanted it *so* bad, Bear."

"Space for what?" I ask.

"Oh, a salon. I'm a cosmetologist. My dream since I

was a sophomore in high school has been to own a hair salon. I'm right there, bear. *Right there*. I know I can do it. I just…I need the right location at the right price. That's the hold-up, though. Real estate on Main Street, where I want to be, is *really* expensive. So either I need to keep working and saving and building up my credit, or I down-size where I live to somewhere cheaper, or I go for a space in a less-than-ideal location. Or all three."

"No sense in compromising on a dream you've been working on for this long," I say.

She groans. "I know. I know. I keep telling myself to just be patient, but it's hard. I've watched four perfect prop-erties come and go in the last year alone. It's demoralizing because they're all *just* out of reach."

"One day at a time. It's all we can do." I hesitate. "When you're looking at a long stretch like I was, you learn to focus on the day in front of you."

She rolls her head on the couch-back. "What was it like? Being in prison, I mean. Mind me asking?"

"Nope. It's…hard. Boring, most of the time. Not much to do to pass the time. Can't trust too many peo-ple. Gotta watch your back. Especially when you're me."

She frowns at me. "Why?"

I tip my head to one side. "New guys like to prove themselves by picking fights with the biggest, baddest dude they think they can take. It's always me. So they'll jump you in the showers, or try to shiv you in the hall or in the chow line. Just to prove a point."

"Shiv means stab, right?"

"Yep."

"You've been stabbed?"

I snort. "Too many times to count."

She sits up and looks at me, concern knitting her features. "Bear, *no*."

I want to laugh at the compassion, the fear for me, the ache for my pain. She's so sweet, so innocent. Instead, I touch the pad of my thumb to her furrowed brow. "None of that. I'm fine."

"But…people just come up and stab you for no reason? And the guards let them?"

I shrug. "They get caught, they do a few days in the box. Lose privileges. To them, it's worth it."

"But… *why*?"

"It's not for no reason. If they can do damage to a guy like me, it proves to the rest that they're not someone you wanna fuck with. Means they're more likely to get left alone by the other guys."

She blinks, thinking. "But…you're bigger than just about everyone, right? Can't you just…stop them?"

I nod. "Sure. Wanted to, I could snap 'em like twigs. That don't do me any good, though."

"I don't understand." She toys with the end of her braid as she looks at me.

"If you get caught fighting, you get punished. Locked in solitary, what we call the box. Or, you lose privileges— time outside, time in the commissary, phone calls, visitation, shit like that. Plus, if you fight a lot you get tagged as a problem. Parole board won't even look at you if your security level is too high, and neither will work release programs like Riley's." That's the most I've said all at once in a long time.

"So what did you do?" she asks. "When guys tried to hurt you?"

"Depends. Usually, though, they'd get one shot in, and

then I'd take the shiv from 'em. By that point, the guards show up and take it from there. They get punished and I don't."

"But that means you just…let them shiv you?"

I shrug. "Sure. One little poke ain't gonna kill me, long as they miss the vitals." I pat my stomach. "I've got enough padding that most shivs can't even reach my organs anyway. Most shivs aren't that long."

She stares at me for a long, silent moment. "And this happened often?"

I shrug. "First few years, yeah. Eventually, my reputation spread around, and new guys knew better and learned to leave me alone."

She lapses back into silence again. "Geez. That sounds awful. People sure are mean."

I snort at that. "Nice guys don't end up in prison."

She peers up at me. "You're nice."

"No. I'm not."

"Bear. You *are*. You've never been anything but kind to me." She rolls into me, half on her side, half lying against me. "Told you my problem was stupid."

"Noelle, your problem isn't stupid. It ain't a competition. It's real to you. It's upsetting to you."

"I guess." A sigh. "You had to worry about being stabbed. My worst problem was a silly fight with my siblings. Hard not to see that as stupid, in comparison."

"What's your family like?" I ask.

She laughs, trailing off into a sigh. "They're a lot. I have two sisters, twins, four years older than me, and two brothers, also twins, four years younger than me. Natasha is the oldest by six minutes, then Nikki. Nat is a pediatric resident at McLaren, Nikki is a news anchor at Channel Four, and Nate and Noah just graduated from Central Michigan and are trying to start a business. So far, they've tried a car wash, a car dealership, and some sort of app. Mostly, they're into partying, playing video games, chasing girls, and off-roading. And giving my parents gray hair with their antics. They're twenty-six going on sixteen."

"And your sisters?"

She sighs. "Annoyingly perfect. Straight-A students, never in trouble, beautiful and thin and popular. Like I said, Nat is a doctor and Nik is a journalist on her way to being the next Connie Chung."

"And your folks?"

"Mom's the principal at the middle school, and Dad teaches psychology at the U-of-M satellite campus here in town."

Successful parents, successful kids.

"You guys get along?" I ask.

She shrugs. "Mostly. I'm the middle kid, which is its own weird, difficult thing." A self-deprecating laugh. "Sorry, that's another complaint from someone who's lived a charmed, privileged life."

"Weird and difficult how?"

She shakes her head. "Doesn't matter."

"Does to me."

She tucks her chin into my shoulder and gazes at me. "Why?"

"Curious, I guess. Never had a family." I long to let my arm slide down and curl around her shoulders, hold her close and never let go. I don't. "Wanna know things about you."

"Well, four years is a tricky gap when you're little. When I was four and old enough to want to play with my sisters, they were almost nine and didn't want me in their way, messing with their big girl stuff. The boys were just babies and took all of Mom and Dad's time and attention, which left me to sort of fend for myself, which meant I played alone most of the time. That's how it was growing up. Nik and Nat had their lives, Nate and Noah had theirs, and I had mine. Now that we're all grown, it's a bit better, but the twins, being twins, have this bond with each other that I just can't even touch."

"Sounds kinda lonely," I say.

She nods. "Yeah, I guess it was. People don't understand how you can be lonely in a family of seven, though." Her voice is slow and sleepy. "Mind if I rest a minute? I was up at five this morning."

"Go for it," I murmur.

She sinks into me, so I slide lower on the couch and put my feet on the table. Her cheek rests on my chest. She lets out a soft, contented sigh and sidles closer yet, snugging her hips and belly against my side, one arm wedged between us, the other curved low across my belly.

"You're very cozy," she whispers.

"Got you, Noelle. Rest."

"Mmm."

My heart pounds in my chest, hammering a mile a minute. What does this mean? What do I do with this, with her feeling so comfortable with me? It feels good. So good. Makes my stomach flip and tighten, makes my heart swell with pride. Makes some part of me way deep down sit up and snarl—daring anyone or anything to threaten this sweet, sexy, beautiful, kind, innocent, trusting little woman in my arms.

Panzer gets up, takes a long, splashing, gulping drink

from his bowl, and then resumes his spot in the open door-way. I should close it so bugs don't get in, but I'm not gonna disturb Noelle for a single goddamn thing.

She sighs sleepily and nuzzles closer, and the slight adjustment in angles draws my arm off the couch back, so I have no choice but to let it drape over her. I absolutely re-fuse to take any kind of liberties with her body, so I make sure my arm rests on her shoulders and my hand on her waist, well away from her hips or anywhere even remotely erogenous.

The hard labor of the day finally catches up to me, and my own eyes begin to droop. "Panzer, Pass Auf." *PAH-ss OW-f*—watch out, be on guard.

Chin on paws, his eyes snap open and his ears prick up—no one and nothing will get within a hundred yards of him without him knowing. Even if he drowses off a lit-tle, he'll keep guard all night long.

I linger in the lulling in-between, not quite asleep and not quite awake for a long time, wanting and needing to relish every second of contact with Noelle that I can get.

If this is all I ever have with her, it's still far more than I could ever hope for, or dream of, and far more than I deserve.

At some point, I fall asleep.

6

Noelle

AWARENESS COMES SLOWLY, GRADUALLY. The first thing I become aware of is a contradiction of sensations: cold and warm. A bird chirps somewhere close. A jet scuds noisily overhead. A car horn blips as someone keys their locks.

I'm not in bed. At first, that's all I know. I'm stiff from being in one position for a long time, but even before I reach full consciousness, I'm aware that I've slept better than I have in a very long time. I just don't know why, yet.

A soft, gentle snore whuffs a hot breath onto me, startling me. Which is when I become aware of where I am, and with whom.

Bear.

His apartment.

The cold is the air around us—a thin fleece blanket has been draped over my hips and legs, but my upper body is exposed. I crack an eye open—the door is still wide open, and Panzer lays in the opening, curled into a giant comma shape, facing the outside. His eyes are open, nose twitching, ears perked up, swiveling. Watchful, alert. God, what an amazing dog. I'm so glad Bear saved him.

The warmth is coming from Bear—he radiates heat as if he's a furnace. He's scooched low on the couch, his butt half off, long legs hanging over the far end of the coffee table, head lolling to one side. My cheek is on his sternum, my hand on his belly. His arm is a heavy weight draped across me like a weighted electric blanket. His hand curls across my belly.

I'm comfortable and warm, covered in a blanket, with his huge body a radiator and a mattress in one, while he, still in jeans and boots, is in what looks like a horribly un-comfortable position, exposed to the cold. He held me all night long rather than move to a more comfortable position.

I take the opportunity to study him. Slack and asleep, his features are boyish and smooth. A small white line bi-sects his left eyebrow. Another peeks out from the line of his beard along his right cheek. Yet another tugs the left corner of his lower lip down ever so slightly. His beard is a ticklish frizz-bomb, and his hair sticks to his lips and drapes off to one side. I use the moment to pinch the ends of his hair in my fingers—split ends, dry strands. I wonder if he even knows how to tie it back.

I wonder if he'd let me clean him up a little? I decide to ask, at some point. I could show him basic hair and beard care.

Somehow, that thought leads to images of Bear in the shower, his huge bulky body bare and wet—bare Bear. I snicker to myself at the wordplay, biting my lip to keep from waking him. I try to dismiss the image of him in the shower, but it's a tricky, demanding image. It makes my belly flip-flop and my core go damp and hot.

I haven't even thought about sex in a long time. After Brennan's betrayal and our subsequent divorce, and then the single idiotic date I went on, that part of me just sort of went dormant. I focused on work and whatever errands and factors my family demanded of me.

Bear is waking up my libido, however. Quickly.

He's unlike anyone I've ever met by several orders of magnitude. Physically, obviously, but in every other way as well. He's unfathomable. I just never know what he's thinking, and even when I ask and get an answer, I sense that for as much as he says, there's ten times more beneath the surface that he just doesn't know how to express or is unwilling to.

His past should terrify me. He's been stabbed more times than he can count? And he just shrugs it off as no more than "a poke." I don't even like getting a darned sliver.

He was in a gang. He's done a lot of bad stuff, enough, according to him, that he felt a ten-year prison sentence was fair for the crimes he committed.

So…why am I so comfortable with him? Why am I so utterly unafraid of him? His life has been violent. He has been violent.

When I hit people, they break.

Yet here I am, having slept in his arms like a baby. Safe. Warm. Content. Protected.

But how could he fit into my life? What would that

look like? My conservative, church-going, straightlaced parents would not understand him. My sisters would turn up their noses, at best. My brothers are wild cards—who knows how they'd react if I brought him home.

The girls—Raina, Ashlynn, and Kyle—love him. They think he's cool as heck, although, in the text thread, they used the F-word instead of heck. I mean, the way he sent those collar-popped dweebs running scared with a glare, a growl, and two words was the highlight of their week. My friends, however, are the most accepting, open-minded, and loving people I know. So it's no surprise they get my attraction to Bear.

Could I try a relationship with him? Would he want that? It's hard to tell. This is the most contact he's ever initiated, and he's asleep. And even asleep, his hand is carefully placed. I have no doubt that's on purpose.

I get the sense that he battles some serious self-worth issues. Which is understandable, given his life: abandoned as a child, homeless, surviving on the streets, forced into a life of violence, and then framed for murder. Goodness knows any felon must have a hard time finding a place in the world post-prison—I know enough to know I don't have the slightest clue what that's like.

Yet, he also seems to know exactly who he is, and what he's capable of. It's a strange juxtaposition.

I'd have to tread lightly, as Gloria advised.

He makes a grumbly sound in his throat and stirs—sounding so ursine that I can't help but sniff another laugh. He's just so much like the animal he's named after. It's adorable, intriguing, funny, and sexy all at once.

Who knew my type was man-bear?

He couldn't be any more the opposite of Brennan, my

only relationship and the only person I've ever had a physical relationship with. Brennan was just over six feet, so he was not short, but he was slender and geeky—a church boy through and through. He could quote long sections of the Bible, loved to debate creationism versus evolution, and the occasional round of golf was as close to physical exertion as he ever got. He was sweet, attentive, and very needy. Sex with him was…well, all I've known, so I have no way of comparing it to anything. I was often—or maybe always—left wanting more, though—I can admit this now, a year after the divorce.

I was with Brennan for a long, long time. We dated all throughout high school, got engaged the year after, and got married a year after our engagement; we were together in some romantic capacity for fifteen years and married for eight. He was a third of my world—work and my family being the other two-thirds.

We did things right—according to my parents' standards, at least. Mostly. We didn't even kiss until after we graduated and didn't go beyond a few heavy make out sessions until after he proposed to me—at which point we'd been together for more than four years. Our relationship was cerebral, I guess. Conversation, debate, companionship. We never moved in together, but we did sleep together regularly once we got married, obviously. The plan was to get married and get his career as a pastor going while I continued as a cosmetologist until we had kids, at which point I would become a stay-at-home wife. I was content with that—cosmetologist and pastor's wife. It was a life I could see.

And then he accidentally left his phone unlocked and open while in the shower after sex one morning. It went off while I was making the bed—rather than a text message, it was a topless photo of a woman. Another came through—her lower half, also naked. With her fingers touching herself.

"Can't wait to have you again, Brenny baby."

I was immediately sick—I'd run into the kitchen to vomit into the sink. Once I'd rinsed my mouth out, I took his phone, locked myself in the spare bedroom, and searched every message and email.

I discovered threads with two more women, all of them graphic and lewd. Lots of sexting, lots of naked photos going both ways. *I can't wait to see you again. Want you inside me. I love the way you "eff" me, Brenny baby.*

All three women were from the church where we went—where he was an usher, deacon, and assistant teaching pastor and in the running to take over as lead pastor when Pastor Johnson retired. One of the women was married with kids.

I'd put his phone on the bed, open to the photo that had begun the whole spiral of discovery, packed my few belongings, and left without a word.

I left the church and haven't been back. I blocked his number. Refused to speak to him. Refused to speak to his parents or his two siblings, who had been like bonus siblings to me my whole life. Filed for divorce, asking for nothing from him but a speedy dissolution.

My one act of…vengeance, I suppose, was to forward myself screenshots of some of the more incriminating photos and texts, print them out in full color, and mail them anonymously to the church, care of Pastor Timothy Johnson.

Brennan had been ousted from his positions,

ostracized by the community, and eventually moved out of Three Rivers in shame.

Perhaps I should feel guilty—a good Christian doesn't deal in revenge, I know that. But goodness, it was rather satisfying, and I don't feel guilty at all. It was no less than he deserved.

My faith, ever since, has been…wobbly, shall we say. I still hold onto my core belief in a God who created the world, his son Jesus, and the Holy Spirit, but the trappings of organized religion have lost their appeal to me. Brennan ruined it. Maybe that's an indictment of my weak faith, but so be it. I just can't bring myself to go back. If someone like Brennan, raised in the church, educated in the Bible, and serving the church faithfully for his whole life, could be a cheating, philandering, butthead, then what does anything mean?

In the year since the divorce, I've felt happier than ever despite my loneliness. I'm learning to stand on my own two feet. Do things for me. Brennan never approved of my friends—especially not Thomas and Colin. Ashlynn, he hated more than anyone—for reasons I'll never understand. She's quirky and unique, takes no crap from anyone, and does what she wants. She's dated men and women. Probably, she just makes him uncomfortable— like Thomas and Colin.

Now, without Brennan and his disapproval, I'm free to enjoy my friends, go out for drinks, and have fun. I've even gotten tipsy a few times. I kissed a stranger. It stopped at kissing and I didn't like it at all, but I can see myself going all the way with the right person.

With Bear.

Speaking of whom—he grumbles again, stirs. His eyes flutter open, and his green-gray gaze finds mine. "Mornin.'"

I smile at him. "Hey, you." I wince as he rolls his neck, popping it loudly. "Sorry, I, uh, sort of fell asleep on you. You should have woken me up."

"Wouldn't do that for anything."

"You can't have slept well in that position."

His eyes search my face, sleepy and gentle. "Rather sleep like that, with you than in a bed."

"Bear." It's a whisper. "You're so sweet."

"Not sure about that. Best feeling in the world is you trusting me enough to fall asleep on me."

My heart melts, pounds; my stomach flips. "I slept great. Better than I have in a long time."

"Good."

"It's Saturday," I say. "What are you doing today?"

He shrugs. "Dunno. Downtime ain't my friend. Was thinking I'd work at the rescue."

"Downtime isn't your friend—what does that mean?" I ask.

"I can't afford to get in trouble. I don't know anyone around here except you and Riley and the guys I work with. I volunteer at the rescue to keep myself busy and out of trouble. And because I like animals more than people."

"Would you…want to spend the day with me?" I ask, my voice a hesitant whisper.

He stares at me, blinking slowly, brows knitted. "You wanna spend a whole day…with *me*?"

I nod. "Yeah." I reach up and brush his coppery locks away from his eyes and mouth.

His eyes flare at the contact—surprised? "What do you want to do?"

I shrug. "I dunno. Whatever. Get breakfast, to start with. We could take Panzer to the dog park and let him play. There are some nice hiking trails a few miles north of town." I hesitate, and then my mouth runs away from my brain. "My family is getting together for a cookout tonight. You could come."

He goes perfectly still—quite a feat for someone as given to stillness as he is. "Noelle…"

I touch his lips. "I understand if you don't want to. No pressure."

He swallows hard. "I…I don't fit, Noelle."

I frown. "You don't fit? I don't know what that means."

"You're…good. Clean. Normal. I…ain't."

My heart breaks a little. "Goodness, Bear. Don't be ridiculous. My family is…we're just people." I keep going before he can say anything. "Just set that aside for now. Don't worry about it."

"'Kay."

I rub his cheek, the fuzz of his beard along his jaw. "Breakfast first. How about that?"

"I could eat."

I smile. "Me too. C'mon. I know a good spot."

Fifteen minutes later, we're parking in the back of the lot at The Good Egg, my favorite breakfast and lunch cafe. It's on the north end of Main Street on the corner of Compass, with outdoor, dog-friendly seating facing the rippling waters of the lake.

Carrying a leash, Bear paces beside me, Panzer at perfect heel, head on a swivel, nose going a mile a minute. We stop at the hostess station and wait.

A teenage girl with curly, mouse-brown hair approaches, nose buried in a tablet, a stack of menus under one arm. "Hello, welcome to The Good Egg-*holy-shit-you're-huge.*" Her wide, shocked brown eyes go to Panzer. "All d-d-dogs must be on a l-l-leash." She squeezes her eyes shut and takes a deep breath. "I'm sorry. Let me try again. Welcome to The Good Egg. Table for two outside?"

"Yes, please," I say.

Her eyes flick to Panzer. "All dogs must be on a leash, please."

Bear hooks the leash to Panzer's collar, but then drapes the leash across the dog's back; his gaze dares the poor, trembling girl to say anything else.

"This way, please." She leads us to a table along the fence near the far side of the outdoor area. "Your server will be right with you."

Bear waits until I take a seat and then sits across from me; Panzer, without needing instruction, curls up into as small of a ball as he can manage behind Bear's chair, out of the way. Within seconds, the big beast is snoring.

"He stayed in that doorway all night?" I ask.

Bear nods. "Yup. Tell him to stay, he stays. No matter what."

"He's such a good dog," I say. "I'm so glad you saved him."

"Me too." He spends a few minutes reading the menu. "Don't know what to get."

"Well, you really can't go wrong with anything, but I'm partial to the stuffed French toast," I tell him.

He finds the item on the menu. "Never had French toast before."

I boggle at him. "What? You haven't?"

"Nuh-uh."

"Well then, that's settled. You have to get the French toast." I peruse the menu a moment or two longer before deciding on avocado toast.

The waitress comes by and we both get coffee; she brings that and takes our orders.

"So you walk everywhere?" I ask after our orders are in.

He nods, sipping coffee. "No car, no license."

"You don't have a driver's license?"

A shake of his head. "Nope. Never learned."

"I can teach you."

He looks down at the table for a second. "That'd be cool."

"We can do that after we eat. The parking lot at the dog park is big and open—it's a good place to learn."

"What's a dog park?"

I laugh. "A park for dogs?" His face twists, and I realize he probably thinks I'm mocking him. "Bear, I'm sorry. I'm not making fun. You just ask funny questions sometimes—I forget how vastly different our experiences are. It's just a fenced-in area where people who don't have backyards can go to get their dogs exercise and socialization."

He nods. "I was a street rat. Until I went to prison, I lived my whole life in the same ten-block radius—the territory my gang controlled. Wasn't a whole lot there, but it was ours."

"What was the gang like?" I ask. "Do you mind me asking questions?"

"Nope. Don't mind."

"You don't ever have to answer, obviously. I'm just curious. But please tell me if I'm being nosy."

"It's cool." He sips coffee, his massive paws making the

porcelain mug seem like a plaything. "It was complicated. They were my family. We took care of each other. Protected each other. Someone came for one of us, they got all of us. Some had families, a mom, or a brother or sister. I didn't. I stayed with whoever I could. Usually, I stayed with my boy Gerard. His mom was nice. She'd feed me. Let me sleep on her couch. I kept Gerard outta trouble."

"You still talk to him?" I ask.

His eyes narrow, flick away. "Nah. He died."

"Oh god, Bear, I'm so sorry." I reach across the table and take his hand.

Bear nods. "My fault."

I shake my head. "Bear, I'm sure it wasn't."

"Was. I was with a girl. Gerard was beefing with this clown from another gang. Wanted me to go with him for backup. Told him it was foolish. Forget it. Let it go. He went anyway, figured he could take the guy himself. Got jumped and beat to death." He looks away, his gaze hard. "Shoulda been there for him."

I squeeze his hand. "Bear, you were trying to keep him out of trouble. You told him not to go."

"Your boy asks you to go, you go. I didn't. He died."

I sigh. "I'm sorry. I know I have no idea how that must feel."

"Feels like shit." He clears his throat. "Done is done. Can't take it back."

"But you can forgive yourself, Bear."

He frowns at me. "How?"

"Understand that you made a choice. Maybe it was wrong, maybe it wasn't—obviously, I have no clue how things work in that world, but you clearly lived according to your own code. You feel responsible for his death.

Maybe you were—it's not for me to say. But Bear, carrying around that guilt isn't going to bring your friend back. Nothing will—you know that far better than I do. I've never lost anyone I care about—not to death, at least. It's in the past, and it doesn't define you. It doesn't make you a bad person."

He regards me for a long time. "I could've saved him."

"You said he got jumped. Wouldn't they have killed you too?"

A shrug. "No."

"How many were there?"

"Dunno. Five or six."

"Were they armed?"

"Sure. Bats, chains, pipes, shit like that. Nothing I couldn't have handled."

I don't know how to process this. "Sorry, but…You could take on six people armed with bats and chains…. by yourself?"

He nods, shrugs one shoulder. "Easy."

"Bear."

"What?"

"I really don't understand."

"Look at me, Noelle. I put on a shit load of muscle on the inside, but I was still a big motherfucker, okay? Stronger than anyone else, even then. My whole life, all I've known is how to take a beating." He spreads his mammoth arms wide, six-some feet from fingertip to fingertip, each bicep at least eighteen inches around, thick and heavy with muscle. "Told you. When I hit people, they break. Takes a whole hell of a lot more than six little clowns to slow me down."

I'm stuck on "all I've ever known is how to take a

beating." His whole life has been pain, suffering, betrayal, violence, and hardship.

All I want is to show him the opposite.

I thread my fingers between his. "Well, that's not your life anymore."

He stares at our intertwined fingers. "No, it ain't. But figuring out what my life is, now…it's tricky. Don't know who I am. Where I belong."

With me.

The words stick in the back of my throat. I barely know him. I'm crazy—diving in headfirst with this guy. But I can't seem to stop myself. I don't want to.

I'm drawn to him. Endlessly fascinated by him. Driven to show him…everything. More of life—life beyond prison, beyond gangs, beyond the narrow, limited, scope of what he's known.

I'm attracted to him.

I'll have to take that slow, though. Even holding hands seems like it's difficult for him.

"Did you have a girlfriend, before?" I ask.

"No. Had a few friends who were girls. But a girl-friend, like going on dates and…and whatever? No." He hesitates, and I sense questions coming.

"You can ask me anything, you know." I finish my coffee as the waitress brings our food, along with a carafe to refill our mugs.

Bear pokes the six-inch-high stack of marbled French toast that's been stuffed to overflowing with creamy ricotta and drizzled with real maple syrup.

He tries a bite, and his eyes flare. "Jesus."

"You like it?" I ask.

"Fuck, yeah. Good shit." He wipes his mouth with a napkin. "It bother you when I curse?"

I shake my head. "No. Not at all."

"You don't curse."

I shake my head, cutting a section of toast, avocado, and egg whites. "I was raised very, very religious. I've moved on from that for the most part, but I never picked up the habit of cursing."

"So you grew up going to church and all that?" he asks.

"Yup. Every Sunday and most Wednesdays."

"Wednesdays too?"

I chew and swallow, sip coffee. "Youth group."

"Dunno what that is."

"Like church but just for kids your age. We'd sing songs, hear a message about God, and hang out. It was fun."

He hums a sound that's neither yes nor no, just sort of acknowledging what I said. "Don't go church at all anymore?"

I shake my head. "No, not really."

"Why?"

I consider what to say and decide that if I'm going to ask him about prison and being in gangs, I can darned well talk about Brennan. "I was married. His name was Brennan. We started courting—dating—when we were freshmen in high school. I loved him. We were together for... gosh, how long? Twelve years? Or close to that, at least."

He blinks at me. "You were with the same guy for twelve years?"

I sigh, laughing a little. "The world I grew up in was... well, as far from the world you grew up in as you can get, I suppose. In my world, you didn't date, you courted. Our first four years of dating, we had chaperones."

"Don't know what that means," he says, around a mouthful of French toast. He's devouring it, inhaling it. "This is the best shit I ever had. Legit."

I grin. "Good! I'm glad you like it." I take my time cutting, chewing, and swallowing. "A chaperone is just someone who goes on a date with you to make sure you remain pure. No hand holding, no kissing, none of that."

"Weird," he mutters. "Sounds lame."

I cackle. "It really was, honestly." I laugh again. "Anyway. After high school, the church we went to went through some changes. Things loosened up a little with the new pastor, Pastor Timothy. Less strict, not as many legalistic rules. After that, our parents let us go on dates alone, as long as we continued to remain pure until marriage."

He does some mental math. "You'd have been…what, twenty?"

I nod. "Yes."

"And your parents still controlled who you went out with and how?"

I nod again. "Oh yes. Very much so. I lived at home. Obeyed their rules." I blush, preparing to discuss things I'm uncomfortable discussing. "We, um, we didn't, you know… um, sleep together, like that, until I was twenty-one."

He shakes his head. "And you were with him for another how many years?"

"We were married for eight years, and together in the sense of dating or courting or whatever you want to call it for fifteen—from the time I was fifteen until I was twenty-nine last year. My one-year anniversary of being divorced is this month"

"A lot of marriages don't last that long."

"I know."

"Why didn't you marry right after graduation?" he asks. "Why wait so long when you'd already been waiting for so long?"

I tip my head to one side. "That was him. I wanted to. He wanted to have our lives set up first. He wanted to be a pastor. He was studying to get his doctorate in divinity."

"Sounds like an excuse to me."

I sigh. "It was. I discovered he was having sexual relationships with three other women."

Bear's face darkens with fury. "Piece of shit."

"He was, very much. A real piece of...poop." I laugh. "I'm lame—I just can't...I can't bring myself to curse, even now."

He shakes his head. "Don't. You don't need to." He polishes off the last of his meal and then eyes me. "What'd you do when you found out?"

"Cut him out of my life, left the church, moved out of my parent's house, and, um...sort of sent evidence of his wrongdoing to his pastor. Which, umm, sort of ruined his life."

Bear snorts. "Good. He around, still? I can cram his face down his neck for you."

I snicker and then turn serious. "No, he's long gone. I wouldn't want you to do that anyway. It's not worth what it would cost you." I look at him. "You would, though, wouldn't you?"

He nods. "In a heartbeat. Dunno how he could do that to someone as perfect as you."

My eyes water and sting—he threw that out so off-handedly. "Bear. I'm...I'm not perfect."

He looks panicked—it'd be comical if it wasn't so sweet. "Don't cry, please. Jesus. But you are."

I duck my head and fight the tears back. "God, Bear. You're too darn sweet."

It takes a few minutes for me to regain my composure—no one has ever said things like that to me. Brennan told me he loved me, but now, in hindsight, I realize he only ever said it when he was pushing me toward sex, or afterward. He never complimented me. Never told me I was beautiful.

Gosh, why was I even with him for all that time? Fifteen years? I spent literally *half of my life* with someone who I'm only now realizing was just an all-around piece of poo.

Piece of shit.

He was a piece of shit.

A liar. A cheater. A scumbag. Fake. Slimy. Horrible. Not even very nice. Was I attracted to him? Maybe, but only because I didn't know any better.

When I shake myself out of my thoughts, I find Bear watching me very closely.

"Lost you there for a minute," he murmurs.

"Sorry, I was just...thinking," I say.

"Care to share?"

I sigh, rub my face. "About Brennan. In telling you about him, I'm just realizing how pathetic he was. And how pathetic *I* feel for wasting so much of my time on him. I think..." I look away, hunting for the truth, and how to put it. "I think I felt like he was what I was *supposed* to want. I was *supposed* to want to marry a man like him. Or a man like I—and everyone else, apparently—thought he was good, righteous, and pure. A pastor. A man of God. But...he wasn't any of that. Not even close. And...I don't think he ever really loved me. He..." I blink hard, trying to hold back tears as the truth tumbles out. "He *never* said nice things to me. Never complimented me. He never told me he thought I was pretty, or that I looked nice in a dress. He thought I was stupid for going to cosmetology school and insisting on working."

Bear rumbles in his chest, his face a mask of outrage. "What a dick."

That makes me laugh. "He *was* a dick." I cover my mouth, sputtering laughter. "Oops. I said a bad word."

For the first time since I've known him, Bear smiles—a full, real smile, with a single booming bark of laughter. It fills my soul.

"Dick barely counts as a curse word in my book, but good for you. Curse his name." He shakes his head. "If I was ever lucky enough to be with a woman like you, I'd tell you how fucking gorgeous you are every single fucking day. Be a crime not to."

"With me? Or just a woman *like* me?" The question slips out before I can stop it.

He licks his lips. "Noelle, I…" He looks away, voice dropping. "Wanting to be with you…it makes me feel like Icarus."

It takes me a long, long time to process what he said, to understand the implications of it.

Icarus, the man who flew too close to the sun with his wax wings. Flew too high. Wanted too much. Wanted something not meant for him.

"Bear," I whisper, eyes stinging all over again.

"Read a lot of books on the inside. One of the guards helped me get connected with a librarian from a nearby high school. We'd email back and forth and she'd send me books to read." He brushes his long, wild hair out of his face—the wind pushes it right back across his eyes. "The librarian, Miss Ellsworth. She helped me get my GED. Taught me a lot."

"That's so cool, Bear. Do you know which school?" I ask.

He furrows his brow, thinking. "Hmmm. No. But if I could get into that email address, I could find out. Somewhere up here, I think."

"You can use my laptop at home," I tell him. "You should reconnect with her now that you're out. I'm sure she'd love to meet you."

He nods. "Be cool to meet her in person."

The waitress comes by with the check, and before I can say a word, Bear hands her cash and tells her to keep the change.

"That was very nice of you, Bear, thank you." I stand up. "So. How about we take Panzer to run around?"

Bear nods. "He'd like that. I think."

Cᴏ

A few minutes later, we're sitting on a bench watching Panzer, all two hundred pounds of him, prance and bound and sprint like a puppy, his booming bark shivering the leaves and terrifying squirrels for miles. The other dogs join him, and soon the whole park is doggy mayhem.

After a good half an hour of play, Panzer lopes over to us, panting, and plops down at Bear's feet.

"I think that means he's done," I say.

Bear nods. "Yep." He looks at me. "Now what?"

I regard him, watching the wind ruffle his beard and plaster his hair across his face, resisting his attempts to control it. "Well, I do have one idea. I don't know how you'd feel about it, though."

"Try me."

"I'd like to do something with…all this." I gesture broadly at his face. "Not cut it off, just…clean it up."

He thinks for a moment. "Okay."

I light up. "Really?"

He nods, shrugging one heavy shoulder. "Sure. Why not? I got no clue what to do with it. Gets in the way most of the time."

I grab his hand and pull him to his feet—or, well, I pull at him, and he stands up. I doubt I could lift so much as one of his gigantic legs on my own.

"The salon is closed on Saturdays, so we'll do it there." We walk hand in hand back to my CR-V, Panzer trotting after us with a big doggy grin.

7

Bear

Lux Locks Salon is in the heart of downtown Three Rivers on Main Street between Tompkins and Brookline. The whole front is picture windows with planter boxes underneath filled with a profusion of colorful flowers. Couldn't say what kind, though. There's an upscale women's clothing boutique on one side and a running gear store on the other.

Noelle unlocks the glass front door, ushering in Panzer and me and then re-locking it behind her. Inside, the space is open and airy and light, with six stations on each side facing each wall. Each station features a black leather chair with chrome accents, a stand for each stylist's equipment, and a large mirror. Along the back wall are another half a dozen weird sinks with chairs in front of them, the facing lip of the sink divoted like an executioner's block. A long, low, sleek leather couch sits under the front windows, and a heavy glass coffee table nearby is stacked with magazines. A small counter with a computer screen and a credit card reader stands near the couch. It smells like shampoo and floral air freshener.

Noelle leads me to the weird sinks at the back. "Have a seat."

I lower myself carefully into the seat, my back to the sink. "What's this?"

"Gotta wash your hair first," she says, and the sound of running water splutters to life.

"Took a shower after work yesterday," I tell her.

She rests her hands on my shoulders, gently guiding me to lean backward until my neck fits into the divot of the sink—the setup makes sense, then. She gathers my hair so it hangs into the sink.

"Oh, I know. But…um." A brief hesitation. "Can I ask what you use to wash your hair?"

"I dunno. Bottle of some shit Riley picked up for me at Target the day I got out."

"And let me guess, you wash everything with the same bottle? Hair, beard, and body?"

"Yeah. Why?"

Water sprays me in lukewarm droplets. "Too hot or too cold?"

"Cold."

The water warms until it's pleasantly hot. "Good?"

"Yeah."

"So, I'm guessing you didn't intentionally grow your hair out? You just sort of never cut it when you were in jail?" She asks, gathering my hair in her hands and dousing it with the hot water.

"Right."

"And you never trim it, or tie it back, or anything?"

"Nope."

"Okay, well, a few things, here. The all-in-one stuff is…convenient, I suppose, but for hair as long and thick and glorious as yours, you need better products. You need a good shampoo and conditioner, for one thing—separate bottles." She pinches a dry strand of hair and shows it to me. "Feel it."

I run my forefinger and thumb over the strands. "Okay?"

She bends over me so her hair dangles over my face. Her scent washes over me, making blood rush to my head…and elsewhere. Lavender and vanilla and roses… and something else that's just indefinably female. And intoxicating.

"Feel mine."

As gently as I can, I slip a lock of her hair through my fingers—it's soft, cool, silky. "Totally different."

"Yours is dry, Bear, that's the only difference. It needs proper hydration. It's just thirsty."

"Water doesn't hydrate it?" I ask, feeling stupid.

She giggles, not unkindly. "Seems counterintuitive, I know, but no. The chemicals in the stuff you use are what dries it out. Good shampoos and conditioners are specially formulated to help your hair stay healthy. The same goes for your beard. We don't stock men's products here, but after I'm done we can swing by Target and I'll help you pick out better stuff. And then your hair and beard will be healthy, shiny, and not in your way all the time."

"Sounds good."

All this time, she's been rinsing my hair, kneading it, squeezing the water out, and re-rinsing. Now, I hear a bottle cap click open, a soft fart sound as she squeezes shampoo into her hand, and then she starts applying it to my hair.

She even lathers my hair differently than I do—I just glop it onto my crown, rub it in for a few seconds, and then rinse it out. Noelle rubs her hands together and then starts at the ends of my hair, scrubbing and lathering her way up to my scalp. Once she gets to my scalp, her strong, nimble fingertips knead and massage all over, from my hairline by my forehead to the back of my neck to around my ears.

It feels fucking incredible. It's so…intimate. Almost sexual in feeling. I want to let out a moan, it feels so fucking intense.

I let my eyes close, sunlight bathing my eyes with yellow warmth, and her massaging fingers dance and knead endlessly over my scalp. Her fingers pinch my ears, running down the cartilage to my earlobes and then pressing in behind my ears, focusing for a moment on the tender dips where ear, skull, and mandible meet.

Which is when a little grunt of pleasure does escape me.

Her soft giggle is close, her breath warm. "Feels good, huh?"

"Fucking intense," I mutter.

"Never had your hair professionally washed and cut, I assume?"

"Nope. Before prison, Gerard's mom would buzz me every couple of weeks. once I went in, I just sorta…forgot about it. Didn't care what I looked like. So it just grew."

"So you've not touched it in ten years?"

"Nope."

"Well, I'm honored to be your first proper haircut." She shifts to stand over me, looking down at me as she begins rinsing the lather away. Her breasts hang a few inches from my face. "There's nothing like a good scalp massage, though, is there?"

I shove my hands under my thighs before they do something stupid, like touch her. "Best thing I ever felt," I admit.

She sniffs a soft laugh. "I find that hard to believe."

"Nah. It's the truth."

She pauses her rinsing to look down at me. "I mean, it can't be better than sex." Her eyes fly wide and her cheeks flush bright red. "Forget I said that?"

I swallow hard. "Been so long I barely remember. All I know is that scalp massage was fuckin' incredible."

I hope she doesn't look at my crotch—I'm fighting arousal. Not sure what it is—her proximity, her smell, the massage—but I'm rocking a partial erection that I can't do shit to hide.

She smiles and resumes rinsing. "Well, good. I'm happy I could give that to you."

She repeats the lathering process with some other product—conditioner, I guess, whatever the hell that is. And then the scalp massage again, and then more rinsing.

Eventually, she's satisfied with how rinsed my hair is and squeezes it out, snaps a towel open, uses that to squeeze my hair dry some more, and then guides me to sitting up before working the towel over my hair a bit more.

"Alright," she says. "Come on over to my station."

She leads me by the hand to a station along the lefthand wall near the middle, littered with jars of scissors and combs in blue liquid, a tangle of cords, a hair dryer, clippers, and a clear plastic tray full of neatly organized guards. There are several framed photographs of Noelle, with who I assume is her family. One is her with her mom and dad—her mom is short and somewhat bottom-heavy, with long, wavy gray hair and a bright, happy smile and the same green eyes and freckles that Noelle has; her dad is tall and whipcord lean, with smile-lines at the corners of his dark eyes, graying blond hair in a neat, classic side part, and a short, neat beard. The other two photographs are of Noelle with her sisters and Noelle with her brothers; her sisters are so alike it's almost freaky, with long platinum blond hair and dark eyes. They're stunningly beautiful in a slender, model-type way—not as sexy as Noelle, though, if you ask me. Her brothers are as identical as her sisters, and they too are tall and lean and blond, with pretty-boy good looks.

Once I take a seat, Noelle drapes a black plastic cape over me and buttons it behind my neck. Standing behind me, close enough that her breasts press against the backs of my shoulders, she runs her fingers through my hair, which is dark, damp, and heavy.

"So, unless you wanted it short, I was thinking I'd just trim some of the length off and give your hair some shape," she says, playing with my locks with a professional eye. "Thoughts?"

I shrug. "Whatever you think. Kinda like it longer, so maybe don't hack it all off."

She presses herself against my back, tits squishing against my shoulders and neck, hands sliding down my chest. "There will be no hacking, you have my word."

Thank god for the cape—it hides my monster

hard-on. I know the press of her chest against me is inno-cent. I know she's just a touchy sort of person and prob-ably unaware of the contact; I feel kinda dumb for even imagining that it could be on purpose.

I do not pretend she's attracted to me in that way. How could she be?

Still. I long to reach up and take her thick braid in my hand, tug her down, and kiss her. I know I'll never be able to. I don't deserve a woman like her. Someone so clean, so good, so generous and kind and beautiful.

She's not for me.

I don't fit in her life.

But it's nice to wish. Being on the outside means I get to wish. I get to hope. I just have to be realistic. A man with my past has no place thinking I could ever *be with* a woman of Noelle Harper's caliber.

She stays like that for a heart-stoppingly long time, pressed against me, hands on my chest, breath against my ear, cheek to my cheek. For a moment, I give in. Let my head sink back against her. She turns her face toward mine, her soft warm cheek against mine. Her lips part.

I could kiss her.

Fuck, I want to kiss her so damn bad it hurts.

"Bear…" she whispers. I smell the coffee on her breath.

I pull a hand out from under the cape. Trace the sharp line of her cheekbone. Her jaw. "So fucking beau-tiful, Noelle."

Her lips slip closer to mine. Hope burns in my chest, warring with disbelief, freighted down by fear.

A sharp knock on glass shatters the moment.

"Darn it," she breathes, sounding irritated. She

touches her lips to my cheek, pressing a soft, slow kiss there. "Be right back."

She glides gracefully across the salon to the door, unlocking and opening it an inch.

"We're closed today, sorry. Private appointment."

"Oh, okay. Thank you."

"I know we have some walk-in slots open on Monday morning, though."

"Wonderful," comes the elderly female voice. "I'll come back then."

"I look forward to seeing you Monday, ma'am. Have a nice weekend."

"You too, dear."

She closes and re-locks the door and returns to her station. "Haircut time."

For the next half an hour, Noelle uses a pair of scissors to snip here and there, pinching the ends between her index and middle fingers and trimming away the extra. No one cut makes anything look different, but when she steps back, sets the scissors down, and feathers her fingers through it, my hair does, somehow, look a hundred times better. Cleaner, lighter, healthier. The shape of it looks... neater. Less like a wild man who just came down from a winter in the mountains.

"Now your beard," she says, spinning the chair around so my back is to the mirror.

She runs her fingers through my beard a few times the way she did with my hair, assessing and scrutinizing. "Yeah, you need some oil and a good brush. Your skin underneath is all dried out. It must itch, huh?"

I shrug. "Yeah, I guess, "I admit, realizing only as she

points it out that I do have a habit of scratching at the skin under my beard a lot.

"For now, I'll just update the shape. I'll show you how to oil it and brush it later."

Standing between my knees, Noelle leaned forward, her scissors snip-snip-snipping away, sending curly red tendrils fluttering to the floor.

Her cleavage is right in front of my face, and the angle of her forward bend means I can see down her shirt, revealing the cups of a black bra and a whole hell of a lot of skin. I fight myself tooth and nail, my selfish desire to see more of her beautiful body at odds with my determination to be respectful. Eventually, I have to close my eyes because I can't seem to look away.

After a while, the snipping stops, and her fingers trail down my cheeks, trace my jawline, and then feather down through my beard. "There, *much* better."

I open my eyes—she's so close, standing between my legs, her hips wedged between my thighs. Her green eyes search my face, a smile on her lips.

"I didn't mind you looking," she murmurs. "But it's super sweet that you didn't."

My cheeks burned as I realized she knew I was staring and why I closed my eyes. "Noelle, I..." I trailed off, unsure what to say. "I can't take my eyes off you."

Her smile brightens, taking my breath away. "The way you look at me, Bear. It's...you make me feel pretty."

"Pretty ain't the word, Noelle. Not even close."

She trails the backs of her knuckles down the side of my face, a gesture that makes it hard to breathe and hard to swallow. "You're pretty dang handsome yourself, you know."

I huff, shaking my head. "Need glasses, if you think that."

She frowns, laughing and shaking her head. "I have twenty-twenty vision, thank you very much." She tugs my beard through her fist. "Can I do one more thing?"

"Anything you want," I answer.

Her fingers work swiftly and nimbly in my beard, gathering sections and braiding them together into the three separate plaits, which she then weaves together into a single thick, complex braid, tied off at the end with a black hair tie. Moving out from between my legs, she stands behind me again and pulls the topmost section of hair around my temples and crown and braids them as well, leaving them to hang just behind my ears. The rest of my hair she leaves loose, but now, with the braided section out of the way, it's out of my face.

She turns the chair to face the mirror. "What do you think?"

I'm speechless. I mean, I'm a man of few words in any case, but the Bear I see in the mirror is a whole different person than the one who walked in.

Before, my hair was a wild explosion, riotous, frizzy, and dry, and my beard was just as bad, bursting down from my jawline in a ragged, unkempt, unruly mop.

I look like a Viking warrior from a TV show that used to play in the afternoons in the dayroom. The braided beard looks cool as fuck, and my hair is clean and silky smooth and shiny, pulled back to expose the angles of my face, letting my eyes show, whereas before, they were often hidden or obscured by my hair.

"Holy shit," I mutter. "Who the fuck is *that*?"

Noelle laughs, resting her hands on my shoulders. "You, silly. I think Thomas would say you're hot as balls."

I meet her eyes in the mirror. "What would you say?"

She swallows hard, gnawing on her lower lip, eyes searching mine in the mirror. "I think you're the sexiest man I've ever met." She runs my hair through her hands. "A good cut and proper styling just reveals how hot you really are."

My heart crashes in my chest at her words. "Noelle, I..." I shake my head, unable to find words. "I don't how to thank you."

Moving slowly, she circles to stand in front of me and then lowers herself to sit on my lap, legs hanging sideways over mine, arms circling my neck. "You just did."

I shake my head. "I feel like a new man. Never looked this good before. Thank you."

One arm across the back of my neck, she runs my beard braid through her fist. "My big, handsome Viking warrior."

Her big, handsome Viking warrior? My heart flips, and my stomach twists, and hope is no longer a germinating seed but a tender shoot soaking up the sunlight of her attention, her touch, her affection.

"I'll never be able to make it look this way on my own, though," I say.

She grins. "Good. That way you'll have to keep me around."

"Your time and your skills are valuable, Noelle. How much do I—"

Her hand covers my mouth. "Absolutely the heck not. Don't even think about paying me. I'd be insulted."

"Don't want to insult you, I just don't wanna take advantage of your generosity."

Her smile is soft and warm and tender. "So sweet and so thoughtful." She cups the side of my face with her palm. "You'll just have to keep spending time with me. Okay?"

Hesitantly, I bring my arms away from the armrests and circle her with them. Inexplicably, this makes her smile burn hotter, and her eyes flick to my lips. "Favorite thing in the world," I murmur, "Spending time with you. So damn lucky to know you."

"I feel the same way," she says.

And then she leans into me, resting her head on my shoulder, one arm around my neck, the other circling to clasp hands on my other shoulder. I hold absolutely still, barely even breathing. My arms circle her soft, warm body, one hand around her middle, the other draping to rest just above her hip. Instinctively, my hand runs across her thigh and back to her hip.

She hums happily, nuzzling closer. "I love the way you hold me, Bear."

My breath is lodged in my throat—I expect to wake up any second and find myself back on the hard bunk of my cell in Holbrook.

"Doesn't seem real, "I whisper.

"What doesn't?" She asks, pulling away to look into my eyes from mere inches away.

"You. This. Getting to…to hold you. To touch you. Feels like it shouldn't be allowed."

For some reason, this makes her eyes water. "Gosh, Bear," she whispers. "You can't say things like that to me. You're killing me."

"Sorry."

This makes her laugh. "I didn't mean literally," she says, bumping her forehead onto my shoulder, laughing. "Geez, you're very literal."

"I..." I frown, shaking my head. "Still don't understand you."

More bubbly, happy laughter. "What's not to understand? I didn't think I was all that complicated."

I shrug. "Keep waiting for you to come to your senses. But you don't. You're still here. Letting me talk to you. Letting me touch you. Don't make any damn sense."

This makes her brows furrow. "We'll have to pull that statement apart at some point. For now, just know that I'm in full possession of my senses."

She lets go of my neck with one hand and runs it down the outside of my arm, caressing my bicep, fingertips tracing the horseshoe outline of my tricep and then gliding down to my forearm. Her hand covers mine. Moves my hand from her waist to her hip. Pinning my eyes with hers, she slides my hand further down to cup the taut curve of her ass.

"Does that clarify things?" she whispers.

My erection goes full-bore. I can't help it, can't fight it down any longer. Surely she can feel it. I keep still, barely breathing, rocked with disbelief.

"Noelle..." I growl. "Crazy woman."

"Why am I crazy?"

"Playing with fire."

"So burn me."

I give in to need—graze the side of her face with my palm, soaking up the exquisite softness of her skin with the rough calluses of my big, hard, clumsy hand. She nuzzles into my palm, and my breath boils in my throat at the movement.

Her beautiful face is inches from mine, her deep, burning, verdant green eyes searching me ceaselessly. Her lips are parted, and her tongue darts along them, moistening them.

Fuck, I want to kiss her so goddamn bad.

All indications point to her wanting me to. I just… it's hard to trust that. Hard to believe she'd want that—with *me*.

I'm a brute. A criminal. A monster with a horrible, violent past. She doesn't know half of it.

She covers the side of my face. "You're not ready yet, are you?"

"For what?"

She doesn't answer. instead, her lips touch my cheek next to my nose. My cheekbone. The corner of my mouth. Teasing. Tempting. Tantalizing. "This."

My dick turns to steel, aching under the firm weight of her lush backside. My hand curls into the soft cotton of her pale green dress, and beneath the thin material, her skin is warm and her curves generous and supple. I can't help but seek more, my hand spreading to greedily cup more of her full, soft bottom.

She lets out a sigh that contains a note of a moan—of pleasure. She nuzzles my jaw with her nose and then kisses my cheek again. "I like that," she whispers. "A lot."

My breathing is ragged, harsh. "Noelle."

"Yeah, Bear?"

"You're too good for me."

"I happen to feel otherwise."

She brings her face in front of mine, noses tip-to-tip,

lips almost touching. I feel her breath. I can almost taste her mouth.

A sudden, sharp, loud trill jars the moment, and she jerks upright, gasping in shock. "Holy crap, that scared the poop out of me."

Without leaving my lap, she reaches past me to snag her phone out of her purse, glances at the screen, and pulls an annoyed face. "Gotta answer it. It's my dad." She swipes the answer slider. "Hey, Dad. What's up?"

A pause as she listens; I can hear him speaking on the other end, but it's muffled and tinny and indistinct. "Yeah, I'm planning on coming, of course. Oh, um…sure. Yeah. Okay, I'll pick it up and be there soon. Okay, yeah. Yup—love you too, bye." She ends the call and leans past me to toss the device back in her purse. "They need a few extra things for the cookout, and Mom wants me to help her prep the food."

"Oh. Okay."

She slides off my lap and stands up, smoothing her skirt down. "I'll need to swing by my house first, though. I need to rinse off and change." She holds my eyes. "Unless you don't want to come."

My chest is tight. "Um. I…" I work my jaw, fighting for breath as the iron band around my lungs constricts. "I don't know."

She unsnaps the cape and whips it off, folds it up, and puts it away. "I get it if you don't want to."

"Not that I don't *want* to. I do. Just…"

She puts the scissors in the jar and then puts her backside to the cabinet, looking at me. "Just what? You can tell me anything."

"It's your family. A family get-together. Not sure I belong." I shrug, looking away.

She gives my beard a gentle, playful tug. "It's an informal barbecue. My brothers and sisters have brought friends and dates over before. No one will think anything of it."

"Don't want to impose. Or…" I shrug and shake my head. "Be in the way."

She just laughs. "You're silly. Let me clean this hair up real quick and then we can go."

"How'm I silly?" I ask, leaving the chair so she can sweep.

She brushes the red curls and commas of my hair into a pile and then into a small trash can-like device that turns on with a whirr and sucks the hair away.

"I'm inviting you. Therefore, it's not an imposition. You will be welcome."

"I guess it's more than that," I growl in frustration as the right words seem to evade my tongue. "It's…who I am. I'm worried I don't…" I sigh. "Fit."

She puts the broom away and comes to stand in front of me, both palms on my chest, gaze soft with understanding. "You're definitely not what they'll expect when I tell them I'm bringing a…a friend. They may have questions, I won't lie, but just remember—you don't owe anyone an explanation. Okay?"

"We're friends?" I ask.

"I mean, I sure hope so. At the very least." She pats my chest. "Don't worry. It'll be okay. Promise."

8

Noelle

BEAR IS QUIETER THAN USUAL, PENSIVE. WE MAKE the short drive from the salon to my house in silence, the only sound is Panzer's soft breathing in the back seat. To be fair, though, I'm kind of lost in thought myself.

He *is* attracted to me. He just doesn't feel like he deserves to be. He doesn't think he's allowed to. He expects me to reject him or mock him—I'm not sure which. Both, maybe.

More than once, he's called me "clean," and I'm starting to understand that doesn't mean physically free from dirt. He means spiritually, existentially. He feels unclean as a person. Stained by his past. By his record.

But good grief, when he does touch me? I feel

combustible. My skin still tingles where he touched me. My lips burn, longing to feel his on them. We were *so* close—had Dad not called when he did, we would have kissed.

I want more.

I want to kiss him. Touch him. Be touched. Held.

Sleeping with him—literally only sleeping—was incredible. So peaceful. Safe. Warm. Connected.

The thought of going home tonight and sleeping alone in a cold bed sounds horrible, now.

Lonely.

I want him. I desire him. And I want him to want me, to desire me. To show me how he feels about me. It'll take some time, though. He needs to be shown that he's not defined by his past. That I see him for who he is now. I'm not afraid of who he was or the things he did. I understand full well that he's only given me the outlines of what his life was like before going to prison: violent and full of struggle.

That's not who he is anymore. He just needs a little encouragement is all.

And I plan to give him that. Show him who he is to me. Who he can be. Hopefully, I can show him that it's okay to want things. To hope. To believe in himself. To allow himself to have…

Well…

Me.

One step at a time.

I pull into my driveway. "C'mon, boys."

Panzer and Bear follow me up the driveway to the side door. I unlock it, and Bear holds the storm door open so I can go in. Panzer follows, and then Bear. My kitchen is small but cute. The cabinets are white, and some enterprising prior tenants with artistic talent hand-painted little flowers, bumblebees, and dragonflies on them in random patterns. The counters are blonde butcherblock, the floors are vintage hardwood stained a few shades darker than the cabinets, and the appliances are newer stainless steel. The first thing I do is get a big mixing bowl, fill it with water, and put it on the floor for Panzer, who slurps away noisily, making a godawful mess—easily cleaned.

Bear follows me into the open-plan dining room and living room. The walls here are a soft, muted moss color, the floors the same hardwood as the kitchen carried through the whole home. My couch is one of the few things I ever splurged on, a soft gray Lovesac sectional framing an antique cherrywood coffee table, with a print of Monet's Water Lilies where a TV would be in other homes.

"You have a beautiful home," Bear says.

"Thank you. I love it." I lift on my toes and kiss his cheek. "Have a seat and relax. I'm gonna rinse off and change. I won't be long."

"'Kay." He settles himself carefully on the couch, his huge frame tense and stiff.

I can't help but laugh, perching on his thighs. "Hey. *Relax.*" I reach up and try to massage his massive shoulders, but it's like kneading granite. "Geez. Talk about boulder shoulders."

He lets out a breath. "I'm just…mixed up, I guess. In my head."

"About what?" I ask.

He just shrugs, looks away.

I grab his beard braid and tug gently. "Hey. Talk to me."

Another vague shoulder roll. "Nothing."

"Bear." It comes out a little firm and scoldy. I soften my tone. "Whatever it is, I want to know."

"Just this whole thing. You and me."

"Yeah?"

He swallows hard. "I'm not sure what it is. Don't know what I'm doing. What to do. What not to do."

"You're doing fine, Mister Bear," I say, emphasizing the mister to make it a teasing joke.

He blesses me with an actual, very rare smile, and a soft huff of laughter. "Not that again."

"That again. You're my Mister Bear."

"*Your* Mister Bear?"

"Well, hopefully not someone else's," I say, pretending to scowl. "Is there something I should know? Someone else in the picture?"

"No," he says quickly. "No. Just you. Only you."

I break into laughter, wrapping my arms around his thick neck and cliff-like shoulders. "I'm teasing. Just teasing." I pull away just a little. "Yes, to answer your question. *My* Mister Bear. *My* big handsome Viking warrior."

He furrows his brow thoughtfully, sighing. "Never been anyone's before."

I can only smile at that. I kiss his cheek again, wanting more than anything for him to take my face in his big hard hands and kiss me breathless.

His eyes search my face. Land on my lips. His thumb brushes ever-so-gently over my mouth. "Pretty little mouth. Soft."

I touch his lips the way he did mine. "Yours too."

He leans closer.

God, please—p*lease* kiss me.

"Noelle, I…" he trails off, swallowing.

"What, Bear? Say it. Ask me anything."

"Wonder what your lips…feel like. Taste like."

"So find out," I breathe. "Please?"

A growl rattles his chest. "No shit? You…you'd let me?"

A hungry smile curves my lips. "Try it and see."

Sitting sideways on his lap, I cling to his shoulders and fight for breath as he moves in, millimeter by millimeter. His hands frame my face, so exquisitely gentle he's barely touching me, as if afraid that one wrong move will shatter me like porcelain. The rough pads of his thumbs brush under my eyes. And then his lips touch mine, and my breath whooshes out of my lungs.

He's kissing me.

So softly, so slowly. So delicately. Tender. A questing question of a kiss: *May I?*

No tongue, only lips. So gentle. The immense power in his hands is reduced to a tremble upon my cheeks.

Gosh, this man.

I lean in, snaking my arms tighter around his neck. Tilt my head and deepen the kiss. A low rumble shakes his chest—shakes me.

I press him back into the couch and clutch his nape in both hands. Part my lips for him—his tongue darts against my lower lip and retreats. His thumbs caress my cheeks. Fingertips trace my ears. He radiates heat. Pulses with power. With coiled strength, with tightly leashed desire.

I feel it in every line of him. In the taut tension of his colossal muscles wrapped around me.

God help me—I need more.

It's been so long. So long since I felt wanted. Since I felt pretty.

Since I felt…sexy.

He gives that to me without even trying.

Makes me feel more like a woman than I ever have—powerful, sensual, desirable. Safe. Protected. Respected. Wanted.

All at once—all of a sudden. Just by being who he is.

I slip my tongue against his, and his whole being tenses, and he rumbles in his chest softly. Pulls away. "Holy shit, Noelle," he breathes.

"I know," I whisper. "Me too."

"Thank you." His hands stay on my face, caressing. Cupping.

I give him a questioning look. "Thank you? For what?"

"The kiss."

I almost laugh but worry he'd take it wrong. "Don't thank me," I whisper. "Just…don't stop."

"Your lips taste like candy."

"Bubblegum lip gloss." I pull back, licking my lips. "Like it?"

"More'n I can say."

I snag my purse where I dropped it on the ottoman, pluck my lip gloss from the inside pocket, and reapply it, rolling my lips to spread it evenly. "There." I move to straddle him. "Kiss me again?"

He doesn't, though—not right away. Instead, he just looks at me. "You're a wonder. A miracle."

"Bear…"

"An angel."

"I'm not."

"You are to me." His green-gray eyes are wild and deep, hinting, as Gloria said, at the waters that run deep beneath his stillness. "Could kiss you forever. Never stop."

"I'd like that," I say.

"You would?"

"Mmm-hmmm. A lot."

He licks his lips and then drifts closer once more, and I close my eyes and wait. Feel his soft, strong lips cover mine. His breath is warm and sweet, and his tongue finds mine. I grab his beard and pull him closer, cupping the back of his head with my other hand. He growls like a hungry, feral beast, and my core spasms, my sex rushing with liquid heat.

I lean into him, crush my chest against his, and push him deeper into the couch. Straddling him, I feel his manhood straining beneath me, a huge hard ridge. His hands carve around my waist and spread to cover my back, just below my bra strap. We pause for a second, both of us gasping. His hands slip lower. Lower. Hesitate, and then retreat upward.

"It's okay," I whisper against his lips. "Go ahead. I want you to."

I hold his eyes, letting him see my desire. Hoping he sees the permission there.

The need.

His fingers dig into the muscles at the small of my back, gathering the bunched-up skirt of my dress, baring more and more of my thighs until my bottom is exposed— my black underwear. I decide to encourage him by doing some exploration of my own. Find the hem of his shirt and slip my hands under it, touching his hard belly. Flatten my palms against his rock-hard abs and his immense, bulging pecs.

He growls again, and his lips slant across mine, and I sigh, whimpering with desire, pleasure, and desperation as he kisses my breath away. His arousal digs into my butt and I tilt my hips to get friction where I need it—suddenly consumed with need.

His hands slip down to my bare thighs, and I gasp at the fire of his touch to my skin. His powerful grip skids softly upward toward my hips. I open my mouth fully and accept his tongue, giving him mine. They dance and tangle, twist and taste. Every breath he takes is a rumble, a growl, a hot, hungry snarl.

Finally, at last, he finds the courage to cradle my bottom in his hands. And I whimper into his mouth at the touch, flicking his hard little nipples with my thumbs.

I pull away with a long low moan. "Bear. My god."

"Hmmm?" he queries, sounding shaken.

"The way you kiss me."

"Was it okay?"

I laugh, letting my smile curve against his lips, and kiss him as I laugh. "So much more than just okay." I rub lip gloss off his lips with my thumbs. "I could stay here and kiss you forever." To start with. "But we have things to do."

"Dumb."

I dissolve into laughter, clutching his face and kissing him through my laughter. "I agree. I'd much rather kiss you, but I need to shower and change, and we need to get to the store."

"You really want me to come with you?" he asks.

I sit back on his lap. "I do. I know you're nervous. But it's going to be okay. I'll be with you every step of the way, okay?"

"Not nervous." He lets out a breath. "Fuckin' terrified."

"Oh god, Bear, honey. There's nothing to be afraid of. It's just my family."

"Barely know you. But…I feel like I do. I dunno."

"I know what you mean. But I promise, it's going to be okay. So just… relax. Breathe. And try to trust me, okay?"

He nods. "You, I trust."

Reluctantly, I slide off of him and to my feet. "Won't be long, promise."

He makes an expression that is the facial version of a shrug. "No rush on my end."

Now that I've tasted him and felt his mouth on mine, I'll never get enough; I bend at the waist and touch my lips to his. "Just one more."

Mistake. Big mistake.

I find myself falling into the kiss all over again, and his hands frame my waist. Slip upward, now. The thin cotton of my dress does nothing to dull the sharp heat of his touch. Higher. Pauses at the lower edge of my bra.

But then, instead of going where I know he wants to, he sinks backward with a growl, yanking his hand away from my body. "Shower. 'Fore I lose my goddamn mind."

I straighten, rubbing both hands over my flushed, flustered face. "Right. Yes. Shower." I let a harsh breath out past clenched teeth. "I don't want to stop, Bear."

His gaze searches my face. "No?"

I shake my head. "Not at all. Not even a little bit."

"Glad I'm not the only one."

Before I start something we really don't have the time to finish, I force myself away from him, heading down the hall for my bedroom. I bite my tongue to keep from inviting him into the shower with me. I do feel his eyes on my backside, and I shamelessly let my hips sway a little extra, just for him.

Right before I go into my room, I steal a peek back at

him—just in time to catch him adjusting himself, lifting his hips and tugging at his fly with a pained wince.

I affect him.

A lot.

I like that. I like knowing I make him feel that way. That he desires me.

I shut my bedroom door and peel my dress off, and then my underwear and bra, tossing them all in the hamper. I twist my hair up onto my head and put a shower cap on while the water heats. Step in, wash up, rinse off—ignoring the damp heat between my thighs, the ache. The pulse of need. Ignore the urge to take the edge off with my fingers—I haven't been with anyone in a very, very long time, but my fingers have been rather busy. A girl has needs, after all.

I wonder if he does that. I wonder if he's thought of me while doing that. I find myself hoping he does. Wanting him to.

I blush furiously as I shut the water off and dry myself, trying desperately to erase the image of Bear in the shower, water sluicing down his huge, heavily muscled body, his big fist stroking down his—

No.

Nope.

Can't go there.

I'm barely hanging on as it is—I've pushed him as far as he can go for now, I think. I have to keep myself in check.

Funny—Brennan always made me feel self-conscious about my sexuality. I can't pinpoint how, it was always just this vague sense that I wanted something he didn't. What, I don't know.

Our physical relationship started very slowly and

stayed slow. It didn't progress past an innocent kiss here and there for *years*. When we did finally actually sleep together on our wedding night, he finished within a minute or two, and I was left frustrated—and felt guilty for feeling frustrated.

There—that's it. That's the source of my negative feelings about my sexual relationship with Brennan: he didn't satisfy me.

I didn't want him.

I wasn't turned on by him.

Not ever.

I wasn't even attracted to him.

It's only now that I know what true desire, true attraction feels like—with Bear—that I can finally understand it. Brennan just didn't do it for me. I wasn't excited by him. I was eager to explore my body, to explore sexuality, and I would have pushed the boundaries with him had he given me even a *hint* that he wanted to. But he didn't. He was the one who always pulled us back when we started to get carried away.

So…when did he start sleeping with other women? Did he think I didn't want him? Was it me? Or was the whole thing with me fake?

Now I kind of want answers.

I push those thoughts away and remove the shower cap, pull my hair out of the braid it's been in since yesterday morning, spray leave-in conditioner into it, work it through my hair, and brush it till the kinks become waves. Deodorant. A touch of makeup. Lotion on my arms and legs.

Now…what to wear?

I pull on a thong—I own several, purchased after the

breakup, but I've never had the courage to wear them. I do so now, and I feel...sexy.

Daring.

Courageous.

Ready.

For what? I don't know. Just...more. Of Bear.

Lies—I do know. I want him. All of him.

I want him to strip me naked and—

Gosh, stop. Stop!

I can't go there. I *have* to get a grip.

I put on the bra that matches the thong—red and lacy, a pushup number that makes my boobs, already pretty darn big, look even bigger. I opt for a denim skirt, the shortest skirt I own. It comes to an inch or two below my butt—my parents will most definitely say something about it. My sisters, too, probably. But who cares? I'm wearing it for Bear.

I want his approval, now—not theirs.

It has a white fringe lining the hem, tickling my bare thighs. I pair it with a white button-down—at first, I leave two buttons open, but then, in a fit of boldness that's utterly unlike me, I undo a third. Prop the girls up, shove them this way and that until they sit just right. A hint of red lace peeks out; I can already feel Bear's gaze sticking there, lingering like a caress.

I decide on a pair of low brown booties with a chunky heel—they make my legs look even longer, and do good things for my bottom.

I check myself out in the mirror one more time, nodding in approval. Not too bad.

A spritz of perfume, and I'm good to go.

I emerge from my room, suddenly nervous to see Bear's reaction. Which is silly—I'm not even dressing up.

I just want him to think I'm beautiful. I want to be beautiful for him. I've always cared about my appearance and always put in effort to look my best, but Bear's attention puts things into high gear.

He looks up as I clomp down the hallway. His brow furrows and his jaw flexes. "Jesus." He stands up, hands tightening into fists at his sides. "Noelle...holy shit."

Butterflies rampage in my belly. "Do I look okay?" Fishing for compliments is not my style, but here I am, fishing.

"You look..." he goes around the couch and stops a foot away from me, reaching for me but pulling his hand back at the last second. "Incredible."

"Really?"

"Not good with words. Wish I could find a better one than that." His eyes rake down my body lingering at my chest, as expected—as planned. "Won't be able to take my eyes off you."

I step into him. "Good. That's the whole idea."

"So fucking beautiful, Noelle. You take my breath away."

"That's okay," I whisper, touching my lips to his. "You can have mine."

He kisses me softly, slowly. "Should I change?"

I pull back and assess: nice jeans, his usual work boots, and a black T-shirt, all clean, if a little wrinkled from sleeping in them last night. "No, you're fine. You look great."

"Changed before going to the shelter—I get dirty at work."

"I imagine you do." I take his hand. "Well. Shall we? Target awaits."

I make quick work of getting the stuff Dad requested:

a package of strip steaks, pre-formed burger patties, a couple of bags of potato chips, and a case of Diet Coke. Bear paces beside me, his gait smooth and light despite his immensity.

I bring him to the toiletries aisle and pick out shampoo, conditioner, beard wash, beard oil, a hairbrush, hair ties, and a beard brush, and then we head for the checkout.

"One sec," he says, as I pull the cart to a halt behind a mom and her two little kids. "Wanna grab something."

"Okay," I say, curious.

A few minutes later, he comes back with a giant bouquet of flowers and a bottle of whiskey.

I give him a look. "You don't need to bring anything, you know."

He shrugs. "Yeah, figure I do." he holds up the bottle. "Wasn't sure if your dad drinks. Figure a lotta church people don't."

I smile, nodding. "He does, on occasion. He'll appreciate that. But you really don't have to."

"It's your parents. Your family. It's important."

This whole thing has gone zero to a hundred in no time, hasn't it? He's meeting my *family*.

Suddenly, I'm nervous. Am I going too fast? Am I pushing things too quickly? Jumping in head first? Especially physically. I'm all in on the physical attraction aspect, and I definitely don't see the value in progressing our physical relationship as slowly as Brennan and I did. But…should we just jump into bed together within days of meeting each other?

Doubts, questions, and concerns storm through my brain.

"Noelle?" Bear's voice is a rumble in my ear, and his hand presses gently into the small of my back. "Our turn."

"Oh." I startle, realizing the cashier is looking at me with impatient expectation. "Sorry. Spaced out for a minute."

The cashier rings up the items as I put them on the belt. At the last second, Bear adds his flowers and bottle and hands the cashier a card, all before I can so much as get my wallet out of my purse.

"Bear!" I protest.

He gives me a look as he pockets the card again. "Got it. All good."

"Well at least let me pay you back for the food," I say, following him now as he pushes the cart toward the exit.

"Nope."

"Bear, that was like a hundred dollars worth of food. You didn't need to do that." I grab a bag, put it in the back of my car, and then turn to grab another one.

Before I can, however, his hand closes around my wrist, and he gently but inexorably guides me to the driver's side door, pulls it open, and guides me into the seat. I open my mouth to protest that it's just a couple of bags, but the look he gives me has me snapping my mouth shut.

"I got it, Noelle."

It feels important to him, for some reason, so I nod and relax into the seat. He shuts the door, and I start the engine and buckle up while he finishes loading. A big, hot, wet pink tongue flaps against my ear, eliciting a surprised shriek from me.

I twist in the seat to say hi to Panzer, only to get another lick right up the center of my face. "Hi, buddy," I say, scrubbing his ears in my hands. "Who's a big sweetheart?"

I wipe at my face while the big dog tries to nuzzle under my hands to give me more slobbery kisses, and soon it's become a game, Panzer nosing under my hands while I laugh hysterically and try to dodge his long, darting tongue.

When Bear lowers himself into the passenger seat, he watches us with another rare, beaming smile. "He likes you."

I wrap an arm around Panzer's thick, iron-hard neck and kiss him on the forehead between the ears. "The feeling is mutual. He's a sweetheart."

I check my mirrors and blindspots and then back out and make for the parking lot exit, wait for traffic to clear, and then make a left onto Division, heading for my parent's neighborhood, which is off of Brookline midway between Main and Division.

Bear eyes me, clears his throat. "What were you thinking about, back there? Looked sorta freaked out."

"It was nothing," I say, but the lie sits like acid on my tongue.

Bear sighs. "Rather have an uncomfortable truth than a pleasant lie, Noelle."

I hesitate and then take his hand. "You're right, I'm sorry. I just…"

He looks down at our joined hands. "You can just drop us off at home. I get it if you're rethinking me coming over."

"No!" I say, squeezing his hand. "No, that's not it. Well, not really. Sort of."

He snorts. "That clears it up."

"Sorry, I just don't know where to start."

A heavy shrug. "Rip off the Band-Aid."

"I guess I'm wondering if… if I'm jumping into things

with you a little too fast. Like maybe we need to spend some time just getting to know each other." I thread my fingers between his, hoping it will reassure him somewhat.

"Jumping into what things?" he asks, looking and sounding genuinely puzzled.

Before I can answer, my phone rings—Dad again. I answer it, holding up an index finger at Baer. "Hey Dad, just left Target with the stuff. What's up?"

"Oh, just checking on you. Thought you'd be here by now. Nat will be here in an hour, Nik in less than that, and the boys are already here."

I laugh. "I'm on the way, I promise. Um, by the way, I just wanted to let you know that I'm bringing a friend with me. I hope that's okay."

A short silence greets this pronouncement. "A friend?"

"Yeah."

"Sure, no problem. The more the merrier!"

"Okay, cool. See ya in a minute."

"Yepper!"

I laugh to myself as I hang up. My dad is such a midwestern dad stereotype. *Yepper!*

I toss the phone back into my purse in the footwell by Bear's feet. "Anyway. Where were we?"

"You were wondering if we were jumping into things too fast, and I asked what things."

"Right, right." I lick my lips, unsure how to proceed with this. "Look. I'm…I'm very attracted to you. Physically, I mean. And, you know, otherwise, as well. Who you are, all that."

He blinks at me in that slow, thoughtful, owlish way of his. "Okay. But?"

"I've only ever had a physical relationship with one

person—Brennan, my ex-husband. And that was a long, *long* relationship. And physically, it progressed very, very, *very* slowly. Much too slowly, if I'm being honest."

"Because of your religious beliefs."

I nod and then shrug, tipping my head to one side. "Well, my parents' beliefs—the beliefs they raised me with. I'm not so sure I agree with all of them anymore, is the thing. See, they believe that sex is sacred. Designed by God to exist exclusively within the confines of marriage. There should be *no* physical relationship before marriage. None. Zero. And even within marriage, there's this…I dunno…a sort of unspoken idea that sex is meant for procreation—making kids. Not merely for enjoyment or pleasure. So, with Brennan and me, I was frustrated for a lot of our relationship. Or, honestly, all of it."

"Frustrated? Sexually, you mean?"

I nod. "Yeah. Well, not just sexually. In every way." I glance at him. 'Sorry, I guess this is probably weird and uncomfortable for you to talk about, huh? Me and my ex?"

He shakes his head. "It's part of you. It's important. I wanna understand."

"Okay, so…" I rub at my face with one hand, hunting for a way to explain what I'm feeling when I'm not entirely sure what I'm feeling myself. "What I'm struggling with is that I don't believe that way anymore. But I don't know what I believe in terms of sex, marriage, and physical relationships. You and I just met. I feel like I know you way more than the amount of time we've known other should allow, though, if that makes any sense."

He nods. "Does to me. I feel the same way."

"I don't think that there's anything wrong with sharing a physical connection with someone you care about,"

I say. "Being intimate with someone you want to explore a long-term relationship with is just...I dunno. Normal? I don't think it has to be only within marriage, either. I think that can complicate things, actually." I sigh and spend a few moments staring at nothing, considering. "I realized recently that I never truly knew Brennan. I still don't understand why he took things so excruciatingly slow and then was so...disinterested in me sexually but was having sexual affairs on the side with *three* other women. That just makes no sense. And it's still messing with my head."

"He's just a liar and an asshole. Nothing to understand." Bear rolls one heavy shoulder. "You were his public face—what he knew he *should* have: a good girl with a good family. The correct relationship. Chaperones. All that silly shit. But he was a liar. Thought with his dick. Wanted to have his cake and eat it, too. Wasn't you, it was him."

My mouth flaps open and closed a few times, shocked. He succinctly summarized the whole issue in a few sentences.

"I..." I look at him, shaking my head, processing what he just said. "Wow. Yeah. I guess I was looking for a deeper meaning or something."

"My experience, men aren't that deep. What happened, if you ask me, was he started off believing in your relationship. But as time went on, he started wanting things he didn't think you'd agree to. Or maybe, things he figured weren't right in the context of your relationship. So he went and got it elsewhere."

I shake my head, disgusted all over again. "I would have given him whatever he wanted. I was always the one pushing the boundaries, and he was the one who always pulled us back. I always wanted more. I tried over and over again to spice things up with him. Try new things. I initiated intimacy all the time. And he wouldn't turn me down, but…" I want to cry. "He just…he acted like he could take it or leave it. And when I suggested we try new things—you know, anything other than vanilla missionary sex, he…he never put it in so many words, but he made me feel…ashamed, I guess. Of myself. For wanting to go farther." I wipe my face. "He just always made me feel so insecure for being…sexual, I guess."

"Fucking prick," Bear growls. "Shouldn't feel that way."

"That's what's confusing me now. With us. I want things with you, Bear. I really, really do. But is it too soon? We just met."

Bear doesn't answer for a long time. He licks his lips and tugs on his beard. "Noelle…" A pause. Starts over. "I got no clue how things like this are supposed to work. Never had a relationship." He looks away, out the window, hiding his expression from me. "I've had sex. I'm not a thirty-two-year-old virgin or anything. I just… things were different for me, the way my life was back then. I was a gang-banger. A thug. Dunno what word you want to use. Not a good person. Did bad things. Hung around bad people. Hurt people. Stole things. Hooked up with girls just because. It was always mutual—I never…I never forced anyone. *Never*." His eyes fix on mine, pleading with me to believe him.

I squeeze his hand as hard as I can. "I know, Bear. I *know*. You wouldn't. I *absolutely* believe that."

He exhales slowly, a sound of relief. "I got no reference point for relationships, Noelle. All I know is that I feel big things for you. I think about you when I'm not with you. Wanna know more about you. But physically, I..." he trails off.

We're less than a block from my parent's house, but I pull over to the curb and hold the brake. "Bear, you can tell me anything. Okay? Anything."

"I want a physical relationship with you, Noelle. Of course, I do. Been locked up with a few thousand other men for ten years. Sorta...sorta forgot a lotta shit about how life on the outside works. What things are like. Couldn't tell you who I was with last or what it was like. Been so damn long it's almost like a...a reset, or somethin'."

"Wow. I, um. that never occurred to me."

He shrugs. "No reason it would. Just saying. I don't expect anything, Noelle. I like spending time with you. That's all I need. If you wanna keep things just friends for a while, I got no problem with that. I understand."

"But you want more."

"Course I do. I mean, fuck. Look at you. You're..." he shakes his head. "Exquisite. Breathtaking. I don't know a lotta fancy words. Just...yeah. I want more. The way you kissed me back there? Noelle, if you never wanted anything else but to be friends with me, I could die a happy fuckin' man because the most beautiful woman in the whole god-damn world kissed *me*. Okay? So don't stress. It's what you want it to be."

My throat is hot, my eyes burning. I can't stop a tear from leaking out and trickling down my nose. "God, Bear."

"Cryin' again? What'd I say?"

I shake my head, laughing through my tears. "I'm not upset. You're just so sweet it hurts."

He frowns, perplexed. "Dunno what that means."

I lean over the console, take his face in my hands,

and kiss him. "It means that was the most perfect answer I could have asked for. And then some."

"I'm not sure what to say."

I pull away from the curb. "You don't need to say anything. I'm just grateful I met you."

9

Bear

WE PULL INTO NOELLE'S PARENTS' DRIVEWAY and she shifts into Park. She shuts off the engine, opens her door, and slings one long, ivory leg out, but stops when she sees I haven't even unbuckled yet.

"Knew I shoulda dressed up more," I mutter.

She huffs, shaking her head. "You're fine."

I gesture at the house. "Look at the place. Fuckin' mansion."

Noelle frowns at me and then sinks back into her seat, pulling her leg back in as she looks at the house she grew up in, perhaps trying to see it through my eyes.

Two stories, it began life sometime in the first few decades of the nineteen hundreds as a simple Craftsman.

Over the intervening century or so, it looks like it has been added onto, renovated, added onto again, and re-renovated. Now, it looks—to my eyes, at least—to be over five thousand square feet and sits on a five-acre lot at the end of a cul-de-sac, with state-owned forest on two sides. Sided in gray, weathered cedar shakes with a green metal roof, it has a deep front porch held up by a pair of river stone pillars, a white bench swing hanging from the ceiling on the left side, and a pair of antique rocking chairs on the right. The driveway extends past the house on the right side a good fifty yards, ending at a big red pole barn. Twenty or so hens run around the backyard, clucking and scratching, while a huge rooster watches, tail feathers arched proudly, cockle-doodle-doing noisily every few seconds.

I frown. "I thought roosters only do that at dawn?"

She laughs. "God, no. That's Boggle. He never shuts up." She pats my knee, smiling encouragingly at me. "It's just a house, Bear. I promise you're fine. My brothers haven't worn anything but joggers and hoodies for like five years."

I blow out a breath. "I'm nervous."

"It's okay. You're okay. Just be yourself."

I snort. "Still figuring out who that is."

"A sweet, smart, strong man who's working incredibly hard to overcome a very difficult past. And succeeding admirably, I might add." She squeezes my thigh. "C'mon, time to go in."

I sigh and reluctantly, nervously unfold from the CR-V, and open the rear door for Panzer, who hops down and stretches forward and backward, yawning prodigiously, shakes off violently, and then waits for my next move.

Noelle heads for the porch as I gather the bags

containing the groceries from the trunk and joins me at the door. As soon as my feet hit the top step, the front door opens and Noelle's mother bustles out, arms open.

"No-No! Thanks for coming early, sweetie." Her arms wrap around Noelle, who returns the hug with similar exuberance.

"Of course, Mom." She turns as I lumber up the steps, Panzer at my left heel. "Mom, this is Bear. Bear, this is my mom, Nina."

Her mom's eyes bug out of her head as she sees me— and then she sees Panzer.

She screams, ducking behind Noelle.

Noelle whirls, grabbing her mom's arms and staring at her in shock. "*Mom*! What the heck?"

Noelle's father appears in the doorway, concern on his face. "What in the *world* is going on?"

Noelle shakes her head. "Mom saw Bear's dog and screamed. I know he looks scary, but he's the sweetest dog you'll ever meet. Relax."

Mom is shaking like a leaf, white as a sheet, still hiding behind her daughter.

Her dad pulls his wife against his side. "She got attacked by a dog the other day. She's still shaken up."

I set the bags down and go back down the steps to where Panzer is waiting, panting, tongue lolling. "Panzer, komm." I lead the dog across the front yard to the huge spreading oak tree. "Platz. Bleib."

Panzer settles onto his belly, licking my hand as I scruff the dog's ears.

"Sorry about that," I say, coming back up the steps. "Didn't know."

Noelle frowns at her mom, who has a hand on her

chest, her breathing finally starting to slow down. "You were attacked? By whose dog?"

Nina nods, swallowing hard. "I was taking a walk like I do every day. Two miles to the Cromwell farm and back. I passed by the Hendersons like always, and their dog jumped the fence and chased me, barking like crazy. He bit me. See?" She tugs the sleeve of her cardigan up to reveal a nasty set of healing bite marks. "I've known that dog since he was a pup. I have no idea what happened. I felt horrible, though. They had to call animal control."

Her dad huffs. "Never trusted that dog. Always thought he had a bit of pit bull in 'im."

I frown at this but hold my tongue; pitties have a bad reputation, which most of them don't deserve.

Noelle takes my hand and gestures from her father to me with her other hand. "Dad, this is Bear; Bear, this is my dad, Nicholas."

I shake Nicholas' hand. "Sir." I offer Nina my hand, and when she takes it, I shake gently. "Ma'am. Sorry to have scared you. Panzer won't hurt a soul, I promise."

She looks at Panzer, who is dozing beneath the old oak with his chin on his paws. "I've always loved dogs. I'm just a bit…shaken up, like Nick said. Will he be okay there? He won't run away?"

I shake my head. "No ma'am. He's a very highly trained guard dog. Tell him to stay, he stays till I say otherwise."

"Was that German?" she asks.

I nod. "They get trained in German. Don't respond to English commands at all."

She watches as a squirrel darts across the yard a few feet from Panzer, oblivious to his presence. Panzer's head lifts from his paws and his ears perk up, his tail tapping, watching the critter scamper around the yard, but he doesn't otherwise move as the squirrel ascends another tree farther away.

"Would you look at that?" Nicholas marvels. "Never known a dog that didn't chase a squirrel."

"Did you train him?" Nina asks.

I shake my head. "No ma'am. Rescued him. His owner died, and animal control didn't realize he didn't know English commands. I guess I sorta bonded with him. We're a lot alike."

"Well, come on in," Nicholas says, gathering the grocery bags. "No sense standing around letting all the cold air out."

Inside, white ceilings and walls are juxtaposed with dark wood trim and dark floors. A staircase greets you as you enter, leading up to the second floor, the banister squared off and thick and worn smooth, with a dark green carpet running up the center of the stairs. Right off the stairs is the library/office. A set of glass double doors stand open, revealing floor-to-ceiling built-in bookshelves lining the walls, with a heavy antique desk occupying the center of the room, littered with papers, stacks of books, a coffee mug full of pens, and a large iMac in one corner. A Tiffany lamp sits in the other corner, with a small glass terrarium next to it. A pair of black leather wingback chairs face the desk at angles to each other.

A narrow, low-ceilinged hallway runs past the library, leading to the sprawling, open-concept kitchen, dining room, and den. The kitchen is on the left, a round, eight-seat antique table in the middle, and a sunken living room on the right, carpeted with a thick, high-piled white carpet; a massive white leather sectional takes up most of the den, with two matching ottomans, a low, glass-topped coffee table and matching side tables. Throw pillows and knitted throw blankets are draped artfully here and there across the back of the couch, and stacks of books lay scattered on the coffee table and side tables. A breakfast nook occupies a rounded bump-out next to the sliding glass doors leading to the expansive deck overlooking the back-yard. A huge griddle grill smolders on the deck, waiting for the meat.

In the far rear of the property, a pair of mini donkeys graze their fenced-off acre of pasture.

I feel Noelle watching me as I take it all in, eyes wide.

"This place is amazing," I say. "Peaceful."

Nicholas pulls the steaks and burgers out of the bags, rips open the packages, places the meat on a large platter, and then goes to town seasoning them with salt, pepper, and garlic. That done, he pulls a platter of chicken breasts from the fridge, and another of corn on the cob.

I watch as Noelle wafts around the kitchen, moving with seamless grace around her parents as they prepare the food. Nina washes a head of romaine and then sets about chopping it while Noelle peels carrots and chops them into small rounds and then moves on to celery. Nicholas grabs two of the platters and heads for the sliding doors. "Mind grabbing the door for me, big fella? You could bring those other platters out, too, if you're so inclined."

"Yes sir," I say, and tug the door open for him and then follow him out with the rest.

Nicholas deftly tosses the steaks onto the left side of the griddle and then uses tongs to lay the chicken breasts on the back, the burgers in neat rows in the middle, and the corn along the right.

That done, he hangs the tongs from a hook on the side of the griddle, opens a long white Yeti cooler, and produces a pair of long-neck beers.

He twists the tops off and hands one to me. "Cheers."

I take it, tap the neck against his, and take a small sip. "Thank you."

He nods, eying me. "So."

I can tell he's about to ask questions; I brace.

"Where'd you meet Noelle?"

"Animal Shelter. I volunteer there after work."

A nod, a sip. "Where do you work? What do you do?"

"Demolitions. I work for Riley Crowe." I take another tiny sip, pretending to take a longer one.

His eyes narrow immediately. "Crowe Demolitions. He runs that convict program."

My heart pounds. "Yes sir."

"You part of that?" His gaze is sharp.

I swallow a lump of nerves—or, try to. The lump stays in my throat, hot and hard. "Yes sir. I am."

Noelle arrives then, a glass of wine in her hand. "Dad, stop. No interrogating my friend."

Nicholas takes a long sip. "Just making conversation, honey."

"It's okay," I tell her.

Nicholas glances from me to Noelle, who's standing quite close to my side—closer than one would expect just a friend to stand. "What happened? What'd you do?"

"Dad. Stop," Noelle snaps.

I touch her shoulder. "Noelle, it's okay. I don't mind." I direct my gaze at her father. "I was involved in an armed robbery that went wrong. Someone was killed."

Nicholas's gaze narrows. "You kill him?"

I shake my head. "No sir. It was an accident. I got charged and convicted for it, though."

"But you were there. You were part of it." The judgment is clear in his voice.

I nod. "Yes sir, I was."

He looks at his daughter. Then at me again. "How long were you in prison for?"

"Ten years, almost eleven. Out on parole, working for Riley."

He nods slowly. "I see." A long pause, his gaze thoughtful. "Learn anything?"

"I did."

"Such as?"

Noelle touches my forearm to hold back my reply, glaring at her father. "Dad, please. He doesn't need to be interrogated."

"Noelle." My voice is firm. "Let him ask his questions. You're his daughter. He has the right to know who you're hanging out with."

Nicholas looks from me to her, waiting for Noelle's answer.

"I'm an adult. I choose who I spend time with," she says. "I know all about Bear's past."

"It *is* your *past*, though, isn't it?" he asks me.

I nod. "Yes sir, it is. I live here in Three Rivers. I work for Riley. I volunteer at the shelter. I got nothin' to do with anyone or anything from that part of my life anymore. I did some bad things, even if I didn't do what I was accused of. I did do other stuff. I was given a second chance, and I plan on doing things right this time around."

Nicholas nods, setting his beer aside to check the food

on the griddle. He notices that I've set my bottle down after only a few sips. "Not a drinker?"

"Not much of one, sir, no," I answer.

"Problems with it?"

I shake my head. "No. But I'm on parole. Doing my best to keep out of trouble." I frown at Noelle. "I forgot to give them the things I got."

She laughs. "Oh! All the excitement with my mom and Panzer. I'll be right back."

A moment or two later, her mother comes out onto the deck with the flowers I got her, already cut and in a vase. "These are lovely, Bear. Thank you very much."

I offer her a small smile. "You're welcome."

Noelle hands me the bottle, and I pass it to her dad. "For you, sir."

He accepts it, examining it. "Balvenie Twelve. Very nice. Unnecessary, but I appreciate the gesture." He sets it aside and gestures with his bottle at mine. "If you're not expected to pass any kind of test, I don't think one beer will harm anything, do you?"

I tip my head to one side, considering. "Probably not. Just trying to err on the side of caution."

He nods. "Wise man. Finish that and we'll switch you to soda, then. I appreciate your being forthcoming."

Noelle leans into my side and looks up at me. "You're okay out here?" When I nod, she lets go. "I should go back in and finish helping Mom."

"Go for it. I'm good."

After she disappears back inside, Nicholas spends a few moments flipping and rolling the food on the griddle and then turns back to me.

"So you and my daughter."

"We're friends, sir."

He looks past me through the glass, watching his wife and daughter work together. "She's always been very innocent. Perhaps a little naive. I don't know what she's told you about our beliefs, but we used to be quite...strict. We've loosened up a good bit over the past few years, though." Here, he lifts his bottle. "Once upon a time, I'd never have allowed myself this, not even one."

"She's talked about it some. Told me about Brennan."

His expression darkens. "That was very rough on her. She's not the same. That whole business really shook her."

I haven't seen that, myself. His assessment of his daughter doesn't exactly align with the woman I know. "I'm not sure about that, sir. I think she's better off."

He frowns. "Perhaps. She's wandered from the faith, however."

"Can't speak on that, sir. Not a church-going man, myself."

"Are you against it?"

I shrug, shake my head. "Not against it, no. Had some long talks with a chaplain, on the inside."

"So, then, what do you believe?"

I consider his question for a while. "Unsure. If there is a god, I've got some questions for him. Her. Or them, or whatever." I watch Noelle throw her head back and laugh at something her mom says; I feel myself smile a little at the way her laughter lights up her face. "I don't think she's wandered. I think she's...learned. Grown. She just believes a little differently than she did. Than you do."

Nicholas regards me for a moment, thoughtful, even if I can't discern what he's thinking. "I suppose that makes sense. Brennan's behavior was certainly inexcusable. It hurt her deeply."

A shout in the distance catches my attention: a pair of horses bearing riders are galloping this way, figures hunched over.

"Oh, there's the boys back from their ride," Nicholas says. "We can pick this up later. Hard to have deep conversations with those two knuckleheads around."

The riders haul the horses to a stop mere feet from the railing of the balcony, tossing the reins over the horses' necks as they hop down. Her brothers are a little older than in the photo at her station. Tall, lean, athletic, and absurdly good-looking, the boys are dressed in joggers, sneakers, and T-shirts, with backward hats and wraparound mirrored sunglasses. While their clothes aren't identical in color, they are the same style. Without different color clothing, I'd never be able to tell them apart at first glance.

They tie the reins to the railing of the deck, chattering at each other and over each other, bickering playfully about who won.

They tromp up the deck side by side, laughing—their laughter trails off when they see me.

"Holy shit, who the hell are you?" one of them says.

"Nathan Harper. Watch your mouth," Nicholas snaps without looking away from the grill.

"Sorry, Dad," the offender mutters; he's wearing gray joggers, a black shirt, and a black hat.

The other one, in black joggers, a white shirt, and a white hat, shoves his brother. "Yeah, Nate. Watch your mouth."

"Shut up, dweeb."

"Boys." It's patient but annoyed.

They both go silent. I hold out my hand. "Bear Olafsson. Friend of Noelle's."

"What kind of friend? A special friend?" This is the other brother, Noah. The one in the white hat.

Noelle comes out with a giant glass bowl containing the salad she and her mother put together. "None of your business, Noah," she says. "Don't be a buttinsky."

"You're a buttinksy," he snarks. "You've never brought anyone to a Saturday cookout before. Sue me for being curious if you're finally back in the saddle."

"About damn time," Nathan says.

Noelle sighs. "It's none of your business whether I'm *back in the saddle.*"

"You gave that cock—" Nathan cuts off, glancing at his father, who looks at him with an arched eyebrow. "That cock-a-doodle-dooo *way* too much your life. I'm just happy you're finally getting back out there."

Noelle smiles at her brother, setting the salad bowl down on the metal outdoor table. "Well, thank you, Nathan." She looks from me to her brothers. "Did you introduce yourselves?"

"Oh, shit—I mean shoot." Noah approaches me, hand extended. "Noah Harper. This is my twin, Nathan."

I shake his hand and then his brothers. "Bear."

"Bear," Noah repeats. "That's your real name?"

"Yeah, it is."

"Cool. It fits you."

Before I can think of a response, the sliding door opens and Noelle's sisters come out onto the deck.

Tall, slender, and classically beautiful, with long, swan-like necks and elaborately curled blond hair, they're both dressed professionally, one of them in a black pantsuit with a pale pink blouse, the other in a long red skirt, matching red high heels, and a white blouse, all but the top-most button done up modestly. Both carry expensive-looking purses and have an air of importance. Or maybe self-importance.

Their eyes widen as they see me.

"No-No, you brought a...friend?" The red-skirted one says.

Noelle joins me, tucking her hand around my elbow; the action has the air of her making a statement. "Yes, I did. Natasha, this is Bear. Bear, these are my older sisters." She gestures at each sister as she names them. "Natasha and Nikki."

Nikki is in the black suit, and Natasha is in the red skirt.

I hold out my hand, and the women both shake mine—their grips are limp and delicate, so I only lightly clasp their hands before letting go immediately. "Nice to meet you both."

Their eyes scan me, assessing me—my clothes, my size, my tattoos, my hair, my beard. It feels like scrutiny and makes me uncomfortable.

Nina comes out, then, bearing a large wooden bowl covered with a cloth napkin. "Noelle, can you fetch the plates and silverware?"

It strikes me as odd that Noelle was summoned early to help, and even when the other siblings arrive, it's Noelle who's asked to set the table. None of the others so much as offers to help as Noelle carries a tall stack of heavy-looking, brightly-colored plates outside.

I hustle over to her and take the plates from her. "Let me help."

She blinks at me. "Oh—um, yeah. I'll get the silverware."

I set a plate at each place as Noelle moves around the table behind me with the silverware.

"How are you doing?" she asks in a soft murmur pitched for my ears alone.

"Okay."

"Sorry about the third-degree," she says.

"Don't be. You brought home a convicted felon. He's gonna have questions."

She stands in front of me, looking up at me. "You're more than that, Bear. A lot more."

I allow a tiny smile—she likes it when I smile, I've noticed. Haven't had much reason to, but now, for her, I'm re-learning how to. "Thank you. I'm just saying, I get where he's coming from."

She shoots a sideways glance at her sisters. "Don't mind them. That's how they always are."

I arch an eyebrow. "Not sure what you mean."

She laughs, leaning into me. "Yes, you do." She pats my chest. "I appreciate you coming. I'm glad you're here."

"Thank you for inviting me. It's interesting to see your family. Where you grew up."

I feel eyes on us—Natasha and Nikki are watching us whispering to each other.

Noelle stares right back, not moving away from me; I get the sense that Noelle is using me to make a point of some sort. Something to ask her about when we're alone again.

The next few hours are…interesting. The food is amazing—the steak is the best I've ever had, not that I've had many: thick, juicy, well-seasoned, and perfectly cooked. With the meat are baked potatoes with all the fixings, corn on the cob, salad, rolls, and a homemade lemon meringue pie.

The one thing that bothers me, though, is my observations of Noelle's role in the family. Baked potatoes? Noelle made them. Dessert? Sliced and served by Noelle while everyone else sat around outside and chatted; once dinner was made, Noelle rose and served dessert automatically, and no one even offered to help her. When dessert was finished, who cleared the table? Noelle.

That's the last straw for me. As she balances a stack of plates in one hand and tries to open the door with the other, I look around the table, trying gamely to suppress a growl.

I don't entirely succeed, and everyone, including Noelle, goes silent and turns to look at me.

I rise from my seat, take the stack of plates from Noelle's shocked and unresisting arms, and draw open the door. I set the stack in the sink, return to the outdoor table, and gather up bowls, dessert plates, and silverware.

Noelle frowns at me. "Bear, what are you doing? You're a guest. It's not your job."

I cast my baleful stare around the table. "Ain't yours either. Don't recall your name being Cinderella." A gasp comes from one of her sisters. I rake my eyes from face to face around the table. "Rest of you folks have hands. Maybe use 'em."

Stunned silence ensues, and I carry the dishes into the kitchen, set them in the sink, and head out the front door.

I don't like the burn of anger in my chest.

It's not safe. Not healthy.

For other people, I mean.

I sit in the grass under the old oak tree next to Panzer, who groans softly and rests his head on my thighs. I scratch his ears, letting the sunlight and warmth settle my nerves.

I hear her approach, feel her sit next to me. Let out a growling sigh. "Sorry, Noelle. Didn't mean to embarrass you."

She lifts my arm, ducks under it to put her head on my chest, and settles my arm around her waist, my hand on my hip. "You didn't embarrass me. You embarrassed my family."

"That's worse. I just…" I shake my head, feeling the ridges of bark roll against my scalp. "Pissed me off how they all seemed to expect *you* to do all the work."

"That's how it's always been," she says. "I'm used to it."

"Shouldn't be. Least, how it seems to me. I ain't ever had a family, so I guess I don't know shit about it, but it seems like everyone oughta help."

She's quiet for a while. "Bear…" A sigh, her gaze going through the open front door to where we can make out movement in the kitchen. "They're in there doing the dishes together. It feels weird to not be the one doing it."

"I'm sorry for embarrassing them. I can walk home. Ain't that far."

I make to get up, but she doesn't move, instead pressing a hand to my chest, looking at me. "I'm not upset at you, Bear. I'm…I guess I'm realizing that you're right. It's been bothering me for a while, honestly, just…I didn't want to feel it. I've always been expected to do more than my siblings. I don't know why, it's just how it is. It's never been discussed or anything. Not in so many words. It just…it's the way it is."

"But not how it should be."

"No, you're right." She tugs at my beard to get me to look down at her. "I've never had anyone stand up for me like that. Thank you."

"Got pissed off. Shot my mouth off."

"Bear, you're fine. It's okay."

I shake my head. "Worked hard to get rid of my temper. Got away from me today."

"You're the sweetest, gentlest man I've ever met," she says.

"Didn't know me, before."

"You're not that person anymore. If that was you pissed off, then I think you're in good shape."

"Wasn't my place to say anything."

She toys with the tip of Panzer's ear. "You're too hard on yourself, Bear." She gives my beard braid an affectionate tug. "Come on back inside."

"Gonna be awkward."

"What's life without a little bit of awkwardness?" She gets to her feet and extends both hands to me.

I take hers and give her a hint of my weight to pull at as I stand up. I follow her up the steps into the cool, dark foyer. Nina stands just inside at the base of the stairs, drying her hands on a pale yellow hand towel, her brown eyes thoughtful as Noelle and I enter.

"What did you say your dog's name was?" she asks.

"Panzer. Means tank," I answer.

She watches out the screen door as a robin hops, utterly without fear or concern, an inch past Panzer's nose as it hunts for worms and bugs in the grass. "I don't want to be afraid. I love dogs."

"Panzer is the gentlest soul you'll ever meet, Mom," Noelle says. "Except maybe for Bear."

Nina's hands shake as she squeezes the hand towel in both fists. "Could…could you call him over here, please? I'd like to try to meet him properly."

"Panzer," I call; his ears perk up and his attention laser focuses on me. "Komm."

He bolts to his feet and trots across the lawn and up the steps. I open the screen door for him, and he enters the home, tail swaying side to side, a big puppy grin on his face. He nuzzles Noelle's hand with his nose in greeting.

"Panzer—sitz," I command. His butt plops to the floor. I look at Nina. "He won't hurt you. Let him sniff the back of your hand."

Nina inches toward the massive creature, who watches her, tail starting to thump. She holds out her hand to him, and he sniffs it, and then nudges her palm with his forehead, begging shamelessly for ear scratches.

Nina laughs, giving him what he wants, earning a happy groan and a noisily thudding tail.

"Awww," she says, bending over to accept a slobbery kiss on the cheek. "He really *is* a dear, isn't he?" She straightens, meeting my gaze. "You were right, you know. We've taken our darling Noelle for granted for a long time." She pats my shoulder. "I think my husband would like a word. He's out in the barn with the boys."

I nod. "I'll go talk to him." I look at Noelle. "Tell him to heel. You remember the word?"

She scrunches her brow in thought, then nods. "Panzer. Fuss."

Panzer circles around behind Noelle and stands at her right leg, looking up at her expectantly.

"Remember the other commands I've used?" I ask. She nods. "I think so."

I look at the dog. "Stay with Noelle."

He gives a single short bark in response and leans his weight against her thigh. "Good boy."

His tail thumps.

I go through the house, onto the deck, and across the yard toward the big red metal structure. There is a large, rolling, overhead door for admitting tractors or boats or whatever and a smaller person-sized door; the former is closed, the latter open. I enter—buzzing fluorescent lights cut the gloom within, illuminating a green and yellow riding lawn mower, a larger red tractor with some sort of mowing implement hooked to the back, an old, dusty, battered red Ford pickup with the hood open, random detritus piled in the bed; piles of reclaimed wood, stacks of cedar shakes, rolling tool chests, coils of hose lay scattered here and there…wherever I look, there's more stuff. There's another large rolling door in the back wall, also closed; along the left wall near the back are a pair of stalls, presumably for the horses, built out of two-by-fours and black powder-coated steel.

Hay bales are stacked against the wall next to the stalls in serried ranks, reaching fifteen overhead, along the wall, and dropping down to the height of a single bale. Nicholas is restacking bales, throwing them up toward the back wall to make room near the front, condensing the footprint.

I watch him for a minute and then move up to help. Each bale of ripe, pungent green hay is bound with parallel bands of dull red twine. Nicholas grabs a strand in each hand, heaves the bale up to his hips, ducks to get under it, and tosses it up to the next rank.

The bales must be heavier than they look—Nicholas is lean and strong, despite being at least sixty.

"Got it," I say.

I grab a bale in both hands and heave—I estimate it weighs at least fifty pounds, if not closer to sixty. Easy. I toss the bale up to the next rank and then grab a bale in each hand, tossing them simultaneously into place.

Nicholas snorts, watching. "Alright then."

Two by two, I move the stacks upward and back toward the wall until the lowest stack is chest height.

Nicholas pats my back. "That's good. Appreciate it." He laughs, shaking his head. "Woulda taken me all afternoon to do what you did in ten minutes."

I shrug. "All good." I dab at my upper lip with my sleeve and then use the hem of my shirt to dab at my forehead. "About what I said, Mr. Harper."

"Nick, please." He crosses to the rear door and presses a button—the door rolls upward, emitting a sliver of sunlight that expands into a huge, blinding square.

A few feet away, the boys are brushing the horses as they nibble at the grass, the saddles, blankets, and bridles nearby.

He watches the boys groom the animals and then turns to look at me. "You care about my daughter."

"I do."

He nods. "She'll give till she doesn't have anything left to give. She's got the most nurturing spirit of anyone I've ever known. Instinctively takes care of people. Wants to please everyone."

"I've seen that."

"We all sort of let her take on that role, I guess. Got used to it." He looks at me again. "The situation with Brennan did a number on her."

"I think she's okay."

He bends and plucks a bent nail from the ground, twisting the rusty tip between his finger and thumb. "You're not who I would have picked for her."

"Of course not." I know I shouldn't say what comes to mind next, but I do anyway. "Brennan was. Look how that turned out. Maybe let her decide."

He snorts, nods. "Wise words." A glance at me. "Her sisters won't be easy to win over."

"Not tryin' to win anyone or anything, sir. She's my friend."

"In my experience, son, there's no such thing as a purely platonic relationship between a heterosexual man and woman. I know she's friends with Thomas and Colin, and I know that's different."

"Up to her to tell you what she and I are or aren't, sir."

He snorts again, smirking at me with a shake of his head. "You're no one's fool, are you?"

"Hope not, sir."

"Boys!" Nicholas calls. "Make sure they have hay and water when you're done."

"We know," Nathan yells back. "Ain't our first rodeo, ya'll." The last part is in a fake southern drawl.

I follow Nicholas back to the house, pausing at the base of the steps leading up the deck, turning to take in the sweeping, peaceful view of their property.

I like it out here.

Another hour or so of chit-chat in the kitchen, and then Noelle declares that we need to go.

I'm on the front porch with Panzer, waiting for Noelle to finish her goodbyes. The solid inner door is open, just the screen door preventing bugs from getting inside. Which is how I overhear Noelle getting cornered by her sisters.

"Noelle, wait." Sister One—no clue which; her voice has a slight rasp to it.

"We need to speak with you for a moment." Sister Two; her voice is smoother and more articulate.

Noelle sighs; it sounds annoyed to me. "Yes?"

"This…friend of yours." Sister One, raspy. The doctor. Natasha?

"What about him, Nat?"

"What are you doing?" Nat sounds…almost disgusted.

"Indeed," Sister Two says—Nikki, the news anchor. "I know the breakup with Brennan was rough on you, getting dumped like that. But you can do better."

"He's a *criminal*," Natasha says.

"We thought you had standards." Nikki.

My stomach twists, acidic. My impulse is to bolt before I hear anything else, but I resist it. My footsteps will tell them I'm here, listening to their conversation. Also, I'd like to know what Noelle says in response.

Her pause before answering is long and tense. "I don't expect either of you to understand. And I don't need your permission *or* your approval."

"But surely you value our advice," Natasha says.

"We only want what's best for you," Nikki adds.

"Okay, several points," Noelle says. "Number one, Brennan did not *dump* me—*I* left *him*. He was cheating on me. He is a lying, cheating scumbag, and I hope he gets STDs. Screw Brennan Engler. Number two, Bear is more than just a friend. I care about him…*a lot*. Number three—I can do better? Go to hell, Nik. *He* can do better than *me*. Number four, he's *not* a criminal. You know *nothing* about him—if you'd taken even five minutes to talk to him, to get to know him, you'd know he's smart, kind, gentle, caring, and thoughtful." She lets out a breath. "I feel safe with him. I feel seen. And he makes me feel brave."

"You barely know him." Nat.

"We just want you to be safe." Nik.

"And he doesn't seem very...safe." Nat.

Noelle laughs, and it's not exactly a kind sound. It's sarcastic, biting. "As I said, I don't expect either of you to understand. You don't know me. You don't know my life." Her voice nears the door. "Now, Bear and I have other things to do. I'll see you later." The door opens and she sees me standing there. "Bear, um..."

Her expression is troubled and concerned. I touch the small of her back. "I heard. It's okay. Let's just go."

Once we're in the car and heading back toward town, she looks at me apprehensively. "Bear, about my sisters."

"They care about you." I wave a hand. "I understand their concerns. It's okay."

"But...they were being judgmental. It's not okay." She takes my hand. "They should give you a chance."

I shake my head. "They had valid points. I may not be a criminal anymore, but I was. We haven't known each other very long. You *can* do better. They have every right to express their concerns to you. Maybe even an obligation."

She lets out a harsh breath. Shakes her head again. "I guess you're right about most of that. But I take issue with the idea that I can do better than you."

"You're smart. Beautiful. Hard-working. Successful. About to own your own business." I swallow bitterness rather than let it infect my words. "I'm an ex-con working demolition. My record ain't going anywhere, Noelle. You may see more in me, and that means a whole fuckin' lot to me, but not everyone else will. I get that. Can't change it, and neither can you."

Noelle squeezes my hand. "My sisters are good people. They just… sometimes have their own way of expressing themselves about things. They've also been through a lot of their stuff. They meant well."

"I know. Can't say it doesn't bother me a little, but that's on me. They didn't say anything that wasn't true. The part about you being able to do better is subjective." I let out a breath. "I like spending time with you. I wanna get to know you. We can back off on the physical stuff till you're comfortable with it. You wanna keep hanging out with me, I'll gladly take all the time you're willing to give me."

She smiles. "I like spending time with you, too, Bear. Very, very much. So you'll see a lot more of me, okay? Promise."

10

Noelle

OVER THE NEXT COUPLE OF MONTHS, BEAR AND I find a rhythm. After he's done working, he goes home to shower and change, and I meet him at the shelter when I'm done. We take Panzer to the dog park, go somewhere to eat, or go to one of the local hiking trails outside town and walk together and talk.

The more I get to know Bear, the more I appreciate the man he is. He's considerate, thoughtful, and sweet. He has a very dry, subtle sense of humor, and is quite articulate and intelligent.

On Fridays, he joins me and my crew for Trivia night, and with his added voice, we win several times.

We aren't alone in private together—which is hard for me. I crave him. It's honestly a little scary how much I want him. Every minute I'm around him, I'm hyperaware of his presence. His warmth. his strength. We hold hands a lot, but that's about as far as it goes, physically. He never pushes. Never seems impatient.

I dream of him. Naughty dreams—kissing him. His hands on me. His mouth.

Frustratingly, though, the dreams never go beyond that—I wake up horny, overheated, and impatient.

And I can't bring myself to bring myself the release I need—it feels wrong to go there without him, even in the privacy of my mind.

I'm not sure what the female version of blue balls is, but I have it. Badly.

Ugh.

I find myself wondering if he thinks of me like that—if he wants me as badly as I want him.

I catch him looking at me a lot—I feel his eyes on me.

Part of me wants him to just grab me and kiss me and not stop. Push me past my hangup. But he's respecting the boundaries I've set.

What a pickle.

When is it enough? How long do I wait?

Around two months after the cookout at my parents, I meet Raina for lunch.

Of my friend group, Raina is the most like me. Raised conservative and religious—her Muslim to my Christian—despite our differences in orthodoxy, we share a lot in common. She, too, left the faith to a degree; like me, she hasn't completely abandoned her beliefs, she just doesn't adhere to the legalistic restrictions she was born into. She doesn't wear the hijab regularly—she does wear it to go to the mosque and when visiting her with her family. She does date, but she's careful about whom and takes things very slowly.

So, if any of my friends can understand what I'm struggling with, it's her.

We meet at The Alt Cafe, an adorable little farm-to-table spot at the south end of town just off Main Street overlooking Crooked Trout River, specializing in vegetarian, vegan, and gluten-free offerings. It's a bright, open, airy space with eclectic, mismatched furniture, hand-made industrial lighting, and local artwork for sale on the walls. Owned by Lainey and Layla Cartwright, sisters a few years older than me, it's a popular hangout for the less mainstream crowd.

Lainey is behind the counter taking orders while Layla makes the food. Most of the tables are full, leaving us a small two-top in the corner. We sip our green juice smoothies while we wait for our food.

At the table next to us, a young woman around our age sits alone. She's got white-blond hair, skin tanned a lovely golden color, wearing a boho, hippy, patchwork skirt and a bandeau around her chest, exposing a pierced belly button. She's reading a giant text on veterinary medicine and taking notes, earbuds in her ear and a pair of knitting needles keeping her long, thick, herringbone-pattern braided hair in a coiled bun. If I had to guess, the vintage VW Bus with all the stickers parked out front belongs to her.

Raina smiles as she glances at our table neighbor. "She must be new in town—I've seen her here several times over the past few months." She sips her smoothie. "So. What's up with you and Bear?"

I sigh, sit back, and rub my face with both hands. "I'm stuck, Raina."

She leans forward, grabbing my wrist. "Stuck how? Tell me everything."

I grin. "Why do you think we're meeting for lunch?" I shake my head, my grin fading. "I just don't know what to do. When we first met, I was…I dunno. All in. Super attracted to him right off the bat."

"He's definitely attractive…if you go for the mountain of a man type. Not especially my type, but I see the attraction." She arches her brows. "So? What's the issue?"

"We kissed, and…well, it was freaking *amazing*. So, *so* good. But we'd just met. I barely knew him. I…I mean, you know how slow Brennan and I took things. And I guess I felt like part of me was jumping in head first too soon. And I felt like I was doing it out of…I dunno. Not spite, but…" I shake my head, frustrated. "See? I'm so mixed up I don't even know how to talk about it."

"Brennan was an asshole who didn't deserve a single minute of your time, let alone the years you gave him. So spite is a perfectly reasonable explanation."

"But not a good reason to start a relationship," I point out.

"Order up for Raina and Noelle," Layla calls. I go up and get my pesto chicken sandwich (organic, farm-raised, free-range, local chicken) and a side of sweet potato tots, along with Raina's green goddess salad. "Thanks, Layla."

She smiles at me, her shoulder-length black hair pulled through the back of a ballcap with their logo on it, her brown eyes bright and friendly. "Of course, Noelle. Good to see you. How's your family?"

"Oh, you know, good."

"Brothers staying out of trouble?" she asks, smirking.

I laugh. "Mostly? I think? They're all over the place."

She glances at me as she works on an order. "What's their latest venture?"

"Honestly, I have no idea. I stopped trying to keep track years ago." I gesture at the cafe. "Things are pretty busy, huh?"

She rolls her eyes. "God, yes. We're thinking about hiring someone to open for us."

"Good, you should! You two have been working open to close every day since you opened, and that was, what, last year?"

"Over a year ago now, yeah. It's been a big push, but everyone has been so welcoming and receptive. It's been great. We've had a lot of support on social media." The printer spits out another ticket, and she snags it and scans it. "I'll let you get back to lunch. Good to see you, Noelle."

"You too, Layla. Thanks for the sandwich. It looks amazing!"

I take our food back to the table and we spend a few minutes eating.

After a bit, Raina eyes me as she stabs cucumbers and avocado slices. "So, what's the issue?"

"I don't know how or when or if to progress things. We've been spending a lot of time together, dating, sort of. We go on walks, take Panzer to the park, and go for hikes. I've been trying to introduce him to different restaurants. It's been great. The more I get to know him, the more I like him."

"But?" She spears a green pepper and pieces of lettuce.

"I want more. I know he does, too. But I don't think he'll push it. He's been very respectful of the boundaries I've set."

"A little *too* respectful, maybe, because you kinda want him to push?" She suggests.

I blush. "Yeah. But that's not fair. *I* told him I wanted to get to know each other; *I* set the boundaries. So I can't then very well sit here expecting him to push against those boundaries. I just…how do you know when it's time for more?"

She grins. "Well, you're blushing. I think you're ready. Is he?"

I shrug, shaking my head. "I have no idea. He told me he hasn't been with anyone in a very long time. Since before prison."

Her eyes bug out. "He's been celibate for *ten years*?"

I nod. "Yeah." I frown. "Actually, more like eleven, if not longer."

"And he's patiently waiting for you to be ready for more?"

"Yeah."

She snorts. "Babe, you gotta throw the man a bone. Good grief. After that long, and with how shy he is, I wonder if he may not know *how* to push for more. How to tell you he's ready. That may not be in his toolbox, so to speak."

I consider this. "Wow, I…I hadn't thought about that. You're probably right."

"So, are you asking my advice? Or just sounding off?"

See, that's what I love about Raina. She doesn't assume things.

"Asking for advice. What do you think I should do?"

"Well, first, what do you see with him? I mean, you like him, you're attracted to him. But do you want a relationship with him? Like, a real one?"

I swallow hard. "Yeah, I think I do."

"You think?" She sets the fork down and takes my hands in hers. "You need to be sure. From what I know of Bear, he's not someone to do casually. Neither are you, obviously. But you owe it to yourself and to him to be *very* clear on what you want." She rubs my hand with her thumbs. "It's been a long time for you, too. Not as long as him, but a while. So just…don't get being horny mixed up with what you do or don't feel emotionally."

"I don't see him every day, but nearly. He doesn't have a car or a phone, so the only way for us to connect is if I go by the shelter after work. And the days I don't see him, I… well, I miss him. All day long I think about things I want to tell him. I feel safe with him. I feel seen. And…I'm also going a little crazy. From, um…wanting him."

"You wanna climb that mountain, don't you?" She asks, grinning and wiggling her eyebrows at me.

"Yes," I whisper, covering my face with both hands. "So darned bad."

"Then I think you can probably think about changing the boundaries. But think about what those will be. Do you want to go all the way right away? Are you ready for that?" She resumes eating; Raina is a slow eater.

I consider this as I drag my last tot through ketchup. "Do I bring it up in conversation? Or just sort of…stop holding myself back and let things happen organically?"

"I mean, maybe invite him over sometime and see what happens. And then have a conversation about it."

"You're so wise, Raina," I say. "Thank you."

She does a mock bow at the waist. "I live but to serve." She giggles, then. "You just have to share at least *some* of the details, if and when."

"It's a deal."

C⌒

The next day, Bear works late and my last client ends up hating what she asked for and I have to spend an hour past close fixing it so she's happy. Which means I'm frustrated, stressed, and hungry. By the time I clean up my station and lock up, it's after seven, I haven't eaten since noon, and I miss Bear.

I'm too out of sorts to go anywhere other than home, though—as much as I'd love to swing by the shelter and let Bear comfort me, I don't want to subject him to my poopy mood.

So I go home, nuke some leftovers, and watch reality TV in my underwear.

I think about my conversation with Raina, and decide she's right. I know I want more with Bear, and I'm pretty certain he wants more with me. But it's on me to progress things. The question is how?

Maybe instead of going for a hike on the trails like we have been lately, we walk in my neighborhood. I'll invite him in, and…see what happens.

My belly twists and my heart flips at the prospect of kissing him again. Feeling his hands on my skin. See more of him—touch him. Connect with him physically. Reach a new level of intimacy.

We've talked just about everything. He's told me about his various foster parents and the abuse he suffered, leading him to run away. He's told me some of the things that happened to him during his years in the gang—and I suspect for every story he tells me, there's something far darker and more violent he's not telling me. Which I get—he's protecting me. I tell him about growing up in a big family. Feeling invisible as the middle child between sets of twins. About my relationship with Brennan, well, more of it, anyway. We talk about books—despite only having a GED, he's very widely read, thanks to that librarian. He's read biographies on various important historical figures like Lincoln, Washington, MLK Jr., Malcolm X, both Roosevelts, and Einstein. He's read sci-fi, fantasy, mysteries, romances, literary fiction...a bit of everything.

You just have to get him talking, I discover—once we find a subject, we have long, meandering conversations that delve into religion and spirituality, social politics and regular politics—the latter of which neither of us has much stomach for—social justice issues, inequality, racism, sexism...

We know each other now. Better, at least. I know he loves Chinese food, Indian, and Italian. He hates lunch meat, brussels sprouts, and mustard. He doesn't have much of a sweet tooth, and even though he's never had alcohol issues, he chooses not to drink almost ever. He's saving money to buy a good car—he could afford one now, but he'd rather wait longer and buy something nice that will last and not waste money on endless repairs. He's never had social media and doesn't really understand it.

Now I'm ready for the next level. Whatever that looks like, however it unfolds, I want it with him.

The next day, Wednesday, is cloudy and overcast, the skies heavy and threatening rain. My last client cancels, which means I'm out of work by five-thirty. I go home, make sure everything is picked up and clean, change into my favorite black leggings, my most supportive black sports bra, and a pale mauve tank top with a lightweight ivory hoodie, and head to the shelter.

Only, he's not there, and Gloria hasn't seen him—he called from Riley's phone and said he wouldn't be in today.

Three Rivers is a small town. Everyone knows everyone. It's gotten bigger in recent years, and new people are moving in every day, it seems like, but those of us who've been born and raised here know each other. Therefore, I happen to know that Riley and Felix have been working in the Creighton Meadows neighborhood, which was intended to be the beginning of a much larger subdivision, only to be abandoned by the developer after a single street, leaving it as a weird outlier, a single street of middling-quality homes, outdated, abandoned, and in desperate need of rejuvenation. The brothers have been buying the houses, demoing them, remodeling, and selling them.

I head there on a whim. When I get to Meadowview Lane, it's after six-thirty, and the crews are all still here, Felix's guys busily hammering and sawing and whatever else in one house or working on the finishing touches inside at another, while Riley's crew handles the demolitions.

I spot Riley's truck outside a small ranch with faded green siding and a buckling roof—guys come and go in a constant stream, hauling out sections of drywall, light fixtures, and wheelbarrows full of detritus. In all the coming and going, I don't see Bear.

I park down the street a bit, feeling nervous, a little foolish, and presumptive.

Riley himself comes out of the house, a white N95 mask covering his face and a yellow hard hat on his head. He tugs the mask down around his throat and puts his phone to his ear.

"Mel? Hey. No, I'm gonna be awhile. We're almost

done with this demo, and we decided to work late until it's done. Nah, I'll grab something after with the guys." He sighs, facing the side of the hood of his truck and slumping over it, frustration in his body language. "Mel, I'm sorry—I'm the boss. I can't just peace out. Yes, I like you. Yes, I want to spend time with you. It's not personal...Mel, *fuck*. Okay, you know what? You knew my hours when we first started hanging out. They haven't changed. Right now, work comes first. My guys come first...Oh, is that so? Cool. Cool. Go for it. Have fun with Johnny *fucking* Ricardo. Yeah, fuck you too."

With a vicious snarl, he stabs the end button, starts to throw his phone, and then just barely restrains himself. He makes a fist, starts to punch his truck, and thinks better of that, too.

He turns in a slow circle, raking his hard hat off and throwing it violently against the side of the big green roll-off dumpster.

Which is when he sees me. "Noelle Harper." He has dirt smeared across his nose and left cheek, a cut on his chin, and pain in his eyes. "What...um, what're you doing here?"

I smile at him. "Hey, Riley."

He winces. "Overheard that, huh?"

I shrug. "Yeah. Sorry, you're going through that."

He shakes his head, sighing. "It wasn't serious, but I liked her. She told me either I meet her for drinks or she'd accept Johnny Ricardo's invitation instead."

I frown. "Johnny Ricardo? *That* guy? I heard he makes drugs or something."

Riley laughs. "He's a notorious meth cook, yeah. Not a good dude."

"Well, it's none of my business, but if she's going out with him, maybe you dodged a bullet," I say, and then glance at a cluster of guys coming out of the house. "I was, um, looking for Bear."

Riley's face lights up. "Bear? You know Bear?"

I nod, hoping my blush isn't too obvious—or my embarrassment and nerves. "Yeah, I do. We, um...we've been hanging out. He's working late, obviously, and we were supposed to meet, so I thought I'd see if he wanted a ride home."

Riley's eyes glint with amusement. "Bear's a tight-lipped one. I've known him for over three years now, and I don't know much more about him than the day I met him. I have to say, I'm thrilled to know he has a...friend."

He's angling for more info, but I just smile and shrug. "Yeah, he's pretty private."

Riley smirks. "Not gettin' any gossip outta you, am I?"

I grin. "Nope. If he wants to share it, he'll share it."

He crosses to pick up his hard hat and places it back on his head. "Honestly, good. He's a good dude. Been through a lot. He deserves someone in his corner."

"He has you. He says your program gave him a second chance at life."

Riley nods. "Appreciate that, Noelle. I'm picky about who I let into the program. For the program to succeed, the guys in it have to succeed, and the guards and warden at Holbrook had nothing but positive things to say about Bear. He's put in the work and then some." He points at a house across the street that has a roll-off in the driveway, overflowing with demolition refuse. "He's in there. He works best alone, I've discovered, mainly because he can do the work of four people by himself. You can go in, just be careful, it's a work zone. He throws that hammer around like he's Thor or some shit." He yanks open his truck door, leans in, and grabs a hard hat and safety glasses. "In fact, put these on, just to be safe. He's a madman when he's working."

I take them, frowning at him. "A madman?"

He nods. "He works like a man possessed. Never seen anything like it." Someone calls his name, and he juts his chin at me. "Gotta go. You'll see what I mean!"

I cross the street, holding the hard hat and glasses and feeling increasingly stupid for this whole thing. I feel eyes on me and glance back at the house Riley went into—several guys stand huddled together by the dumpster, sharing cigarettes and whispering…about me, probably.

Hopefully, I haven't caused any problems for Bear.

The front door is open, and I hear music playing—hard rock from the local station. I hear smashing, creaking, crashing.

Placing the hat on my head—it's too big, wobbling like I'm a kid wearing a fireman's helmet—and the glasses on my nose, I go up the steps.

A low snarl greets me, and a dark shadow appears from the haze of swirling dust: Panzer.

"Hey boy, it's me. It's Noelle." I stay where I am and wait for him to get closer, that vicious, guttural snarl turning my guts to water. A second later, the snarl cuts off, and Panzer is nuzzling my thigh, tail whipping dangerously. He yips once, looking up at me happily. I crouch and let him kiss my face as I rub his ears. "Hiya, handsome boy. Hi, hi, hi." I stand up, wipe slobber off my face, and follow the dog into the house.

It was once an average mid-century ranch, the front

door opening into a sunken postage stamp foyer and the living room and dining room, a low half-wall separating the kitchen, a sliding door going to the backyard, and a hallway with the bedrooms and bathroom. Now, it's been opened up, the walls taken back to studs and wiring, the floor nothing but bare subfloor, with a blue tarp covering the space where the sliding doors were. The sound of work is coming from one of the hallway rooms.

Panzer turns in three clockwise circles, one counter-clockwise, and then lays down in the foyer, content that I'm allowed to be here; his duties done and scratches received, he goes back to his nap.

I follow the sounds to the bathroom. It's early summer now, and it's been pretty hot lately, in the high seventies and low eighties. The air in the house is still and stifling, full of dust and dirt—it's hot.

Therefore, it's not a surprise to see that Bear has taken off his shirt—he's tucked it into the back of his jeans to hang down like an odd white tail. His back is impossibly broad, his shoulders endless and cliff-like, rippling with lay-ers of muscle and tapering to his waist. Sweat drips down his spine in glistening rivulets.

He has a giant sledgehammer in his hands, a yellow hard hat on his head, and he's swinging the hammer at the ugly canary yellow tile on the bathroom wall like he hates it. His arms ripple, and with each crashing impact, tile shat-ters, and the wall disintegrates a little more.

My tongue stuck to the roof of my mouth, I'm frozen in place, riveted.

He uses his whole body to swing the hammer, his feet braced wide, massive thighs bulging as he moves, hips twisting, torso torquing—the huge, heavy hammer whistles through the air and smashes into the wall again and again and again, each strike precise, moving him along the wall with startling speed, leaving piles of shattered shards of tile in his wake.

I watch until he reaches the end of the wall, at which point he sets the sledge upside down on its head against the wall and yanks his shirt out of his jeans, wiping his face with it.

"Bear!" I call over the jarring racket of hard rock music coming from a heavy-duty industrial radio.

His head jerks up, eyes wide. "Noelle?"

As he turns to face me, I'm stunned speechless by the vision of him.

For some people, it seems like God just went a little extra, a little overboard. When he was making Bear, He seemed to have forgotten to stop adding muscle.

The man is profoundly mammoth. His pecs are like slabs of granite carved into the upper portion of his chest with an artisan's chisel. I wouldn't say he has a six-pack, which has never done it for me anyway. He has a definition, but his abs are more like massive blocks of stone, thinly padded. His tattoos ripple colorfully on his immense, sweaty, rippling arms, and his chest, stomach, and sides are mazed with scars.

Sweaty, out of breath, muscles swollen from labor, Bear looks like he could rip I-beams in half with his bare hands.

My skin tingles, my nipples go hard behind my sports bra, and my thighs clench together. It's hard to breathe. Hard to think.

This was a mistake.

But good grief—I'm glad I came.

I unstick my tongue and look for something to say—arousal seems to have scorched the sense right out of my idiot brain.

"Bear. I…hi."

He wipes his face with his shirt as he shuts off the radio. "You're here."

"Sorry to show up like this," I say. "I…I'm not sure what I was thinking."

"No, no, it's fine. I'm just surprised to see you here." He grabs a gallon jug of water from the floor and takes several long, glugging swallows. "Want some?"

I grin, shaking my head. "No, I'm good. I just…" I swallow hard. "I wanted to see you. I thought maybe we could go for a walk at my house. I was gonna make pork chops."

He licks his lips and smooths his hand down his beard—he's taught himself how to braid because his beard is clumsily braided in a single thick queue down his chest. His hair is back in a low ponytail. "That sounds great. I'm pretty much done here."

I shift my weight from one foot to the other. "I hope it's okay that I came. I went by the shelter, and Gloria told me you had called in. I happened to know that Riley and Felix are working here, so I took a chance and just sorta…came over." I'm babbling from nerves. Why am I so nervous?

Oh, right. Because I plan on kissing Bear. And…stuff. Hopefully.

Maybe.

God, I'm a mess.

He gives me a small, quick smile, stepping close to me, a big hand drifting close to my face but stopping short.

"Always glad to see you, Noelle. You're the best part of every day."

I can't help it. "And the days you don't see me?" Fishing, fishing, fishing. Gosh, I'm shameless.

"Boring. Like flat soda."

"I hope my coming here doesn't create issues for you with the guys," I say, shuffling closer to him.

"Nah. They may tease me, but they're good dudes. Most of 'em." He shrugs. "You see Duane, though, I want you to give him space. Guy ain't all there."

"Which one is Duane?" I ask. "So I know who to avoid."

"I'll point him out." He glances at the shirt in his hand. "Sorry, I got hot."

"I don't mind," I say, unable to suppress my grin. "At all."

He frowns as if having to figure out what I mean by that. "Oh…okay." He shrugs into the shirt, which sticks to his sweaty skin and muscles. And that's almost as yummy a sight as him shirtless. "I probably don't smell too great."

I shrug. "Maybe I'm weird, but I don't mind."

He juts his chin at the piles of broken tile. "Just gotta clean that up and we can go."

"I'll wait in the car, get the A/C going."

"Cool." A pause, as I turn away. "Noelle? Thanks for coming."

I shrug. "Missed you."

He swallows and nods his head. Chews on the end of his mustache. "Missed you, too." He rubs the back of his neck. "Be right out. Won't take five minutes. You can have Panzer come with you. You know the commands by now. He listens to you."

I nod. "We're buddies. See you in a minute."

He nods, grabbing a wide-bladed, short-handled shovel from the corner and scooping tile shards into a two-wheeled wheelbarrow.

I head out to the front door, already glad to be in the fresh air—I don't know how he stands being in there all day.

I pat my thigh as Panzer eyes my approach. "Panzer, Komm. Fuss."

He hops to his feet and walks with his hard ribs against my right thigh, panting happily. The rest of Riley's crew is gathered around the trucks, taking off gloves, hard hats, and glasses, smoking cigarettes, and putting away tools.

I set the hat and glasses on Riley's hood.

"Man, why we ain't got no pretty girls visitin' us?" one of the guys says—a big Black man only a little smaller than Bear, with kind brown eyes, a short beard, shaved head, and a friendly grin as he elbows the guy next to him. "Ol' Brer Bear barely says two words all damn day, and he got a visitor. My man's got game."

Another guy, this one less friendly looking, with long-ish, greasy dirty blond hair and a scruffy goatee, his eyes beady and quick and unreadable, eyes me up and down. "Hell, if I know, but a dish like that's wasted on that big oaf."

The Black man slugs his companion on the shoulder—*hard*. "Man, shut the *fuck* up, Duane. Bear hears you talkin' about his lady friend like that, he'll pull your skinny white ass apart. An' he won't need that dog, neither."

"I ain't afraid of him," Duane says—I see why Bear warned me about this guy.

"Well, you an idiot, then. He likes *me*, and he scares me to fuckin' death. You wanna talk shit about his girl, be my guest." He grins at me. "Just tell him Darius wasn't part of it, alright?"

I laugh, grinning at Darius. "I will. I'm Noelle Harper."

He comes toward me, removing a work glove and offering me his hand. "Darius Thibodeaux. Nice to meet you, Noelle Harper." He grins back. "So, you're sweet on the big man, huh?"

"Something like that, yeah."

"Good, good. He's a real one, y'know? Works like a dog."

Duane snorts. "Dogs don't work. Stupid thing to say."

"Used to, didn't they? Sled dogs and shit? Shepherd dogs? You're just salty because Bear makes the rest of us look like we standin' still." Darius shoots a look at my car—I head for it, taking the cue. "Nice to meet you, Darius."

"You too, Noelle Harper. Take care of our boy, y'hear?"

"I will!"

"What, not gonna introduce yourself to me?" I hear Duane mutter. "Bitch."

Panzer snarls, and Duane pales, hurrying away into the open trailer, where he busies himself putting things away.

I bring Panzer to my car, open it, give him the command to jump up and in, and then get it going, air conditioner on full blast.

I wait for Bear, watching the other guys clean up and get ready to go.

Duane stops every so often to glare at me, an ugly sneer on his face that sends shivers down my spine.

Not a good dude. Not all there.

Indeed.

I'll *definitely* be steering clear of him from now on.

A few minutes later, Bear emerges, shuts the door behind him, attaches a lockbox, and then heads my way, waving at the others.

He settles into the passenger seat, filling my tiny car with his presence, heat, and masculine smell.

Sweat, yes, but not stink. Or if it stinks, I'm nosebleed or something because it doesn't bother me at all.

"Ready to go home?" I ask, smiling at him.

He nods. "Sure am."

It only occurs to me later that when I said home, I meant my home, but used it in a collective "we" sense. *Our* home.

I wonder if he caught that.

The closer we get to my house, the more my nerves jangle and clang in my belly, butterflies soaring and fluttering, skin tight, nipples hard, core damp and slick.

I don't know what's going to happen between us tonight, but I'm ready for it.

I just hope he is.

11

Bear

SOMETHING IS DIFFERENT. I DON'T KNOW WHAT, and I don't know how to ask.

I didn't miss the way she looked at me back at the worksite—the only word I can find is "ogle," but it feels weird to apply that to me. I knew a few girls that would hook up with me back in the old hood, but I was never a ladies' man. Too shy. Too fucked up. Those girls knew the score, too. We had a good time, I went my way, she went hers, and that was it. If we hooked up again some other time, cool, but there was never an expectation of more—*more* simply didn't exist for us in that world. For me, at least.

And I've never felt like the type of guy a girl is gonna ogle, or stare at—not that way, at least. But she did.

She was looking at me like she couldn't get enough of looking.

That does weird shit to my insides. Twists my head all around. Makes me feel like…I dunno. I just don't know how to feel.

I wish I knew how she was feeling—what she was thinking. We've gotten way closer and gotten to know each other pretty well over the last couple of months, but I still can't always read her. Especially where the idea of "us" is concerned. I've tried hard to keep the line clear—we're friends, no more. We hold hands, which confuses the issue, sure, but…what does that mean?

Then today she shows up at work, looking at me like I'm something to eat. Picking me up from work, taking me to her house, talking about cooking dinner?

What am I to make of it?

I decide that it's foolish to try and guess, so I'll just take it as it comes and see what happens. Follow her lead.

The ride across town to her place is quiet, the radio low and tuned to country music. I feel dirty, grimy, and smelly and I'd love a shower, but I'm not about to suggest a change in plans. She doesn't seem to mind my stink, so whatever.

We pull into her driveway, and I let Panzer out—he trots in circles and then lifts his leg on one of her bushes. She unlocks the side door and lets us all in. Panzer jogs around the house excitedly, sniffing.

"You up for a walk?" she asks. "I get it if you're not—you just spent all day working."

"A walk sounds good."

"Cool. I've got some pork chops marinating."

Panzer accompanies us back outside into the dense,

still, humid evening—the sky is leaden and heavy, and I smell rain.

"Probably can't go too far, huh?" Noelle asks, glancing up at the sky.

I shrug. "Just rain."

She threads her fingers in mine, Panzer choosing to walk at her side rather than mine. We walk at a fairly slow pace—this isn't exercise, just an evening stroll in a quiet, peaceful neighborhood. Occasionally, we pass a house where someone's sitting out on their porch; we wave, and get a wave back.

After a mile, a few drops start sprinkling.

Noelle looks up at me. "Turn back?"

I shrug. "Sure. If you want. Gonna get wet either way."

And, as we make the turn that'll take us toward her street, the sprinkle becomes a steady rain and then a downpour. At first, Noelle shrugs her shoulders up around her ears, pulls her hood up, and speeds her pace. When I don't, she looks back at me, confused.

I just shrug. "Already as wet as we can get, Noelle. It's just a little rain."

She halts, thinking. She then pulls her hood back, turns her face to the sky, and laughs. "There's a freedom in it, isn't there? Just accepting the wet?"

I nod. "Yep. Sure is. Always liked walking in a summer rain."

So we walk hand in hand, soaked to the bone within minutes. Panzer is happy as a clam, splashing in puddles, occasionally taking a quick slurp from the rain running along the curb toward storm drains.

Her hair is plastered to her head and sticking to her cheeks and neck, her clothes molded to her body; her yoga pants were already skin-tight, perpetually drawing my gaze to the luscious sway of her firm, round ass—the rain has pressed her shirt to her chest, however, and the material is thin and light, turning translucent, revealing a black sports bra.

She's so fucking beautiful, it never ceases to amaze me that she wants anything to do with me, that she cares about me, even just as a friend.

I know myself. I know who I am. Among men, I know my place. I'm unbothered by posturing and bravado because I know what I can do. At work, I'm confident in my skills, strength, and work ethic. Among the guys at work, I'm among equals. Even with Riley, my boss, I feel as if we're friendly, even friends, in a boss-employee way.

But around women? Not so much.

I'm not sure what I have to offer, if anything.

I don't know what's going on with Noelle and me other than friendship. I know I enjoy her company, I know I think about her all the damn time. I dream about her and wake up with a hard-on I refuse to touch while thinking of her—she's worth more than that.

I guess in my mind, she's this perfect, pure creature of light and wonder, and I'm… just me. Big, broody, quiet, with a violent history, no education beyond the GED, a criminal record, and a questionable future.

But she sees something in me. What, I don't know. I keep hoping that at some point, I'll figure that out and learn how to see it in myself.

I'm comfortable with her, that much is true. More so than with anyone else I've ever known, man or woman.

She looks up at me, expression soft and quizzical. "Penny for your thoughts?"

Rain drums on my head, trickles down my neck. "Ummm." I opt for the truth. "I was just thinking that I've never been comfortable around most people. Never had a lot of close friends." I squeeze her hand gently. "Never had a friend like you, Noelle. Someone I feel at ease with. Means a lot. A whole lot."

She blinks rapidly. "God, Bear, you really have a way of hitting me in the feelings, you know that?"

"Sorry?" It comes out like a question—I'm not sure if I'm supposed to apologize for that or what.

She laughs, leaning against me, head on my arm. "No, no, no, silly. It's a good thing! You just say the sweetest things." A quick pause, her tongue swiping raindrops away; my eyes follow her tongue across her lips. I remember the way she tasted, the way it felt to kiss her. "You've become one of my best friends, Bear."

That makes my heart flip.

We reach her house a minute or two later, right as the rain slackens to a steady drizzle. Nolle just laughs as she opens the door for Panzer, following me in.

"I'll get a towel for the dog. Stay here."

I can see him preparing to shake off. "Panzer, Nein."

He whines but doesn't shake. A minute later, Noelle returns with a stack of navy blue towels, and we scrub, blot, and dab Panzer as dry as he can get and then spread them out on the kitchen floor for him to lay down on. She fills a bowl with water for him, too.

"Our turn," She says, taking my hand. "Come on. The bathroom is this way."

She seems nervous for some reason.

Her bedroom, which I didn't see last time I was here, is a calming, peaceful space. The walls are a soft, oceanic turquoise, a shaggy white rug covering the wood floor beneath her bed, which is antique with tarnished wrought iron headboard and footboard, a thick white duvet, and roughly fifty different pillows of various colors picked to complement the wall color. A white chest sits at the foot of the bed, a dove gray throw blanket folded and placed on it at an angle. A five-drawer bureau, old looking, solid, and thick, once probably stained oak, has been painted a bright, vivid sapphire with a matching oval mirror on top.

In addition to the bathroom in the hallway, she has an en suite, the doorway on one side of her bed, a door to her closet on the other, that door closed. The bathroom is more white, with subway tile on the walls, and long, narrow, rectangular tiles on the floor in a herringbone pattern. A square mirror ringed with bare lightbulbs is mounted on the wall over a deep porcelain sink, the hardware burnished copper. A freestanding tub dominates the space, deep and high-sided with more bronze hardware. A narrow shower stall takes up the far back corner, glassed up to the ceiling, with a toilet opposite.

I admit to being confused though—we're in her room. I expected her to give me a towel, or show me the guest bathroom in the hallway.

Instead, she draws me by the hand into her bathroom, stops, and turns to look up at me.

My heart is pounding out of my chest.

Her teeth are chattering.

"You should get changed," I tell her. "Take a hot shower. I'll dry off soon enough. I'll wait with Panzer."

"Bear...wait." Her voice is soft, barely audible. "Stay."

"I..." I look into her eyes, searching—and all I see

is nerves…and need. "You want me to…stay? In here? With you?"

She nods. "I have no idea what I'm doing right now, but…yeah."

I can't swallow past the lump in my throat or the jangling, screaming nerves in my chest. Bats flap around in my belly.

"Okay," I whisper.

She reaches for me, hands hesitant, fluttering near the hem of my shirt, and then she finds her courage and lifts the hem. Rises on her toes and peels it off my head, letting it drop to the floor at my feet with a wet plop.

Her fingers touch my chest, one hand on each pec. "God, Bear. Do you have any idea how sexy you are to me?"

I can only shake my head.

She runs soft, quick fingertips across my chest, making my breath come in short quick puffs of searing nervousness—I haven't been touched like this…ever.

"Is…is this okay?" she asks, looking up at me.

"Yes," I say, my voice raspy, grating, gravelly. "Here for you, Noelle. Whatever you want. Whatever you don't want."

She flattens her palms against my pecs, presses her fingertips in, dimpling, testing, feeling. Down over my diaphragm. My abs. "Does it feel good?"

I try to swallow past my tongue, which is thick and dry in my mouth. In the end, I can only nod. "Yeah," I manage, a hoarse, gritty syllable.

She slides warm, smooth, soft hands along my sides, around to my back, leaning into me, her clothes wet and cold against my chest; up my back, and down, and back up to my shoulders. Down my arms, back up to my shoulders, to my pecs again.

"So big," she whispers. "So strong."

There's nothing to say to that. My heart is crashing in my chest, and my stomach is flipping. My cock is an iron bolt in my jeans, which I struggle furiously to ignore.

She finally takes my hands in hers. Looks up at me as she guides my hands to her waist. "Will you help me?"

"Do what?" I ask, knowing what she meant, but feeling stupid for thinking it. There's no way that's what she means. Not me.

Her smile is teasing, kind, amused, eager. "With my wet clothes."

Her thin black hoodie is unzipped; I peel it down her shoulders and let it join my T-shirt. She waits, gaze expectant on mine.

I lick my lips, so unsure, so nervous, filled with so much raging need and desire and pent-up everything that I don't know what to do with it. I slip my fingers under the hem of her shirt, and then hesitate.

She nods. "Go ahead. It's okay."

Swallowing hard eyes again, I peel her pale purple tank top up; she raises her arms over her head as I tug the wet garment off.

"My turn, now," she whispers. "You okay?"

I nod. Dip my head to one side, shrugging. "Little nervous."

"It's okay. So'm I." She gazes up at me with a look I can't quite decipher—soft, tender, sexual, affectionate, apprehensive…a world of emotions. A universe. One that mirrors my own, I suppose. "We're in this together."

"Together," I echo.

She steps close to me, breasts bulging against the wet fabric of her black sports bra, pushing against my chest. Rests her hands against my pecs. Steps closer yet, smashing herself against my front, and every inch of her soft curves mold against my frame. She rests her chin on my chest, and looks up at me.

"I want to kiss you, Bear." She licks her lips. "But not yet."

"Why not?" The question emerges unbidden.

"Because I won't want to stop, won't be able to stop. And I want to take this one step at a time." She turns her head so her cheek rests on my skin, and my hands lift on their own to cradle her shoulders.

Drift down to the hot bare flesh of her waist; at my touch, she shivers, gasps. "Your hands! They're so warm. And...rough."

She leans back—just her torso, not her lower half—and pulls my hands around, examining them one at a time. Traces my calluses—the ones from the barbell along the pads just beneath my fingers, the ones on my palm and heel from swinging hammers and using shovels without gloves. My hands are similar in texture to cinderblock.

"Sorry," I mutter. "Probably don't feel good."

She smiles, shaking her head, and puts her cheek to my palm. "No. Not at all. Just the opposite, actually."

I frown down at her. "Really?"

She nods, pushing my hands downward to her waist. "Really. I mean, yeah, they're rough, but..." her cheeks flare with a bright blush. "I...I like how it feels."

I caress her back below her bra strap, her shoulders above it. "You like this?"

She nods. "Very much."

"So fucking soft," I growl, heart clogging my throat.

She nibbles her lower lip. Steps back from me an inch or two, looking down at my jeans and boots. Up at me, nerves apparent in the way she searches me. "Um…okay, " she whispers. "Boots." I bend to unlace them, but she pushes at my chest. "Let me, please."

"Uh, okay?" Again, my statement emerges as a question.

She crouches, her slender back rounding, the curves of her chest, waist, and hips like the body of a violin—not just any violin, one of those special ones. Stradavary-something.

Her nimble fingers unknot the laces and tug them loose, working downward from the tongue to the toe. I balance, lifting my foot, and allow her to remove my boots one at a time.

"Oof," she says, snorting. "Wow."

"Yeah. Not letting you touch my socks. Smell like a science experiment gone wrong."

"No arguing with you on that one," she says, straightening to her feet.

I rip off my socks and toss them near the door, away from us, along with my boots. "Sorry," I mutter. "Feet tend to get a little ripe."

She brings her soft small body back up against mine, a tender, bright smile playing on her lips. "Nothing to apologize for. You work hard." She licks her lips, eyes moving, searching. "You know, watching you work…it was…" she swallows, giggles nervously. "Kinda hot. Or…or a *lot* hot."

I can't help but smile a little, shaking my head. "It was, huh?"

She nods. "Yeah." Her hands go to my arms, trying

vainly to wrap them around my biceps, rubbing up and down. "Mainly just because it was you."

"You're weird," I mutter, letting my smirk stay on my lips; she seems to like it when I smile.

She makes me smile. No one else ever has, not the way she does.

She's pure joy.

Light.

Goodness.

Her light burns away the darkness in my soul. Pushes the shadows away. Keeps the demons at bay.

"Bear?" Her voice is that tiny whisper again, delicate as lace, ephemeral as dew drops.

"Hmmm?"

"Can I see more of you?" Her deep, expressive green eyes convey her thoughts clearly, now. Her emotions.

Need. Desire. Fear—or nerves, at the very least.

"Whatever you want, Noelle. Here for whatever you want."

She drags her fingernails down my chest, ghostly and tickling, sending shivers of effervescence down my spine and into my balls. "I'm here for you, too, Bear. Okay? Hear what I'm saying to you?"

I gotta give her the truth. "I hear you. Scared, though. Hard to…hard to believe. Hard to trust this. Not you—I trust *you*. Just…" I growl, frustrated with my inability to say what I mean in moments like this. "Doesn't feel real. Dunno how to put it."

She takes my hands and places hers palm to palm against mine. "Bear, listen to me." She lifts on her toes and touches a tiny, delicate kiss to the tip of my chin. "This is me telling you, and hopefully showing you, that I...I want more with you. I'm scared, too. Nervous. Unsure."

"Don't wanna do the wrong thing. Say the wrong thing." I let my hands find her waist again.

The soft flesh there is so warm, so silky. My heart lurches and my gut tumbles at the privilege of having this woman's body in my hands.

Her trust.

He affection.

"You won't, Bear. You can't." She's breathing fast, breasts swelling and rising with each swift inhale, pressing against me. "You won't ever hurt me. And if there's a misunderstanding, we'll talk about it. We're honest with each other. Open. Brave. Right?"

"Tryin' like hell," I say.

Her tongue slides along her lower lip again, sticking at the corner for a moment. I'd give anything to kiss that spot.

So, I do.

I test her.

Dip closer, cradling her beautiful face in my rough workman's hands. Touch my lips, as softly as I can, to the spot where her tongue was, that little corner of her mouth.

She gasps, a sudden sharp inhale, and her hands clap against my chest, fingernails digging in. "Bear," she breathes.

Pulls back just a hint. Runs her nails down my chest, down my abs. Hesitates. Slowly, slowly, she slides the button of my fly free from the opposing buttonhole. I stop breathing. My lungs burn, my skin burns—everything is on fire, so superheated I'm half-worried she'll combust upon contact.

She keeps her eyes on my face as she tugs the zipper

down, down, until it rests at the bottom of the V. My aching, straining, painful erect cock pushes into the opening. She steals a glance down, eyes flying wide and then returning to mine, lower lip caught in her teeth. She says nothing, however. Hooks her fingers in the belt loops at my hips and tugs my wet jeans down until they sag loose—I step on a cuff and yank my leg free, and then the other. Now I'm in nothing but a pair of tight gray boxer briefs, and there's nothing to hide my arousal.

"Your turn," she whispers.

I sink to my knees in front of her, and she cups my cheek, brushes a thumb over my lips, and then frees my hair from the ponytail, slicking her fingers through my hair until it's loose.

Hands shaking, I wrap them around her waist, which I can't quite span, but almost. Soft skin, pale skin. Beautiful, perfect skin.

Unable to catch my breath, I hook my fingers inside the stretchy waistband of her yoga pants, careful to make sure her underwear stays in place. Look up at her—she nods. Runs small, clever hands over my head, petting my hair with such tenderness it makes my lungs seize all over again.

Tug down, peeling the skintight black fabric inside out, baring a lacy black thong, the triangle covering her sex—the damp, black material sticks to her skin, framing the outlines of her seam. High hipbones and the silk of her inner thighs. Her belly button is tiny and shallow. Long legs. Powerful legs. Thick, smooth, luscious thighs.

Small, delicate feet, toenails painted bright red.

She steps out of the pants, toes them aside, pressing her thighs together, eyes wide, shimmering.

I stay on my knees in front of her, shaky hands hovering above her thighs. Boldened by the kiss, and further by her allowing me to help her out of her pants, I settle my hands on her thighs, wrapping my hands around as much of their generous, lush curves as I can. Her breath catches, eyes wide even as her brows furrow, lips parted—a sensual, wild, fraught expression.

"Keep going," she whispers. "Please."

"So fucking gorgeous," I grate, throat raw with the fire in my lungs. "Take my breath away."

She fists my beard and leans down. "Then have mine."

Her lips meet mine, and her tongue is soft and wet and hot in my mouth all at once, and her breath is in my lungs, cooling the burn, stealing the ache. Greed for her skin, her curves, her soft flesh surges through me and takes over.

I do what I've longed, yearned, and dreamed of doing since the moment I laid eyes on her: I let my hands slide up the outside of her thighs, pause, shaking, and then glide up to cup her ass.

She whimpers into the kiss, and then gasps. "*Yes.*"

"Perfect," I growl. "Fucking incredible."

I want to weep at the feel of her ass in my hands—hot, silky skin, round and plump and firm. I explore it, the curves of it, palming the delicate weight of each awe-inspiring cheek, lifting and releasing, kneading, clawing, desperate to touch, fearful against reason that she'll suddenly come to her senses and make me stop.

"God, Bear." She cradles my face, tilts my head up to hers. "The way you touch me. It takes *my* breath away."

"Then have mine," I say, echoing her words.

"Yes, please," she breathes.

Her breath is sweet, her tongue nimble, daring,

darting. Tasting, teasing, probing. Demanding mine. She pulls away just enough to allow words to emerge, lips moving on mine, her voice barely a breath. "Keep going, Bear. All the way."

"Noelle," I mutter, my voice so deep it's coming from my toes. "You're sure?"

Her lips curve in a smile against mine. "*So* sure. I *want* you to." She slides her hands over my shoulders, down my back, scratching and caressing. "And then it's my turn."

"All the way?"

"All of me, Bear. You can have *all* of me. Please."

Still on my knees, I sink back to sit on my heels, searching her for signs of nerves, of refusal, of hesitation.

All I see is her desire.

How is that for me?

How is she real? How can she stand to have my blood-stained hands on her perfect skin?

Have to ask her, someday. Not now. Don't dare ruin the moment with my self-doubt.

I slip two fingers inside the strip of lace around her hips; my breath shakes, my hands shake. I hold her eyes, moving slowly, giving her all the time in the world to change her mind.

Instead, she slides her fingers into my hair at my temples, watching me. I draw the scrap of black lace down an inch at a time. The desire-damp material clings to her sex, sticking where her thighs touch.

"Oh god," she breathes.

I stop instantly. "You okay?"

"I'm okay. Just...nervous." She licks her lips. "Please don't stop. I'm just scared."

I pull the lace down a few more inches, past the

sticking point where her thighs meet, and then the underwear falls free. Her scent greets me, sensual and erotic. I clutch her thong in my hand, amazed and awed that this is happening.

I have a wild urge to sniff the underwear, to see if it smells as good as her sex. I can't seem to stop myself.

"Bear!" Noelle cries, laughing. "Did you just…smell my underwear?"

My cheeks burn. "Yeah."

I set the black lace aside and fill my hand with her curves, sliding my touch up her thighs to her butt. Press my face to her belly, forehead against her diaphragm. Her breath makes her belly swell against my face, and I can't help but kiss her there.

I inhale deeply. "You smell so fuckin' good, Noelle," I murmur. "Sorry if that was creepy. You just…fuck. You smell so goddamn incredible."

"Ohmygod, Bear," she breathes. "You mean my…I smell good…*down there*?"

"Yes," I growl, longing to taste her.

Kiss her left thigh, just below her hipbone. The other side. Her belly again, just below her sweet, adorable little navel—I kiss her there, too, and catch a giggling gasp from her.

Press my nose just above the soft thatch of curly red fuzz, hands cradling her ass. Take a long inhale of her scent, heady and dizzying and uniquely hers and so fucking arousing I could crawl out of my goddamn skin with need.

"Your pussy smells like fucking heaven, Noelle." I press my eyes into her belly. "I've got a filthy mouth. I'm sorry. You deserve better than to be spoken to like that."

Her gasp at my words is shocked, shrill; at my apology,

she murmurs a wordless sound of negation. Smooths her hands over my head, gently tilting my face up to hers. "No, honey. No. Don't apologize." She kneels and presses her mouth to mine, kissing her words to me instead of speaking them. "I like your filthy mouth. I liked it…what you said." Her cheeks flame red. "It was hot."

She moves to her feet, tugging me up with her. Brings my hands to her belly and guides them to slide up around the lower curves of her breasts.

Honey.

I'm stuck on that. The sweetness of it, the affection that sinks hooks into my heart. Into my soul.

I'd do anything—any fucking thing at all—for this woman; this fact rifles through me and lodges at the core of my being. I may not deserve her, but I'll be damned and double goddamned if I ever stop trying to be worthy of her.

All because of that one word—and the intent and emotion behind it.

She senses something or sees it in my face. "Bear? What is it?"

Where do I start? What do I say? It's too much. Too big.

"You called me honey." It's the best I've got, right now.

Her expression melts, and she sinks against me, soft thighs pressed against one of mine, sex against my taut quad, her pubic hair a delicate scratch against my skin. "You liked that?"

"Broke something in me. Or rebuilt it. I dunno."

"Bear…" Is it a question, the way she says my name? A statement? Neither, both.

The way she says my name is everything.

She hooks her fingers in the waistband of my underwear at each hipbone. "Take my bra off, Bear. Please."

I growl, a wordless rumble in my chest—anticipation, fear, need...all of it is so overwhelming in me that all I can do is let out that one growl.

She shivers at the sound. "Love it when you do that."

"Growl?"

She nods, shaking her head. "I'm not sure why. It just...it drives me a little wild."

"Wild? How?"

"Crazy. For you."

I slip my fingers under the wide elastic band running around her middle. Tug upward. The fabric cups catch at the weight of her breasts, and I pull upward further. Huge, tear-drop breasts fall free, bouncing and swaying—lifting as she raises her arms so I can draw it off and toss it aside.

"Ohmygod. Ohmygod. Oh god." She's breathing hard, almost hyperventilating.

I wrap my arms around her, marveling that she's naked for me, and pull her soft warm body against mine. "Breathe. Just breathe, Noelle. We can stop if you're not ready."

Her cheek goes to my chest, and she slows her breathing. After a minute, she tucks her chin against my breastbone and looks up at me. "Sorry. I just...I freaked out a little. I'm...I guess I'm feeling sort of self-conscious now that I'm naked."

"Should I leave?" I ask, the question burning a hole in my gut; I'd walk through fire if she asked, so there's no hesitation in me if she were to say yes.

"No!" She cries. Her fingernails dig into my back. "Please don't leave. I just...I haven't been naked with anyone for a long time."

"Noelle…" I frame her face, keeping her body pressed against mine so the sight of her perfect breasts doesn't distract me. "You're a gift. Priceless. Perfect." I ever-so-carefully free her hair from the long braid—it falls free around her shoulders, a cascade of coppery sunfire and luminous gold. "Kill me now and I'd die a happy man because I got to see you like this, just once."

She digs her fingernails into my pecs and buries her face in my chest, shaking her head—I feel wetness. "The things you say to me, Bear. You're a poet. You make me feel like…god, I don't even know how to say it. Like I'm the only woman in the world. Like I'm the most beautiful woman in the world."

"You are."

She backs away, out of my arms. Stands a few feet away, inhales deeply, the heavy globes of her breasts lifting, and then lets it out with a shake of her hair. Hands at her sides. At ease. Waiting.

Letting me just look at her.

"So…fucking…beautiful," I growl each word, and she shivers at each growl. "Don't deserve to look at you. So goddamned perfect."

I just look.

Toes to hair. Soak in her beauty. Every inch, every curve. Her fingers wriggle at her hips, moving to cover stretch marks there. I cross the space between us.

"Don't." I catch her hands. Put them to my lips. "Don't. Don't hide a fucking thing. Ever. Not from me. Every inch of you is perfect."

Her eyes water and she shakes her head. "I'm not."

"You are to me."

She swallows hard, tears sliding down. "You really mean it."

"To my fucking bones, Noelle."

"God, Bear, you're killing me." She slides her hands out of mine and cradles my neck. Pulls me close. "In the best way."

Without a word, without warning, she slips her hands down my arms, to my ribs, down my sides to my hips. Hooks her fingers into elastic and runs them around to my navel, pulling away. Tugs down, past a raging erection so hard I could use it to drive nails.

My hands curl into fists at my sides as she lowers my underwear until they drop, and I step out of them.

Naked with her.

Holy shit.

I meet her eyes—she's locked on my gaze, nibbling at her lower lip. Slowly, she drags her gaze away from mine and down.

"Oh," she breathes. "Oh…my…*god*."

Her eyes are wide, shocked. "Wow. Just…*wow*."

Cheeks burning, lungs frozen solid, I have no clue what to say, how to react. So I don't—I just try to breathe and hold still.

She blinks, gnawing on her lip. "Bear…" she shakes her head. "I don't know what I'm gonna do with all that."

"Don't have to do anything you don't want to," I say.

"Have to?" She steps closer, hands going to my ribs. "*Want* to. *Get* to."

"Noelle," I growl. "Killing me."

"Talk to me." She leaves a little space between us, just the tips of her breasts touching my chest.

"Want you. Need you. But I've got no fucking clue what to do."

She sighs, a sound of relief. "I'm so glad you said that, because me either." She licks her lips. "Let's take a shower. I'm freezing."

12

Noelle

DEAR LORD, HELP ME.

It's a prayer, not an epithet.

I have absolutely no clue what I'm doing. We're naked together, and I'm scared out of my mind, and he keeps saying the most perfect things to me, settling my nerves the moment they flare. Touching me like I'm spun glass, reverent and worshipful. Kissing my belly.

Sniffing me—scenting me, like I'm perfume.

But his…um.

You know.

It's freaking *enormous*. I mean, I sort of had the idea that it would be—no part of him is small.

But holy Moses.

That thing is *huge*.

Having no frame of reference besides Brennan, I don't know how it compares to the norm, but my guess is that since every other part of him is beyond the pale, this is, too.

I shy away from figuring out what to call it, even in my own head—dratted hyper-religious upbringing.

I want to be daring.

Bold.

Sexy.

Naughty.

A little dirty.

I just…where do I start?

He's watching me, staring at me, gaze greedily going to my breasts, my sex. He can't look away, and bless him for trying—he keeps finding my eyes, but his gaze goes back down.

I turn, open the shower, twist the water on—within a minute it's skirling whirls of steam, and I catch Bear's hand as I adjust it so it's not scalding.

I pull him in after me and he shuts the door—he's nervous too, hesitant. Standing against the rear wall, he fills the admittedly not huge shower stall with his massive presence. The water beats on my back as I face him, and the heat leaches into me.

I pull him toward me, and I'm thankful that the shower head is mounted up near the ceiling, so he doesn't have to duck. "Stay close to me."

I slick my wet hair back, and pull him forward so the stream hits his chest—I unbraid his beard and toss the tie aside. He ducks under the stream to wet his hair.

"Can I ask you an embarrassing question?" I ask, my voice small and hesitant.

"Anything."

I look down at his huge…thing. "What do you call it?" At his frowned, silent question, I feel compelled to elaborate. "The way I was raised, we didn't talk about sex or body parts. So…I don't know what to call it."

"Yours."

I can't help a laugh. "For real, Bear. It's an honest question."

"Cock."

My cheeks burn. "I don't know if I can say that."

"Try." He rests a hand on my ribs, just below my breasts—which I now realize he hasn't touched yet.

I swallow hard. "Cock." I cover my mouth with my hand. "Another really stupid, embarrassing question."

"Not stupid or embarrassing."

I rest my forehead against his chest. "It's really big, isn't it? Your…your cock?"

"Um." A shrug. "Dunno. Not much for comparing."

"Something tells me that's because there *is* no comparison."

He shrugs again. "You don't have to worry, okay? I won't ever hurt you."

"I know, Bear." I capture his hands. Guide them up. "Don't you want to touch me?"

"So fucking bad."

"I want you to."

I hold my breath as he gently scrapes his cinderblock hands up my skin—the rough scratch of his hands is delicious, delirium-inducing. He cups my breasts in his big hands, cradling their weight. Lifting. Cupping. A low growl of masculine pleasure rattles the shower stall.

"Incredible," he whispers. Looks at me, awe in his eyes. "So fucking exquisite."

My breath is on fire my throat, in my lungs. "Bear."
It's a plea.

I need more.

So much more.

Everything.

The sandpaper grit of his thumbpads roll over my nipples, eliciting a shocked gasp from me. He squeezes the globes almost roughly. He holds my eyes and then dips, pressing his lips to my chest just below my throat. Roughly cupping, squeezing, and kneading one breast, he lifts the other and suckles my nipple into his mouth. I arch my back and give voice to a moan; I'm shocked at the sound that comes out of me.

Not once in my entire previous relationship did I *ever* make such a sound; I refuse to even say his name, now. That person is erased.

Bear is all that exists.

His touch. His kiss.

He lifts my other breast to his mouth and kisses it while playing with the first.

Finds my eyes. "Too rough?"

I shake my head. "Incredible. Perfect." I pull him back down. "Please, Bear. More."

He goes to his knees, framing each breast in his big hard hands, his touch so gentle, so loving. Kisses one breast, the other. Lets them settle to hang naturally; his hands go to my butt, and his mouth suckles my nipples, one and the other, kissing, licking, tongue flicking. With each touch of his tongue, I whimper, cry out, and gasp, each new sensation wild and maddening. A burn fills my belly, swelling into an inferno of pressure and heat. Each kiss and lick of my nipples sends fire into my belly, pressure behind my sex.

"Bear," I whisper, pleading for I don't know what.

Well, actually...I do.

I just don't know how to ask for it.

"*Please*, Bear."

"What do you need, Noelle?"

I shake my head, breathing hard. "I don't know how to say it."

He caresses my bottom with tenderness, gazing up at me as the shower stream splatters off my shoulders. The tile must be hard under his knees, and he must be cold not under the hot water, but he doesn't seem to even notice.

He brings his hands around to my hipbones. His thumbs brush the delicate hollow where my thighs dip in toward my sex. "This?"

I nod, stroking his wet hair. "Please, Bear. I feel..."

"Tell me."

"Crazy. Wild." I swallow hard. "I need...*you*. I need *more*. Touch me. *Please* touch me."

"Fuck, Noelle." He slides those thumbs inward, and I hiss as they touch my lips. His voice is shaky. "Ask me again. Please."

I touch his chin so he looks up at me. "Need to hear it again?" He nods. "Please touch me, Bear. Please. Help me..." I swallow hard and force the dirty, forbidden words out. "Help me come."

"Hot as fuck, hearing your sweet, innocent mouth say that." He swipes one big thumb down my seam; I jerk at the touch, a shrill gasp torn from my mouth. "Can't believe this is real."

"It's real," I assure him.

"Don't wanna wake up back in the cell," he growls, his voice gritty and guttural. "Terrified I'm gonna snap out of it and be back there."

I cradle his face. "No, no, no. Bear, Honey. Look at me." His expression is so fraught, torn by need and fear. I smooth my hands down his cheeks, brush my thumbs under his eyes, wipe at the corners. "You're here with me. Feel me? Feel me touching you?"

"Feel it," he whispers, the sound delicate and awed. "Feel you."

"I'm real. This is *real*."

"Don't fucking deserve you," he murmurs.

"I don't want to hear that again," I scold him. "Never again. Promise me."

He frowns up at me. "Promise." He swallows hard, his gaze going to my sex. "So sexy."

"Show me," I whisper. "Please."

"Need you to help me make you feel good, Noelle. Been a long time. Don't know what I'm doing." He brushes a thumb down my seam again, and touches his lips to my belly, below my navel and above my pubic hair.

Should I have shaved? Or at least trimmed? I never have. It never occurred to me to do so, until now.

"Bear?" I whisper. "I have another question."

He kisses lower, lips grazing my skin, my coppery curls down there. "Mmmm?" It's a rumbled query. "Anything."

"Do you…" I exhale a shaky, scared sigh as I look for the words—which seem to flee my brain. "Do you wish I'd…um. Shaved? Down there?"

He growls. "Fuck no."

I frown. "You…don't?"

A shake of his shaggy head. "Hell no." He kisses my

thigh, the hollow next to my sex, his cheek and jawline brushing the outer swell of my nether lip, teasing. "You're a woman, Noelle. All woman. Real. You ask me, a woman's got curves. Soft. Natural." He traces the pads of his fingers down my center, over the curls, one fingertip brushing me where I'm most sensitive, making me jump and cry out. "Love this, Noelle. Every inch of you is fucking incredible."

"Okay." It's a breath, shaky still—this time from the touch.

His hands glide up my belly, gather my breasts in his hands, and his lips touch just above my sex. "Your body drives me wild, Noelle."

His gruff growl shakes me to my core, makes the heat and pressure build to a frenetic boil, and only his touch will give me what I want—yet he takes his time, learning me, exploring me. He lifts my breasts again, thumbs rolling over my nipples, which are diamond-hard, erect, and as sensitive as I am down there.

"These big beautiful tits."

Lifts on his knees, kneading one breast while kissing the other, then he switches—after a moment, he kisses my belly, my navel, my pudendum, and then lower, lips now covering my tender, aching sex. A single flick of his tongue is where I want it most.

"This sweet, perfect pussy." I gasped at the word, shocked and aroused. His tongue flicks me again. "Clit is sensitive, isn't it?"

I nod. "Yes. Very." I moan as he closes his lips over me, there, suckling. "Nipples, too."

"Oh yeah?" He rises, sucking a nipple into his mouth, gently nibbling and scraping with his teeth and flicking with his tongue until I jerk and gasp. "Fuck yeah, you're sensitive." He looks up at me. "Do something for me, Beautiful?"

I swallow hard, aching everywhere, desperate for release. "Anything."

"Touch yourself."

"Where?"

He covers my sex again, tonguing. "Pinch those pretty pink nipples."

His eyes are hooded, heavy-lidded, wild with arousal; he's enjoying this. That only makes me feel even wilder, ratcheting my own arousal to new heights—to a fevered pitch.

He watches as I hesitantly cup my breasts. "Play with your tits, Noelle."

I love this version of Bear—commanding. Confident. Telling me what to do. God, I could come just from his voice, from his dirty, beautiful words.

I cover my nipples with my palms, the pressure against my nipples freezing my breath in my throat. I slide my palms against the erect little buttons, and then, slowly, hesitantly, pinch them between my finger and thumb.

"Show me how you like it," he murmurs.

Swallowing a whimper that's equal parts nerves and need, I pinch harder, rolling them; a hot line of arousal sizzles in a searing line from my nipples to my sex, and a shrill gasp slips past my clenched teeth. I do it again, harder. A sharp bite of pain threads through the pleasure, and my hips jerk as an intense wave of need pushes through me, making me moan.

"Fuck," Bear snarls. "So hot." He licks me—up my sex, tongue tip tripping against the apex, stopping to swirl over the bundle of nerve endings.

I cry out, my knees dipping—helpless to stop myself, I pinch my nipples again, even harder, and he flicks me with his tongue at the same time and now the wave of pleasure is a sudden sharp blast, and the heat is nuclear within me, the pressure titanic. My cries emerge in a series of rough, throaty, staccato moans and whimpers, each one louder and wilder than the last as Bear's tongue and lips ply my sex, flicking and swirling and circling and tweaking my hypersensitive center. My nipples ache and throb as I pinch and roll them, squeezing hard enough that the sharp sting of pain makes my gasps breathless and my knees threaten to give out.

Bear's hands cradle my bottom, pulling me against him, and now his tongue swipes up relentlessly, fast and greedy. The pressure increases inside me in ramping waves, the heat billowing like an out-of-control wildfire, and all I can do now is ride the waves, knees dipping, hips pushing against his devouring mouth.

"Oh god, Bear. Oh god, oh god, oh *god*—Bear!" I barely recognize my own voice; it's rough and ragged and raw, thick with arousal. "I need to come. Please. Please. Ohgodohgodohgod—*please*, Bear, I need to come."

Who is this Noelle, saying these things, begging this man for an orgasm?

I can't stand upright on my own—I hunch forward over Bear, bracing myself on his massive, rock-hard shoulders, knees bent, hips grinding, back against the wall.

It hits me all at once.

My climax is so powerful it rips a full-throated scream out of me, a scream worthy of a slasher film. My hands clutch at Bear's head, my hips flying, flexing, thrusting as the orgasm shatters me and shatters me, pieces of my soul flung to the farthest corners of existence as his mouth covers my sex and sucks hard, and now I feel pressure against my seam, something thick and hard nudging my opening—pressing, slipping between my slick lips, arousal leaking out of me, coating me, drenching me. The orgasm continues to wrench my body into contortions of ecstasy, the scream fading into gasps, groans, and whimpers, and that pressure against my opening becomes penetration—his finger sliding into me, centimeter by centimeter, and my jaw drops open, and my eyes fly wide. I look down and find his eyes. He pulls away, lips and beard glistening with my essence, shower spray dotting his face and beard, droplets rolling down his shoulders as the stream batters his broad back. I watch, rapt and awed and breathless, as his middle finger fills my sex, splitting me open, taking the wild crescendo of climax into something else, something beyond mere orgasm.

Another wave bursts in my belly as his finger drills deep into me, curling, scraping against some secret place that rips another sudden scream out of me—another smashing, shattering climax shearing me into sobbing, weeping, boneless pieces.

My knees give out totally, and Bear catches me. I'm dizzy, disoriented, gasping raggedly. I'm floating, drifting. Cold air washes over me. Something soft and warm wraps around me. I'm settled onto my bed, mind spinning, my whole body twitching and spasming as aftershocks seize me like mini-earthquakes.

A moment later, his hot hard chest becomes my pillow, his arms wrapped around me, sheltering me from the storm of orgasms still shuddering through me.

I must pass out for a moment because I find myself

blinking my eyes open—daylight has faded, and Bear's breathing is slow and soft and deep. But when I crane my neck to look up at him, he's awake. His gray-green eyes are tender and warm on mine.

"Hey." His voice is low, a smile playing at the corners of his lips. "There you are."

"Did…did I…pass out?"

"Mmm-hmm."

"How long was I out?"

"Not long. Twenty minutes. Maybe thirty."

A throw blanket covers our naked bodies.

I roll against him, and look into his eyes. "Bear, I…." I press my face into his chest, cheeks burning. "I'm at a loss for words."

"Don't have to say anything."

I swallow hard, a lump of emotion in my throat. "I didn't know it could feel like that." I shimmy up his body until I can capture his mouth and claim his tongue. "I don't know what you did, but it was incredible. *Beyond* incredible. I've…I've never…" I bury my nose and mouth in the side of his throat, shake my head as I hunt for words that will express my feelings at this moment, and come up short. "Nothing has ever felt like that. Not even close."

"Giving that to you…" he ghosts a thumb over my mouth. "Greatest privilege of my whole fucking life." His lips touch mine, whispering. "Thank you, Noelle. Thank you for trusting me with your perfect body."

I can't help but laugh. "I should be thanking *you*, Bear."

"Told you. It was my privilege. Getting to touch you. See you. Be with you. Hear you scream. Knowing you picked me, of any man in the world, to give you pleasure…."

fuck. Nothing better in the whole wide world. Not a single goddamn thing."

My eyes burn. "God, Bear."

Another ache takes root inside me. Another, different kind of need. This one is not for my release now, but his.

I slide the blanket down around our hips, baring the hard, rippling expanse of his chest and abdomen. A thick smattering of rust-red curls covers his chest, narrowing to a thin line trailing down beneath the blanket. His nipples are flat buttons surrounded by tan ovals, the pecs massive and hard and bulging with power. I trace a long keloid scar line. Touch a round, puckered one. A burn under his ribcage on the left side.

Tug the blanket lower, kick it away entirely—his manhood, not erect at this moment, is long and thick, curled against his thigh, a profusion of copper pubic hair surrounding the thick root and heavy balls.

"Noelle, you…you don't need to—" he starts.

I cover his mouth with my hand. "I want to. I *want* to touch you. I wanted to touch you in the shower. I'm just sorry I was so selfish."

He shakes his head. "Nothing selfish about that. It was beautiful."

I slide my palm over his stomach. "And this will be beautiful, too. I want to give you as much pleasure as you gave me."

"Got all the pleasure I need, making you feel good."

"Bear," I say. "Please let me touch you. I don't just want to—I *need* to. I need to. Please." I let my hand drift lower. "Don't you want me to?"

He nods hesitantly. "Course."

"Have you…thought about this? About me touching you?"

A slow nod. "Couple times. Didn't feel right. Felt like I was using you or something. I dunno." A shrug. "When we decided to take time to get to know each other, I tried to put that aside."

"I know what you mean." I rest my cheek on his chest and watch my hand slip down to his left thigh. "Gonna make you feel so good, Bear. Just…just relax and let me touch you. Trust me, okay?"

He nods. "I do." His hand curls around my shoulders, tightening as my touch inches closer to his manhood. "Here for you, Noelle. Whatever you want. Whatever you need."

"What I want and need right now is…this." I cover the slack comma of his manhood.

At my touch, I feel it harden, immediately thickening, hardening, straightening.

Memories assault me, unbidden, unwanted, of the fumbling attempts in the past. Barely a handful at full erection, he would be done within seconds of me touching him. He'd make me feel bad about it. Like I did something wrong in making him come too soon.

It got to the point, toward the end of the relationship, where I'd lost interest in the act. With him, at least. Alone, I'd help myself find the release I needed—daydreaming and fantasizing about…well, exactly what Bear just gave me: time, attention, affection. Focusing on me. Making me feel good. It's not just good—it's *amazing*. And no matter how wild or detailed the fantasy, nothing came even close to the reality of how Bear made me feel.

Now, a new hunger rises in me. I remember the wild

need I felt as a teenage girl, a young woman eager to explore her body and sexuality. I remember feeling feverish and half-crazed with want. I remember making out and being shaky with the desire to feel him, to touch him, to explore.

All that comes to life within me again, stronger than ever, a kind of renewal of those girlhood needs, quashed and killed then, now resurrected by Bear's sweetness, patience, kindness, and devotion. By all that he is. By his touch.

I circle his thick, erect organ with one hand—my middle finger just barely meets my thumb. I place my other hand above the first, and he's long enough that the tip protrudes above my upper hand, a bulbous pink head, the slit weeping clear fluid.

I look at him—his jaw is tensed and flexing, his chest rising and falling with slow, powerful breaths. His eyes are locked on my hand, his erection.

"So big," I whisper, gently sliding one hand down from tip to root. "Beautiful." I hold his gaze for a moment. "You're beautiful, Bear."

His brows lower, and his head shakes, but he says nothing, only swallows hard, breath coming faster.

"Talk to me, honey," I whisper. "I want to know what you're thinking, what you're feeling."

"Been a long, long time since I've been touched like this. Not sure how long I can last."

I nibble his earlobe. Whisper in his ear. "I don't *want* you to last. All I want is for you to feel good."

"You touching me…feels fucking amazing. Unreal."

I caress his length again, the ridges of skin and veins slipping and stuttering against my palm, past my fingers.

His abs tuck in and harden, and his hips tense subtly. "It's real," I whisper.

"Oh god, Noelle. Feels so fucking good." His voice is rough and guttural and low. "Please don't stop."

"Never." I feel…powerful.

Strong. Bold.

Maybe it was the orgasm, maybe it's just him, the things he says, but I'm emboldened to let my desire take over. I give myself permission to be naughty. To let my deepest, wildest, most hitherto forbidden fantasies come true—because I know I'm safe with Bear.

I cup his taut, red-fuzzed, heavy balls in my hand, toying with them. They're fascinating and strange. At my touch, he jerks, thighs bunching, a ragged growl pushing past his teeth.

"Love how you growl for me," I whisper. "Love the sounds you make."

I plunge my fist down his length again, ever so slowly, inch by inch, twisting around the top, scudding down the thick hot shaft, and curling around the root, my other hand cradling and cupping his balls.

"Ohhhhhh fuck, Noelle."

"Feels good?" I breathe. "You like how I touch your cock?"

The word drops from my lips, and excitement makes me shiver and shudder—I can say anything. He won't judge. He'll only encourage.

"Fuck yes," he growls. "Love how you touch my cock. Feels so fucking good."

"I want you to come for me," I whisper in his ear. "Show me how I make you feel, honey."

Faster, then. I shove my hand down his length and

then slowly drag it back up, rolling my thumb over the tip, smearing the clear fluid over him. Tease the slit with my fingernail, making him jerk and jump and growl. Another swift plunge of my fist.

He snarls wordlessly, hips lifting off the bed. "Gonna come soon, Noelle."

"Good," I say. "That's what I want."

I don't know who I am right now, but I like her. Scratch that—*love* her. I feel more alive than I've ever been. Like I've been asleep—or half alive. Bear giving me not one but two—at least—incredibly potent orgasms broke a spell, shattered chains I didn't know were binding me.

He brought me to life.

A ravenous, greedy, sensual, erotic beast has been woken inside me.

I can do anything. I can have him. I can give myself to him. Show him all of me. I can accept everything he is, and demand more because I can give more.

A thought percolates and takes root.

A desire.

A dark, hidden, dirty, secret fantasy—something I touched myself while imagining. Trying to picture what it would feel like if I were ever able to do that with someone. In the fantasies, the man was nameless and faceless, and the act was forbidden, sinful, and shameful.

Now...

The prospect of allowing myself to live out that fantasy with this wild, beautiful, immense, powerful, kind, wonderful man?

Excitement and wonder and desperate need thrill through me—I'm consumed. Shaking with energy, with want.

I slide my cheek from his chest to his diaphragm, slowly caressing his hot length.

His breathing is rapid and shallow. "Noelle?"

"Sssshhh." I twist to look at him. "Just enjoy it, Bear."

Heart slamming frantically in my chest, I slip lower. Lower. The plump, straining tip is right in front of my face, now. A bead of clear liquid dots the slit. I hesitate, and then stick out my tongue and lick it away. The flavor bursts on my tongue, unexpectedly potent. He groans at the touch of my tongue, and the ragged, desperate sound gives me the courage to go further. To take more of what I want—to give him more.

I kiss the tip, lips against the soft, tender, warm skin, flitting my tongue over the slit, earning me another raw, guttural moan. "You taste amazing," I whisper.

"Noelle...*fuck*." The disbelief in his voice sears my soul. "Feels so fucking good."

His praise fills me with pride, further emboldening me to keep going. Give more; take more.

I hold his cock in my hand and part my lips, open my mouth. I taste flesh on my tongue, salty and hot and slippery smooth. His fingers dive into my hair, gather the long, braid-kinked tresses in his hands, clutching, holding, knotting, tugging at the scalp. The slight pinch of pain at the tug drags a groan from me—apparently, that's a thing for me, now.

I stroke his length from the root to my lips.

Down...and back up, so slowly.

Again.

Again.

He growls, wordlessly, feral snarl of masculine pleasure, and his hips buck. I moan at this, loving his response.

He knots his fists in my hair. "Noelle—fuck. Holy shit. Holy fucking shit. Your mouth. God, your sweet fucking mouth."

"Mmmmm…" I moan. "Mmmm-hmm?" Pull away, the tip popping free from my lips with a sound like a bursting bubble in a cartoon. "Tell me how it feels, baby."

Baby?

Where did that come from?

He groans—at my stroking hands, perhaps, or at the term of endearment. Or both. "Heaven. Feels so fucking amazing. Hot, wet, tight mouth. Soft lips. Soft hands. My god, Noelle. Please, fuck, please don't stop."

"Mmmm-mmm," I hum the negative, kissing the fat round head again, licking, tasting. "Never. Not until you come for me."

"Almost," he murmurs. "*So* fucking close."

I fill my mouth with him. Dare more—slide my lips around his jaw-stretching shaft and then back to suckling around his tip. This makes him jerk, shoving his hips helplessly upward, driving his length into my mouth again. I let him—and even drive down to take more of him as he thrusts. He gasps in ecstasy, shocked, ragged, and wild.

"Oh god, Noelle. Oh god." His fists clench hard in my hair, tugging at my scalp with a delicious tinge of pain.

I let my hands both wrap around him, then, plunging down and sliding up, faster and faster, while my mouth suckles around his tip, pushing down inch by inch, swallowing as much of his cock as I can take.

His hands spread to gently cradle my head, and his heels dig into the mattress, pushing his hips up, and he groans, long and low.

Faster.

I taste sweetness and musk, tang and smoke. Moan the flavor of him.

He growls, my new favorite sound—my core spasms with arousal as he cuts loose a vicious, ripping snarl of ecstasy, and every muscle in his great, massive, mighty body quivers, lost to the mercy of my two little hands, my mouth.

Me…

I'm giving him this.

I feel him shake, tensing all over, the growl becoming a breathless, wonder-filled gasp. "Noelle!" For a split second, his fingers tighten with merciless strength around my head, but in the same instant he releases me and his touch returns, delicate and gentle.

How do I tell him I like it a little rough, that I like a little bit of a bite with my pleasure?

A worry for later.

At this moment, I crave his release. His utter, abandoned, pleasure.

"Noelle," he grates, his voice raw and raspy. "Gotta come. Fuck—fuck, fuck. Oh god, Noelle. *Noelle.*"

I have no idea what to expect when he comes. I've never done this before. I fantasized about it, daydreamed of it, fingered myself while imagining it. I understand, mentally, what's going to happen, but the real, physical experience of something is never equal to the idea of it.

I'm scared, for a second. What if—

I push the doubts away. Bear is gasping my name on repeat, chanting my name as he nears his release. He's all the matters. This moment. This connection. This act that I can give him.

I taste his essence on my tongue, and I feel his cock pulsing in my hands, throbbing against my lips. I cradle his balls in one hand and stroke his length with the other, lips wrapped around the head, tongue swirling, lapping, flitting, smearing.

"Ahhhh god, fuck, Noelle—" he thrust off the bed, a wordless roar torn out of him as he finally unleashes his orgasm.

A hot flood washes out of him, filling my mouth. I taste him, the flavors of his seed exploding on my tongue as I swallow and swallow and swallow frantically. He arches, hands shaking on my head as he bellows again, another rush overwhelming my mouth—I can barely swallow it all before he comes yet again, and now I can't take it all. It leaks out of my mouth, trickling down my lips to my chin.

Again and again, his hot, thick, pungent seed fills my mouth, shockingly intense, and seemingly endless.

Finally, the flood ends, and he's gasping, groaning, panting raggedly. I keep going, desperate to milk every last droplet of his pleasure out of him as I can. As I continue to stroke and suckle, he spasms yet again, and this groan seems almost broken, shattered.

He's softening in my hands, and I no longer taste his seed seeping out of him, so I move away, letting his organ pop out of my mouth to flop softly against his belly.

I sit up, hyperaware of my body, of the way my breasts sway, how my nipples stand out hard—aroused at his pleasure, and, yes, at the power I feel knowing I can make such a massive, mighty man shatter into desperate ecstasy. I wipe my lips and chin with the back of my wrist, staring down at him.

He looks absolutely stunned. "Noelle. Dear god."

I giggle, licking my lips, grinning at him. "Hi."

He jackknifes upright, brawny arms snaking around me and hauls me down to him. "C'mere, you."

I sigh happily, enveloped by him, held, protected. "Yes, please."

For a few minutes, he just breathes, his panting slowly reducing to normal breaths, his heartbeat slowing to normal as well. "I don't know what to say."

I rub his chest. "Whatever is on your mind. You can always tell me anything."

"Sorta stunned right now."

"Then you don't have to say anything. Just hold me."

"Wanna savor this moment." He runs his hand over my shoulders, smoothing it down my spine, capturing the upper swell of my backside and back up to my shoulders, caressing me in a long, slow circuit. "Can't quite believe you did that."

I giggle. "Me either, actually." I bite my lip, hesitate, and then tell him the truth. "Never done that before."

"What?" He sounds shocked. "Never?"

I shake my head. Cheeks flushed, I continue to admit the truth to him—scary and liberating all at once. "I…it's been a secret fantasy of mine for a long, *long* time. Part of me never thought I'd ever feel brave enough to try it. But you…Bear, you give me courage. You make me bold. I know I'm safe with you."

"What a gift," he breathes. "What a priceless gift."

"That's how I feel about you, Bear."

He rumbles—a sound of disbelief. "I'd honestly given up on…on life. On myself. On love. Sex. Spend the amount of time I did locked up, you gotta find ways to cope. For me, it was putting that part of myself away. Killed it. I focused on reading and lifting. I just…I never thought, even after I got out, that anyone would want me like that. I felt like…like a reject."

"Bear, no. *No.* You're not. You're so far from being a reject."

"You changed everything," he says. "Changed me. Gave me a reason to not just live but to want more out of life. I want more. I wanna *be* more—for you."

My eyes sting. "You already are more." I roll onto him, resting my breasts on his chest, hands folded on his breastbone, chin on my hands, gazing into his beautiful, endlessly deep eyes. "I need you to understand something, honey. I have never, ever, *ever* felt the way you made me feel, just now. I'm talking about the way you made me come, first and foremost. I've never come like that. To the point that I'm not entirely sure I ever *have* actually come. But getting to make *you* feel good? That was *so* hot for me. I'm still so turned on it's crazy. Making *you* feel good makes *me* feel good."

He slides his fingers into my hair along my temple. "Noelle. God, Noelle. This all feels like a dream."

"For me too." I smile at him. "The best dream I've ever had. May we never wake up."

"Amen to that." His eyes droop, heavy.

I shimmy higher so I can nuzzle my face into the side of his neck, most of my body on his, greedy for his warmth, his solidity, his strength. His hand cradles my bottom.

"Close your eyes," I tell him. "Rest with me."

His only response is a soft, happy little growl.

The last thing I think before dozing off is that I'm very much aware of one fact: I'm absolutely falling in love with my big, handsome Bear.

13

Bear

I WAKE UP ALONE IN NOELLE'S BED TO THE SCENT OF frying meat.

A small digital alarm clock on her bedside reads 7:55 pm. I remember it reading just before seven when I dozed off. I stretch, yawning.

God, I'm still shaken to my core by the wild, wonderful, unexpected experience with Noelle. Simply having the privilege of getting to strip her lush, sexy body naked, piece by piece, was overwhelming and amazing. But then to be able to touch her? To have those huge, luscious tits in my hands? To kiss them? And her ass. Her pussy. Everything about her is fucking perfect. And she allowed me to touch her. She let me make her feel good. Let me give her an orgasm. I followed instinct, listened to the sounds she made and the way her body responded, and just tried to give her everything I possibly could. I feel like I succeeded—according to her, anyway, I certainly did.

But good god in heaven—being touched by her? Her small soft hands wrapped around my cock? Her mouth? I never in a million years would have expected that.

I'm lost in thought when she comes into the room. I sit up, raking her with my eyes. She's wearing nothing but an oversized T-shirt. It doesn't quite cover her butt, so the lower curves play peekaboo as she walks. Her tits sway behind the cotton with every step, and her long thick legs are bare and smooth.

"Hey you," she says, carrying a tray to the bed. Her gaze takes me in—the blanket shifted off me as I slept, rucked around my thighs. I tend to run hot when I sleep, so I often end up uncovered. "You're smiling."

"I am?"

She giggles, nodding. "Yep. Big ol' grin. Never seen you smile like that."

She sets the tray on the bed, revealing two plates, each bearing a huge pork chop, a pile of rice, and broccoli sprinkled liberally with seasoning and parmesan cheese; also on the tray is a bottle of wine, an opener, and two goblets, as well as silverware and strips of paper towel for napkins.

"What's got you grinning for the first time in your life?" She asks, her voice light and right, happy, teasing.

"You." I jut my chin at the tray. "What's all this?"

She shrugs. "Dinner." She crawls onto the bed on all fours, snuggling in beside me, sitting up. "I, um…worked up an appetite, if you know what I mean." Her cheeks flush, her grin widening.

"Why do you think I'm smiling?" I say, reaching for the tray and pulling it close. "But…I woulda helped."

She cups my jaw. "I wanted to do this for you. Bring you dinner in bed. You make me so happy, Bear. And when I'm happy, I like doing things for the people I care about. I enjoy cooking." She hands me the bottle and opener. "Can you open this, please?"

"Sure."

Never opened a bottle of wine before, but I've seen it done on TV in the dayroom, where a TV was always playing something. I figure it out easily enough, and the cork comes free with a pop; I pour some of the ruby red liquid into each goblet.

She takes one and clinks it against the one in my hand. "To us," she says. "And our future together."

"To us," I echo, but my mind is stuck on the second part of her toast.

Our future together.

I like the sound of that.

"What's that future look like?" I ask. It's not a question I would have even thought to myself just two or three months ago.

She slices a piece of meat instead of answering right away, but I can see her thinking as she chews. "I don't know. I guess that's what I'm excited about—figuring that out with you."

I try the porkchop: it's incredible, unsurprisingly. Juicy, tender, well-seasoned. I force myself to eat slowly, savoring each bite.

"What about you?" she asks. "You have any ideas about the future?"

I shrug. "Dunno. Haven't given a lot of thought to it."

"You should." She dabs her lips with the napkin, scoops rice, and then nibbles a piece of broccoli. "You have a future, now, Bear. A bright one. What do you want it to look like?"

"Today." The answer pops out unbidden. My cheeks burn. "Not just…sex. Everything. Being with you. This— eating together."

She smirks at me. "But also the sex."

I nod, letting my smile answer hers. "Definitely that."

"And a *lot* of that, hopefully." She spends a while eating, and then looks at me again, setting her fork down. "Is it okay if we…um…keep taking it slow? Sex, I mean. I want our relationship to be…strong. Based on the right things."

"Absolutely," I say.

She rushes to speak. "The only reason I say that is because I feel sort of…I don't know. Crazy. About you. I just…I don't want to get caught up in the physical and lose sight of our emotional and mental connection. Maybe I'm overthinking it."

I take her hand. "No. Slow is good, Noelle. There's a lot of transitions in my life. Freedom. Work. And now you—us. It's a lot. It's all good—great. But I…" I trail off. "I guess I sorta want to…savor each step with you. Like today. What we did together. I want to savor the memory, the feeling." I sigh. "I want you. Need you. But I don't want to rush. And I'm glad we waited. Got to know each other more."

"You understand me," she says, her eyes misting.

"Hey, don't cry," I say. "Can't handle you crying."

She laughs, shaking her head. "Not all tears are bad. I'm just emotional, I guess. But I'm happy. So freaking happy. And that makes me a little weepy, but it's a good thing."

"Oh." I brush at her eyes. "Then, I guess just let it out?"

She sniffles a laugh, nodding. "You make it safe for me to show you my emotions. All of them." She sighs, wincing. "I haven't always felt that way. Or ever, really. I mean, with my friends, yeah. But with...before—with my ex. I've decided not to even think of his name anymore, by the way. I always felt like...like my feelings were too big. Too much. He couldn't handle everything I was. I wanted sex too much, wanted to know what he was feeling too much, and tried too hard to love him. The harder I tried and the more of myself I gave to him, the more he seemed to just...I dunno. Pull away. I've never gotten it. But it hurt. It made me feel—I don't know. Poopy about myself. Like I'm just too much. Like no one will ever be able to accept me for everything I am. I always have to hold back."

"Maybe it's selfish, but I want all of you," I say. "I guess because I know exactly how you feel. I've always been...a lot. A social worker, when I was ten or eleven, before my last placement, she told me what she knew about my origin."

Noelle sets her plate aside and turns to focus on me. "Will you tell me? Please? I want to know everything about you."

"Wasn't much. I guess my parents were very young immigrants from Iceland. Came over when they were nineteen. My mom was already pregnant with me when they got here. Dad had trouble finding work. Had a job lined up, but it fell through, and he didn't know much English. Things got hard for them. Eventually, he got a job in a factory, but he was killed in an accident about a week before

I was born. Apparently, according to the social worker, I was so big at full term that she had to have an emergency C-section. She almost died in the process—some sort of complication, I dunno. She never recovered. Not all the way. Kept getting sick. Couldn't take care of me. So, she gave me up for adoption when I was only a few months old. Turned me over to the state."

"God, Bear. That's so hard. I'm so sorry."

I shrug. "All I remember from my early childhood is this tiny house with an overgrown backyard. Lotta other kids. And then having to leave. A new family, a new house. Had to carry all my stuff from house to house in this black garbage bag that had my name written on a piece of duct tape. I got made fun of a lot. Being so big, plus my name. I mean, Bear was bad enough, but Bear Olafsson? With red hair?" I shake my head. "Kids were cruel."

Her eyes go misty again, and she snuggles closer to me, trying to get her arm around my chest. Eventually, she gives up and straddles me, naked bottom and sex sliding over me, and she presses herself against me, arms around my middle, cheek on my chest—a full-body hug.

"Keep talking," she says. "Don't mind me."

I set my empty plate aside near hers and scratch her back in lazy circles as I tell her the story I've never fully told anyone.

"Got in a lot of fights in school. I was angry. Alone. Confused. A lotta fosters were abusive." I find the scars on my right shoulder and bicep, little round burn marks in a neat line down my arm. "One foster father did this. Put his cigarettes out on me. If I made a sound, cried out, flinched, anything, he'd kick the shit outta me. So I learned to keep quiet, no matter what." She shudders, sniffling. "I'm okay. I'm okay. It's old."

"Not to me," she whispers.

"That was how it went. My last foster was the worst. The mother tried to…do things to me. I was already pretty big and strong, even at eleven. I fought her off and ran away. Got picked up by some gangbangers. They took me in and took care of me. Had to do some bad shit, but at least I sort of belonged. I just…I never felt like I could be me. In the gang, I had to be…bad. Scary. Hurt people. Not who I am but how I had to be. And then, in prison, it was all different. Same, but different. At first, I thought I had to be the tough guy. But I learned eventually that if I made friends with people and kept to myself and stayed out of trouble, it was better. I didn't have to be the tough, hard-ass, violent guy."

Noelle sighs. "I'm glad you learned that. I can't picture you being violent."

"Glad you can't. Hope you never see it." I swallow hard. "Only reason I'd ever be that guy again is if I have to protect you. And if I do, I'll stop at nothing to keep you safe."

She nods against my chest. "Good thing my life is safe and boring, then, huh?"

I laugh. "Safe and boring is good." I can't help but cradle her ass in my hands. "Nothing about you is boring, though. Hope you know that."

She sits upright, her breasts swaying behind the shirt, hair loose and wild around her shoulders, a cloud of red like the setting sun. Freckles dot her neck, chest, thighs, and cheeks. I trace them and connect the dots with my fingertip, wishing her shirt was off so I could connect those dots across the rest of her beautiful body.

"Thank you for sharing that with me," she murmurs.

"You too. About…him. How you feel." I hold her eyes. "Want you to know that you can…be you. totally. Don't ever hold back. I know you I don't wanna hear me say this, but I gotta, once more. I don't always feel like I deserve the woman that you are, but since you seem to have chosen me for reasons I'll never understand, all I can do is promise you that I can handle everything you are. All your biggest feelings, your fears, your needs. Gimme all you got, Noelle. God made me big, made me strong. Guess if I believe in that God, then I believe he made me this way for a reason. For you."

Misty eyes flicking side to side, searching me, she swallows hard, sniffling. "God, Bear—there you go again, making me cry with how darned sweet you are." She wipes at her face with both hands, shuddering a sigh. "You can't know what it means to hear that and know it's true."

"I can imagine," I say. "Feel the same."

"It is. It is the same." She takes my hands, kisses each of my palms, and then presses them to her face. "I'm not big and strong like you. But I have a lot of love to give. I want all of you, too. All of you. I don't want you to hold back, either. You're not too much for me. You're not too big." She tangles our fingers together. "You won't break me. You won't hurt me. Okay?"

"Okay."

"Good. Now that that's settled." She rolls to her stomach on the bed and reaches across me, shirt riding up to expose that luscious ass which I can't help but play with, earning me a little giggle, she opens a drawer in her bedside table and produces an iPad connected to a charger; she unplugs it, opens it, finds a streaming service app, taps it, and hands it to me. "I'm gonna make popcorn. You pick a movie."

"What do you like?" I ask.

"Not telling. I wanna know what *you* like."

"I don't know."

She laughs, pausing in the doorway. "Exactly the point! Pick something that interests you."

We stay up way too late, sipping wine—not my favorite, but she likes it, so I drink it—and eating popcorn and watching a movie. I pick one called *Three Hundred*, which she claims to have not seen before. When that's over, I insist she show me her favorite movie, which turns into a long discussion of *which* favorite because she has several. She picks *The Princess Bride* but falls asleep around the time when the giant is fighting the man in black.

This time when we fall asleep together, it's in her bed.

Best sleep of my life.

⟡

The weeks that follow are amazing.

We work, meet at the shelter, go on walks, eat dinner—either out or at her house. I spend as many nights with her as I do at my own place.

We make out a lot. On a few memorable occasions, I use my fingers and mouth to make her come, and she does the same for me.

But we're in no rush.

I'm enjoying just being with her. I don't need more.

I *want* more.

I want to make love with her. I want that full connection. But I sense she's not ready. She needs this interlude period. And, to be honest, so do I.

On a couple of occasions, she brings lunch to the worksite—bags of burgers and fries from a local place, with enough for all the guys on the demo crew.

She, Darius, and I form a friendship—I'm closest with him of all the guys. On one such day, some six or so weeks after that life-changing rainstorm, she brings dinner for the crew—this time, it's homemade chimichangas, several casserole dishes full of fat little tortillas stuffed with meat, beans, rice, and cheese, topped with more melted cheese, sour cream, and salsa. We're working late, trying to finish the last two houses on the block of the ones Riley and Felix own.

We're sitting in clusters on the curb, eating, laughing, teasing each other. The food is delicious, and it's a warm, beautiful summer night. When the food is gone and everyone is stuffed, Noelle gathers the dishes, paper plates, and silverware, packs it up, and brings it to her car while the guys resume the last of the cleanup.

I'm outside the house I've been working on, emptying a wheelbarrow into the dumpster. I've got one eye on Noelle as she plays with Panzer in the yard a few dozen feet away.

I notice someone else watching her, too.

Duane.

And the look on his face is ugly.

Evil.

Jealous.

Later, on the way home, I squeeze Noelle's knee. "You have a run-in with Duane?"

She nods, frowning. "Yeah, once. The first time I met you at the site. Why?"

I shrug, not wanting to worry her. "I don't like him. I don't like how he looks at you."

"Me either. He said some nasty things, but Darius set him straight." She waves a hand. "He's just lonely, jealous, and insecure. Don't worry about him."

My gut tells me otherwise, but I keep that to myself. I can't exactly beat him up for looking at her. I might have, once upon a time. I'm not that person anymore, though, so the best I can do is keep an eye on him.

C᠆ꜱ

Two weeks later, we're at a grocery store not far from her house, shopping for dinner. We're in the produce section, and she's selecting a bag of apples while scanning the list in her hand.

"Hey, Bear, honey, can you go grab some sour cream? I forgot it when we were over there."

"Sure."

I find the sour cream section easily, but she neglected to mention how many different brands and sizes there are and which she wants, so I pick the biggest tub and head back to where she is.

Only, she's not there anymore.

I roam the aisles one by one, finding her eventually in the far back corner near a rack of sale items and the door to the back. Duane has her cornered.

"You won't even give me the time of day, but *him*? Oh, of *course*. I ain't so bad once you get to know me." His voice is filmy, wheedling, and evil.

"Duane, please just leave me alone." Her voice is firm, but I hear fear in it.

Rage fills me, and I struggle to contain it. My hands shake, and I know I have to be very careful with what I do next. I prowl up behind Duane, grab him by the back of the neck, and toss him backward. I only use a fraction of my strength, but he's a skinny little guy, and he goes sprawling half a dozen feet away. I stomp toward him, fighting the urge to rip his head off his shoulders.

He must see the murder in my eyes because he scrabbles backward on his butt. "We—we was just t-t-talking," he stammers. "Didn't mean nothin' by it."

I grab him by the shirt front and haul him off the ground and onto his feet—he's airborne for a second. "You don't come within ten feet of her. Ever." I shake him. Once—hard. His teeth rattle. "You don't fucking speak to her. You don't talk about her. You don't even *think* about her. You do, I'll tear you into little pieces and feed you to the fucking seagulls."

I toss him again, but this time gently enough that he can keep his feet. He staggers backward, pale and shaking. With one last glance at me and Noelle, fearful and small and vicious and ugly, he runs off, tripping over his feet.

I close my eyes once he's gone, and try to find my center, my calm.

I can't breathe. I'm shaking with rage, a red haze obscuring my vision.

She was scared—of him.

That rage fills me all over again, terrifying in its potency. My muscles spasm, wanting to destroy something.

"Bear?" Her voice is small, tiny. She tentatively touches my arm. "Hey. It's okay. I'm fine."

I shake my head. "Don't—don't touch me. Not…I'm not safe right now."

She ignores that, circling in front of me and standing on her tiptoes to get close to me, pressing against me with her warmth and softness. "Hey. Hey. Breathe, baby. Breathe with me." She sucks in a long breath, holds it, and lets it out—I follow along, and my heart slows, the rage subsiding. "Look at me, honey. Touch me. Feel me. I'm *fine*. I'm not hurt. I wasn't even really scared—I knew you'd find me and take care of him. It's okay, now. It's okay."

"I wanted to…" I shake my head. I can't put it into words. "I'm sorry you saw that side of me."

She wraps her arms around my neck, nuzzling my throat. "I'm not. You protected me." She strokes my beard, my jaw. "You didn't do anything bad, Bear. You scared him a little. Or a lot. Which he deserved. You controlled yourself. I'm proud of you."

Her words burn through the haze, clearing my mind. "You…you are?"

"Yes!" She pats my chest. "I saw how mad you were. You could've really hurt him, but you didn't."

I shake my head, staring at the way Duane went. "Don't like him. Gotta talk to Riley."

"Okay. Maybe he can talk to him about keeping his distance and behaving himself." She grabs the cart and smacks me on the butt. "C'mon, you. Let's go home. Steak and potatoes won't cook themselves."

The following morning, when Noelle drops me off at work, I'm the first one there. Felix arrives next in his big, gold pickup with the bullbar and light rack. He hops down, blond hair shaggy around his collar, a scruffy beard shadowing his jawline, mirrored, wraparound Oakleys on his face. He and Riley look a lot alike, opposite hair color aside—sharp, rugged jawlines, eyes so pale blue they're almost white, high cheekbones, and lean, athletic builds. Felix is heavier and more densely muscled in contrast to Riley's hard, shredded build.

Riley, despite being the clean-cut one, is the bad boy, the brother with a reputation as a ladies' man—to put it nicely—whereas Felix, the shaggy and unkempt one, is the golden boy, the football star in high school, pillar of the Three Rivers community, with his construction company providing luxury housing across the area. Felix's company, Crowe Construction, in addition to homebuilding, also installs play structures at schools and parks in the area as a charitable donation, as well as maintaining a tiny home community for the local homeless population.

Felix is widely adored by the Three Rivers population, and since he's perpetually single, he's considered the most eligible bachelor in town—all this is according to Noelle and her friends, during Trivia Night gossip sessions.

Riley is the black sheep. The one who went to prison for an offense I've never learned, squandering a full-ride scholarship to a Big Ten university for hockey. He's always got a girlfriend, but they never last long and often end in messy, public blowouts that see him going on a bender and having to be collected by his brother.

Despite all that, his work-release program is a darling in the city, beloved by most residents as an ideal second-chance opportunity, a means of rehabilitation rather than punishment. People see the good it does; the inmates who go through it often stay in Three Rivers and become liked and respected members of the community. Not everyone feels that way, obviously—there's a small but vocal faction who think prisoners should stay in prison where they belong, fearing us.

Felix waves at me and goes to the trailer hitched to his truck, opens the tailgate, and starts to organize equipment. A few minutes later, his guys start showing up, and then Riley arrives with Eddie in tow, along with the rest of the crew. Duane hops out of Eddie's truck, sees me, lip curling into a vicious, vengeful sneer, and scurries away to open the house they're starting on today.

Now that we've finished the demo, our job is to assist the construction crew, filling in gaps and cleaning up after them. No one likes this part of the process—it makes us demo guys feel like second-stringers. But the brothers like to have the crews working in tandem, so it's the way we do it.

I approach Riley as he shrugs on his hi-vis vest and snags his hard hat. "Got a minute, boss?"

He tosses the hard hat back onto the rear bench. "Sure, man. What's up?"

"Figured you oughta know. Noelle and I had a run-in with Duane last night at the store. He cornered her, talking shit to her. Guess he did it once before, too, the first time she came around the site."

Riley glances at Duane as the scrawny, greasy, weaselly little man gathers tools from the trailer and carries them inside. "Seems in one piece."

I shrug. "Tossed him around a little, threatened him. But I don't like it. Don't like him. He ain't right."

Riley nods, brows lowering. "You're not wrong. He works hard for the most part, but he's always given me skeezy vibes." he winces. "I can't just fire him, though. Need a better reason. Did he put his hands on her?"

I shake my head. "Not that I saw."

"I'll keep an eye on him. I guess just try to keep him away from your girl, and you give him space, too. Neither of you needs any shit—you especially. You've got too much to lose now." Riley claps me on the arm. "Felix asked if I could loan you to his crew. They're putting in a bunch of marble today, and he needs your help. You up for it?"

"Whatever you need, boss."

"Good man. Report to Fee, and I'll catch you for lunch." He snags his hard hat and heads inside to the build our crew is doing cleanup in—it's been framed out and drywalled, and flooring has been put in, and now it needs to be cleaned up so cabinets, counters, and finishing touches can go in.

I find Felix at the next house over, he and four other guys struggling with a giant slab of marble that must weigh several hundred pounds. "Heard you needed me," I say.

The men all set the slab down together, wiping their brows and panting.

"Thank fuck." Felix gestures at the marble. "Make room, fellas." He juts his chin at me. "Grab the end. You're the base."

"Got it," I say, circling to the end opposite Felix.

There are suction handles attached to the slag at regular intervals at the top and bottom, providing handholds. I grab a pair on one side at the end, brace my legs, and wait for the count.

"On three," Flex calls. "One…two…three."

I heave upward—a little too fast; the other guys need a second to catch up.

"Holy fuckballs, dude," the dude next to me says, laughing. "You got it by yourself? Shit."

"Probably could," Felix grunts as we carry the huge slab down the hallway toward the kitchen. "Why do you think I—pivot, careful—why d'you think I borrowed his big ass from Riley?"

By the time we get the monster chunk of marble into the kitchen, even I'm huffing and sweating…but to be fair, I've got the whole back end by myself while the rest take the front and middle, focusing on guiding it around the narrow turn into the kitchen. After a brief rest, we get it up into position.

I watch as Felix measures, re-measures, and measures a third time before using a special water saw to cut holes for the sink, faucet, and sprayer. "Still need me?" I ask.

He looks up at me, nodding. "Oh yeah." He gestures at the kitchen and the acres of open space above the lower cabinets where counters have to go. "Strap in, big man. We got a lot of work to do."

And so goes my day—lugging slab after slab of marble inside, placing it, and repositioning. I take an interest in the cutting process and end up Felix's assistant as he cuts, places, and joins the sections seamlessly.

By the end of the day, I'm flat-out exhausted but exhilarated. I didn't just destroy shit today, I created something.

Feels good.

Felix and I sit on his tailgate sipping water as the other guys take one last smoke break before cleanup and go time.

He eyes me. "Great work today, man. Woulda taken twice as long." He watches his brother laugh and rough-house with Anthony. "Love to have you on my crew, to be honest. Not sure if my little bro will let you go, though."

I frown. "Yeah, maybe not. But I…" I scrub my face.

"I liked the work, today. Building. Creating. Demo is a great outlet, but…"

"You're ready for more," Felix finishes, nodding. "I'll talk to him. See if I can convince him to let you do a few shifts on my crew. How long do you have left in the program?"

"Well, my parole with the state is separate, obviously. You a total of five years in the program, and I've done three and a half. After that, I'm good to go wherever. Most guys stay with the crew, though."

"What about you?" he asks.

I mop my face with the hem of my shirt. "Just starting to think about that, to be honest. Been just putting one foot in front of the other. Noelle, though…"

Felix grins, pawing through his wild mane of shaggy blond hair. "Makin' you consider the future, huh?"

I nod, grinning. "Yeah, man. She really is."

He laughs. "A good woman'll do that. Make you feel like you can reach for the moon, long as she's with you." His laugh fades, some old sorrow taking its place. "Lose that, though, and you lose the moon."

"Speaking from experience?" I ask.

He nods. "Yep. Had a woman like that. Fucked it up." He picks at a thread at the knee of his jeans. "Someday, maybe, I'll find another one."

I snort. "They don't grow on trees."

He cackles. "Wow, thanks for that nugget of wisdom, dude."

"Sorry, I just meant—"

He slaps me on the back. "Nah, I got you. You're right. I just mean I'm hoping someday I'll get another chance."

"With her, or…?"

A slow shake of his head. "Hell nah, man. She's *long* gone. Got a husband and kids now. Lives in a big ol' mansion in Bloomfield Hills."

"Swanky."

"Right?" he laughs, not quite bitterly, but sort of. "She deserves it. Good woman."

"Take it from me, Felix, second chances come around when you least expect them." I clap his shoulder. "Back to it."

"Yup." He juts his chin at me. "Good talk. I'll have a word with Riley about you pulling shifts with me. Teach you how to build a house."

"I'd like that. Thanks for the chance."

"You're a good man and a hard worker. Riley's lucky to have you."

Buzzing with possibilities, I help Felix's crew with cleanup, putting away tools and locking up. I'm in the back of Felix's trailer, putting things away when I hear Duane's obnoxious, reedy voice complaining—as usual.

"I just don't see what those pompous bozos see in that big dumb oaf. Sure, he's strong, but they act like he shits sunshine and farts roses. Now he's on *Felix's* crew? It ain't enough he gets special treatment, rides from the boss, gets to work alone and play whatever music he wants, and don't even get me started on that goddamn *dog* of his." He hawks and spits. "And that fuckin' girl of his, man. He's got that fine little piece of ass wrapped around his dumbfuck finger. He ain't shit, man. Somebody oughta show him his place."

Someone laughs—Miguel, I think. "And you think it gonna be you, ey, *esé*?" Another laugh—it's Miguel. "You tell me when you teach him this lesson. I will sell tickets."

"Aw, fuck you, Miggy. He ain't so tough. Catch him

just right, he'll go down like anyone else. Then maybe I'll show that pretty little redhead of his what a real man is like."

Miguel spits. "*Estupido gringo*. He kill you. You stay away from him, and very much stay away from his *linda pelirroja*."

"Yeah, well, I didn't ask you, did I, shithead?" He follows this with a muttered slur.

Miguel sighs, disgusted, muttering imprecations in Spanish, and the sound of their footsteps recede in separate directions.

The unease in my gut grows into a knot of anxiety.

I think Panzer is going to be spending time at the salon from now on.

14

Noelle

BEAR HAS BEEN DISTRACTED THE LAST FEW DAYS. When I ask him about it, he shrugs it off, saying it's nothing. Despite this continual brush-off of my concerns, he's taken to insisting Panzer go to work with me.

Fortunately, the salon has a big office where he can sleep out of the way. Otherwise, I'd be worried he'd scare my clients. As it is, Kelly, the owner, isn't hot on the new arrangement, not being a dog person.

But when I again ask Bear what's going on, he just shrugs, shakes his head, and refuses to answer.

I suspect it's something to do with Duane.

And, honestly, I'm glad to have my big, furry friend—there's construction happening in the lot where we all usually park, meaning we now have to park down the street in a narrow, dingy alley; the usual lot is being turned into a parking garage, which is going to be nice when it's done but means several months of parking in a seedy, poorly lit alley. With summer in full swing, it's still light out even on the nights I work late, but I don't like the alley, and I don't like walking there alone at night. With Panzer at my side, however, I feel perfectly safe.

Two weeks pass like this—Bear broody and closed off and worried, me taking Panzer to work. I figure I'll give Bear another week to sort his issue out, and then I'm calling a sit-down. I want my sweet, cuddly, smiling Bear back. I don't like this brooding, terse version very much.

Maybe it's time to move things to the next level. I've been thinking about it. It's been good for me to have this time to get used to my own renewed sex drive. I want him all the time, but I don't want sex to be the only thing connecting us. We talk a lot, and he's been sharing a new dream he has—he wants to help Felix build houses. He's worried about Riley's reaction, of course, but the shifts he's spent over the last few weeks on Felix's crew have given him the builder bug. He enjoys creating, he's discovering.

I've been encouraging him to pursue this; not that demo isn't a worthy endeavor, but Bear has so much more to offer the world than merely destroying things just because he's so big and powerful. He's starting to see this in himself, finally. He's starting to reach for more, to believe in himself, to look for more of life beyond the narrow scope of what he's known up till now.

I'm immensely proud of him.

Yes, I decide, as Panzer and I reach the alley lot where I'm parked, it's time to let myself fully invest in Bear, and in our relationship. I've been afraid, I'm realizing. Holding back.

I love him, but I'm afraid to let myself love him fully. I'm afraid of being let down. Having my heart broken again.

Even though I know, mentally, that Bear would never betray me, not in a thousand years, not for anything, my heart still clings to the fear of brokenness my ex-husband's betrayal seeded in me.

Panzer growls, breaking my train of thought.

I stop a few feet from my car and look around: the rear of the Main Street buildings are on my left, an unbroken line of two-story structures fused together stretching from intersection to intersection, with the backs of the First Street businesses on my right. First Street runs parallel to Main, with the alley sandwiched between them. The First Street businesses are more separated than the ones on Main, broken up by employee and public parking lots and businesses with their own dedicated parking areas.

The lot my car is in is tiny, wedged between a bank on one side and a three-story office building on the other, housing lawyers, accountants, and financial planners. Both the bank and the office building feature rear entrances and a few alley-side parking slots. Dumpsters, piles of pallets, and the discarded odds and ends of the various businesses line the backs of the buildings on both sides, and despite the dying golden light of dusk on Main Street, back here, it's dim, shadowy, and cool.

My skin crawls as Panzer growls, pressing his big, solid body against my thigh—his growl vibrates against me.

"I know, buddy," I mutter. "I don't like it here either." I reach my car and blip the locks, open the rear driver's side door for Panzer. "Komm rein," I command, and he leaps up into the car.

I close the door after him and grab the handle of my door, but my phone rings, so I hesitate, digging the device out of my purse and answering it, hand still on the door. "Hello?"

Panzer starts barking wildly, paws scrabbling on the window.

"No-No," comes Mom's voice. "Hi, baby. What're you up to?"

Puzzled and worried at Panzer's uncharacteristic behavior, I wedge the phone between ear and shoulder. "Hang on, Mom. One sec. Panzer is going nuts."

I reach for the handle of the rear door, intending to open it and calm him down.

That's as far as I get.

A cold, clammy, viciously strong hand claps around my mouth, cutting off my scream. I'm yanked backward, off balance. nasty, hot, sour, alcohol-stained breath huffs on my face. "Finally got you away from that fuckin' dog and that big fat stupid fuckin' oaf," an icy, evil, rage-filled voice grates in my ear. "Time to teach your snotty, uppity little ass a nice long lesson in *respect*."

Duane.

Panic smashes through me—I struggle and kick, screaming into the gritty, cold, strong hand clamped down on my mouth and jaw. I'm thrown to the ground, the back of my head cracking against the concrete; stars of white light burst behind my eyes, dizziness washing over me.

"Now, now, none of that." A wicked slap rocks my head to the side, pain searing through my cheek. "That was a warning. Don't wanna have to ruin this pretty little face." Something sharp and cold trails down my cheek.

"Bear…" I whimper. "Don't. Please. Don't."

Panzer is going apeshit, barking and snarling, smashing into the window and door, rocking the whole car so its shocks squeal and protest at the mad force of his attempts to get to me.

"Think your big dumb boyfriend is gonna magically appear and save you?" The knife tip slides under my shirt at my belly and slices upward, cutting open my shirt and severing the front of my bra; he flicks the garments aside, exposing my chest; I squeeze my eyes shut, not breathing, not moving as the knife tip pricks the underside of my chin. "Got him taken care of. Permanently."

The knife moves away, and I thrash anew, eyes springing open and my blurred vision clearing—Duane is wearing a red bandana over his mouth and nose, a ballcap and sunglasses hiding the rest of his face, clad in dirty denim and a filthy T-shirt. The reek of booze on his breath turns my stomach.

He slaps me again and then presses the blade to my throat. "Hold the fuck still or I'll start cutting. I'll fuck your corpse if I have to."

I gag, gasp, and go still, wheezing and whimpering.

Panzer is still going nuts, and I hear the window crack. The car is only a few feet away. If I can get away for even a split second, I can yank the door open and let Panzer have Duane.

I have to time it just right.

I go still, watching with a revolting stomach and hammering heart as Duane knees astride me, pointing the knife at me while fumbling at his belt with the other hand.

He's drunk, and his hand is unsteady, working in my favor.

He looks down for a moment, struggling to get the prong of his belt out of the hole. I buck, dislodging him and making him wobble backward; I yank my feet back and kick at him with all my strength, screaming as my feet connect with his chest. He flies backward and lands on his back, gagging for breath.

I scramble backward on my backside, away from him and toward the car, toward Panzer.

"Oh no, you fuckin' don't, *bitch*!" Duane snarls, jack-knifing forward.

He stumbles to his feet, staggers unsteadily sideways, and then lunges for me as I scramble desperately backward, reaching for the door handle.

He stands over me, swiping at me with the short-bladed folding knife; the tip whistles past my face. I grab the handle, but his fist cracks across my face, smashing into my nose, loosing a freshet of hot, salty blood down my face.

With another scream, I lash out with my foot, catching him in the crotch. He doubles over and I kick him again, missing his crotch but getting his thigh, sending him to a knee as he wheezes, eyes bugging out in agony.

I yank open the rear door an inch; Panzer smashes it open with his shoulder as he leaps, clearing six feet in a single bound. His teeth latch onto Duan's knife hand, the blade clattering to the ground. The man screams, a gargling howl of pain.

Panzer snarls, shaking his head—a wet crack echoes through the alley: Duane's arm breaking in several places.

I tug open the driver's door and haul myself in by the

steering wheel. My purse is still slung around my torso, and I dig for my keys frantically as Panzer thrashes and savages the screaming, howling Duane. I hear another crack of breaking bone.

I get my keys free and shove the key into the ignition, starting the motor. "Panzer. Komm Rein." I can barely manage the words past the blood flowing out of my nose and filling my mouth, staining my chest and throat.

Panzer releases Duane and hops up into the car, panting. His brown muzzle drips red.

Duane is on the ground, moaning, rolling. His arm is mangled and unrecognizable, bone protruding in several places. I don't want to be responsible for his death, but I'm not upset that he'll never use that arm again.

A groan of agony escaping me. I reach into the back, yank the rear door closed, and then gun the engine out of the parking lot.

It never occurs to me to call 911, or anyone else. All I care about is Bear—Duane's words echo in my head: *Got him taken care of. Permanently.*

I race at reckless speeds toward Bear's apartment complex, knowing that's where he'd be at this time—showering and changing between work and the shelter.

Tires squealing as I fishtail into the lot and screech to a halt at an angle in front of his building, I shove open my door and race, panting and sobbing, for his unit.

I trip and lurch up the stairs, slicing my palms bloody as I cut them on the metal stairs. "*BEAR!*" I scream.

His door stands open. Bodies litter the floor, six or eight of them—my first thought is that they're all dead. But then I hear a chorus of ragged moans and realize they're all still alive.

Panting, hanging against the splintered doorframe, I survey the scene.

Bats, chains, knives, and brass knuckles lay discarded near their erstwhile wielders. I see one arm broken, bent at a horrible angle, white shards protruding from ragged flesh. A jaw is dislocated, hanging loose. A leg is bent horribly inward at the knee. One man rolls to his side, vomiting—I see teeth amid the puddle of bile and blood.

Nauseated at the gory scene, I turn away.

A trail of bloody dots leads away from the apartment. I follow the dots down the stairs, Panzer at my heels, whimpering.

"I know, boy," I whisper. "We'll find him. He's okay. he has to be."

The trail of blood leads part of the way across the parking lot, abruptly stopping near a pair of tire marks.

Out of options and desperate to find Bear before he does anything else, I fumble my phone out of my purse and call Riley—I've spoken to him a few times to coordinate picking up and dropping off Bear.

He answers after two rings. "Noelle, hey. What's up?"

I'm hyperventilating, my broken nose making me slur and spit blood. "Bear—attacked. Apartment. Help. Please help."

"I'm not even five minutes away. Hang tight. be right there."

Hyperventilating, choking on blood, all I can think about is Bear—where he is, how badly he's hurt. I pace back and forth and in circles until I see Riley's silver pickup fishtail around the corner and barrel toward me, skidding to a halt.

Panzer puts himself in front of me, growling viciously, until he sees it's Riley.

"Ruhig," I mumble; *ROO-ihg*: quiet. "Platz." Panzer goes silent and lowers himself to his belly onto my feet.

"Holy fucking shit," Riley shouts as he leaps from his truck. "Noelle, what the *fuck*? You said *Bear* got attacked!"

I point at the apartment. "In—in there."

"Yeah, but what in the fuck happened to *you*?" He whips off his shirt, approaching me warily, since Panzer, even lying down, is rumbling softly, daring Riley to make one wrong move.

"Duane," I mumble.

The adrenaline leaches out of me all at once, and I collapse to my butt. Heedless of the fact that my chest is exposed, ignoring the blood still dribbling from my nose, I cling to Panzer's neck, sobbing.

"Hey, hey." Riley crouches in front of me. "Let's get this on you, yeah?"

I nod. He gently slides the shirt over my head, and I shrug it on over the ruins of my cut-open top.

"Be right back," Riley says, jogging up the steps toward Bear's unit. A peek in, and he trots back down to me. "Bear's not there."

I shake my head, pulling my arms in and wriggling out of the cut-open shirt and bra, pull the remains out, and re-insert my arms into Riley's oversized T-shirt. I use the scraps of my shirt to pinch my nose and sop up some of the blood. "I dunno where he went. I guarantee you he knows it was Duane. Probably looking for me." I grab Riley's wrist. "We *have* to find him before he does anything, Riley. He *can't* go back to jail."

Riley helps me to my feet. "Come on. We'll find him."

I command Panzer into the back seat of the truck and let Riley help me up into the passenger seat.

Riley turns toward me. "Can I set your nose? It'll help."

"Okay," I mumble, dazed and panicking.

"Just make sure Panzer doesn't, you know, eat my face. It, um…it'll hurt at first and then feel better."

"Panzer—bleib," I command, as Riley puts his hands on either side of my face, earning a warning rumble from Panzer. "Ruhig."

"Ready? On three. Deep breath. One—two—*three*." On three, he jerks his hands backward, away from my face.

A bright bolt of white light and lancing agony blast through me, and I scream. Moments later, though, the throbbing pain subsides to a dull ache.

"Let's check your house and your work first," Riley says.

I nod.

He guns the engine, driving recklessly fast. He taps a speed dial entry on his phone, putting it on speaker.

It rings once, and then I hear Felix's voice. "Riley, what's—"

Riley cuts in. "Noelle got attacked by Duane, and Bear got jumped in his apartment. He fuckin' wrecked the shit out of them—fuckin' eight of 'em, man. They're alive but royally fucked up. Now he's missing. I've got Noelle, and she's in bad shape too, but we gotta find Bear before he does something he can't come back from."

"*Fuck* me," Felix growls. "I'll check the salon, you check her house."

"Got it. Call you back." Riley ends the call and keeps the phone clutched in his hand as he slams his brakes to haul us around the corner onto First and then into the alley behind the salon. A quick glance tells us that he's not here—the salon is quiet and dark, no sign of Bear. Riley peels out and whips past the front on Main, just to be sure, and then re-dials his brother.

"Not here," he says after Felix's snapped greeting. "Now what?"

"He'll look for Duane," Felix guesses.

Riley looks at me. "What kinda shape is Duane in?"

I shake my head. "I...I don't know. Bad. Panzer got his arm. I called him off before he killed him."

"Shoulda let him," Riley mutters.

"No, she shouldn't have," Felix snaps back. "That's the *last* thing anyone needs. He needs to be brought to proper justice, not mauled to death by a dog."

"You haven't seen her," Riley snarls in response. He looks at me. "Did...did he...?"

I shake my head, pulling the scrap of shirt away, re-folding it, and pressing it to my nose, which isn't gushing anymore but still dribbling a little. "No. I fought him off until I could get Panzer."

"How'd he get past Panzer in the first place.?" Riley asks.

"*Rye*," Felix says, his voice whips sharp. "She can give a statement to the police. She doesn't need a goddamned interrogation. We need to find Bear. *Focus*. Where would Duane be?"

"He wouldn't go to a hospital," Riley says. "The man doesn't trust any institution. Probably home."

"Where does he live?" Felix asks.

"Fuck. I don't know. I've got files on everyone at the

yard." Riley's face clears, and he guns the engine. "Bear knows that's where the files are: the yard. Come on!"

A few minutes later, we're skidding to a halt in the gravel lot in front of Riley's and Felix's equipment yard—a U-shape of three long, low, steel-sided buildings with large bay doors, with a single smaller office as a dot in the opening of the U. The front door of the office hangs open, smashed inward.

Riley hops out, and I follow him—Panzer scrambles over the console and leaps out after me, ears picked and swiveling, head low, eyes roving, body pressed against my side.

Riley pauses at the door, whistling in awe. "Holy fuck, man. He didn't just kick this in, he smashed the whole fucking frame right out of the goddamned wall."

I see what he means—the frame has come away from the wall itself, the whole door frame hanging askew, daylight streaming between frame and wall, the door dangling open at an angle. The office is tiny, a single room containing three desks in a U, a row of filing cabinets along one wall, computer monitors on the desks, a large map of Three Rivers and the surrounding area on one wall, and pins of varying colors in different locations. A dark doorway reveals a bathroom; the office smells of old coffee.

One of the filing cabinets is open; the drawers yanked open despite the locks keeping them closed, the metal warped and ripped with the force of Bear's pull. Files are scattered everywhere, papers strewn in piles.

A single manila folder lays open on the nearest desk, with Duane's mug shot, a separate, newer headshot, and a printed sheet of details, including his record, biological data, and last known address. A large, bloody fingerprint smears the last known address.

"Got the address," Riley says, still on the line with his brother; he rattles off the address. "Meet you there."

"Riley, if you get there first, you gotta be smart. You've got a record, too. Don't do anything stupid."

"And don't you go calling the goddamn cops, Dudley Do-Right," Riley snaps. "Not till we know what's happening."

"Fine," Felix answers. "Just…be smart. Please."

Riley ends the call with a savage snarl and a stab of his index finger, and then we're back in the truck and racing across town to Duane's address.

We arrive at Cooper's Hollow, a trailer park on the far southeastern edge of town; it's rundown, overcrowded, and dangerous. A lot of residents routinely call for it to be leveled and rebuilt, but the occupants of the trailer park up a right about that, stopping any action from being taken.

The lots are narrow, and most of them are weedy and scraggly, others bare dirt, the trailers ancient single-wides with sagging porches and bowed roofs and crumbling cinderblock stairs. Junk is strewn everywhere, and the streetlamps, what few of them there are, flicker and strobe, casting jumping orange light on the buckling blacktop road that winds around the trailer park.

"Should be just ahead," Riley mutters, his brights on to illuminate the street numbers on each trailer; night has fallen in the time since my attack, shadows lengthening as sunset fades.

A shotgun blast rings out ahead.

"Fuck," Riley growls. "Looks like we found him."

Another shotgun blast rings out, and I scream. "Bear!"

Riley's truck skids to a halt, just in time for a third concussing blast to shudder through the still, warm night. The trailer is long and low, once white and now a dirty off-white, with cinderblock stairs, a leaning fragment of black metal railing, and filthy, grime-smeared windows. A gray, twenty-year-old sedan is parked in front, the lights on, the engine running and the driver's side door open, the chime dinging repeatedly. Light sprays upward in narrow, pin-thin streams from the ceiling of the trailer; a fourth blast creates more holes.

Felix's truck halts an angle near Riley's, and Felix jumps out. Riley hops out too, glancing back at me. "Stay in the truck."

"Bear," I whimper as yet another blast goes off, more holes appearing in the ceiling.

A split second later, a shotgun sails through the front window of the trailer and lands in the dirt at Riley's feet.

Despite Riley's instruction, I get out, but I shut the door to keep Panzer inside. "Do something!" I shout.

A bellowing roar shudders the trailer—Bear. Pain. Anger. Animal rage.

Riley and Felix trade looks. "I'm not going in there. My money's on Bear," Felix says.

"He'll kill him!" I scream. "Stop him!"

Both men stare at me. "How the hell are we supposed to stop him?" Riley asks.

A crash shakes the trailer.

Another.

A man howls—Duane. The already shattered window splinters out of the walls as an entire Lay-Z-Boy recliner flies through it, bowing the wall outward and causing the whole structure to lean precariously.

"Holy shit," Riley mutters. "Glad I'm not Duane."

A pistol goes sailing through the window to land in the dirt—it's bloody.

Bear's roar of rage echoes again, and Duane himself staggers past the opening where the window used to be. Bear follows, reaching for him.

"Bear!" Riley shouts. "Stop!"

No answer.

The door of the trailer, already hanging askew, smashes backward, hits the exterior wall, and falls to the ground. Duane flies backward through the open doorway, slams hard into the dirt with an agonized screech, and rolls another six feet, flopping to a stop nearly a dozen feet from the door.

Bear appears in the doorway. Hulking, chest heaving, his face a rictus of murderous rage, his once white T-shirt is tattered and crimson-stained. A knife handle protrudes from his back near his shoulder. His nose is broken, sluicing blood down his front, and his torso leaks blood from several wounds to his chest and stomach.

He stomps out of the trailer and leaps off the porch, striding with grim intent toward Duane's prone, sobbing, pleading form.

Riley's arm circles my waist, hauling me back. "You can't get near him in that state, Noelle."

"LET ME GO!" I screech, thrashing. "*BEAR!*"

I fight against Riley's hold as violently as I did to get away from Duane, if not harder.

Felix rushes at Bear, grabbing at his arm—Bear doesn't seem to see him or recognize him. He brushes Felix off as if he's no more than a buzzing fly, shoving him absently aside; Felix, all six-two and two hundred pounds of him, goes sprawling in the dirt.

Bear reaches Duane, fists his shirt one-handed, hauls him to his feet, shakes him once like a rag doll, and then takes two spinning steps like an Olympic hammer thrower and hurls Duane six or eight feet into the side of the trailer. Siding cracks, the frame splinters, and the roof caves in where the structure has been compromised. Duane lands heavily in the dirt at the base of the trailer, sprawled awkwardly, limp.

Desperate to stop Bear before he kills Duane, I bite into Riley's arm. He lets me go in shock, and I sprint across the dirt lot.

I grab Bear's arm and haul on him. "Bear! *STOP!* It's me. Stop. Stop. Please stop. Please stop."

He registers my presence, at least, his eyes flicking to me, recognition fluttering in his gaze. "Move." His voice is ragged and raw, guttural and grating.

He pushes past me, and his titanic strength and size brush him past me as if I were no more than a piece of paper. Undeterred, I run ahead and circle in front of him, putting myself between him and Duane.

"Stop, Bear. *Stop.* No more." I hold out my arms as if to create a barrier.

His eyes clear a tiny bit, flicking over my bloody face, and Riley's oversized T-shirt. "He hurt you."

"I'm fine, Bear," I say, inching closer. "I'm okay. Let it be over. Please."

His gaze goes past me to Duane, who, while broken and battered, is still alive, watching in abject terror. "He raped you."

I shuffle closer, inches from him now. "No. No, he

didn't. I promise you. I fought him off. Panzer got him. He didn't. I'm okay."

A shake of his head. "He touched you." His voice is flat with terrible finality. "He dies."

Another long stride carries him closer to Duane, who tries to crawl away.

With no other options left, I'm beyond desperation now. I sprint around in front of him once more and leap onto Bear, latching my legs around his waist and my arms around his neck. I bury my face in his throat, heedless of our blood smearing on each other, mingling

"Please." I grab his beard and jerk his face to mine, hard. "Bear. Listen to me. Look at me, baby. Look at me. Please."

It's the "baby" that gets him. He stands still, eyes moving almost robotically down to mine. His hands are fisted at his sides, chest heaving; my weight clinging to him is nothing whatsoever. "Noelle?" That soft, quiet growl, finally, his eyes clearing of the haze of rage.

"There you are," I whisper. I cling to him all the harder. "Take me home. Please, Bear. Please. I want to go home. Let it go."

His hands uncurl from the fists and lift to my butt, supporting my weight. "You're hurt."

I shake my head. "It's nothing. Broken nose. Bumped head. I'm fine. I promise you I'm okay. He didn't touch me like that."

"He was going to."

"Yes," I admit. "He was. I fought him off, and Panzer stopped him."

"Panzer." He blinks, looking around. "Where is he?"

"Riley's truck."

Sirens howl in the distance, approaching us. At the sound, Bear tenses. Looks at Duane. At me. "Should've let the dog have him."

"I couldn't. I had to get to you. I...I didn't want his death on anyone's conscience. Not mine, not yours, not Panzer's." I shake my head. "I know dogs don't have consciences, but still."

Felix and Riley approach us.

"Bear?" Felix meets Bear's gaze, his voice low, calm, and hesitant. "I know Sheriff Mannix personally, okay? He's my friend. I called him and explained the situation. It's going to be okay. Just stay calm and follow my lead, okay?"

Bear nods and looks at me. "Give me a second."

I hesitate to let him go. "Leave him alone."

"Won't touch him," he promises.

I slide down his front to my feet, and Bear crouches in front of Duane, who cringes away, whimpering pathetically, trying to scrabble under the ruined trailer.

"Thank her for your life." It's a command.

"Th-th-thank you," Duane says, past missing teeth and split lips.

"Don't give a fuck what the police do with you," Bear growls. "No one in Three Rivers ever sees you again. Understand?"

Duane nods, curling into a smaller ball. "Understand."

Bear rises to his feet and comes back to me. His face is troubled, now, sorrowful. "They were a distraction. So he could get to you."

"I know," I say.

"I wasn't there."

"Bear." I lean into him. "You can't be with me every moment of every day. He'd have found a way somehow."

The sirens are close, now—arriving. Two squad cars and two ambulances skid to a halt behind Riley's and Felix's trucks, lights flashing, sirens going silent.

Four officers approach Bear, hands on their weapons. Bear takes a deep breath and looks at me. "I'm sorry."

He steps toward the officers, wrists together in front of him, his body language resigned.

The officers, however, move past him. Two of them grab Duane by the arms and haul him to his feet. "Duane Murphy, you're under arrest for assault and battery, attempted rape, conspiracy to cause bodily harm…" the list goes on, followed by his Miranda rights, as they drag him to the ambulance, where he's handcuffed to a gurney and loaded inside. The ambulance departs, leaving behind the second ambulance, the other two officers, and a very puzzled Bear.

15

Bear

PANIC BOILS INSIDE ME AS THE COPS SPLIT WAYS— two of them follow the ambulance away, and the other two approach me.

I wait for them to arrest me, desperately resisting the urge to run, to fight for my freedom.

I can't go back.

I can't.

They stop in front of me, one of them pulling out a notebook and pen while the other watches with his hands hooked into the front of his bulletproof vest.

"Need your statement," the officer with the notepad says.

He's a few years older than me, with close-cropped blond hair, a short, neat beard, and piercing brown eyes. He's muscular, fit, and intensely good-looking, his gaze hard but not unkind as he takes in my size and bloody appearance. The nametag on his left breast says "Mannix" and a gold star emblem indicates that this is the county sheriff himself, Cole Mannix.

"Statement?" I say. "I...I'm not being arrested?"

The officers exchange glances, and Sheriff Mannix shakes his head. "Seems to me like you got jumped, kidnapped, and fought your way free. Self-defense." His eyes go to Noelle, anger filling his gaze at the sight of the blood on her face. "That piece of shit should never have been allowed out. It was only a matter of time before he did it again."

Riley steps forward. "Wait, *again*? His sheet only has petty theft, grand larceny, and grand theft auto."

Mannix shakes his head. "Duane Murphy is an alias. He's wanted in Arizona under the name Philip Bradshaw for several counts of rape."

"How can he have gone to jail under an alias?" Riley asks.

Mannix shakes his head, shrugging. "Somebody fucked up big time, somewhere. The Duane Murphy alias is paper fuckin' thin. A blind kid could see through it. Not sure how he got through the system at all under it, let alone through a fucking work release. Philip Bradshaw is a nasty, nasty motherfucker. Done time in three states for sexual crimes. Arizona is only the latest."

Riley falls to a crouch, head in his hands. "Jesus *fucking* Christ. How did I miss this?" He looks at Noelle with agonized eyes. "I'm so fucking sorry, Noelle."

"It's not your fault," Noelle tells him, her voice quiet and calm. "The legal system failed, not you."

"I knew he was creepy. I just...I figured I'd keep an eye on him. If I'd known—" Riley trails off, shooting to his feet and kicking the dirt. "*Mother*fucker. I *fed* that man. Gave him a job. He was in my fucking *house* with my fucking *MOTHER.*"

Mannix claps his hand on Riley's shoulder. "Miss Harper is right, Riley. You couldn't have known. He's going to prison for a long, long time. Won't ever get out if I have anything to do with it."

The officer turns back to me, looking at his notebook. "So, according to my notes, here, you were in your home getting ready to work at Three Rivers Animal Rescue when eight men armed with bats, knives, chains, and brass knuckles broke in and began assaulting you. You disarmed them, but they incapacitated you and brought you here, where you managed to escape and fight your way free. Is that correct?"

It's a leading statement—it's very obviously not what happened at all, with major holes in the story, but Felix has somehow managed to massage things in my favor; how I don't know, but relief floods through me as it starts to sink in that I'm not going back to prison.

I frown, glancing at Riley and Felix—Felix nods subtly. "Yes, sir. That's correct."

The officer flips the notebook closed. "I think I have what I need for now." He turns to survey the trailer. "Fuck me, man. Glad I'm not that poor bastard." He glances at Noelle. "Good thing you were here to stop him. Had it gone any further, there wouldn't be much I could do."

She takes my hand, threading her fingers into mine. "Thank you, Sheriff Mannix. Thank you so much."

The officer looks her over. "You need to get checked out."

She shakes her head. "I'm fine. He needs attention, not me."

I grumble, annoyed. "I'm fine."

Noelle looks up at me, exasperated. "You have a knife sticking out of your back, honey."

I roll my shoulder, only then realizing she's right. I glance over my shoulder, wincing at the twinge of pain. "Oh. Forgot about that."

Sheriff Mannix shakes his head. "How the hell do you forget about a whole-ass knife?"

I shrug—a mistake. It does hurt now. A few other injuries begin to make themselves known now that I'm no longer disassociating, as the prison therapist called it.

A medic approaches me, a tiny waif of a woman with black hair in a tight braid against her head. "Can I take a look at you, sir?"

Noelle answers for me. "Yes, you can." She guides me across the yard to the back of the ambulance and nudges me, an indication that I should sit. "Let her help you, honey."

The medic climbs into the back of the vehicle and crouches behind me, examining the knife. "Short blade, in the muscle. I can take it out. Ready?" She touches blue-gloved fingers to my back when I nod. "Here we go."

She slides the blade free and hands it to the waiting officer—the other one is bagging and tagging the other weapons I took away from Duane.

"You'll need sutures," she says. "You should let us take you to the ER—plastics can do a better job than I can here."

I shake my head. "Nah. Just sew it up."

She clears her throat. "I, um, I actually ran out of topical numbing agent on my last run."

"Don't care. No hospital. Just stitch me up, doc."

"Bear," Noelle says, "Let's just go in."

I shake my head. "No. Don't like hospitals. Nothing is life-threatening. I should know."

The medic sighs. "Fine. I'll have to remove the shirt, though."

I rumble a laugh. "Not much left to remove."

"No kidding," she mutters, slicing it off.

A few moments later, I feel the pinch of the needle as she sutures the wound.

Noelle watches me as the medic works. "That doesn't hurt?"

I lift a hand in a version of a shrug since my shoulder is being sewn up. "A bit. Done it to myself a few times. She's got a nice light touch."

The medic pauses, looking at me over my shoulder. "You've sutured yourself?"

"Yep. Couple times. Medics wouldn't come to the hood where I was, and no way I was going to no damn hospital."

"Oh." She resumes suturing, ties it off, and snips. "Okay. All set. Anything else I need to look at?

Noelle again answers for me, correctly guessing I'd try to get out of further treatment—I just want to go home, and my stupid little owies will heal on their own soon enough.

The medic brings her bag around and sits on the step-bumper next to me. "Face me, please." I turn to face her, and she hisses. "Holy hell. What *happened* to you?"

She shakes her head as she assesses the extent of my injuries—a long shallow cut to my ribcage, a bruised or cracked rib on my left side, and several places where Duane's birdshot didn't quite miss, not to mention extensive bruising.

"You don't fight off eight armed dickheads and not get hurt a little," I say by way of explanation. "Not too bad, though. Been through way worse."

"No kidding," The medic says. "I see the evidence." She looks up at me. "You've been through some shit, huh?"

I shrug. "A bit." I look at Noelle, my heart filling with gratitude and awe—she fought like hell to save herself, but her first thought was for me. "Better now. Got an angel looking out for me. A reason to live a good life."

The medic sees my look, and her face melts into a sappy grin. "Awww, my god—if that's not the sweetest thing I've ever heard."

After more stitches, she pokes and prods. "Well, you've got a banged-up rib, but I don't think it's broken. You'll be sore for a while, though. You really should get it X-rayed, but since I assume you won't, just keep an eye on it. If it gets hard to breathe or anything, you *have* to go in. A cracked rib can break all the way, splinter, and puncture your lung. To be clear, that's a *very* bad thing. It's not something you can just shrug off."

I tap my ribcage on the right side, where I have a scar. "I'm aware."

Noelle frowns at me. "You've had a punctured lung?"

I nod, shrugging. "Sure. Wasn't fun, but I survived. Thus my dislike of hospitals."

The medic snorts. "A punctured lung wasn't fun. Jesus. Who are you, man? The Incredible Hulk?" She pats my arm very gently. "You're good to go, big fella. Try to go easy on that rib, okay?"

I nod. "Thanks, doc."

She smiles up at me. "I'm a medic, not a doctor, but you're welcome." She looks at Noelle. "Get him home and take care of him."

Noelle nods. "I will."

I look at Noelle, noticing a smear of blood at the back

of her head; I meet the medic's eyes. "Can you look at her, too, please? She's bleeding from the head."

"Sure, no problem." She moves around behind Noelle, putting on a fresh pair of gloves and gently probing the injury with professional fingers. "This is okay—just a small contusion, no longer bleeding." She moves around to look at Noelle. "Any dizziness, blurred vision, or nausea?"

Noelle shakes her head. "I was dizzy and blurry when it happened, but not anymore. Cracked my head on the ground when he threw me down."

After applying antiseptic ointment, the medic takes Noelle's hand. "Do you need a rape kit?"

Noelle shakes her head. "No, he didn't get that far, thankfully." She looks at Panzer, watching us from the back of Riley's truck. "Thanks to him."

I growl. "You fought him off, like the badass you are."

She smiles at me, soft and sweet. "It's over now. I'm okay."

After checking her out, the medic strips off her gloves and announces that we're both good to go.

The officers, having finished their assessment of the scene, clap me on the shoulder and shake my hand. "We're adding gun charges," Sheriff Mannix says. "None of the guns here are legal. We've got him on a laundry list of shit. He's going away for a good, long time." He looks at Noelle. "We'll need your statement regarding the attempted rape, but that can wait."

She shakes her head. "No, I'd rather get it out of the way now. I just want to go home and get cleaned up."

"Okay." He pulls out his notepad and pen. "Can you tell me what happened? I know it's hard, but I need as much detail as you can provide."

She squeezes my hand, her eyes going vacant as she recalls. "I work at Lux Locks Salon on Main Street."

Mannix nods. "My sister goes there. Loves it."

She grins. "Oh! Callie Mannix. I know her."

He smiles, nodding. "That's her. " The grin fades back to the professionally blank face. "So, you left work…"

"That garage is going up, so we've had to park next to the First Federal there on First. I cut through the alley." She points at Panzer. "Bear has been insisting I take him to work. He was growling as I approached the car, but I guess I didn't think much of it. I should have—he never growls without a reason. I guess I just figured it's a creepy alley, and he saw or sensed something he didn't like." She shakes her head. "Anyway. I got Panzer into my car, and I was about to get in when Mom called—Mom! Oh my god!" She claps a hand over her mouth. "I was on the phone with her when he grabbed me. I must've dropped the phone—she probably heard everything! She must be worried sick!"

"On it," The other officer says. "I'll send someone over to explain." He paces away and mutters into his radio.

"So, he grabbed you?" Mannix prompts. "How?"

"From behind. His hand was over my mouth." She demonstrates, hand across her lips. "He dragged me backward a few feet and threw me to the ground. I fought and kicked, but he slapped me. Before I could do anything else, he put a knife to my face, and then he cut my shirt and bra off." His voice wavers. She sucks in a deep breath. Squares her shoulders, lets it out, and keeps going, voice steady once more. "I…he slapped me again and put the knife to my throat, warned me to hold still or he'd kill me. Said he…" She trails off, voice shaking. "He said he'd fuck my corpse if he had to."

I growl, that red haze washing over my vision again.

She turns into me, palming my face. "Hey, no, no, no. Stop. I'm *okay*. It's just hard to recall. I'm okay. I'll be okay." She lifts on her toes, pulling my face down to hers. "Breathe. Don't go back there."

I touch my forehead to hers, following along with her as she takes long, slow breaths in, holds them, and lets them out. "Okay."

She rubs my lips with her thumb. "Okay." She turns back to Mannix. "I…I waited until he was unbuckling his belt. He was drunk. Clumsy. I saw a chance when he got distracted by his belt and kicked him. Fought my way over to the car and opened it so Panzer could get out. I…" She pauses to breathe. "I was worried about Bear. Duane told me he had you taken care of permanently. I was worried you were going to kill someone. I couldn't stand it if you went back to prison, so I…I called Panzer off and drove to your complex. I saw the bodies, and I…" she shudders. "I thought they were all dead at first. I called Riley, and we figured out that you came here—the yard, the files."

Sheriff Mannix arches an eyebrow at her. "You were worried not that he was in danger but that he'd kill someone?"

She shrugs, gesturing vaguely at the crumbling, collapsing single-wide and the Lay-Z-Boy recliner on its side near the rust-bucket early-aughts sedan I stole from the thugs who jumped me and drove here. "Well…yeah."

Mannix closes his notebook. "I've got what I need, I think." He glances at Panzer and then at Noelle. "Probably for the best you called off the dog, you know. Death by guard dog cases can get seriously complicated legally, even in cases of clear-cut self-defense."

Noelle exhales, rubbing her face with her hands,

smearing and flaking the drying blood, then looks at her hands with a wince. "I just…I remember thinking I don't want someone's death on my conscience, even if it may have been well-deserved."

"Can't unring that bell," I say. "Damned hard thing to forget."

"Facts," agrees Sheriff Mannix, his own gaze distant. He shakes his head. "Well, like I said, I've got what I need for now. I know how to find you both if I have any more questions, but I doubt I will." He claps me on the shoulder as he passes me on his way to his squad car, nudging me a few steps away from Noelle. "Get her home and run her a bath. It's gonna hit her like a fuckin' Mack truck any minute, and she'll need somewhere safe and familiar to process and decompress."

I nod. "Yes sir, thank you, sir."

He surveys the damage I did and grins at me, shaking his head with a huffing laugh. "Never seen anything like it, man. You're a beast." He pats my shoulder again. "Good job keeping your shit on a leash. You obviously could've ripped his arm off and beaten him to death with it."

"The hardest thing I've ever done," I admit, my voice pitched so only he can hear me. "Wanted to…" I shake my head, growling a sigh. "Wanted to do really bad things to him."

"But you didn't." Mannix holds my gaze, nodding. "That's what counts."

"Thank you, Sheriff Mannix. You ever need anything…"

Mannix grins. "You know, me and a few other guys get together to play football couple'a times a month.

You're welcome to join. Officially, it's touch, but every once in a while, someone gets a proper tackle in. By accident, of course." He winks. "All friendly fun. Crack a few beers, toss around the ball, shoot the shit. Felix and Riley tag in once in a while. You should too."

Play football with a cop?

What a weird world I've found myself in.

I nod at him. "Sounds like fun. I'll give it a try sometime."

Mannix's radio crackles and the dispatcher rattles off a code and a car request. Mannix keys his radio and responds. "Gotta go. I'll have the Crowe boys bring you to the next meetup." He jogs to his squad car, and they peel out, leaving Riley, Felix, Noelle, and me alone in the night.

Noelle comes up to me and all but collapses against my chest, her hands together under her cheek. "I wanna go home."

"Me too." I bend and scoop her up into my arms.

She rests her head on my shoulder. "I can walk," she mumbles, making no effort to get down.

"Course you can. Not gonna, though," I answer, carrying her to Riley's truck.

Riley opens the rear passenger door and I settle her on the seat; Panzer immediately pounces, resting his bulky body on her thighs and frantically licking her face and throat.

She holds onto his head, eyes closed, and lets him lick. "Thank *God* for you, boy," she whispers.

"Her house," I growl at Riley as I shut her door and open the front passenger one. "Now, if not sooner."

"Roger that, pal," Riley says.

I pause, shooting Felix a look. "Thank you for what you did."

He nods. "Glad we could have the best possible outcome from a shitty situation."

We make the twenty-minute drive in fifteen. Riley parks in the driveway of Noelle's house, glancing at me. "Not the time for the full discussion, obviously, but you should know I talked to Felix. About you switching crews, I mean."

My gut flips. "Riley—"

He grabs my shoulder and squeezes. "We'll figure something out, brother, alright? I hate to lose you, obviously. My productivity will tank without you. But you deserve it. You've worked damned hard to turn your life around."

My eyes burn—not so much at the praise as at the word "brother."

I can only nod, throat tight. "Appreciate you... brother."

Riley clears his throat, jerking his head backward at Noelle, who has nodded off, her head resting on Panzer's side, whose head rests in turn on her thighs. "Get your woman inside. Take care of her. She says she's okay, but she went through a traumatic situation. She's telling herself it could've been way worse, which is true, but that don't negate what she did experience."

"Speaking from experience?" I ask.

He nods. "Long time ago, yeah." His expression is distant and troubled. "Something similar happened to someone I cared about." A sigh. "With a...slightly less favorable outcome for everybody involved." He waves a hand. "Forget it. Get outta here. I've got a bottle of Jack at home calling my name."

"Riley," I start.

He shakes his head. "Don't start, man."

I can only nod—it's not my place. "See ya tomorrow."

"Nope. You're taking the day off. So's Noelle."

"Alright. Thanks for everything. For showing up for her. For me."

He nods as I gather Noelle in my arm; Panzer, against training, hops down without being commanded, whining as I move Noelle away from him.

"I've got her, boy," I murmur to him. "C'mon."

Despite everything that happened, Noelle's purse somehow remained slung around her torso the whole time, even after her shirt was cut away. She's partially awake, groggy and mumbling incoherently as I set her on her feet long enough to rustle her keys out of her blood-stained purse and unlock the door. That done, I pick her up again and carry her inside. Into her room, lay her on her bed over the covers and toss a throw blanket over her.

"Bear," she mumbles.

I cup her cheek, standing beside her. "I'm here."

"Need you."

"Not goin' anywhere. Just locking the door. Right back."

Panzer slumps to the floor on her side of the bed, the side closest to the door, putting himself between her and the door. Dozing back off, she rubs her nose and then her hand tumbles to hang off the side of the bed. Panzer licks her fingers a few times and then rests his chin on his paws, ears alert, eyes watchful.

I crouch beside him, hugging him. "Good boy, Panzer." I ruffle his ears. "Good boy."

He licks my chin, cold wet nose nuzzling my cheek.

I check every room, every closet, even the small, low-ceilinged, unfinished basement. Lock the side door we came in.

As I'm heading for the bedroom again, a headlight swings around to shine in through the front bay window. I peek out—Noelle's mother and father.

I go out onto the front porch. "She's asleep."

Her mother stops at the bottom of the steps. "I need to see my daughter, Bear."

I cross my arms. "I'm sorry, ma'am. She's been through a lot. Not waking her up for anything."

Her father pushes past his wife to stand on the step below me, glaring up at me. "Move aside, son. She's our daughter."

I cross my arms. "No. Sorry. She needs to rest. Second she's awake and up for it, she'll call you."

Nina's lip trembles. "Our baby girl was…she was attacked, Bear. I need to see that she's okay."

"Promise you, she's physically fine. Broken nose, meanin' black eyes. Roughed up a little. Seeing her right now won't make you feel better." I force myself to soften—this is their daughter, even if my protective instincts are raging at me to destroy anyone who comes within fifty feet of her. "She needs rest. Needs to get cleaned up."

Nicholas sighs. "The second she wakes up…"

I nod. "I'll tell her you want to see her. I swear."

They trade glances, and then Nicholas nods. "Okay. I guess it's good she has you to take care of her."

They get back in their Forester and back out of the driveway. When they're gone, I go back inside, lock the front door, peel my dirty, blood-crusted jeans off, boots and socks, too, and climb into the bed next to Noelle.

She mumbles in her sleep, sensing my presence, and wriggles toward me. I bring her onto my chest and hold her close.

Despite my own exhaustion, I know I won't sleep any time soon.

C⌒⊙

I'm shaken from my fitful, restless quasi-sleep by Noelle thrashing and crying out.

"No! Please—don't. Don't! No!"

I let her thrash, even when her fists bludgeon my face and chest and her feet kick my shins. "Noelle," I say, voice low and soothing. "Wake up, Noelle. You're dreaming. You're safe. Wake up."

"No! Let me go!" She thrashes again, fist smacking my nose hard enough to re-break it.

"Noelle!" I say a little louder, shaking her gently. "Wake up. It's a dream. It's not real. You're safe."

"No! Bear!" She twists and thrashes again, clocking me in the temple. Jackknifing upright, her eyes sweep the room frantically. "Bear?"

I wrap my arms around her and pull her to my chest. "You're okay. You're okay. You're safe."

A sob wracks her body, and she slumps into me. "Bear," she whispers, her voice tiny and lost. "I was back there. On the ground in the alley, and he was….he was—"

I squeeze her, nuzzling my lips against her temple. "Safe now. I've got you."

She sighs, the fight and the tension ebbing out of her. "Fuck."

The curse is shocking coming from her—it's one of fear, anger, and frustration, a million emotions all mixed up together into a Gordian knot of trauma.

I dab my nose with my wrist, not wanting to bleed onto her or the bed. I pinch the bridge of my nose and reset it with a soft growl.

Noelle lifts up. "What? You're bleeding. What happened?"

"Nothing. I'm fine." I wriggle and wrinkle my nose, wiping my forearm under it, and then the heel of my palm, and then my bicep, until the blood starts to clot.

She sits up further. "Bear—did I do that?"

I tuck a strand of her coppery curls behind her ear. "You were having a nightmare. It's okay."

Her eyes water. "I hurt you."

I smile. Shake my head. "No, you didn't."

"I re-broke your nose," she protests.

"You have any idea how many times it's been broken? Don't give a shit, honey. All I care about is you."

She shudders, and the shudder becomes a shiver. "Cold all of a sudden."

I shift toward the edge of the bed. "I'll run you a bath."

"No!" She cries out, fear and desperation making her cling to my arm. "Don't leave me."

"Never," I promise.

I scoop her up and carry her into the bathroom, sitting on the edge of the tub with her on my lap, clinging to my neck, shivering and whimpering. Twist on the hot water and plug the drain. I sit there and hold her as the tub fills with steaming water. Once it's nearing full, I add cold water bit by bit until it's steaming hot but not scalding.

"Noelle, sweetheart," I whisper, the term of endearment emerging unbidden, rising from the depths of my love for her. "Let's get you in the bath, okay?"

She nods.

Doesn't move, doesn't let go of me. "Cold."

"Water's piping hot, okay?" I touch her face, turn it so she's looking at me—her eyes are tear-wet, not seeing me but that alley, most likely. "Gonna help you out of your clothes so we can get you clean, okay?"

She nods, straightening on my lap so I can peel Riley's now stiff-with-blood shirt off. A thin red line mars her throat where Duane's knife pressed; killing rage bubbles up inside me, but I squash it down viciously, lock it away in the dungeon of my soul. She doesn't need my rage anymore. She needs my touch, my love.

There's no sexual excitement in me at the sight of her bare chest—not in this moment. Nor as I help her out of her socks and sneakers, jeans and underwear. I move to help her into the tub, but she clings to me desperately, clawing at me to get closer.

"No!" she whimpers. "Need you. Please." The last word is hissed, shaking.

I strip off my underwear and then cradle her against my chest as I sink gingerly into the hot water with her. She hisses as the water rises around us, her body stiff and tense, muscles shaking, every fiber of her being trembling.

"Got you," I whisper. "You're safe, now."

For several minutes, she just clings to me, shaking and shivering and trembling, an occasional sob escaping past her gritted teeth.

Slowly, slowly, she begins to relax as the hot water tinges pink. Her breathing settles back to normal from the ragged panting.

I rest my head against the back of the tub, marveling that this thing is big enough to contain not just my giant ass but both of us. I hold her, trying hard as hell to project calm, peace, and safety.

The water cools.

I pull the plug and let it drain around us, and then twist on the water, adjusting the taps until it's hot but not too hot. Between the tub and the wall—a gap of eighteen inches or so—is a marble pedestal with a bowl on top, which contains a plethora of mysterious girly bath shit. Plastic-wrapped balls, tubs of flaky white shit, tubes of goop, bottles of goo, and squares of colorful soap.

I grab one of the balls and look at it—it's wrapped in crinkly plastic with a circular sticker on it; pastel pink with cursive writing, the sticker says: "Rest, Relax and Rejuvenate," across the center, and "Bath Bombs by Bathing Beauties" beneath it.

I don't have a clue what a bath bomb is, but I figure she could do with some rest, relaxation, and rejuvenation right about now, so I unwrap it as the hot water refills.

I toss the bath bomb into the water at my feet. For a second, nothing happens. And then suddenly the water is fizzing wildly, frothing with crazy, colorful, pungent, foam that swirls throughout the water.

"The fuck?" I mumble.

Noelle giggles against my chest. "Bath bomb, silly."

"What's it do?"

"Smells good, mostly. They're all different. They have

different minerals and stuff that do different things." Her voice sounds more normal, now.

"Is it okay that I used it?" I ask.

She nods. "Of course. I like it."

"Good."

A long silence.

"Bear?" Soft, quiet, hesitant.

"Yeah?"

"I was so scared." She shudders, trying to burrow into me. "I fought him. I *really* fought him as hard as I could."

"I know. You fought the bastard off."

"Panzer saved me."

"Yup."

She's quiet again, but I hear a quiet sniffle. "I'm t-t-trying to be s-s-strong, Bear. I-I-I j-j-ust…"

I curl my arms right. "Don't gotta be strong, honey. I'm here. I've got you. Nobody and nothing is getting near you. You're safe." I tilt her face to mine, her wet eyes shimmering and wide. "Let it out. Let yourself be whatever you need to be."

For a second or two, she's frozen and silent. And then she sniffles. again. And then her frame shakes with a silent sob.

"Give it all to me," I whisper. "I can take it, honey. I can take it all."

She dissolves, then. Silent sobs become great, wracking, heaving ones, guttural and gut-wrenching. She screams once, drawing Panzer to investigate—he pokes his head into the bathroom and then slumps heavily to the floor just outside it, seeming content that I've got our girl taken care of but still determined to keep his eyes on her.

It's hard to know how long she weeps—it feels like a

good half an hour or so. Eventually, the sobs subside into sniffles and shuddering breaths.

The water's gone cool again, and our fingers and toes are pruned.

"Can we get out?" she whispers.

"Gotcha. Let me get a towel."

I climb out and towel off as fast as possible, then wrap the towel around my waist; Noelle is crouched in the tub, arms around her knees, wet hair stringy around her bare shoulders. Her eyes follow me as I snag a fresh towel. She wobbles to her feet, bracing against the sides of the tub. I wrap her in the towel and sweep her off her feet.

"I can walk," she protests.

"Nope."

I carry her to the bed, sit on the edge with her on my lap, and use the towel to dry her body, then squeeze the worst of the water out of her hair the way she showed me.

I yank back the blankets, discard our damp towels, and bring her into my arms again under the covers.

Cheek on my chest, she burrows against me. "Maybe I'm not as okay as I thought," she whispers.

"That's okay. You don't have to be."

"Don't leave me, okay? Please?" The raw, terrified desperation in her voice shakes me to my core.

"Not a fucking chance in hell," I promise her. "I've got you. Always."

Her fingers touch my cheek, the bridge of her nose against my jawline. "Always?"

"Always."

16

Noelle

THE FOLLOWING DAYS ARE HARD.

Bear stays with me, never leaving my side for anything. I have to promise I'm okay long enough to use the bathroom alone.

He's touching me at all times, in one way or another. A hand on my back, waist, or shoulder, or my thigh, or hip.

He's endlessly patient with me when I'm hit by waves of fear when I wake in the middle of the night with nightmares. The morning after our bath, he tells me my parents came by demanding to see me, but confessed he wouldn't let them in. I lost my phone at some point—in the alley, most likely. I use the landline my landlord insists on keeping on the wall near the side door, and I use that for the first time since moving into this place to call them. I reassure them that I'm okay, which isn't a total and complete lie, just mostly.

I just can't handle them right now. I can't handle anyone. My sisters come by as well, but Bear fends them off, much to their indignant frustration. My brothers must have gotten the memo somehow because they leave a giant gift basket on the porch, a wicker basket full of fresh fruit, bags of my favorite candy—sour gummy worms—bars of chocolate, candles, and, just because it's them and they're weird little jokesters, a bag of cannabis gummies.

At some point, Darius and Miguel bring my car over. The girls from the salon bring by cards and casserole dishes of pasta bakes and other easy-to-reheat meals. Kelly tells me in no uncertain terms that I'm not to come back to work until I'm ready for it. Raina, Ashlynn, Kyle, Thomas and Colin come by as well with bottles of wine and sandwiches from The Alt; I promise them that once I'm up for visitors, they'll be the first to know.

I just…I can't handle anyone except Bear.

After three days of hibernating at home, watching TV on the couch curled up on Bear's lap, I'm finally ready to take a walk around the neighborhood. It feels good to be outside under the sun and blue sky, even if I am a little jumpy.

On day five, just past noon, the doorbell rings. I stay on the couch, content to let Bear send whoever it is away—I've decided I'm going to give myself a week and then I'll start reconnecting with all the friends and family who've reached out to me.

Bear mutters quietly with whoever's there for a minute and then turns to me. "You, uh, you may want to see this person."

I frown. "Who is it?"

He comes over to crouch beside me. "A therapist who specializes in sexual trauma."

I blink. "Here? At my house?"

"A friend of Sheriff Mannix's, I guess. She heard what happened. Says she wants to help." He searches my face. "Up to you. I can send her away, or I can let her in and give you two space."

I swallow hard. "What do you think I should do?"

He blinks at me, puzzled. "You're asking me?"

I nod.

"I think you should talk to her," he says.

"Okay," I say, sitting up higher. "Let her in. But...don't go far. Okay?"

He kisses the back of my hand. "I won't. Promise."

He rises and opens the door. The therapist is a woman in her early forties, with wavy, beautiful brown hair and light brown eyes, dressed in jeans and black heels with a white blouse and black blazer.

Her smile is friendly and warm as she approaches. "No, please, don't get up," she says when I start to rise. She takes a seat on the other end of the couch from me. "I'm Britt Hofstetler," she says. "I'm a licensed and board-certified therapist and counselor. I specialize in trauma recovery, domestic abuse, and sexual assault." She hands me a business card with her name, degrees, and certifications and the address and phone number of her practice here in the Three Rivers.

I manage a small smile. "Noelle Harper. Thank you for coming, Britt. I understand you're a friend of Sheriff Mannix's?"

"Something like that, yes." She glances at Bear, who's

hovering in the doorway to the kitchen. "I just thought maybe it would help to have a little talk with me. I can help you process things, and give you some tools and strategies for coping with what happened."

Bear shifts his weight. "Okay, Noelle?"

I nod. "Yeah, I'm good."

Panzer has been even more clingy and protective than Bear—he won't leave my side even in the bathroom. He settles on the floor by the couch near my feet, eyes watchfully assessing Britt.

Bear leaves, somewhat reluctantly, going out to the backyard; I hear the mower start up.

Britt looks at Panzer, then at me. "Quite the pair of guardians you have."

I smile. 'Yes, I know."

She echoes the smile. "Are they suffocating you?"

I laugh. "No, god no. I…" I sigh, the laughter fading. "I wouldn't let Bear leave my side at all for the first few days. I'm a little better now."

"That's totally normal and understandable," she assures me. "It's good you have a loving and supportive boyfriend."

I realize he is my boyfriend only when she says that—we never talked about it or put labels on things. But I realize I like it.

"I really do." I reach down and scratch Panzer's ears. "Two of them."

Britt laughs, her gaze searching me as the laughter subsides to professionally assessing concern. "So, Noelle. How are you feeling about things?"

I sigh, considering. "I…I'm not sure. Mixed up, I guess. I'm having nightmares every night. I couldn't even leave the house until just the other day. I couldn't handle seeing anyone but Bear—not my family, not my best friends, no one." I swallow hard, a hot lump forming in my throat. "I...I feel sort of...guilty?" It comes out as a question.

Britt hands me the box of Kleenex from the coffee table. "Guilty about what?"

"I mean..." I try to swallow but can't. My words tumble out, hesitant and awkward and stilted. "I just—nothing—nothing happened. You know? Like...yeah, he hit me. Hurt me. Threatened me. He would've...he was going to—but he didn't."

"The more you avoid the words you fear most, the more power you give them, Noelle," Britt says, her voice low and smooth and comforting.

"Duane didn't rape me." A sob escapes. "And I...I feel like I shouldn't be so...so upset. Like, nothing happened. But I'm...I'm reacting like it did."

Britt toes off her shoes and tucks her feet under her thighs. "Noelle, something *did* happen. You were *attacked*. Your attacker may not have sexually penetrated you, but it was sexual assault all the same. He violated your autonomy. He took away your choices. He hurt you." Her eyes go to my throat, to the scabbed-over cut. "Will you tell me what happened?"

I recount the assault for her, hesitantly at first, and I have to pause a few times to catch my breath as sobs rip through me. I go through piles of Kleenex. When I start crying and shaking, Panzer sits up and burrows his head onto my lap, and I curl around him, rocking as I work through the event for Britt.

By the time I'm done, I do feel lighter.

Britt spends a few moments thinking when I'm done. "What you experienced, Noelle, was a horrific and traumatizing event. You absolutely should *not* feel as if you're not allowed to be traumatized by it just because it wasn't fully rape. It was still sexual assault, full stop. No matter what you may be feeling, it's valid. The first thing you need to do is give yourself permission to feel whatever you feel."

I nod, sniffling, dabbing my nose as I scratch Panzer's ears. "I guess that makes sense."

She gestures at Panzer. "Use him. He's clearly very empathetic, and he obviously brings you comfort. Let him." She smiles as the dog nuzzles my palm before settling onto my lap again. "I'm not a vet, obviously, but I think the experience was hard for him, too. Not being able to get to you? For a dog bred and trained to protect, he probably feels some canine version of guilt that he couldn't get to you sooner."

Tears start again as I realize how right she is, and it makes sense of why he's been so clingy ever since. I curl over him, kissing his fuzzy forehead. "It wasn't your fault, buddy. You saved me, didn't you?" He whines in his throat. "Yes, you did. You're the best boy, Panzer."

Britt clears her throat, and I focus on her again. "Where are you with Bear?"

I frown. "What do you mean?"

"I mean in terms of your relationship. Events like this can have an impact on romantic relationships, especially newer ones."

"Oh." I shrug. "He's been amazing. He takes such good care of me."

"But you, Noelle—how are *you* feeling about things?"

I sigh, allowing myself to fully examine my feelings for the first time. "Conflicted, I guess. Or…maybe confused is a better word."

"How so?" she asks. "Why? Can you explain?"

I shrug. "I...well..." I shake my head. "It's a lot. And it's not all necessarily to do with the...with my assault." It's a little less hard to put the words to what happened now. "We, um...I don't know how relevant this is, but we actually haven't...um...been intimate."

She frowns a little. "So it's really new, then."

I shrug and nod. "Yeah, I guess. I mean, no, not really. We've been together, sort of, for several months."

"But you haven't had sex?"

I shake my head. "Not yet, no. We've done...other things a few times, but we haven't had sex yet."

"It *is* relevant, Noelle. Would you mind elaborating a little?" She has a yellow legal pad and a pen and has been taking notes while I talk. Now, she clicks the pen to retract the point and focuses on me.

"I'd have to go back and explain my previous relationship for it to make sense," I say.

She nods. "That's okay. We have all the time you need."

I frown. "I thought these things were on an hourly basis? We've been talking for over an hour already. I'm sure you have other clients."

She smiles, shaking her head. "Well, for one, I'm not charging you. I provide counseling to trauma victims for free after the event because they need it. Not to make money off of them. I've blocked off the whole day, Noelle. I'm here for as long as you need me."

"God, really?" She just nods, and I sniffle. "That's amazing. Thank you so much."

She just smiles. "We all do what we can, don't we? This is something I can do." She clicks the pen again. "So. Your last relationship."

I tell her about Brennan, our courtship, the expectations placed on us by our parents, and then on me by Brennan. Our marriage—how unhappy I was even if I didn't realize it until after the fact. His infidelity, how I discovered it, and my reaction. Leaving him. Its effect on my faith, and on my sexuality, and on my belief and trust in love.

As it all pours out of me, guided and prompted and nudged along by probing, carefully crafted questions, I find myself admitting things I hadn't even realized myself:

That I had—or have—hangups about sex.

That I struggled with being able to trust myself, and anyone else.

I realize that while I trust Bear on pretty much every level, I've held a certain part of myself back from him. I know I love him, but I've still held back. I haven't told him how I feel. I need him—especially lately, after what happened. I can't imagine life without him, now.

But what Brennan did, along with the beliefs I had drilled into me as a child and teenager…all of that left with me a deeply rooted distrust in and resistance to allowing Bear all the way into my heart.

Which is why I've held back from being fully intimate with him, Britt explains. Because there was such a strict emphasis placed on sex, compounded by Brennan's betrayal, even though I am attracted to Bear and feel comfortable allowing us to do some things together, I've been holding back out of fear. And for me, sex and love are inextricably linked.

I sit in silence, stunned. "How did I not know any of this about myself?" I ask.

Britt flips her pen around her middle finger. "It's not uncommon. We don't like to examine this kind of thing in ourselves. And when it's so deeply rooted in our childhood and adolescent years, it's even harder to see."

I nod, thinking. "So…what do I do?"

"About?" Britt asks.

"Bear. Our relationship." I swallow hard. "Sex."

She smiles gently. "Give yourself time. Talk to him. He's waited this long, right? He hasn't pressured you?"

"No!" I say, a quick outburst of a word. "Not at all."

"Then I have a feeling, considering how supportive you say he's been throughout this whole experience, he'll be understanding." She pauses a moment. "Do you want to move forward with that aspect of your relationship? Do you want to have sex with him?"

There's no question. "Yes. God, yes."

"Then talk to him. Communication is key, Noelle." She pauses as Bear enters the kitchen through the side door, grabs a bottle of water from the fridge, and goes back outside. "Often, especially in men with…shall we say… well-developed instincts for protection, events like this can make them afraid to initiate sex, even if you may be ready— even if you *tell* him you are. He'll be worried he'll trigger you. And honestly, he may be right. You have to go slow, take things one step at a time, and give yourself grace if you try and find out you're not ready. Be patient with yourself. Don't set unrealistic expectations. It doesn't seem like this is something you'll have to worry about, but don't let him place any expectations on you, either."

We talk about this a little more, and other things— picking apart how my upbringing may have colored my view of sex, and how I can move past that.

Eventually, after more than three hours, the conversation winds down.

"Well, Noelle, I feel like you've made a lot of very important progress today. Would you agree?" Britt asks.

I nod eagerly. "Oh yes, very much so. I can't thank you enough, Britt."

Her smile is bright and warm. "Absolutely—my pleasure. You have my card—please call me anytime. And understand that these things take time, Noelle. It won't be resolved in one conversation. I have room in my schedule—we can get you in for weekly or biweekly appointments. Okay?"

She stands up and gathers her things. She embraces me and takes her leave. Once she's gone, Bear enters hesitantly.

"Hey," he says. "How'd that go? You guys talked awhile."

I go to him and wrap my arms around his middle. "It was so good, Bear. So good. I have to find a way to thank Sheriff Mannix for sending her to me." I put my chin on his chest and look up at him. "Thanks for giving me that time."

"Absolutely. Of course. Whatever you need. You know that." His lips brush my forehead. "Anything."

I let out a sigh. "We have some things I want to talk about, but not right now. I'm all talked out."

He frowns. "Okay."

I smooth the frown lines on his forehead. "Good things, honey. I promise."

"Oh," he breathes. "I'd understand if you need space or something."

"No!" I cry, squeezing his middle as hard as I can—hard enough that he grunts in surprise. "The opposite."

"Oh. Right. I just….I don't want to crowd you or… or get in the way if you need something to heal that I can't give." His voice is low, rumbly, deep, hesitant.

Emotions bubble up in me again, and I laugh through

a half-sob. "God, Bear, stop. No. You're giving me everything I need." I rub his chest. "In fact, I...I actually sort of
feel like I'm not giving you enough. That's what I want to
talk about."

He touches my lips. "Don't. You're a gift, Noelle.
Everything about you is a precious, priceless gift."

"But we haven't—" I search his face, his eyes. "I've
made you wait so long, and—"

He silences me with a kiss, soft and chaste, but ef-
fective. "*Stop*, Noelle. Don't even think about that. I don't
need that."

"But don't you want—"

"Of *course* I do." He cups my face. "More than I know
how to say. But not until it's right. If you're not ready, then
I don't want it. If you can't do anything at all for—whatever. Days, weeks, months. Years even, I don't fucking care.
You're all that matters. Having you in my life. If you want
to just kiss and nothing else, okay. If you want to do what
we were doing before what happened, okay. If you need
to back off and I just hold you, that's okay too. I'm not impatient. I won't be upset. I won't be anything except here
for you, for whatever you need and whatever you want."

"But you're a man, Bear. You have needs."

He just laughs. "I spent ten years in prison, surrounded
by a few thousand other men. I can wait as long as you need.
So don't even think about me, Noelle. All I care about—
the *only* thing I give one single solitary fuck about is you.
Your happiness. That's it."

Tears bubble out, and I sniffle a laugh around them.
"I'm so sick of crying."

"So let's watch something funny," he suggests. "You
pick."

I sigh, caressing his cheek. "You're the most amazing man I've ever known, Bear. Truly. I'm so, so thankful for you."

He just shakes his head. "*I'm* thankful for *you*. You changed my life. Believed in me. Your strength, your resilience, your wisdom. You amaze me. I could spend the rest of my life trying and never feel fully worthy of the woman that you are."

This only makes me cry harder. "God, Bear, stop making me cry, dammit!" I laugh, wiping at my face. "You are worthy. More than worthy." I cover his mouth with my hand, silencing whatever he was about to say. "How about you put in a bag of popcorn while I find us a movie? I can't deal with anything else heavy right now. I need you to hold me while we watch something dumb and funny and not think about anything."

"Sounds pretty perfect to me," he says. "Be right back."

We spend the rest of the day watching comedies, stuffing ourselves with junk food, and snuggling.

In the back of my mind, though, I'm working on the things I talked to Britt about. My past, my beliefs and hangups about sex…and what I want.

How to get there from here.

One step at a time. One day at a time.

C⌒

The next day, my parents come over—at my invitation. We spend a couple of hours talking, and I reassure them that I'm okay, that I've spoken with a therapist and plan to continue to do so. Satisfied that I'm actually okay, they head home.

Nat and Nik show up the following day with a bottle

of tequila and a copy of *Practical Magic*, a favorite movie of ours and one of the few points we have in common. Poor Bear is once again evicted, although this time I encourage him to spend it away from the house entirely—he hasn't left since that day.

Reluctantly, he does—he calls Riley, who shows up with Felix, Darius, Eddie, and Miguel, and they drag him away for some football game or something equally macho.

I let my sisters ply me with tequila while we watched the movie, get Mexican food delivered, and act ridiculous. They do not once bring up what happened, and it's exactly what I need.

I hug them after the movie—and a bonus feature of some made-for streaming rom-com Nikki chose. They leave, and I feel closer to them than I ever have; they knew exactly what I needed, which does leave me with questions that I decide to ask them at some point. I have an inkling of why, but they were a good bit older than me when whatever happened to them happened; I wasn't informed of it, and they refused to talk about it.

Bear returns covered in dirt and mud from head to toe, bruised, limping, and grinning.

I eye him as he stands outside the side door. "What the heck happened to you?"

He toes off his sneakers. "Well, it started out as touch football. Felix, Riley, some of the guys from both crews, as well as Sheriff Mannix, a few other cops, and a handful of firefighters."

I arch an eyebrow. "It started as football and ended up...mudwrestling?"

He laughs, a big booming beautiful sound. "It ended

up in a contest to see how many guys it took to take me down. They formed teams and took bets."

I laugh. "Only you. Geez. Who won?"

"Felix's team."

"How many did it take?"

"They did it with only six. They cheated though. Grayson tripped me."

I roll my eyes. "Only six, huh? And they had to cheat to win?"

He wipes his brow with his forearm, only succeeding in smearing mud even more. "Pretty much." He grins at me. "How about you?"

I wave a hand. "We had a great time. Nik and Nat got me buzzed and we watched a couple of movies. It was fun. I needed it." I put a hand on his chest, stopping him from coming inside. "You are not bringing those filthy clothes in this house, Bear Olafsson." I allow him past the threshold, pointing down into the basement. "Take them off down there."

I follow him down, butterflies in my stomach. His shirt is stiff and molded to him, and resists coming off, and I end up having to help him peel it off. For the first time in nearly two weeks, I feel a flutter of desire ripple through me at the welcome sight of his big, brawny, heavily muscled body.

He turns away from me, pushing his filthy sweatpants down around his hips.

I step in front of him, catching his hands. "Hey. Hold on, now. Where are you going?"

He rolls a shoulder, not quite looking at me. "I didn't want you to think I was expecting—"

"Bear," I interrupt. "I think this is a good time for what I need to talk to you about."

"Okay," he says, hesitant, cautious.

"I talked to Britt about a lot of stuff. Not just the attack." I move closer to him, running my hands over his scarred, muscular, beautiful chest and abs. "We talked about Brennan. How I was brought up. We talked about how I feel about sex."

He shifts side to side, uncomfortable. "I told you—"

"Yes, you did," I say, touching his lips. "But now I need you to listen to me, okay?"

"Yeah," he says. "Okay. I'm listening."

"Good. Like I said, we talked about sex, both in the context of the attack and outside of that context." I slide my hands down to his waist, gazing up at him in the dim gloom of the unlit basement. "It's nothing I haven't already told you, but what she helped me realize is that even before the attack, I was holding back. I was mentally framing it as taking time to get to know you and then wanting to take things slow."

"Which makes total sense with what you told me," he says.

I nod. "Yes, of course. And there's an element of truth to that, but it's deeper than that. Brennan didn't just break my trust in him; he broke my ability to trust anyone." I touch the center of his chest. "I trust you more than I trust anyone. But what Britt helped me realize is that I was holding back because I was scared. And also pretty confused about who I am and what I want."

He gazes down at me thoughtfully. "I can see that. And now?"

"Well, obviously the attack changed things."

"How could it not?"

"Exactly," I say. "But...I guess what I'm trying to say is that I don't want to hold back anymore. I refuse to be afraid anymore."

"It hasn't even been two weeks, Noelle," Bear says. "You can take—"

"I know," I interrupt. "I'm not saying let's do it on the floor right here right now."

Bear looks around, frowning. "That wouldn't be very much fun, I don't think."

I laugh. "No, definitely not." I rest my hands up on his shoulders. "What I am saying is that I want to...I want to try. Britt warned me that I might have to sort of...I don't know, take my time, like don't be surprised if I have a flash-back or something."

Bear frowns even harder. "I don't want to do the wrong thing. Make things worse, or harder."

"She told me about that too—that you may have a hard time with it. What I'm telling you, Bear, is that I *want* to be with you." I hold his eyes, hoping he sees the truth in mine. "I want everything with you. I want to make love with you. I want to give you every last part of me. What I'm saying is that I *will not* let Brennan *or* Duane keep me from being with you. You'll probably have to keep being patient if things don't exactly get off to a great start—I admit I have no idea how I'll react. Right now, I feel fine." I let my hands trail down his chest, tracing his pecs and each of his abs. "I feel...I'm crazy attracted to you. I want to kiss you. I want you to touch me. I don't know how far I'll be able to go, but I want to try."

Bear reaches for me but stops short of touching me

since his hands are covered in dried mud. "Then we take this at your pace. I'll follow your lead."

I nod. "Thank you." I lick my lips, looking up at him as the butterflies in my stomach do flips and loops. "And one day, hopefully very soon, I'm going to want *you* to take the lead."

"Me?"

I nod. "Yes, you. I mean, we'll need to see how I react first and take things one step at a time, but yeah. I want you to show me how you feel. Show me you want me."

"You may have to help me understand what that looks like. I've always tried to be very careful and respectful of you."

My heart melts a little. "And you absolutely have been, to a degree that honestly stuns me. It's part of how I..." I swallow hard, choking on the words; this isn't the time, place, or circumstances I'd imagined saying them to him, but I can't not. "How I fell in love with you."

Bear rocks backward on his heels, shock registering on his face, in his body language. "Noelle—"

I cover his mouth. "You don't have to say anything, Bear. I've known it's true for a while, I just...I was scared to admit it to myself, much less out loud to you. But I can't avoid the truth of it, and you deserve to know." He tries to speak again, but I shake my head and press harder on his mouth. "I don't *want* you to say it back right now, Bear. I want you to just take it in, and know that it's true. I'm in love with you. And if you feel the same way, find your own time to say it. Okay? Does that—-does it make any sense?"

"Yes," he whispers, sounding shaken. "You....you *love* me?" Tears shine in his eyes, and my heart somehow manages to shatter, expand a thousandfold, and heal all at once.

My eyes sting, and my own tears fall. "Yes, Bear. So damn much it terrifies me."

He bends at the knees, and his hands scoop under my butt, lifting me. I latch my legs around his waist and cling to his neck. His face buries in my throat, and I feel his hot wet tears on my skin. His huge shoulders shake.

"Bear…" I whisper.

"Good tears," he growls, burrowing against me.

"Okay," I whisper, caressing his head and cradling his face against my chest. "Okay, honey. Let it out."

It's not a long cry, but it's an intense one. His shoulders shake raggedly, and he doesn't utter a sound. His hands grip my hips with bruising force—I let him bruise me and hold him all the tighter.

After a few minutes, he sighs, a deep gusting exhale. "Sorry—I'm sorry."

I pull away and grab his face, making him look at me—he tries to hide his wet cheeks, but I refuse to let him. "Hey, no, no, no. No hiding and no apologizing." I hunch lower to hold his wavering, uncertain gaze. "Thank you for giving that to me, Bear. It's beautiful. It means *everything* to me that you felt safe enough to let me have that."

He swallows hard, holding my butt with one hand while wiping at his face with the other. "I just…" a shake of his head.

I wipe at his eyes for him, and then kiss under his cheeks, tasting salt. "Tell me. Please."

He buries his head in my neck again, shuddering another huge sigh. "It's a lot."

"That's okay. I can handle it. I want to hear it."

"No one's ever told me that they love me," he says in a small whisper. "I never really expected to hear it. I mean,

I know you care about me, but…love? Part of me just…
I've always felt…." A ragged exhale between pursed lips.
"Unlovable."

My heart breaks for him all over again, and my love
for him rushes into the cracks, sweeps up the shards, and
builds something new, something beautiful. Something
magical.

"You're not unlovable, Bear Olafsson," I tell him, cupping his face and holding his gaze, thumbs brushing under
his eyes. "You're so far from it. I *love* you." I touch my forehead to his. "*I love you*. Hear me?"

"I hear you," he murmurs.

I grab one of his hands and move it from my backside to my stomach, slide it up my chest and over my heart.
"Feel that?" I press his hand against my heartbeat. "Feel
my heart beating?"

He nods. "I feel it."

"It's beating for you. Only for you."

He closes his eyes, hot rough hand against my heartbeat. When his big gray-green eyes open and find mine,
they're clear and strong.

"I don't need to wait. Don't need to think. I don't need
my own time—this is my time."

"Bear—" I whisper.

"I love you, Noelle."

My eyes burn all over again. "I really want to kiss you,"
I say, laughing through my tears. "But you're so dirty."

He growls, frustrated. "Of all the times to not be able
to kiss you."

Everything inside me burns for him.

"Fuck it." I slam my mouth against his, tasting dirt
and tears and love.

His tongue sweeps against mine, and the wet beautiful warmth of his mouth subsumes me, drowns me, and I moan.

"Take me upstairs," I whisper.

He carries me upstairs to my room—our room. I wriggle, and he sets me down. I step away from him, keeping hold of his hands.

"Go rinse off," I tell him. "Quickly."

"Noelle, I…"

"Trust me to know what I want, okay?" I grip his beard, pull him down for a kiss. "And what I want is you. Clean. And all for me."

His answering growl does its thing—makes my sex drool with desire, makes my stomach flip and my nipples go hard. "Noelle," he rumbles. "I want you so fucking bad." He tangles his fingers in my hair and kisses me. "Need you."

I break away and push him toward the bathroom. "Then get clean and come back to me."

He backs away, into the bathroom. "Won't be long."

"Better not be," I answer. "I need you too."

He shuts the door, and I hear the shower turn on.

I wash my face off in the hall bathroom and then decide to do this right.

I peel out of my clothes and get ready for Bear.

17

Bear

I'M STILL IMPLODING AT THE FACT THAT NOELLE loves me.

I scrub myself clean, wash and condition my hair and beard, and then wash again, rinse off, get out, and dry off. Run a brush through my hair and beard. Wrap the towel around my waist.

I have no clue what to expect.

I'm nervous.

Eager.

And more than a little embarrassed that I actually cried in front of her. On her. I haven't cried since I was a little kid. I just…hearing her say those three incredible, magical little words was so unexpected that it just broke something inside me.

I open the bathroom door, letting steam swirl out. It's late, almost ten, and the summer sun has set. I'm not sure what I expect, but it's not what greets me.

The room is dark, the lights off, and the blinds shut. The only light is a flickering orange glow from a dozen candles Noelle has lit around the room —on the bedside table, her dresser, and the window sill. The candlelight creates a warm, welcoming, romantic ambiance, drawing me further into the room. A small Bluetooth speaker on the dresser plays soft, inviting acoustic music—guitar, a mandolin, a piano…I don't know. All I know is the music is lovely and soothing. Romantic.

Romance has never been a part of my life. I don't know shit about it. But this?

It tells me everything I need to know. And I know I'm going to give her this as often as I can, now that she's shown it to me.

It's yet another gift she's given me, one of so many. My heart feels so big and full in my chest that I'm half worried my ribcage can't hold it.

Noelle is at the side of the bed, lighting one last candle. She turns me, and my breath lodges in my lungs, catching and sticking at the hot hard dense lump that has formed there at the sight of her.

She's wearing a thin white robe that's covered in pink cherry blossoms. It doesn't quite reach mid-thigh, leaving her beautiful, creamy, milky thighs bare. Belted loosely around her waist, it drapes open in a wide V, exposing the inner curves of her perfect breasts and a hint of a sapphire bra—just a snippet of lace around the lower curves of her breasts. She's brushed her long copper hair until it shines, hanging in loose waves over one shoulder. She's put on a little makeup, her lips vivid scarlet, eyes rimmed in black, making the shocking kelly green pop.

"Fuck," I growl. "Fucking gorgeous, Noelle."

She sets the long-neck lighter on the side table and glides toward me, her hips swaying in a sultry, seductive rhythm. "You haven't even seen what's under the robe, yet."

I'm speechless, tongue adhered to the roof of my mouth. My cock goes ramrod hard behind my towel, and I cling to the knot at my belly button, holding it in place, instinct making me try to hide the bulge of my arousal.

"Noelle." It's a breath, a prayer. "So perfect."

She moves closer. "I'm ready, Bear." She looks up at me from a foot away. "I need you."

My heart slams in my chest, my pulse pounds in my throat. I can't breathe. "Jesus." I reach a trembling hand toward her, and her eyes brighten as I rest my hand on her hip. "There aren't words to describe how fucking beautiful you are." I put my other hand on her hip, and her big, full, heavy round breasts swell with a deep breath at my touch. "How bad I fucking need you. How much I love you."

She trails her fingernails down my chest, making goosebumps crawl all over my body. Her fingers dance over my abdomen, playing and toying with the grooves and blocks of my abs. To the knot of my towel. "So don't tell me." She rubs her palms back up, scraping her smooth hands over my nipples, making me suck in a sharp breath. "Show me."

"Fuck." I caress her face, brush my thumb over her lips. "Don't know where to start."

She looks up at me from under her eyelids, long lashes thick and dark against her pale, freckled flesh. She rolls her thumbs over my nipples again. "Earlier, you said I'm a gift, right?"

I nod. "You are. The greatest gift I could ever get."

"So unwrap me." She rests her hands on my waist, a sly, eager, sexy smile on her lips. "Start there…my love."

My eyes burn—her endearments ravage me to the core of my soul every time. The way she says them—they're not just words, cheap and overused. They're deeply, passionately meant.

Grasping her waist, I spend a moment longer just looking at her.

"What are you waiting for?" she whispers.

"Memorizing this moment," I answer. "You, looking like that—for *me*. Soft and sexy and so goddamned beautiful in the candlelight." I shake my head, catch my breath in a rushed inhale. "Gonna remember this forever. You, like this. Treasure it. Cherish it."

"God, Bear," she says, in that tearful yet exasperated tone she gets when I say shit like that. "So damn sweet."

I grin, touch her lips. "Love it when my good girl curses."

"I am your good girl, aren't I?" she breathes. "All yours. All for you." She lifts on her toes, and her soft lips, tasting of bubblegum lip gloss, ghost against mine in an almost-kiss. "Unwrap me, Bear. Please." She grips the knot of my towel and grips it with white-knuckled fingers. "Get me naked and make me yours."

I growl, so aroused it hurts, so in love I don't know how to contain it. My hands shake as I tug the tie of her robe. The simple bow-knot comes loose and the robe drapes open.

My breath is hot as fire in my throat. "Jesus, Noelle."

She nibbles her lower lip nervously. "Bought it a long time ago. I've never worn it."

A complicated, mind-boggling thing of sapphire lace, the lingerie she's wearing makes my already impossibly-erect cock stiffen so hard I suck in a pained breath. It dives down between her thick, luscious thighs to just barely cover her sex with a narrow slice of lace, leaving her hips naked, leaving exposed the creases where her thighs angle in to her sex. Hugging her tucked-in waist, the lace scoops to frame her breasts, pushing them up from below and squeezing them together from the outside, putting them on mouth-watering display, big lush globes of ivory flesh laced with blue veins that my mouth waters to taste, a semi-circle of areolae peeking around the edge of the lace.

"Fuck," I breathe. "Holy god in heaven."

Her hesitant gaze lifts to mine at my breathless curse, at the awe in my voice. "Bear…"

Need savages me, my chest heaving as I barely restrain myself from grabbing her and ripping the thing off.

I reach a trembling hand toward her, reverently touching the cleft between her breasts, tracing the outer curve of them. "Perfect tits." I step into her, crushing them against the wall of my chest, and reach down to cradle her backside. "Perfect ass."

"Bear," she whispers again, almost as if she doesn't know what else to say. It comes out shaky, a gasp of a syllable.

I slide my fingers through her silky cool hair and then pinch her chin between my finger and thumb. "Perfect everything."

I dip down to her and claim her lips. Kiss her until the hunger rips through me with such wrecking-ball force that I have to back away, hands clenched into shaking fists.

She opens her eyes, mouth still parted from the kiss, confusion in her eyes. "Why…why did you stop?"

I growl, words abandoning me. I don't know how to

describe what I'm feeling. I'm worried I'll scare her if I let her see the primal ferocity of my desire for her.

I shake my head, breath coming in short, frustrated snarls. "I…fuck, Noelle."

Her hands glide warm and delicate up my stomach. "Talk to me, baby. Tell me."

"Worried I'll scare you."

"What would scare me?"

"Me."

"What about you?" Her eyes seek, hunt, pierce mine. "This is when you give me the unvarnished truth, Bear. Whatever it is. Just tell me. I *promise* I'll understand."

I shake my head. "Not like that." I can't control my hands—they grasp her hips, caress her thighs, her ass. "I… fuck. Fuck!" I force myself to let go. "Too rough." I close my eyes, and finally, something like a coherent explanation emerges. "I want you so *goddamned bad*, Noelle. Waited for you. Knew you needed time. And I don't regret it—I'd wait a century. An eternity."

"Bear, I—" she starts, but I touch her lips to silence her.

She goes quiet but gently and playfully seizes my finger in her teeth, grinning up at me.

"Let me get it out."

She keeps my finger in her teeth, nodding, and then closes her lips around my finger, her gaze burning with playful, seductive heat, tongue licking and teasing my finger; she mimes the act of oral sex on my finger, her eyes on mine, heated and aroused.

Her eyes draw the rest out of me. "You're a work of art, Noelle. Exquisite. Perfect." I hold up my hand, showing her my rough, scarred, callused palm; she lets go of my finger and nuzzles my hand, very much like a dog would, all nose, playful, her bright green eyes full of joy and arousal and eager fervor. "And me? I'm…rough. I could hurt you so easily. But I…I fucking *need* you. Need you so bad it feels like…like madness. It scares me."

She presses her palm to mine, her body flush against me, all doe-eyed beauty and sensual splendor. "Tell me about it, Bear. How it feels. Tell me exactly what your need is like. What it tells you to do."

I shake my head, not a denial exactly. "When I took that robe off and I saw you in this…" I trace the lace along the side of her breast. "I was consumed by this…this urge to—-"

Her doe eyes plead with me. "To what?"

"Rip it off you. Shred it. Pick you up and…" I swallow the rest.

"And what, baby? *Tell me.* I want to know. Tell me, please." She tucks her fingers between the towel and my skin, behind the knot; my stomach tucks in automatically, my body betraying me, begging for her touch. "Pick me up and do what to me?"

"Fuck you," I whisper. "Make love to you. But not… gently. Not sweet." My teeth grit and grind on the words. "Hard. Rough. Get you on your hands and knees and…" I'm lost to the image, the fantasy that I've tried so fucking hard over the last few months to forget. "Pound inside you until your ass shakes. Make your big perfect tits shake. Make come so hard so you see Jesus. I want to fuck you and never, ever stop."

"Ohhh…" she breathes. "*Fuck.*" It's a hissed epithet, barely a breath. Barely heard.

"See? I…" I cup her face. "You're… you're everything. Perfect and beautiful and delicate and lovely. The only reason

I believe in God is there's no way something so fucking incredibly gorgeous as you could be anything other than an intentional work of art. And I'm scared I'll hurt you."

Her eyes are wide and shimmering. "Bear, I beg you—I'm *begging* you to hear what I'm saying right now. I mean it down to the bottom of my heart and soul. Okay?" She takes my hands in hers, squeezing them with all her strength. "I am *not* made of glass. I'm not. I'm *strong*. I know exactly how much power you have in these big, strong, rough hands. I've seen what they can do. They can create. They can destroy. But you know what? I know you won't. I know—I *know* as well as I know my own name—I *know* down to my soul that you cannot, will not ever, *ever* hurt me. Are you listening to me right now, my love?"

I nod. Swallow hard. Breath is on fire, body tense, shaking. "I'm listening."

"Take what I'm saying to heart. I'll repeat it as many times as you need until you understand. Until you trust it." She lifts on her toes to get closer to me. "What you just described? What you said you wanted to do?" She tugs me down by my beard roughly. Lips to my ear, whispering. "I *want that*."

Shock leaves me stunned. "You…do?"

"*God* yes," she breathes. "I want it all. I want it sweet and slow. I want it hard and rough. I want it in between. I don't know how I want it, I just know I want it." She digs her nails into my sides. "I…I need to confess something, and I'm scared to."

"Don't be."

I hear her swallow, see the scarlet flush of her cheeks. "When you're a little rough? When you pull my hair, or… or grab my—my ass and squeeze hard? I like it. I don't want to be *hurt*. But when you're a little bit of rough?" She nibbles on her lower lip, teeth sinking into the crimson-painted flesh, her eyes wide and shimmering and scorching with undeniable arousal. "I don't just want that, Bear. I freaking *need* it."

I hold her eyes with mine, breath coming in long, grating gusts, almost growls. My hands, having been loosely resting on the bell curve of her naked hips, slip down and around to the taut silk glory of her ass. I grip hard, squeezing and kneading the plump, juicy cheeks with enough force that I'm pretty sure she'll have fingerprints bruised into the flesh.

Instead of a cry of pain or a shift away, an erotic whimper falls from her parted lips, and she crushes herself against my body, and her fingernails claw into my chest, leaving crescent-shaped divots.

Encouraged and further aroused by the intense sensuality of her response, I'm emboldened to test her a bit more. See how much of my full, true, rabid, primal need she can handle.

It's a beast I've never given free rein, always kept mostly shackled, too fearful of my own power, my ability to accidentally cause pain, especially in the throes of release.

Now, after almost eleven years in prison and months of pent-up sexual desire, attraction, and need, I feel a very real, very manic, and almost insane level of need. For her.

I bend at the knees, curl my hands around her thighs below her ass and lift—it's an almost violent movement, yanking her airborne and against my body. Her cry of surprise is shrill, breathless, and eager, and her thighs wedge around my waist, heels hooking at my ass, tits at face level, arms resting on my shoulders, hands burying in my hair.

She slants her mouth across mine, a whimpering gasp accompanying the demanding, hungry kiss. I growl and thrust my tongue into her mouth, and our teeth knock together. I stagger forward a few steps, dizzied by the ferocious hunger I feel Noelle giving me. As rough as I am, she only seems to want more.

The door rattles in the frame as I slam her against it, pinning her to it with my body. Kiss her harder, deeper, tongue sweeping her mouth, my hands crushing into the sweet, generous curves of her ass. She moans low in her throat, knotting her hands in my hair, the sting at my scalp only fueling the flames of my arousal.

Pinning her to the door with my hips, I lean away and cover her tits with my hands, cupping and gripping—her head thunks against the door as a gasp rips out of her at my ungentle caress.

I yank the lingerie down past her shoulders, and her huge, lush, ivory tits spring free, bare and quivering, heaving and shaking and swaying with her frantic breaths. I scrape my palms over her nipples and then scoop the heavy globes into my hands and lift them to my mouth. Suckle a pert, thick, pink nipple into my mouth with my teeth, earning me a hiss of shocked pleasure. Her hands tighten in my hair and shove my face against her chest, and her hips gyrate against my belly, the knot of my towel a hard wedge between our bodies.

God, I need more of her.

Thoughtless, now, lost in the fiery haze of unbridled need, I grasp the edges of sapphire lace in my hands just below her gasp-shaking tits.

"Tell me I'm too rough," I plead, desperate to hear

her deny my demand. "Tell me not to rip this goddamned thing off your body."

"No," she breathes. "*Fuck* no. Never."

It's the curse that breaks the chains of my control.

With a snarl, I shred the lace apart with a savage yank, and the garment splits open down the middle, hanging open to the apex of her sex, hanging loose around her hips. A shrill gasp at my barbaric action makes those tits bounce hypnotically.

My eyes rake over her beauty, down to her sex. "Sweet little pussy is dripping wet," I growl, and who the fuck is this speaking this way?

"So wet for you," Noelle breathes, and she swipes her two middle fingers through her seam, whimpering at her touch, gathering her essence on her fingers, which she slips into my mouth. "Taste me, Bear."

A raspy, tight-throated moan escapes me at the sugar of her on my tongue. Who is she? Who is this wild woman, this unabashedly wanton, erotic creature in my arms?

Mine.

She's mine. This primal, demanding sexuality is only for me—pride and a savage, jealous possessiveness surges through me, demanding I claim her, mark her as mine.

I pivot, and she shrieks at the abrupt swing, giggling breathily and clinging to my neck, grinning madly and laughing as I march to the bed and fling her onto it from several feet away.

She flies airborne for a moment, lands heavily on the mattress, bounces once, curves jiggling and quivering, making my cock spasm. She lands sideways on the bed, and before she can gather her wits or move or even laugh again, I grab her ankles and drag her across the bed to the very edge. I tear the tattered remains of the lingerie off of her and sink to my knees and throw her legs over my shoulders and bury my face between her thighs, the tender silk of them against my face and neck. The pungent scent of her desire fills my nostrils, eliciting a hungry growl from me as I thrust my face into her pussy, tongue driving inside her, my mouth fusing to her lips.

Noelle cries out, spine arching off the bed as I devour her, all savage desperation and no technique. Within seconds, she's bucking and grinding against my mouth, so aroused she comes almost instantly, screaming and tearing at my hair, shoving me harder against her. She comes and comes, and before she can find the other side of her release, I slip two fingers into her slick tight channel, drawing an arching, grinding cry from her. I shove my fingers into her, deep, quick, hard, curling to find her sacred center, that place that makes her shatter. I suck her clit and drive my fingers in and out, and she quakes arrhythmically, so totally thrown into ripping, merciless peaks of orgasm that she can't even thrust, can only shake and shudder and ride it out.

With scream after scream, Noelle comes apart for me—again and again, endlessly, until she's sobbing and gasping and trembling, limp and helpless in my hands, her juices painting my lips and cheeks and chin and beard.

With sudden, desperate strength, she pushes me away from her sex, every inch of her body trembling. For a few fraught moments, she just lays on the bed, legs wrapped around my face, gasping, fighting for breath. dazed, shell-shocked eyes find mine, burning with carnal pleasure.

"Bear," she whispers, tears slipping down her cheeks. "My god."

I grin, proud and satisfied. "Noelle, my love."

Her heavy-lidded eyes dart and search, shimmering wet and blazing with a myriad of complex emotions.

"God, you're incredible," She breathes. "The way you make me come? Unreal."

Moving slowly, she levers upright, thighs uncurling, slipping down around my shoulders, finding the floor. She sits on the edge of the bed, toes pressing into the floor, heels lifted. She spreads her fingers wide over my pecs, and then her fingernails dig into the muscle with sudden force. She pushes me backward, and I trip as I find my feet, lurching upright. She surges after me, breasts smashing against my chest, fist in my beard yanking me down so she can crash her mouth on mine, one hand wrapping around the back of my neck so I can't escape the kiss.

She curls her fingers against my belly inside the rolled and knotted towel. Her tongue sweeps into my mouth, and with a rough jerk, she tears the towel open, flinging it away. With another hard shove, she sends me slamming into the wall beside her door, lunging after me. Her hands wrap around my cock and plunge down, drawing a ragged groan from me.

She leaps, trusting me to catch her. I do, and she presses the wet seam of her pussy against my belly, clinging to my neck with one arm, the other reaching down between our bodies to grasp my erection. Thumb and forefinger circling my shaft, facing down toward the root, she caresses my length, mouth wide against mine as she gasps breathlessly, shrill with erotic tension.

"Bed," she demands. "*Now*."

I march forward, clutching her ass and groaning as she

greedily strokes my cock. I reach the mattress and bend forward, dropping her onto her back.

She bolts upright and off the bed, shoving me forward onto it. I hit the blankets and roll to my back, shifting upward to get my whole body on and oriented to the pillows. She crawls after me on all fours, heavy tits swaying, ass gyrating side to side with each prowling movement. Her explosion of glossy red hair falls over one shoulder in a coppery cascade, brilliant green eyes hungrily raking my body, halting and fixing on my straining erection.

Fists pressing into the bed at my hips, she runs her tongue up the length of my cock, pauses to grin up at me, and then takes me in her mouth to the back of her throat in a single long wet hot slide.

"Ohhhhhfuck," I growl. "Jesus."

My hips leave the bed, pushing me into her mouth, and she gives me another slow, tongue-swirling ride of her lips from tip to root, or as much of me as she can handle, at least.

With a loud pop of freed suction, my pre-cum-leaking head leaves her mouth, and she continues her seductive prowl up my body until she's above me, hair drifting in sunfire waves around my face, breasts draped onto my chest, thighs framing my hips.

She slashes her lips across mine, gasping into my mouth as I grasp her ass with both hands, gripping hard enough that I know she'll have bruises later. I feel her shift her weight to brace on one arm, and she fits her fingers to her sex, circling her clit with swift, eager swipes.

She whimpers, lips quivering against my mouth as she touches herself, ass tensing as she flexes her hips into the rhythm of her swirling fingers.

A moment later, she cries out, head dropping down between her shoulders. She clutches my cock and guides me to the wet cleft of her pussy, pressing my tip to her lips.

Her eyes find mine, brows furrowed and eyes wide, mouth open as her orgasm shudders through her.

There's no warning.

She crushes her ass down toward my thighs, and the tight heat of her pussy wraps around my cock—-impossibly hot, dripping wet, slick and soft, and so fucking tight.

I shout, a guttural cry of ecstasy. I feel her still coming, shaking and clenching around me as she slides slowly down my shaft—taking me inch by inch.

All the way, until her ass settles against my hips.

When I'm fully buried inside her, she braces her hands on my chest, panting and whimpering. Her eyes pinch shut, her mouth working silently as she adjusts to me.

And then her eyes snap open, fix on mine with a fierce, ferocious, wild, erotic gleam.

"Finally," she breathes.

"Fuck," I gasp. "Noelle. Jesus."

She wriggles her hips to push lower, taking me deeper yet. "Don't hold back," she demands, fingers digging into my muscles. "Promise me you'll give me everything you've got—everything you are, my love. *Promise* me."

I rake my hands up the violin shape of her hips, waist, and chest, fingers diving into her hair to frame her face. "I swear," I growl.

She takes my mouth in a savage kiss, ending with my lower lip seized in her teeth. "Then *show* me."

18

Noelle

STRADDLING HIM, MY HEART SLAMS A MILE A minute behind my ribs, my pulse thundering in my ears. I'm awash in a chaos of sensations—my skin tingles, flushed and prickling with a raging flow of blood, my arousal rampaging through me like wildfire. His chest hair scratches deliciously rough against my tender, erect, sensitive nipples, sending hot lines of arousal pulsing through me.

His cock fills me…

Overfills me.

Stretches me to a stinging burn, even after several pounding heartbeats of adjustment. The ache is glorious, incredible. Earth-shattering.

I didn't know—I had no idea I could feel this way.

That I could be this full—this glutted on ecstasy. I can barely draw a breath, he's so huge inside me, at the very cusp of too big.

My eyes water with the burn of struggling to stretch around him, arousal pulsing like liquid fire in my veins.

Gasping for air, I claw my fingers down his chest, leaving red welts on his skin as I find a new angle, bracing my hands on his belly directly in front of our joined bodies.

I can't stop a moment of awareness—that he…my previous and only other partner, never wanted this position. He liked the control. And the only position he liked was missionary.

But this?

My god.

This is what I've craved my whole adult life, since the moment I became aware of my sexuality as a young teenage girl first experimenting with the forbidden, sinful pleasures of self-touch. All throughout my marriage, I craved something. I never knew what and couldn't ask for it; I didn't have the words, the courage, or the self-awareness to know what I wanted, and I knew my relationship wasn't a safe place to express my needs and desires even if I could have found the words.

This is it—everything I've ever wanted, ever needed.

Bear.

His primal power, his wild, barbaric strength, his savage need, finally given the freedom to be expressed—in so doing, giving me what I never knew I craved.

His hands scrape down my spine, the cinderblock texture over my skin sending ripples of sensuous need through me. He cradles my ass in his rough, huge hands, gently for a breath and then kneading with gruff, possessive power.

Despite his rough treatment of my body, his eyes are gentle and his words gentler yet: "Okay, baby?" He lifts, sitting up to take my mouth in a soft kiss. "Am I hurting you?"

I shake my head, gripping his beard to hold him close for the kiss until need takes over and I shove him back to the bed.

He flops back down and he paws at my breasts, and then cups them, thumbs rolling over my nipples, dragging a gasp out of me.

Balancing upright on him, I grab his hands and crush them against me, loving the harsh scrape of his calluses, the grit of his thumbs on my nipples, his fingernails flicking, tweaking.

I need to move—I *have* to. I still ache and burn with the size of him, but it's the best thing I've ever felt, cracking my soul apart with love and wonder and pride and pleasure, making my heart slam all the harder with anticipation of how it'll feel to finally know the glutting size of him sliding through my clenching sex.

I fall forward, hands landing on his chest, and I draw my hips forward, hissing as he slices through my lips. He's holding utterly still, hands gripping the crease of my hips, thumbs pressing to the tender skin just above where we're joined. His inhales in synch with the upward slide, and then I sink onto him, crying out with a shrill shriek as he splits me open all over again. The burn, god the burn, the ache, the sting. My eyes water, and I gasp helplessly, head hanging, taking him inside me until my bottom slaps softly against his hips.

Again—pull upward. Hesitate with the head of him almost spilling out of me, and then glide myself back down his shaft, now slick with my leaking essence.

"Bear!" I whimper, gagging on a choked cry as he fills me to the brim and then more and more.

He only growls, that beautiful, animal snarl of arousal shivering into the core of me. His hands tighten around my hips, digging in desperately as he tries to hold still, to give me time to adjust, to accommodate him.

"Fuck," he grates, voice rough and guttural. "You feel...*fuck*, so fucking good. So perfect." He pushes me down by my hips, driving his hips up to sink deeper inside me. "Gotta move, my love. Fuck, I *have* to."

"Please," I beg him. "Take me. Show me what you need."

An orgasm hovers in my belly, coiled low and ready to seize me, ready to smash through me. I don't know that I can handle another one yet, so I try to hold it off.

Bear grabs my ass cheeks, a greedy double fistful, bruising with power, sending more delicious ripples of stinging pain through me. he pulls me apart, opening me. Sinks deeper yet, until I can take no more because I have every last thick, ridged, veiny, glistening inch of his glorious cock inside me.

I cry out, a hoarse wail, head hanging. "Bear! Yes!"

Now, he lifts me with that rough grip, dragging himself almost out of me. Pushes me down onto him. I scream, then. Not a soft scream, either—a real, true scream that burns the back of my throat.

My orgasm throbs behind my navel, soaking relentlessly down into my sex, pulsing behind my pussy and into my clit. I angle forward, shifting my hands to his shoulders, tipping my sex against him and my ass higher. And now, when he drags me up his shaft and drives me back down, the slick length of him scrapes and stutters and slides against my clit, sending ragged, helpless shudders through me.

Building and expanding within me, the climax is now titanic, terrifying, explosive—and still growing.

I hold it off.

"More," I gasp, hoarse. "Harder. Give me everything."

"Ahh god, my love, my Noelle. My heaven. My goddess." He whispers, his praise emerging in a rhythmic chant. "You want it harder?"

I fall against him, arms snaking around his neck, breasts crushed fall between us, sink my teeth into his earlobe, gasping and whimpering as he thrusts into me slowly and softly and gently, letting me grow used to the burning slide, the stretching slick ache of him filling and withdrawing—a thrust, and another, and another, and I gasp short ragged moans with each one, breathless with erotic wonder, lost in delirious disbelief that anything in this world could feel as good as Bear inside me, moving in me, taking me.

"Fuck me and don't ever stop," I whisper, the naughty words pulled out of me—I give myself over to this new, wild, and free version of Noelle Harper, a woman who takes what she wants and says what she wants. A sexual creature, a wanton woman, not a lady, not proper, not righteous or good or Christian.

A woman who fucks her man and loves every second of it.

I'm *free*.

I scream again as his brawny arms squeeze me with pythonic power, his hands gripping my ass and tugging the globes apart so he drives deeper, taking more of me.

His hips pump against mine, my soft belly pressed

into his, our heartbeats matched and slamming madly. He grunts now as he fills me again and again, and I groan with him, the sounds feral and crazed.

God, I love this.

I cling to his neck and pant in his ear, and then the first wave of orgasm breaks through me, and my lips fall to his neck, stuttering wetly down the side of his throat; another wave hits, and I sink my teeth into the thick cord of muscle along the ridgeline of his shoulder, growling rabidly as the waves come faster and faster. My hips work on their own now, and I pull my arms in and push against his chest, sitting upright on him and then leaning over him, seeking—I'm not sure what. A new angle, a different position.

More of him.

Deeper.

Harder.

God help, me, I can't get enough—I'm absolutely mad with desire for more and more and more and more of this man who has become everything to me.

I find it, a ragged cry of triumph tripping out of my throat: sitting upright on him, hands on his belly, leaning forward, I sink onto him, slamming myself down hard until he's buried to the hilt, and then I work my sex and hips in a slow sinuous roll, hard and relentless. He tries to meet the rhythm, but he can't—I'm going too fast now, and all he can do is grip the spill of my ass on his thighs and hold on tight as I ride him through the crashing tidal waves of climax.

I can't manage a breath anymore, my lungs frantically spasming for air as scream after silent scream is ripped out of me, each sliding pound of his cock into me smashing me to new heights of ecstasy.

My tits sway and bounce, and I love how his eyes can't look away from their movement. I feel it, then—the true breaking.

My whole being shatters with a nuclear blast of heat and pressure, unleashing and unraveling, a desperate scream finally shredding out of me as I suck in blessedly cool oxygen to line my burning throat.

If I was orgasming before, this is some other, hitherto unknown realm of ecstasy and agony. Bear is giving himself to me fully now, prying my ass apart and slamming up into me as my rhythm falters, no longer able to sustain the sinuous roll. I dissolve into sobbing, gasping whimpers of tattered, shredded bliss, collapsing forward onto him and clutching his neck and pressing tear-damp lips to his.

He draws his knees up, feet bracing into the mattress, legs falling apart, and his hands lift me by the ass, and his whole body arches up off the bed as he drives into me, pounds into me, roaring like his namesake.

His release pours into me in a hot wet flood, triggering my white-hot orgasm into yet another universe of pulsing, plashing, dizzying, demolishing union. Again and again, he comes inside me, bellowing and slamming, each rough pounding thrust slapping noisily, beautifully.

His roars fade to raw grunts, my hoarse wails soften to breathless whimpers, his thrusts slow, and my climax tapers off, and our movements slow, stutter, and stop.

"Holy…fuck," I rasp, panting harder than I ever have in my life. I let my head thud onto his chest. "*Fuck*."

He has to pry his hands out of my ass. Smooths them up my back, caressing my spine, my shoulders, my sides, my hips, my ass, everywhere he can reach. "I fucking love you so goddamned much," he whispers, sounding as shaken as I am. He cups my face and pushes, so I have to lift up on shaky arms to look at him. "Did I…." he swallows hard. "Did I hurt you?"

"Perfectly, beautifully yes," I answer, nuzzling his cheek and then taking his mouth in a breathless kiss. "You fucked me into oblivion, my love."

His breathing is still ragged. "You took everything I've got. Everything I am." He sounds awed, rocked with disbelief. "You're *sure* you're okay?"

I laugh, nodding against his chest. Draw my thighs up, knees high, and wriggle my butt. It's silly and pointless, and I have no idea why I did it, but it makes him gasp and flinch. I do a pushup on his chest, hair framing his face, creating a curtain of isolation around us. "Quite literally, my love, I have never, *ever* been as absolutely, deliriously, madly happy as I am right now."

He laughs, and that sound is the most beautiful thing I've ever heard, along with the way he calls me "my love," the song of his grunts and growls as he loves me, and the beautiful, heart-rending things he says.

"I can't believe you're real, Noelle. That I can…I can just be myself. I can…" he chokes on his words with a ragged sigh that's almost a sob. "I can give you everything I have, and I don't have to be afraid of breaking you."

I kiss him, all hungry tongue in his hot mouth, a deep moan from both of us braiding our souls into a new union. "You didn't break me, Bear. You set me free. You gave me what I've craved for as long as I can remember. You gave me permission to let loose. To be completely and totally whoever I want to be." I rest my forearms on his chest and shoulders, straddling him, our bodies still joined even as he slowly goes slack inside me. "I went a little crazy," I say, giggling. "Did I scare you?"

"A little, yeah," he admits. "But it was the hottest fucking thing ever."

An exhaustion unlike any other washes through me all of a sudden, and I let myself settle on him, sinking into his embrace. "Hold me, my love. Hold me and never let go."

"I won't," he promises. "I've got you."

I drowse then, and drift.

At some point, he rolls me to my side, his heat and solidity abandoning me. I whimper. "Bear. Come back." It's a sleepy mumble.

"Blowing out the candles before I fall asleep."

"Mmm," I acknowledge. "Hurry."

I vaguely hear him blow them all out, and then the bed dips with his weight. He scoops me in his arms and cradles me against his huge body, and I feel him toss the blankets over us.

I fall asleep to the slow rhythm of his heartbeat under my ear, safe and warm and content and very, very, thoroughly plundered.

I know I have a smile on my lips as I drift off, despite the slow sticky seep of his seed leaking out of me.

C⌒

I wake up to the dim gray light of pre-dawn filtering in through the blinds. I close my eyes again, sighing happily as I take stock.

I'm on my side facing the door, and Bear's big hot body is spooned behind me, one heavy arm draped over my waist, his hand wedged under my boobs. His breath huffs on my back in a soft, cute little snore. His hard hips press against my ass, the thick ridge of his cock wedged between my cheeks, semi-hard.

And ohhhhh…my…*god*, am I sore.

I giggle softly to myself, trying not to wake him. I've read about this in romance novels, where the heroine wakes up the next morning after a good hard fucking, and she's "deliciously sore in all the right ways" or some such phrasing. I always thought it was nonsense, overly romantic gushy tripe made up for sexy novels.

Oh no. Nope. Most definitely a *very* real thing. It just turns out I was never the recipient of the kind of vigorous loving required to leave me sore like this.

I couldn't be happier about it.

I doze happily in Bear's embrace, his warmth tugging me gently back down into quasi-sleep. After a measureless time, he stirs, making soft grumbly noises as he wakes up. His hand twitches, curling to grasp my breast. I wiggle my butt against him, giggling when he makes a quiet sound of surprise and confusion.

It quickly becomes a sigh of…joy? Relief? Something of both.

"Real." His voice comes from the bottom of a well, sounding like rocks scraping together.

I thread my fingers through his where it cups my boob. "I am real. So was last night." I roll over in his arm and nuzzle up to him, a smile dancing on my lips. "Hi, you."

His eyes glitter with untold happiness. "Mornin', gorgeous." His eyes slide closed as he sweeps his hand down my back to caress my bottom. "Love how soft you are."

I wriggle closer yet, stealing an arm over his middle to play with his butt, something I've yet to enjoy. And lordy, what an ass the man has. I squeeze one of the rock-hard cheeks. "I'm soft, you're hard. Match made in heaven, if you ask me."

"Agreed."

His eyes open and meet mine. "Noelle, last night was..." he sighs, shaking his head. "I don't have words for how fucking...god, I don't know. Mind-blowing it was."

"I couldn't agree more." I kiss his chin. "And I can't wait to do it again—see if it's just as good the second time around." I wrinkle my nose. "I might need a minute to recover, though. I'm a little sore." When his mouth opens and his brow furrows with frown lines, I shut him up with a kiss. "Nope. Don't even say it. I feel amazing. Incredible. I feel loved. Wanted. Desired. You made me yours in the most incredible way possible."

He closes his eyes again, absorbing and processing what I've told him. "I still can't quite believe...well, any of it. That you love me. That you want me. That you let me touch you, kiss you, make love to you. Especially how you were last night." His head shakes, a soft laugh huffing from his lips. "Fuckin' wild woman."

I blush hard, burying my face in his chest. "I'm actually a little embarrassed. I just...I don't know. I went a little nuts."

His finger tips my chin, so I have to look at him; I give my eyes and see nothing but that love, as enormous as he is, and that desire, as deep as the ocean. "That was the hottest fucking thing ever, Noelle. Do *not* be embarrassed. Be proud. I *loved* it. I fucking loved how you shoved me around. Took what you wanted. Demanded everything I had and still wanted more." He shakes his head, awe blazing in his eyes. "Fuck, honey. You showed me a whole new world."

I dissolve into laughter, somewhat hysterical. When it fades, I can only kiss him. "I don't even know why I'm laughing. I guess I'm just so damn happy I can't help it. You made me come *so* hard, *so* many times. If it hadn't happened to me, I wouldn't believe it was possible. I lost count, baby. That's how good it was." I bite my lip with a grin. "How good *you* were."

"God, I love you," he whispers.

"Love you more," I whisper back.

His lips find mine, and then we just kiss for a while— not to lead anywhere, just for the sake of sharing our joy. I know I have morning breath, and so does he, but I don't care. I just can't get enough. I never will.

When we finally come up for air, He rolls me to my back and levers over me, his hair curtaining around my face. For a second or two, he just stares at me, memorizing or just appreciating—I don't know. I just love the way he looks at me.

But his expression slowly morphs into a troubled frown.

I rub the frown lines between his eyebrows. "Hey, what's this? A frown on the best morning of my life?"

He swallows hard. "I just realized something."

"Okay?"

"Last night. We didn't…" he winces, shakes his head, and then drops his face to my chest, words coming out muffled. "We didn't use protection. It never even occurred to me. I didn't ask if you were on birth control. I didn't—I just got…consumed in how bad I needed you, and…" he lifts his head, worry and fear and self-flagellation warring on his face. "I didn't take care of you like I should have. I'm so sorry, Noelle."

"C'mere." I pull him to me, cradling his face against my breasts.

He gives me some of his weight, and I cuddle him close, wrapping a thigh over the back of his, caressing him wherever I can reach. I stroke his hair, his shoulders, his back.

"Bear, baby, it's fine. It's okay." I kiss his forehead and then resume cuddling and caressing him. "I didn't stop to think of it either, and it's *my* body. I should have too, but I didn't. So it's not all on you—it's not just your responsibility, it's mine, too. One could even argue that it's more my responsibility than yours to make sure my body is protected."

"But I—" he starts.

"Hush." I cover his lips. "It's okay because I've been on birth control since I was fifteen. It was a whole thing with my parents—they were against it, vehemently. At all, let alone for a fifteen-year-old. But my periods were absolutely brutal, so birth control was the only way to make them manageable. I don't miss it—I never have. I have an app that tracks my cycle and reminds me to take my birth control every day. Which is why I didn't think of it—I knew we were covered."

"Oh," he mumbles.

"And as far as diseases or whatever, that's not a concern either. Obviously, there's no way you have anything, right?"

"Celibate for eleven years, till now. So yeah."

"And I was only with one person, ever, and there wasn't anyone after him till you. So me either." I sigh. "After

I found out that he was cheating on me, I went and got tested because who knows how many other church skanks he was screwing. So I do know for a fact that I'm clean. Okay? Do you feel better now?"

He nods against me. "Much. Thank you."

"Can we get back to being deliriously happy again?" I ask.

He laughs, a soft snort. "Yes, please."

"Good." I shiver with a frisson of pure joy and squeeze and shake him against me. "I love you so much it's crazy."

"Can I stay here like this forever?" he mumbles. "You holding me like this. It's…" he trails off, voice thick with emotion. "Stupid. Cryin' like a damn baby—*again*. Don't even know why."

"It's not stupid, Bear. Not at all. You trusting me with your tears means the whole world to me." I turn his face to mine and press kisses all over him, soft, slow, wet kisses to his cheeks, his wet eyes, his lips. "It's not weak to cry, Bear. Not at all. Just the opposite. It's showing me vulnerability, which requires strength and courage."

For I don't know how long, then, I just hold him like that, caressing and occasionally kissing him.

Eventually, he rests on an elbow over me. "Thank you, Noelle."

I shake my head. "That's how this works, honey." I run my hand along his jawline. "We take care of each other. Share. Communicate. Accept and understand and love."

He just rumbles a pleased sigh and leans down to nuzzle my cheek. His mouth finds mine and steals a kiss, and that kiss turns into another, and then that becomes a daisy chain of slow, sweet kisses. His hand grazes over my belly and cups my breast. My nipple hardens under his palm, and I feel him grow erect against my thigh.

He breaks the kiss, staring down at me, pulling his hard-on away. "Just have to kiss you. Not tryin' to start anything—I know you're still sore."

I catch the corner of my lower lip between my teeth in a sly, shy grin. Shift more fully beneath him, framing his hard hips between my soft thighs. Now his long, lovely erection nestles against my seam.

I reach down between us and grasp him, stroking his length a few times, grinning as he groans at my touch, head lolling onto my chest.

"Noelle," he murmurs.

I slip his tip into my sex, letting out a long, hissing gasp as I take him into me in the single, slow, slick slide. Wrapping my legs around his waist, I tilt myself up against him. "Maybe I'm not as sore as I thought."

"Ahhhh god, honey," he growls. "The way you feel—fuck."

I nibble his earlobe. "I want it soft and slow and sweet this time, okay?" I reach down and cup his hard ass. "Make it last forever, please."

And my god, he does.

One thick, brawny arm under my neck as my pillow, the other framing my face, he makes love to me slowly, easing into me by inches at a time, each thrust in and pull out so smooth I can't tell where one begins and the other ends. By the time my climax reaches its peak, I'm panting in his ear, the intensity having ratcheted and ramped up so gradually and so slowly that I'm crazed with it, gasping breathlessly in his ear as we reach our orgasm together, in perfect unison. He comes inside me on a quiet exhale, his huge body going tense and taut above me, driving in and staying there as he releases while I continue to thrust against him through my own.

At long last, he collapses to his back, taking me onto him as we pant together, sweating and sated.

C⌾

We spend the day together, never apart for more than a few minutes. We shower together—a long, soapy, sexy, orgasm-filled shower—and then cook breakfast. Take Panzer for a long walk. Lounge in front of the TV watching cheesy action movies and silly-sweet rom-coms until dinner. Make love again, this time on the couch, again slowly, because I *am* getting quite sore. I just...I can't resist him.

Raina, Ashlynn, and Kyle text that they're swinging by, and they demand an hour or two of girl-only time. Bear playfully grumbles about it, but leaves Panzer with me and meets Riley and Felix downtown for a drink or two.

Before he leaves, he gives me a kiss. "Girl time means talking about shit, yeah?"

I nod, shrugging. "Yeah, but what we have is sacred to me, Bear. I wouldn't share details."

He just shrugs, grinning. "Don't mind if you do—whatever you are comfortable with. They're your friends, honey."

"Thanks for understanding. We will talk, and I might share some stuff, but..." I shrug. "Not everything. Wouldn't want to make them jealous." I shove him out the door. "Go see your friends. Give us like two hours and then come home to me."

After he's gone, the girls drag me into the living room,

shove a freshly blended margarita into my hand, and crowd around me.

"Tell us everything," Raina demands. "We just came to see how you were doing, but it's obvious from that little scene that you two got *cozy*."

Ashlynn grins madly. "We need details, sister."

"Such as," Kyle says, "is he as big as I want to believe?"

I take a long drink of margarita, coughing as I swallow. "Holy shit, that's strong."

"Holy shit, you said holy shit," Ashlynn exclaims. "You must've gotten dicked down something *good*."

I frown at her, voice hoarse as I catch my breath. "Ashlynn—that's unbelievably crude. I did *not* get *dicked...down*." I say in an arch, prim tone.

"Then why are you glowing?" Raina asks.

"Because," I singsong, pausing for more margarita. "We made love. Vigorously. Several times." I dissolve into giggles because I'm either still delirious from my amazing night and day with Bear, or the margarita is hitting me hard and fast. Or both, most likely.

"How vigorously?" Kyle asks.

"Hold on." I set my margarita down and grab the lingerie from the floor of my—our—room, where it still lay after Bear ripped it off and threw it aside.

I toss it on the table as if dropping a mic and take my seat, letting the shredded garment say all that needs to be said. Just for good measure, I pull my leggings down and proudly show them the fingerprint bruises dotting my bottom.

Ashlynn holds up the pieces, and her jaw slowly drops open. "Shut...the *fuck*...up."

I blush furiously, giggling into my glass, unable to

meet their shocked eyes. "*Very* vigorously," I answer. "At least, the first time. The second and third times were…." I sigh dreamily. "Slow and sweet."

"I've never had ass bruises," Ashlynn grumps, tossing the remains of the lingerie back onto the coffee table.

"You never answered my question," Kyle says. "Please don't kill my dreams. Please, please tell me he's packing a whole-ass side of beef down there."

I splutter. "Kyle. Good grief, woman. Have some respect." I sip. Keep them in suspense a bit longer as I decide what to say. "Let's just say…I'll be walking funny for a while."

Raina cackles. "You *did* hobble to that bedroom, girl."

I sigh, laughing. "He does not disappoint, and we'll leave it at that. I'm a happy, happy woman. A very sore, very happy woman."

Kyle gazes at me softly. "You love him?"

I know my eyes blaze with my answer. "So fucking much. If you can love someone too much, that's where I'm at. I'm delirious."

"Because you got dicked down," Ashlynn says. "Finally."

"I'll never not hate that phrase, Ash," I mutter. "But yes."

Raina takes my hand. "I'm happy for you. You deserve this."

Kyle and Ashlynn squeeze in and surround me in a group hug.

"You said fuck," Kyle says. "That's how I know you got it good, girlfriend. He fucked the good girl right out of you."

I snicker. "Yes, yes he did."

"Does he have any brothers?" Raina asks. "Asking for a friend."

"Nope."

"Cousins? Anything?"

I laugh. "Nope. He's one of a kind, and he's all mine, ladies. You'll have to get your own."

19

Bear

FELIX AND RILEY ARRIVE TOGETHER IN FELIX'S truck right as I'm walking up to Callahan's Pub, a traditional Irish pub at the corner of Brookline and Main Street.

They both pile out at the same time, bickering as only brothers can about some sports fact or another. They both stop at once when they see me, staring with identical confusion.

I frown. "What? I got something on my face?"

"Yeah," Riley says, "A grin. It's weird. Stop."

"Ah, fuck off," I say. "Can't a man be happy?"

Felix whacks me on the back. "Sure you can, bud. And we're happy for you—right, Rye?"

Riley slings an arm over my shoulder. "Well sure, it's

just weird. I've never seen you so much as crack a smile since we met three and a half years ago. Now you're grinnin' like a fool. What gives, man?"

Felix shoots his brother a droll look. "Isn't it obvious?"

Riley stops in his tracks in the middle of the pub. "You got laid!"

I backhand his chest gently, and he stumbles backward. "Don't gotta tell the whole damn town. Jesus."

Riley rubs his chest. "Watch it, He-Man, shit. Not all of us were born on Mount Olympus."

Felix snorts. "I'm not even gonna touch that mixed metaphor."

"Sorry," I mutter.

We find a booth in a back corner where's it less noisy; a cute little waitress sashays over to us and bats her eyelashes at us; she's got curly blonde hair and light gray eyes, built svelte and slender. "What can I get you, boys?"

"Pitcher of Coors," Felix says. "Anyone want snacks?"

"Hell yeah," I say. "Hungry as fuck."

"Bet you are," Riley teases. "Pretzel sticks and some chicken wings?"

We all agree and the waitress hustles off. Riley, I notice, watches her tiny little butt as she vanishes. I shove him, careful to do so softly. "She's too young, man. No way."

He rolls his eyes. "Sasha is twenty-four, I'll have you know."

"Sasha, huh?" I say. "First name basis?"

He shrugs, not meeting my eyes. "Guess so."

Felix snorts. "What he's not saying is he's already screwed her."

"Once," Riley protests.

"Yeah, exactly," Felix says. "*Once*."

"Hey, now. *I* was down for more. *She* ghosted *me*." Riley shakes his head. "Sweet girl. Great in bed. Not really my type, though."

Felix throws a Splenda packet at Riley's head. "Female, legal, and willing. Pretty much your only type, there, bro."

Riley tosses it back, missing. "Fuck you. I have standards."

"You screwed Amy Goddard." Felix says this as if it's all there is to say.

I look from brother to brother. "And?"

Riley seems distinctly uncomfortable with the tack of the conversation. "Shut up. Not—another—word. I was *drunk*."

Felix just laughs. "Amy Goddard. Oh man. Year after our high school graduation, a party out in the Mannix backfield."

Riley glares at his brother. "Why do you hate me?"

Felix only laughs harder. "Let's just say Amy Goddard, while a very sweet girl, was, um...god, how do I put this nicely?"

Riley grumbles. "No nice way *to* put it. She was homely."

"Dude." I fish the packet off the bench and toss it at him. "*Homely*?"

Felix shrugs. "That's as nice as it can be put, Bear. For real. Again, she was super nice to everyone, wicked smart, just…objectively speaking, not an attractive person."

"I felt horrible about it, okay?" Riley says. "It was a dick move. I was an asshole back then, and I was drunk."

"You're still an asshole," Felix says. "Just a little less of one."

"Was it at least consensual?" I ask.

Riley's gaze snaps to mine, angry. "Fuck you. Yes, it was fucking *consensual*."

"Oh, it was," Felix says. "Everyone just assumed it was either a dare or some sort of fucked-up pity fuck thing. She moved away not long after."

Riley smacks the table, rattling the glasses. "Okay, *enough*, asshole. It was neither. We were talking. She's easy to talk to. Smart, like you said. I was drunk; she was drunk. It just happened. And you know what? It was pretty damn good, too. So fuck you both. And she didn't move because of me, or what happened, or what people said, she moved because she got a full fucking ride to U of M for molecular biology."

Felix grabs his brother's shoulder. "Alright, alright. I'm sorry, Rye. Didn't realize it was such a sore spot. I was just fucking with you."

Riley rolls a shoulder miserably. "I still feel shitty about it—she was hurt by what people said. And she did confront me before she left asking if any of it was true. I'm not sure she believed me, though. It really was just… something that happened."

Felix looks at me. "He's sensitive about his reputation. But yet, he can't seem to keep his dick in his pants."

Riley groans, staring at the ceiling. "Can we talk about Bear, now?"

"Not much to talk about," I say. "Yeah, Noelle and I…yeah."

Riley grins at me. "You know, I had a hell of a crush on her all through high school. And beyond, actually. But she was with that fucking shitbox cuntbucket dickwaffle, Brennan fucking Engler. And then, after she left his sorry cheating ass, I just knew she was out of bounds. You done good, son."

"Shitbox…cuntbucket…dickwaffle." I eye him. "Tell me how you really feel."

"That was the nice version. None of us ever knew what she saw in that fuckstain." He sighs. "Noelle was always way too good for him."

"Wasn't so much her as it was the expectations of her parents," I explain.

"Makes sense," Riley says. "Her parents were pretty damn strict."

"So, enough about Brennan Engler. You and Noelle." Felix grins at me. "Good? Great?"

"Man spent ten years in the pen," Riley quips. "A wet hole in the ground would be *good*. Noelle Harper?" he whistles. "Man's grinnin' like a fool for a reason."

I frown his way. "Watch it, man. That's my girl."

He just grins wider, holding up both hands palms out. "I've got all the respect in the world for her, my guy. Told you, I never made a move on her, even when she was single. She's way too good for the likes of me, and I know it. Doesn't mean I can't appreciate one of Three Rivers' finest examples of female beauty."

I shrug. "Just watch how you talk about her."

Felix chuckles. "Rye, take the hint. You saw what he did to Duane."

I growl in warning. "Not talking about that."

Riley holds up his hands again. "Alright, I'm done. I'm just happy for you. And for her. She deserves to be happy, and you seem to make her happy."

"Hope I do," I say. "Think I do. She says I do."

"You do," Felix says. "Saw it even before you guys hooked up. If she's grinnin' like you are, then yeah, you make her happy."

"I just gotta know," Riley says. "On a scale from one to ten…how epic was it?"

"Forty-seven…million."

Riley bursts into laughter, clapping his hands. "Hell yes, brother. Hell yes. Good for you."

Felix glances at Riley, and they share a look, and then Riley turns serious. "So, about this whole switching crews thing."

I sigh. "I don't wanna put you in a bad spot, but I want to…" I shrug. "Do more with my life. Especially now that Noelle and I seem to be building something together."

Felix claps me on the back. "If you're game, we've agreed that you can apprentice for me. I'll teach you everything I know about house building. I think you've got the eye for it."

"But," Riley puts in, "I may need you once in a while. Help catch up if we get behind."

I think about it, even though I don't have to. "I think that's fair—more than fair." I look at Felix. "I appreciate the opportunity. I won't let you down."

Felix just shakes his head. "Don't doubt it, man." A small laugh. "You're so damn earnest, Jesus. Chill, man. You're good."

Riley cackles. "*You* calling *him* earnest is rich, bro. You're the textbook definition of earnest."

They bicker like that for a while, and I let it wash over me, thinking about the future.

ONE YEAR LATER

All the other guys have been gone for at least an hour, but I stayed behind to finish putting in the last of the tile in the laundry room. After this, cabinets and counters go in, and then it's finishing touches.

This is the third home I've done with Crowe Construction, and while I'm still the most junior member of the crew, I work the closest with Felix, learning the trade as a whole rather than becoming an expert in one particular aspect. Thus, I've gotten to spend time on each facet of homebuilding, from digging and pouring the foundation to framing, drywalling, flooring, overseeing the subcontracting of plumbing and electrical, to finishing. I'm not the best at any of that, but I've memorized the legal codes as well as our particular standards and know how to spot when something's been done incorrectly or under our standards. I'm learning to read blueprints, how to spot a faulty design, how homes flow best, and how to choose the right materials in order to not scrimp on quality yet keep costs down…it's endless, and I fucking love it.

Officially, I'll still be on parole for, well, a long goddamn time, but I'm finished with Riley's program, and in addition to my position as Felix's apprentice, I also serve as Riley's inmate supervisor and liaison between our crew and the staff at Holbrook, helping Riley choose candidates for the work-release program and assisting him in monitoring their progress through the program.

Noelle found her storefront for her salon, right on Main Street near Compass at the south end of town. She just finished renovations a month ago and had her grand opening last week, having done a soft launch over the previous three weeks to iron out any kinks.

I let go of my apartment and moved in with her about two months after what will always be the most memorable night of my life; it would have been sooner, but there was a situation with the landlord. He suffered a heart attack and was forced to sell his properties so he could focus on his recovery—he was going to sell the house out from underneath her, but she managed to convince him to turn her lease into a rent-to-own, giving her time to scrounge the funds for a full purchase. Part of the negotiations included much-needed repairs she'd been after him about for months, which meant she actually moved in with me in my apartment while the repairs and renovations were underway. Once she was officially the new owner, the first thing she did was finish the basement, giving me a workout space and a temporary space for her to work out of—she left Lux Locks once the basement was done and began building her clientele in preparation for finding her storefront downtown.

All in all, it's been a hectic but productive year.

I made my first significant, adult purchase six months ago—a two-year-old Ram 2500, in cash. It's not the fanciest truck around—double cab, long bed, cloth seats, AM-FM radio—but it's clean, low mileage, with a heavy-duty tow package and a beefy diesel engine; I added a backrack, a spray-in bed liner, and upgraded tires and wheels, and now I have a truck that'll hopefully last me a good, long time.

Another reason I went for that particular truck was because I got a killer deal on it, leaving me a decent amount of cash left over.

I saved over the next month and made the second major purchase of my life, a small but significant object chosen with the assistance of her friend crew.

An object that currently sits in the center console of my truck, burning a figurative hole as I decide on the best moment to give it to her.

Or, rather, offer it to her. The yes isn't guaranteed, but I can't see her saying no.

God, I hope she says yes.

I've gone through a billion scenarios and come up with a billion ways to ask. I've planned elaborate dates at fancy restaurants across the state, destination vacation proposals, simple ones at home…nothing has felt right.

I have my earbuds in and a podcast on righting wrongful convictions playing, and I'm not expecting anyone. Therefore, I'm startled half out of my skin when I feel a tap on my shoulder.

"God, baby, I'm sorry," Noelle says, hanging on my back as I stand up. "Didn't mean to startle you."

She slides to her feet and moves around in front of me, her arms circling my neck, her lips touching mine in a soft, quick kiss.

"All good, babe. Didn't hear you." I glance at my watch. "Oh, shit. Didn't realize how late it was."

She shrugs, smiling. "It's okay. My last client went late, so I'm just now done myself." She looks around. "Got a lot done since I was last here."

I nod. "Yeah, we should be done in another month or two."

"When do you break ground in EastBroook Estates?"

"Mmmm, they're still moving dirt around. The planned timing is to be able to break ground once we're done here." I spread the last of the grout over the tiles in front of the door's threshold. "Done in a minute, here, baby. We doing dinner at home or what?"

She doesn't answer, so I finish what I'm doing and turn to look at her—she's staring off into space, frowning thoughtfully. I decided to let her think while I finish, so I hustle the last stretch of grout, and then stand up and stretch the kinks out of my back.

She's still lost in thought, staring out the laundry room windows at nothing. She doesn't seem upset or worried, so whatever she's thinking about likely isn't bad news.

"Hey," I say, nuzzling her cheek with my beard. "Thinking big thoughts?"

"Mmmmm." It's a non-answer—she didn't even really hear me.

"Noelle?" I ask, touching her chin and dipping at her knees to get her attention. "Hey."

She blinks and shakes her head. "God, I'm sorry, honey. Did you say something?"

I smile. "Just asking about the big thoughts you're thinking, down here."

She looks at the floor. "Oh, you're done?"

"Yeah. Wanna get out of here?"

"Sounds good," she says.

She threads her fingers into mine and we head for my truck—her salon is only a couple blocks from this build, so I've been dropping her off in the mornings and she and Panzer walk over when she's done and we go home together.

Panzer is napping on the grass beside the truck, popping up to his feet when we come out. I kneel at his side and ruffle his ears, kiss his forehead between his eyes. "Heya, boy. Take good care of our girl?"

He ruffs softly and licks me from chin to hairline in answer. I get him in the backseat, and then we get in and I head for home.

Before I get out of the new sub and onto Elk Street, however, she looks at me. "Can we go for a little drive?"

I grin and shrug. "Sure. Anywhere in particular?"

She shakes her head. "No. Well, somewhere we can watch the sunset?"

The sun is approaching the horizon, which means we've got a few minutes before the real event begins. I've learned the area pretty well since getting my own wheels, so I know a good spot north of town.

It's a short drive, and within ten minutes, I'm pulling off the two-lane highway into a small lake-side park—it's nothing more than a parking lot and a stretch of grass with some picnic tables and coal grills, and then the rocky beach, but it overlooks the endless rippling blue of Lake Michigan. I park and we take seats on the bench nearest the water while Panzer trots the waterline, sniffing and frolicking with puppy-like exuberance.

I let her ruminate, knowing she'll open up when she's ready.

"So..." She twists on the bench and I do the same so we're facing each other, and she takes my hands. "I've been thinking."

"You're pretty good at that," I say, grinning.

She tosses her hair playfully. "I know." She giggles and then sobers. "For real, I...I guess I'm a little nervous because I don't know how to approach this."

"Sweetheart, you know that whatever it is, I'm with you and I'll support you."

She gnaws on the corner of her lower lip. "It's...it's not so much a *me* thing as an *us* thing." She looks at me, searching my face. "About us. Our future. And it's something we haven't discussed yet."

My heart pounds. "Okay."

"Um. So. We've been together for over a year, and we've lived together for a few months." She halts, nerves apparent in her eyes, body language, and tone.

I lift her hands and kiss her knuckles. "Hey, breathe, baby. I love you. I'm all in, no matter what."

I may or may not have let her get out of the truck first so I could snatch the ring out of the console, because this could very well be a perfect opportunity, depending on what she's about to say.

She nods. "I know. I know. I just..." She exhales shakily. "I grew up very traditional, you know that. There's a set-in-stone order to things. Courtship, engagement, marriage, and then kids."

The ring heats in my hip pocket. "I know."

"But I...I've sort of let go of a lot of that. I...want to be married. I want to have kids."

"Me too, sweetheart." I slip my hand into my pocket and close my hand around the black velvet box.

She looks at me with apprehension in her eyes. "I, um..." She covers her face. Blows out a shaky breath. "How would you feel if I said I want to go off birth control and... um...see what—what happens?"

The breath whooshes out of my lungs. I slip my hand out of my pocket, keeping the box hidden in my fist.

It's my turn to go shaky and clammy-handed, breath hot and lumpy in my throat. I know she's waiting for my response, her beautiful green eyes frantically hunting my face for signs of my reactions.

"Bear?" It's a tiny whisper.

"I guess I'd just have one question to ask you."

She licks her lips, tears shining in her eyes. "Okay?"

I slip off the bench and onto one knee in front of her, the hot lump in my throat bobbing as I attempt to swallow past it.

I open and hold up the ring box. "Noelle, will you marry me?" A thousand other thoughts and questions rampage through my brain—excuses, declarations, pleas. None of it will come out properly. "I…I've planned this a hundred different ways, and thought about what to say a million times. I love you so fucking much, and I just…I love you. I want to be with you forever. Please, Noelle. Marry me?"

Her hands clap together over her mouth the moment I go to one knee, tears spurting down her cheeks as I show her the ring. By the time I've gotten the last syllable out, she's sobbing and nodding.

"Yes?" I ask.

She leaps off the bench and slams into me full force, knocking me backward to the grass on my back, her arms around my neck.

"*YES!*" She shrieks, breathless and laughing and sobbing at once. "Yes, yes, yes—god yes. *Fuck* yes."

I stand up, and she comes with me, leaping up into

my arms, legs going around my waist. "Fuck yes?" I repeat, laughing.

"How many different ways can I say it?" She says, peppering my face with kisses. "Yes. Yes, please. Yes forever. A thousand times, yes. Fuck yes." She palms my face and kisses my mouth until my cock goes hard in my jeans. "Yes, Bear Olafsson. I will absolutely, one hundred percent marry you. Do you have a pastor in your pocket? I'll marry you right now."

"Maybe you should at least try the ring on?" I ask, laughing.

She leans back, blindly trusting me to support her weight one-armed as she takes the ring from the box and slides it on her ring finger. I shove the empty box in my pocket and cradle her backside as she clings to my waist with her thighs, her left hand on my chest, the sunset glittering scarlet-orange fire off the diamond.

She's crying as she stares at it. "God, Bear, it's incredible."

"Remember when Tommy and Colin took you to Charlevoix for brunch?" I ask; she nods, frowning. "Raina, Ashlynn, and Kyle took me ring shopping and helped me pick it out."

It's a diamond solitaire, a full carat, round, with a white gold band that splits into two narrower bands that cross to become an infinity loop.

"It's so beautiful. I love it so much." She rests her hands on my shoulders. "But...you didn't answer my question."

I lean in and kiss her. "I figure you'd want to process my question first. But the short answer, my love, is *yes*. Whatever the timing is, yes. You wanna start now? I'm in. You wanna wait till we're married? Let's plan the wedding."

She sniffles, twisting and holding her hand at a different angle so the sunset catches the ring. "To be honest, I don't want to wait. I love you. I love our life. And...I've wanted to be a mother..." She drops he head, sniffling again. "For a long time. A very, very long time. And now that we have things sort of figured out more—you working with Felix and me opening my salon, I don't see a reason to wait. I just...I...we never talked about how you feel about kids."

I sit on the bench, and she shifts to straddle me, shins folded under her thighs. "Noelle, I..." I shake my head. "I haven't really thought about it. I honestly never expected... any of this. To fall in love. To have a career I'm passionate about. A life—a *real* life. I didn't have parents. So, I guess If I'm being honest, it's a scary prospect. I don't know the first thing about being a dad. But I know as long as I've got you, I can figure it out. You just may have to show me the way."

She cups my face, strokes my beard. "Bear, my sweet love. You will be the best father. There is no doubt in my mind at all—you have *so* much love. Such a big heart. You may not have had a father, but that just means you get to be the father you wish you had."

My eyes sting. "What if I mess up?"

She laughs. "You're going to. So will I. We're going to fight. I'll probably make you sleep on the couch at least once and you'll want to yeet me into the bay at least once."

I snort. "Yeet?"

She rolls her eyes. "Yeah, not sure where that came from." She kisses me. "Are you saying you're ready to...not try, but not stop it from happening?"

I nod. "That's what I'm saying. I love you. I want this life with you. All of it. I want to be your husband. I want to watch you have our baby. All of it. Even if I'm scared. I love you so fucking much, and I'm ready for all of it."

She leans in and nips my lower lip in her teeth. "Then take me home and see if you can put a baby in me on the first try."

"Doesn't the birth control take a while to go out of your system?" I ask.

She shrugs, nodding. "Well, yeah. If I stop taking it now, my cycle will come back in about a month and I'll be fertile again after three months or so." She grinds her butt against me. "But I figure we should practice, you know?"

I carry her to the truck, calling for Panzer. "We should definitely practice. A *lot*."

I race home and spend a good portion of the night practicing.

Late that night, drowsing half awake, moonlight streams silver and glitters off the ring, her hand resting on my chest as she sleeps in my arms.

And I find myself thankful.

Not just for her, but for each and every event that led me here, to her, to this moment. To this life. I wouldn't change one thing—none of it. Because all of it brought me to her.

Out of the shadows and darkness…

Into the light.

EPILOGUE

Felix

TODAY WAS A ROUGH ONE.

    With Bear officially my new crew foreman, I now have a bit more free time. What do I decide to do with it? Buy a handful of acres a few miles north of town and build myself a house.

It's something I've been meaning to do for a long time, and I've had the acreage picked out for at least two years. I just haven't had the time to do anything. There hasn't been anyone I trust enough to run the crew in my absence, so I've had to be on-site for every build as well as splitting my time checking on the other builds in progress—I spend the bulk of my time at the newest build, leaving the finishing crews to wrap things up without me—cabinet pulls, outlets plates, appliance installs, paint, easy shit like that.

Now that Bear has a full year on the job as my apprentice plus a good three months performing probationary foreman duties without any mishap, I'm feeling comfortable finally taking a day off here and there.

I splashed out for the acres a week ago, signed all the closing paperwork, and I'm now the proud owner of ten point four acres of land—it's mostly dense pine forest, with a nice little natural clearing near the middle, and a slice of the Michigami River running through the back. The clearing is around three or four acres of rolling meadow, with a perfect spot for a walk-out build. I've had the basic design finalized for over a year, and now I'm almost ready to start breaking ground.

Aside from the peaceful beauty of the property, buildable location, and proximity to town, the other major factor in purchasing this particular parcel is the fact that it already has utilities run to the very spot I plan to build on—someone in years past must've planned to build, got started, and then had to abandon the project and try to sell. It's been for sale for over five years, so I got a sweet deal on it, leaving the bulk of my saved cash for the build itself.

Today, I staked out the build site and got started clearing the driveway; it'd go faster if I hired a tree removal service, obviously, but that would cost a small fortune, and I'm in no hurry, so I borrow the Bobcat from the yard, load up chains, a chainsaw, and some other equipment, and get to work.

Tree clearing, without the fancy machinery, is a hell of a lot of work. I mark the path with stakes and flags, and then start at the edge of the clearing and work my way toward the road.

Fell the tree, de-limb, and buck into fourteen- to

eighteen-inch lengths, which I then stack; later, I'll gather up all the stacked logs and move them to the site for firewood.

Each tree I down takes a long-ass time, which means it's gonna be a month of days off here and there spent just clearing the trees out of the driveway path. Then I'll have to break the ground, clear the grass and dirt, grade and level, and spread the gravel. Only then will I be able to get the heavy machinery back in there so I can break ground and start on the foundation.

I expect this project to take a couple of years at least, but I'm excited about it. It's been my dream since I was a teenager just starting to work for my dad on the framing crew—buy acreage and build my own house from the ground up with my own two hands.

I've spent every waking minute of my life learning the skills, building the company, and saving every dollar I can, all for this dream.

And now it's finally starting to come true.

So by the time the sun is starting to set, I've made a decent dent in the trees, and I'm sweaty, dirty, exhausted, ravenous, and ready to kick back in my condo and watch ESPN until I fall the fuck asleep on the couch.

I'm only partially paying attention to the road as I head back toward town—I'm on a narrow dirt road a good mile or two from the highway in an area that sees little to no traffic. I mean, there's nothing out here. The dirt road heads east away from the lake for a good fifteen or twenty miles before simply dead-ending randomly in the middle of nowhere. Most of the land around the road is either state-owned parkland or giant swaths of acreage privately owned as hunting grounds for down-staters. So, I don't expect to see anyone.

I'm zoned out, my bro country playlist blasting, windows open, driving on autopilot. A little too fast, maybe. I dunno, like I said, I'm not really paying attention. There's no one out here.

I round a long, sharp, blind curve; a blur of bright orange in the middle of the road has me shouting a surprised curse as I stand on the brakes, my truck fishtailing wildly in the dirt before coming to a halt in the swirling dust.

My bullbar rocks less than six inches away from the vehicle stopped in the center of the road…and the woman bent over with her head in the engine compartment.

I shove the shifter into Park, muttering curses under my breath. A gust of wind rifles through the trees and clears the dust, giving me a better view of what, and who, I almost just hit.

A violently orange vintage VW bus plastered from bumper to bumper with stickers. The front end is pointed west, away from me, the tail and the engine compartment in the rear facing me. Bent over, head and shouldes in the compartment, is a woman.

I mean, all I can see is her ass, but Good Lord above and all his precious saints, what an ass it is. Full, round, taut, and firm, it's spread in a beautiful curve as she hinges at the waist to get deeper into the engine compartment, swaying and jiggling as she bends her knees and twists and flexes in an attempt to reach something. She's wearing an ankle-length skirt of some thin, slippery material that clings to her ass, stretching around the lush curves of her hips, thighs, and butt. The skirt is royal purple paisley, the comma-shapes of the paisley pattern in every color under the sun. She's barefoot in the dirt, and I can see her toes digging and flexing as she reaches for whatever is giving her fits in the engine compartment—each of her toenails is painted a different color.

Even though all I can see is her lower half, I can tell she's pretty short.

I get out of my truck and head for the van. She doesn't seem to have noticed my last-second stop or my approach on foot. Is she deaf? Or maybe has earbuds in?

I rap my knuckles on the side of the VW and step back, so as to not crowd the woman and scare her.

At my knock, she jerks backward, cracks her head, and emerges more carefully, cursing floridly.

"Goddammit, motherfucking piece of shit, that hurt you ass-fucking pile of moldy dicks…" The stream of creative invective continues until she's fully upright.

My heart stops beating entirely, my mouth goes dry, and swallowing becomes impossible.

She's the most gorgeous creature I've ever laid eyes on.

Barely over five feet, maybe five-three or -four at most, she's all soft, luscious curves. That incredible ass is just the beginning. The wind swirls, lifting her thin skirt up around her hips, baring momentarily short, thick legs. She's wearing…I don't know the word for it. It's not a tank top or tube top, but something like it. A band of stretchy fabric around her chest. That's it. It covers her boobs, but that's about it. And those things are…fuck. I can't rip my eyes away. The white fabric strains in a futile attempt to contain her enormous, perfectly teardrop-shaped breasts. Her nipples are pert and obvious, poking against the fabric, stiffening as the wind knifes past.

With a shake of my head, I force my eyes shut to break

the spell and then open them again to get a look at the rest of her. Her belly, waist, and upper torso, bare, are tanned to a dusky golden brown—the color of naturally pale skin that's been tanned from long hours outside under the sun. She has a glittery purple bauble piercing her belly button, with thin gold chains wrapped around her waist, connecting to the piercing and vanishing up under her top to loop around her throat, a few inches of chain hanging down her chest, another smaller purple pendant dangling just above her cleavage.

Bracelets of infinite variety are stacked on both wrists halfway up her forearms—jelly bracelets, Pandora bracelets with dozens of charms, hand-braided friendship bracelets by the dozen in every possible color and pattern, jangly silver and gold hoops, some with dangling charms and some without.

Her hair is white-blond—not dyed platinum but rather so naturally pale it's nearly old-person white; it's been done in a thick, elaborate braid that wraps around her head like a crown, with feathers, charms, and beads worked into the braid. Gold hoops line her ears from tip to lobe, and a third purple piercing glints on the left side of her nostril.

Her eyes…fuck me.

Silver.

I mean, technically, I suppose you'd call them extremely pale hazel, but the downrange effect is silver. Shocking, vivid, piercing. Assessing, intelligent, wild, proud…

And full of sorrow.

And anger.

Her face is heart-shaped, with high, sharp cheekbones

and plump, kissable lips with a pronounced Cupid's bow. Not a speck of makeup, her lashes are as white as her hair, her lips naturally pink, her skin golden and smooth and clear complected.

"What the actual fuck, dude?" She glares at me angrily, her voice too loud—she does have earbuds in her ears.

I point at my ears, and her eyes fly wide.

"Oh shit! Forgot I had them in." She plucks the earbuds out of her ears, tugs her top away, and drops them between her breasts. Her eyes finally go to my truck, angled across the road, less than a foot from her, and understanding washes over her expression, swiftly changing from anger to mortification. "Oh. Um. My bad?"

"Yeah, your bad," I snap. "I almost hit you. Parked in the middle of the road at the top of a blind curve? To quote you—what the actual fuck, *dude*?"

Her expression goes back to thunderous. "Okay, well, a couple of things here, Kayce Dutton on steroids—one, I'm not *parked*, I'm *stopped*. As in dead. It just conked out and died, and I couldn't even get it to the side of the road. Which leads me to point number two: Do I look like I can push this thing to the shoulder by myself? Number three, this road goes *from* nowhere *to* nowhere, and there's not so much as one actual house on it, so I wasn't expecting some bro in a jacked-up truck to come flying around the curve like an asshole."

Kayce Dutton on steroids? The fuck?

"I'm not on steroids." Stupidly, it's the first thing that comes out of my mouth.

Her lips thin and pull in as she bites down on a laugh. "*That's* your comeback?"

"Don't know who Kayce Dutton is, either."

She gives me a puzzled, disgusted look. "Yellowstone? Luke Grimes? You look like him, just bigger and beefier and bro-ier."

"Bro-ier is not a word."

A roll of those intoxicating silver eyes, and a shrug that does downright hypnotic things to her gigantic tits. "It is now, *bro*."

I close my eyes to rip my eyes off of them, and then find her eyes. "Cool." I jut my chin at her van. "Need a hand?"

"You an expert in VW engines?" she asks.

I shrug, shake my head. "Not especially, but I know my way around an engine." I hold up my hands. "Just offering assistance. You don't want it or need it, cool. I wasn't making any assumptions. Just tryin' to be nice."

She looks away, her beautiful face going through a range of emotions—her face is incredibly expressive, her feelings obvious and easily readable: annoyance, embarrassment, and then resignation.

She holds out a wrench. "Fine. I can't get the fucking bolt free." She turns and leans into the engine compartment. "Stop staring at my ass."

Guiltily, I jerk my gaze away, because I *was* staring. "Sorry."

She snickers. "You're not subtle about the staring, in case you weren't aware." Her voice is muffled, and I hear metal on metal. "You stared at my tits for a solid thirty seconds."

She emerges again, straightening, and rubs at her cheek, smearing grease on it.

"Hard not to stare at perfection," I say, and then bite my tongue—she gives no sign that she heard me.

I wedge myself into the engine compartment, finding where she'd put the wrench—it's at a really tough spot, with no leverage and very little room to work. I grunt through gritted teeth as I strain at the wrench—after straining till my arm and shoulder shake, I feel it starting to slip.

"Come on, you *bitch*," I snarl, and then the bolt comes loose all of a sudden, smashing my knuckles and ripping my skin. "*Mother*fucker."

I finish removing the bolt, and I see the issue she's working on—a snapped belt.

"Got the replacement?" I ask. "I'll swap it out while I'm in here. Unless you'd rather do it yourself."

A pause. "Fine. Thanks. Here." I feel a tap on my right shoulder, I worm a hand out, feel the new belt hit my hand, and then spend the next several minutes replacing it.

When the repair is done, I work myself out and straighten. "All set."

I glance at my knuckles—the skin is torn, blood coating the back of my hand and mixing with grease and dirt.

Her eyes go to the cut, and she frowns. "Let me help you with that."

I shrug. "Meh. It's fine."

She frowns, annoyed. "It's not. It'll get infected. Just get your big macho ass in my van and let me doctor your little boo-boo, okay? It's the least I can do as a thank you for fixing my van."

"Uh, sure. Yeah. Okay." I follow her around to the passenger side.

She tugs open the sliding door, revealing the interior—it's been retrofitted from the skin out, transformed from a '60s passenger van into a miniature RV, with the newest fittings and furnishings to make it into a home on wheels.

A tiny kitchenette takes up half of the wall behind the driver's seat, with a bed in the rear and storage between the tailgate and the sliding door.

She steps up into the van and points at the bed. "Sit."

I stay on the ground. "I'm filthy."

In the process of rummaging in a cabinet, she pokes her head out and assesses me. "Oh, yeah, you really are. Nevermind. Just…just sit there." She points to the lip of the door.

I sit, and she sits beside me with a first-aid kit on her lap. She uses a wet wipe to clean my hand of dirt, grease, and blood, and then pours isopropyl on the cuts, adds a dab of Neosporin, and then Band-Aids across each cut.

While she's doing that, I examine her bus.

It's obvious she lives in it. A sports bra hangs off a cabinet, a mint green lacy one hanging over it. A pile of folded clothes sits on the bed. A wooden box sits on the floor at the foot of the bed—it's the size of a shoebox and looks handmade, overflowing with jewelry. A suitcase lays open on the floor as well, overflowing with skirts, shoes, tops, leggings, underwear, bras, bandanas, and who knows what else. The kitchenette features a small two-person booth, and bowls are stacked in the sink.

In the front passenger seat, I see a cardboard box overflowing with clothes—men's clothing. I can almost make out the writing on the side—*DONATE*.

She glances at me, following my gaze. A pulse of energy comes off of her—sorrow. Her eyes mist over, and she blinks furiously, swallowing compulsively.

A moment later, she eyes me curiously. "Not gonna ask?"

I shake my head. "Not my business. You wanna tell me, I'll listen."

She stares into my eyes. "I respect that answer. Thank you." Her chin lifts, her deep, beautiful silver eyes clearing of the sorrow. "I'm Ember."

"Ember?" I ask. "Like Amber, but with an E?"

"Yeah. Ember, as in a spark from a fire."

"Beautiful name," I mutter. "For a beautiful woman."

She goes blank. "Thanks." A glance at me, not exactly disinterested, but cautious. "And you are?"

"Felix Crowe."

She smiles at me, but it doesn't quite reach her eyes. "Nice to meet you, Felix."

She's beautiful—stunning.

Mesmerizing.

Fascinating

And so, *so* sad.

I'm in love.

ALSO BY
Jasinda Wilder

Visit me at my website: **www.jasindawilder.com**
Email me: **jasindawilder@gmail.com**

If you enjoyed this book, you can help others enjoy it as well by recommending it to friends and family, or by mentioning it in reading and discussion groups and online forums. You can also review it on the site from which you purchased it. But, whether you recommend it to anyone else or not, thank you *so much* for taking the time to read my book! Your support means the world to me!

My other titles:

Forbidden Fruit

Wild Ride: Biker Billionaire

Delilah's Diary

Big Girls Do It:

Big Girls Do It
Married
On Christmas
Pregnant
Rock Stars Do It
Big Love Abroad

The Falling Series:
Falling Into You
Falling Into Us
Falling Under
Falling Away
Falling for Colton
The Ever Trilogy:
Forever & Always
After Forever
Saving Forever

From the world of *Wounded*:
Wounded
Captured

From the world of *Stripped*:
Stripped
Trashed

From the world of *Alpha*:
Alpha
Beta
Omega
Harris: Alpha One Security Book 1
Thresh: Alpha One Security Book 2
Duke: Alpha One Security Book 3
Puck: Alpha One Security Book 4
Lear: Alpha One Security Book 5
Anselm: Alpha One Security Book 6
Sigma
Gamma

The Houri Legends:

Jack and Djinn

Djinn and Tonic

The Madame X Series:

Madame X

Exposed

Exiled

The Black Room (With Jade London)

The One Series

The Long Way Home

Where the Heart Is

There's No Place Like Home

Badd Brothers:

*Badd Motherf*cker*

Badd Ass

Badd to the Bone

Good Girl Gone Badd

Badd Luck

Badd Mojo

Big Badd Wolf

Badd Boy

Badd Kitty

Badd Business

Badd Medicine

Badd Daddy

Goode Girls:
For a Goode Time Call…
Not So Goode
Goode To Be Bad
A Real Goode Time
Goode Vibrations
Dad Bod Contracting:
Hammered
Drilled
Nailed
Screwed

Fifty States of Love:
Pregnant in Pennsylvania
Cowboy in Colorado
Married in Michigan
Christmas in Connecticut

Billionaire Baby Club:
Lizzy Goes Brains Over Braun
Autumn Rolls a Seven
Laurel's Bright Idea

Club Sin:
Rev
Kane
Chance
Silas
Saxon
Solomon

Blood Heir

Blood Heir
Blood Bonds
Blood Reign
Blood Bonds

Standalone titles:

Yours
The Cabin
The Parent Trap
Wish Upon A Star
Big Hose

Non-Fiction titles:

You Can Do It
You Can Do It: Strength
You Can Do It: Fasting

Jack Wilder Titles:

The Missionary

JJ Wilder Titles:

Ark

To be informed of new releases, special offers, and other Jasinda news, sign up for Jasinda's email newsletter.